HALO

Halo Hearts Book 1

MOIRA DARLING

Kaia

THE TOUR BUS SMELLS like citrus cleaner, stale popcorn, and the collective bad decisions of four women who've been awake for too many time zones.

Someone—Jules, obviously—has strapped a pair of rhinestone sunglasses onto a plastic skeleton's face and buckled it into a seatbelt, like it's part of the group. Mina named him Craig, and he's wearing a Midnight Halo lanyard like he belongs.

Craig is currently vibing in the aisle, head lolling with every bump in the road like he's nodding along to our impending doom.

I press my forehead to the window anyway, letting the cold glass steady me.

Outside, dawn bleeds into the sky in thin washes, bruise-purple fading to pale blue, the world rinsed clean and quiet. Pines flash by, their branches glazed with frost. And even through the sealed bus, I swear I can taste the coast coming: salt and kelp and a sharpness that lives in the back of the throat.

Home.

I haven't said the word out loud. I don't plan to.

The bus hums under me like a living thing, the tires singing a low note against the road. Every few miles, a streetlight flashes past, turning the cabin into a strobe of half-seen faces: Mina curled up in a hoodie too big for her, Remy sprawled across two seats with her boots on the armrest, and Jules... Jules is upside down in her chair, legs kicked over the back like a gymnast who never learned to sit normally.

Jules catches my eye, grins, and mouths *homecoming queen*.

I flip her off.

Her laughter is silent but contagious. Mina snorts awake, blinking at us with bleary suspicion.

"Are we fighting?" Mina asks, voice rough with sleep. Her chin-length hair is an explosion of blond and static. She has a face that reads as innocent until you've watched her slice a demon in half with a sword and then ask for an iced coffee.

"No," I say. "Jules is just being... Jules."

"So that's a yes then," Remy murmurs from the shadows of her hood. She has her arm over her eyes, but her voice is sharp, awake.

Jules rolls upright, her bun listing to one side like it survived a storm. "Excuse you, I am being *supportive*. Our fearless leader is returning to the cradle of her humble origins. We should make a wreath. We should—"

"We should *not*," Blaire cuts in.

Blaire, our manager, sits with the calm, immaculate posture of a woman who has survived everything from demon attacks to fan wars to last-minute wardrobe malfunctions with the same serene expression. Early forties, perfect hair that's pulled back into a low ponytail, black coat that somehow always looks crisp, headset around her neck like she's in permanent command mode. She scrolls through a tablet with the focus of a general.

Every so often she takes a sip of her iced coffee and mutters little schedule blessings under her breath. And sometimes she reprimands us.

"We're on a tight schedule," she continues. "If you attempt to craft anything with the emergency bandage tape again, I will personally throw it into the sea."

Jules looks wounded. "You wouldn't."

Blaire's eyes flick up. Flat. Unblinking. "Try me."

Mina's grin flickers on. "Blaire would do it. She has ocean-throwing energy."

The corner of Blaire's mouth twitches, then she dives back into her tablet.

I let their voices wash over me like a tide. It helps. It keeps the sharp edges of my thoughts from cutting too deep.

Because outside the window, the first sign for Harbor's Edge is coming up in a few miles. I can feel it like a bruise you keep bumping.

The bus shifts lanes. A strip of ocean flashes between the trees—dark, glassy, endless. Somewhere out there is the breakwater where we used to sit with our shoes off and dare each other to jump. Somewhere is the beach where I learned how to breathe around heartbreak by pretending it was just cold air...

Jules points at my reflection in the window. "Our fearless leader is staring dramatically into the distance again."

"I'm not—" I start.

"You are," Mina mumbles, voice thick with sleep. "You're doing the Kaia Thing."

"What's the Kaia Thing?" Jules asks immediately, delighted.

Mina cracks one eye. "The intense jaw. The tragic ocean-girl vibe."

Jules interjects, "The 'I am fine and definitely not emotionally compromised' stare!"

"I am not emotionally compromised," I firmly say.

Jules leans over the seatback, chin on her hands, eyes bright. "That's exactly what an emotionally compromised person would say."

I turn my head slightly, just enough to catch her smirk. "Go back to sleep."

"I don't sleep," Jules says. "I recharge by being annoying."

"That explains so much," Remy mutters.

Blaire clears her throat softly. It has the same effect as a stage manager tapping a mic: not loud, but everyone feels it.

"Ten minutes until we hit the town limits," she says. "When we arrive, we do the arena walkthrough, quick safety check, then soundcheck. There's a closed briefing with Council reps before noon. No one wanders off."

Jules pouts. "Define 'wander.'"

"Define 'off,'" Remy adds, deadpan.

Blaire doesn't look up. "Define 'consequences.'"

Mina sits up with a groan, rubbing her face. "Council reps? Already?"

"Already," Blaire confirms. "There's been an uptick in demon activity with the Harbor Lights festival approaching. We'll be briefed soon enough."

I don't say anything. I just keep my gaze on the window and let the familiar weight settle in my ribs.

Some people are born with a Spark—an invisible predisposition to feel the world's energetic current and *shape* it, instead of just adding to it. Untrained, it leaks out in small ways: lights flickering with moods, weird coincidences, animals going skittish, and dreams that feel half-real.

The Council calls them Resonants—people whose souls hum at the right frequency to move magic instead of merely feeding it.

Most never get fully lit. They stay a little strange, a little sensitive, kinda witchy, but manageable.

We're the ones they trained and turned into a bonfire.

I keep my gaze on the window. The road curves toward the coastline.

Harbor's Edge is coming.

My fingers slip into the pocket of my jacket before I can stop them.

Paper. Soft, worn. Folded down into a tight square, edges rounded from years of being pressed, unfolded, refolded. A diner receipt, grease-ghosted and faded, like a relic from another life.

On the back, in looping teenage handwriting with too many exclamation marks, it says:

KAIA RHEE'S OFFICIAL "DON'T PANIC" RECEIPT!!!

1. *breathe (yes you have lungs. use them.)*

2. *drink water (not energy drinks! water!)*

3. *if you forget the words, just smile and point at me. i'll scream them for you.*

4. *if anyone is mean, i will bite them.*

5. *after: fries. extra salt. no arguing.*

PS: your voice is my favorite sound. don't tell anyone i said that or i'll deny it forever!!!!!

Evie's handwriting.

My thumb rubs over the words like I can erase them by touch. Like I can sand down memory until it stops cutting.

I should have thrown it away years ago.

Jules notices the shift in me the way she notices everything she can turn into a joke.

Her grin softens, just a shade. "You're really from here," she says, like it's a revelation she keeps trying to make feel less heavy.

"I told you that," I say.

"You told us you're from 'a small coastal town,'" Jules replies. "That could mean anything. That could mean, like... a quaint postcard village. Or a cursed fog-port where fishermen disappear."

Remy adds, "And you say 'the ocean' like it's a person you're avoiding eye contact with."

Jules leans forward, elbows on the back of her seat, grin sly. "Also you change the subject every time someone says the words *high school.*"

"That's because high school was bad," I say.

Jules' eyes brighten. "Was it? Because I am sensing *lore.*"

Blaire doesn't look up. "Jules."

"I'm just curious," Jules says, all innocent teeth. "Kaia's like... the team mom. The responsible one. The one who always has extra throat spray and knows where Mina left her charger and—"

"—and who will murder you," I finish.

"See?" Jules says, delighted. "Lore."

Mina giggles, then clamps a hand over her mouth when she realizes how loud it is in the quiet bus. "Jules, don't poke the bear."

"I'm not poking," Jules says. "I'm *bonding.* It's team-building."

Remy shifts, the hood of her sweatshirt shadowing her face. "If this is your idea of bonding, I'm requesting a transfer."

I roll my eyes at both of them and glance out the window once more. The particular curve of the road. The way the pines thin and the sky opens. The smell of salt rising stronger now, pressing against the window like a hand.

And in the middle of all of it, a quiet, vicious awareness I keep trying to swallow down: Evie is here.

Don't look her up.

Don't ask about her.

Don't make this about you.

Evie is better off not seeing you.

Mina's gaze flicks to my face, then away, like she's giving me privacy while still letting me know she's there. Mina is gentle like that. Quietly. When she wants to be.

"Kaia," she says softly. "Are you okay?"

"I'm fine," I answer automatically.

Remy murmurs, "That's not a real answer."

Jules points at Remy like she's won a prize. "See? Even Remy agrees."

Remy's voice stays flat. "I agree that you're annoying."

Jules beams. "You love me."

"I do not," Remy says, but she doesn't sound like she means it.

Mina's eyes stay on me, patient. "You haven't been back in a long time, right?"

"No," I say. Then, because honesty is a splinter you can't ignore forever, I add, "Not since... before."

Before Midnight Halo. Before Eon. Before the first time I stood onstage and felt the crowd's love slam into me like a wave, bright and intoxicating and dangerous.

Before I stopped being a girl from Harbor's Edge and became something people could project onto.

Jules's voice turns quieter without losing its warmth. "So this is a big deal."

"It's a job," I say, and my tone tries to make it true.

Remy huffs a soft laugh. "Sure."

Blaire glances at me, just a quick check, like she's reading a pulse. She doesn't push. She never pushes in front of the others. She saves the hard conversations for hallways and closed doors.

"Remember," she says instead, smooth as a practiced line, "Harbor's Edge adores you. Keep it clean. Keep it kind. And for the love of—" her eyes flick to Jules "—don't start any chants in the arena tunnels."

Jules puts a hand over her heart. "No chants. I swear."

Remy mutters, "Liar."

Jules snorts. "Well, what kind of chants are off-limits?"

"The kind that summon chaos," Blaire says.

"The kind that make security cry," Remy adds.

"The kind that make Kaia do the jaw thing," Mina finishes with a devious smile.

I glare at all of them. "Stop talking about my jaw."

Jules laughs. "But it's so expressive."

"It is not."

Remy's voice is faintly amused now. "It is."

I should be annoyed. I am annoyed. But the warmth of it—of them—keeps my ribs from locking completely shut.

The bus crests a low rise, and the town spreads out ahead of us.

Harbor's Edge unfurls like a painting that's been left out too long: weathered, salt-warped, and stubbornly familiar. The bay curves around it like an arm. Rooftops cluster tight against the shoreline. The boardwalk is a thin line, the ferris wheel a dark skeleton against the brightening sky.

Something in my chest twists painfully.

Then, near the base of the hill, I see it. A sign in faded red letters: The Lighthouse Diner.

My throat tightens so fast it feels like I'll choke.

Jules follows my gaze and squints. "That place definitely calls you 'hon' while judging your life choices," she says. "Cute."

"That's not funny," I snap.

Silence drops for half a beat, stunned by the sudden edge in my voice. Jules's smile fades, and for once she doesn't make a joke out of it.

I hate myself for the reflex.

I exhale, forcing the air out slowly. "Sorry," I say. "Just... old landmarks."

Jules nods immediately, accepting the boundary like it's sacred. "Okay."

Remy, mercifully, doesn't dig. She just says, low, "Yeah. Landmarks'll do that."

The bus rolls downhill, closer now, and the morning wakes up around us: a fisherman's truck rumbling out early, a dog walker bundled in a scarf, a coffee shop tugging its blinds open. It all looks ordinary.

And then the first festival posters start to appear.

Bright paper on lampposts that feature stylized lanterns strung over the boardwalk and a lighthouse rendered like a fairy-tale. Bold letters promising HARBOR LIGHTS FESTIVAL – A NIGHT OF LIGHT AND WISHES like it's a blessing and not a magnet for demons.

My skin prickles.

Not fear, but something subtler. A hum at the base of my skull, the way wards feel when you pass them. Looks like the Council has been putting in some work.

Mina rubs her arm, frowning. "Do you feel that?"

Jules's grin is gone now, replaced by something alert. "Warding's already up?"

Remy's voice is quiet, all edge. "Early."

Blaire's gaze flicks toward the posters as the bus passes, then back to the road. "That's what the briefing's about," she says. "Council says there's an active demonic presence building in the area."

Mina's voice dips. "What kind of demon?"

Blaire hesitates just long enough for me to notice. "They're calling it a recurring cluster pattern," she says carefully.

Remy's mouth tightens. "Like our Seoul show."

Jules leans forward, suddenly serious. "The splintery one."

Blaire doesn't even blink. "Yes," she says. Her tone is pure manager mode—clean, practiced, the kind that makes panic sound like a scheduling problem. "We took out that cluster demon, but that wasn't the only one. If the environment keeps feeding the same emotional frequency, they can form. Council tracking shows a similar signature in the vicinity."

Jules flicks a look at me—checking in, like she always does when the air shifts from joking to dangerous—before focusing on Blaire again. "So, tonight's concert is the bait, right? End it before the festival?"

Blaire nods once. "Burn off the build-up, draw it in, cut it out for good."

That's how it is, being a Resonant. Emotion and attention turn into power whether anyone means it to or not—concerts, festivals, riots, a thousand hearts beating in sync. Most people just feed it. They laugh, cry, scream, and the world gets a little brighter, a little stranger, and they never know why.

Resonants? We're trained to catch that energy and amplify it.

Demons feel it the way sharks feel blood in water. Big crowds make it louder. Make *us* louder.

Lightning rods.

We draw the worst of the demonic presences in, trap them inside the ward lines, and cut them down before they can slip out into the streets and start feeding on someone who doesn't even know what's happening.

And tonight, apparently, we're killing a cluster demon.

Mina's brows pull tighter. "If it's so dangerous, why not—why not just... cancel the festival?"

Jules makes a face like she's tasted something sour. "Because money."

"Because tradition." My voice stays even, but my stomach twists anyway. "Even if you cancel the official event, the town will still celebrate. People will still hang lanterns and crowd the pier."

Blaire nods.

"Exactly," she says. "So we don't try to stop the tide—we cut the rot out early, before it can swell." Then her tone shifts, softer without losing the edge. "And you're not alone. Council will have support on the ground. Eon security is doubling perimeter checks. We're not walking into this blind."

Jules lets out a breath she's been holding and forces a smile back onto her face like it's a weapon she's practiced wielding. "Cool. Love that for us. Nothing like demon hunting before breakfast."

Remy lifts her hood higher. "I hate breakfast demons."

Mina's mouth twitches despite herself. "All demons are breakfast demons if you don't sleep."

Jules points at her. "That's poetry. Write that down. Put it on merch."

Mina laughs. "No way."

The bus slows as we approach the town's weathered welcome sign at the limits—salt-warped wood, peeling paint, the letters stubbornly hanging on. It reads: WELCOME TO HARBOR'S EDGE.

My lungs feel too small.

Harbor's Edge used to feel like the whole world. The streets, the boardwalk, the rusty carnival rides that only worked when someone kicked them just right. The Lighthouse Diner with its cracked vinyl booths and the sign that buzzed like it was always about to give up.

Evie used to sit across from me in those booths, elbows on the table, chin on her fist, watching me like I was something worth studying.

... I shouldn't be thinking of Evie right now...

I straighten in my seat, forcing my shoulders back. Leader posture.

"Alright," I say, voice steady enough to fool even me. "Game faces."

Jules salutes with two fingers, but her eyes stay sharp. "Game faces."

Mina nods, swallowing her nerves. "Game faces."

Remy's answer is almost a whisper. "Game faces."

Blaire taps her tablet once, satisfied, like she's sealing a deal with the universe. "Good," she says. "Because the second we step off this bus, you're Midnight Halo again. We go straight from drop-off to arena tour to morning briefing. You can catch up on doomscrolling after soundcheck."

The bus takes the turn toward the arena, tires whispering over the freshly paved road. Banners are already up on the lampposts:

Eon's stylized logo, the Harbor Lights emblem, and our faces blown up three stories tall.

MIDNIGHT HALO: HARBOR'S EDGE HOMECOMING

My smile on the banner is the same one I'm wearing now: perfect teeth, soft eyes, hair caught mid-swoop.

Evie used to tell me that I smiled with my whole face, not just my mouth. But that was before the stylists and media training taught me how to smile for the cameras.

The bus hisses as it brakes, air suspensions sighing like it's relieved to be done carrying us.

Security and staff converge towards the bus in their black jackets, hands at their earpieces. A few fans managed to slip around to the back; they press up against the barriers, holding signs and chanting our name.

Blaire is up first, like she always is, already halfway through a phone call before the door even opens.

"—yes, we're here. No, she doesn't need the second option. I said *no*—" She flicks two fingers in our direction without looking back, a silent *move*. "We'll be inside in three minutes. Keep the corridor clear."

"On your marks," Blaire says to us. "Kaia goes first, then Jules, Remy, Mina. Sunglasses. Hoods. Smile like we love them, move like we've slept. Ready?"

"Ready," I chorus with the others.

I'm good at this part. The doors hiss open, and I flip the switch.

The morning air hits my face, cold and smelling faintly of salt and coffee from somewhere nearby. The fans scream. I wave, that practiced open-palmed motion that makes it look like I'm reaching for them individually. My cheeks lift, my eyes crinkle, the smile comes out on command.

"Welcome home, Kaia!" someone shrieks.

Home.

Flashes pop. Security moves us through the little gauntlet of bodies and cameras toward the service entrance. Jules pauses to blow a kiss; Mina makes a heart with her fingers; Remy does a half bow.

The arena looms ahead, a squat oval of steel and glass with our tour logo plastered across the front. In one of the wide street-level windows, the reflection of the bay catches my eye. For a second, if I squint, I can almost see the crooked outline of the pier where—

No.

I look down at my boots and keep walking.

Inside, the fluorescent-lit guts of the building smell like paint and sawdust, like every other venue on the tour.

We fall into formation without thinking about it: Mina close to my left shoulder, Jules drifting like a comet near my right, Remy a step behind like she's watching for ambushes. Blaire leads. Craig the skeleton remains in the bus, seatbelted and abandoned, a martyr to scheduling.

"Quick walk-through before we do the briefing," says a woman in a sleek black suit as she falls into step beside us. Eon, not Council—her shoes are too nice. "I'm Director Han, local operations. We're honored to host you in Harbor's Edge."

"Thank you for having us," I say automatically. "We're excited."

I remember to add, "It's good to be home," because someone in PR will yell if I don't.

She beams. "We've coordinated with the Council. Everything's in place for tonight's... performance."

There's a tiny hitch between "tonight's" and "performance" that tells me she's one of the ones who knows more than she lets on.

As we're led to the arena, Blaire and Director Han fall into conversation about the hotel arrangements.

On the far side, beyond the arena, I catch a slice of coastline: gray water rolling in, foaming white at the edges. A strip of beach I used to run on as a kid. The curve of it is the same.

The memory hits me like a shove: Evie sprinting ahead of me, laughing, hair whipped by wind, turning around to yell something I can't hear now because the years have blurred it into the sensation of wanting.

My fingers dip into my pocket.

Receipt.

Don't Panic List.

My thumb presses the paper hard enough to crease it deeper.

Don't.

Don't look.

Don't reach.

Better off.

"Hey." Jules bumps my shoulder lightly, a private nudge. "You just went somewhere."

"Nowhere," I say.

Inside, the arena is a cavern of echoes.

Even empty, it feels alive—the way big spaces do, the way they hold sound in their bones like they're waiting for permission to roar. The air smells like metal and dust and the faint chemical bite of fresh paint. High above, catwalks web the ceiling. Rigging hangs like dark vines. The seats curve up in long arcs, rows of emptiness that will be full of bodies tonight.

Our footsteps on the concrete corridor sound too loud.

Director Han gestures toward a wide set of doors. "Main bowl. Stage is set. You'll enter from house left."

Blaire nods. "Security sweep done?"

"Last night. Again this morning. Council added wards."

Director Han swipes a keycard, and the doors swing open.

The stage sprawls out, half-lit by work lights. The main screen is dark, but smaller panels glow softly with diagnostics. Crew members move with quiet purpose—headsets, tool belts, coffee cups clutched like lifelines.

For a second, I just stand there.

This is what I do. This is what I am.

But my chest still tightens the way it always does when I step into a venue before a show—like the space is taking my measure, deciding whether I'm worthy. And if I focus, I can feel the residue of old shows—local bands, school graduations, sports rallies—dusty echoes layered into the air. A thousand small joys and embarrassments and bored nights.

Mina takes one step forward, then stops, face pinched. "Do you feel—"

"Yes," I say, because I do.

It's subtle, but it's there: a low hum in the air, like a note just under hearing. The wards.

Council work always feels like that to me—structured, measured, built from rules. A net of sigils woven into the arena's skin. Protective. Comforting.

Blaire's hand touches the small of my back for half a second, a grounding signal.

"Walk the space," she murmurs. "Then soundcheck. Then we talk."

We move onto the stage.

The moment my boot hits the center platform, my magic wakes like it's been waiting.

It's not dramatic—no lightning, no sudden flare. Just a warmth in my bones, a slow ignition in the chest. Like my body remembers: *here, you burn.*

Jules bounces on the balls of her feet, testing the spring. "This floor is delicious."

Remy's mouth tilts. "Weird sentence."

"Everything is a weird sentence if you're brave," Jules says, then pivots into a small spin, arms out. "Hello, Harbor's Edge!"

A crew member near the monitors snorts, unable to help it.

Blaire gives Jules a look over her shoulder that says *behave.*

Jules winks at her like she's being polite.

Mina drifts toward the edge of the stage, peering out into the empty seating like she's trying to see ghosts. Mina's sensitive. She Sees more than the rest of us do, even with our Resonance.

"What?" I ask quietly, moving closer.

She shakes her head, but her eyes don't stop scanning. "Nothing. Just... it's big."

"It's empty," Remy corrects.

Mina's lips press together. "Empty isn't always empty."

Remy's gaze flicks to her. "You Seeing things again?"

Mina flinches like she's been poked, then forces a smile. "No. Just... vibes."

Jules makes a face. "Vibes are real, thank you. I'm basically powered by vibes."

Remy almost glares at her. "You're powered by attention."

Jules rolls her eyes. "Same thing."

The stage is set up for tonight's kickoff—extra pyrotechnic rigs, the lantern-themed light structures hanging above, special effects machines tucked into corners. Eon Entertainment wants spectacle. They always do. Especially with the festival coming up in a few days.

The Harbor Lights Festival is built on yearning. On tradition. On people coming back year after year to feel like the world is bright and safe and beautiful, at least for one day.

And nostalgia? Yearning? That energy is like drugs to demons.

Blaire steps away to speak with Director Han and a pair of Eon security guards, voices low. I catch fragments: "Council arrives... increased incidents... keep routes clear..."

I turn toward our tech team at the soundboard. "Can we get mics hot?"

A thumbs-up. A headset nod.

A stagehand hands me my in-ear mic set like it's a sacred object.

The weight of it settles into my palm. Familiar. Solid. A focus. I attach it to my ear, clicking it on, as the others are handed theirs as well.

"Check. Kaia. One, two," I say.

The sound comes back through the monitors, clean and bright.

My magic threads into it without permission—just a faint shimmer in the air, a sensation like heat above asphalt.

The crew member at the board nods, satisfied. "Levels are good."

Mina's voice follows, soft but clear. "Mina, check."

Her sound carries differently—less heat, more clarity, like a bell. Her magic always feels like moonlight to me: cool, reflective, deceptively sharp.

Jules grins. "Jules. I am here. You're welcome."

Her magic is all flare and spark, a playful crackle that dances in the air for half a second before she reins it in.

Remy's check is low, controlled. "Remy. Check."

Her sound doesn't shimmer; it cuts. A straight line of force. When Remy's magic rises, it's like a blade being drawn.

"Alright," I say, because it's easier than thinking about anything else. "Run the chorus on 'Halo Burn.' Just once. No full output."

Jules groans. "Just once? You're starving me."

Remy murmurs, "Good."

We fall into position without discussion, the choreography of our bodies as practiced as breathing.

Three... two... one...

We sing.

Even a partial run sends a pulse into the empty arena. It's like throwing a stone into a still lake and feeling the ripples hit your skin. The harmonies knit together, familiar as muscle memory. My voice anchors, Jules' lifts, Mina's threads through like light through glass, Remy's cuts clean and exact.

The magic follows, subtle, controlled.

A faint aurora of light blooms above the stage, then folds back in. Heat rises and dissipates. The air tastes briefly of ozone.

It's contained. Professional.

It's what we do.

When we stop, the arena seems to hold the last note for a heartbeat before letting it die.

For a moment, there's a hush so complete I can hear the distant tick of rigging cooling.

Then Mina inhales sharply.

I look to her immediately.

She's staring up.

Not at the lights.

Not at the catwalks.

Higher, into the rafters where shadows collect like secrets.

"Mina?" I keep my voice low, calm. Leader voice, even when my pulse spikes. "What is it?"

Our magic shouldn't have been enough to attract anything yet, but the way Mina stares at the rafters has me on edge. Mina doesn't answer right away. Her pupils have gone slightly wide, the way they do when she's trying to focus on something only half there.

"Mina," Jules says, suddenly not joking. "Hey. Talk."

Mina blinks once. Twice.

"There was—" she starts, then stops. Swallows. Shakes her head. "I thought I saw something."

My stomach tightens. "What kind of something?"

Mina's voice drops. "A shadow. But... like—" She gestures helplessly up toward the rafters. "Like it was sitting there. *Watching.*"

Jules cranes her neck, squinting. "I see... dust."

Remy's gaze is sharp, scanning every beam, every dark pocket. "I don't see anything."

I don't either.

But the hair at the back of my neck is rising anyway.

"Can you describe it?" I ask Mina.

Mina's brow furrows like the memory is slippery. "It was... huge. Distorted. Like if you took a person-shape and stretched it until it didn't make sense anymore. But it was *really big.*"

Remy's eyes narrow. "Big shadows are always bad."

Jules tries to lighten it and fails. "Okay. *Hate* that for us."

Mina drags a hand down her face. "It was only for a second. It's gone now."

Blaire has noticed the shift. She's striding back onto the stage, headset bouncing lightly against her collar. "What happened?"

"Nothing," Jules says automatically. "Mina saw a demon ghost in the rafters."

Blaire's expression doesn't change much, but her attention sharpens. "Mina?"

Mina's voice is smaller now, embarrassed by being the focus. "I—I thought I saw something. Something big... But it's gone."

Director Han appears at Blaire's shoulder.

"There is no 'something big,'" she says, calm to the point of insulting. "Our monitors would have flagged anything of substantial size, plus the Council laid down wards that would have detected anything."

I look from Director Han to Mina. Then I step closer to Mina, angling my body so it reads like casual proximity instead of protection, and lower my voice.

"Do you feel anything? Residual?"

Mina closes her eyes for a beat, like she's listening with something other than ears. Then she shakes her head. "No. It's... quiet."

Blaire nods once, decision made. She turns back to Han, who's hovering at the edge of the stage with polite concern that doesn't quite reach her eyes.

"Please inform the Council we want another sweep of the rafters and catwalks," Blaire says.

Han's jaw tightens. The smallest flare of irritation—like being asked to re-check work she's already blessed. "It's unnecessary."

"Do it anyway," Blaire replies, still smooth. Not loud. Not rude. Just immovable.

A beat.

Han exhales through her nose and gives a clipped nod. "Fine. I'll relay the request."

"And tell the Council," Blaire adds, as if she's offering a favor, "we're ready for the briefing as soon as they are."

Director Han nods once and turns on her heel, already pulling out a phone—no doubt to relay Blaire's "requests" like they're her idea.

I still don't know where the exact hierarchy falls—whether Blaire technically outranks her in Eon's ecosystem, or whether Han just assumes she does because she's attached to us and we're valuable. But I've watched Blaire walk into rooms full of people with titles and make them adjust their posture without raising her voice. She has leverage. She knows it. And she isn't above using it.

I respect it.

Mina exhales, shoulders dropping like she's been holding herself upright by force.

Jules steps closer and bumps her hip gently. "Hey. You're okay."

Mina's mouth twitches. "Am I?"

Remy's voice is low, almost kind. "If you saw something, you saw something. Don't let them make you feel stupid."

Blaire claps once, crisp. "Alright. Soundcheck done. Go drink water. Council briefing in fifteen."

Jules salutes. "Yes, ma'am."

Remy's attention doesn't leave the rafters even as she follows us offstage.

One of the security guards leads the way. We file down a corridor toward the green room area, the air colder here, concrete sweating faintly. Festival posters line the walls—Midnight Halo faces everywhere, bright and fierce, smiling.

My own face looks back at me in glossy perfection.

I hate her a little.

We pass a staff entrance with a window that looks out toward the parking lot and, beyond it, a sliver of street. For a second, I catch sight of a familiar diner sign in the distance—red letters, one bulb dead.

The Lighthouse Diner.

My chest tightens.

I force my gaze away.

Don't look her up.

Don't.

Because if Evie is still here like I suspect—if she's still in this town, living her life within reach of me—

I don't trust myself not to reach back.

The thought is a hook in my ribs.

I swallow it down like I've swallowed worse.

In the green room, Jules immediately raids the snack table with the determination of someone preparing for war. Remy drops into a chair like she's been unplugged, still scanning the ceiling corners. Mina sits near her, curling her hands into her sleeves like she's trying to make herself smaller.

I obediently reach for a bottle of water, drinking some as I stare at the snack table—neat rows of Eon-approved fuel in glossy wrappers.

For no reason that makes sense, I want kimbap so badly it hurts.

Not the fancy kind. The simple foil-wrapped rolls my mom used to make on festival mornings: sesame oil, salty seaweed, the sharp bite of pickled radish. The kind she'd press into my hands before a big day and say, *Eat first.*

Jules rips open a protein bar with her teeth. "If the Council makes us do another 'grounding exercise' in a room that smells like incense, I'm suing."

Remy's mouth twitches. "You can't sue the Council."

"That's what they *want* you to think," Jules says, already digging for something salty. "Eon at least gives you a hotline and a latte if you're having a breakdown."

Mina murmurs, "Eon gives you a latte so you can keep smiling on camera."

Jules points at her with a cracker. "Okay, valid. But also: latte."

I swallow another mouthful of water.

Mina is right though.

Eon Entertainment is technically our label. They handle the world everyone sees: tours, contracts, cameras, the manufactured mythology of Midnight Halo. They build the stage, sell the story, count the profit.

The Council handles what the world *can't* see: training, wards, intel, containment. Weapons. Cleanup. The things that happen when the emotional power plant of a crowd turns into an open door.

Two entities, one machine. And we're the moving part that makes it run.

Jules sighs dramatically. "I miss when my biggest problem was whether my eyeliner was even."

"You say that," I mutter, "but you cried for ten minutes when our makeup shipment got delayed in Tokyo."

Jules gasps, affronted. "That was a *spiritual* injury."

I keep my expression flat, but something tight eases in my chest anyway. This is what we do: joke until the dread gets bored and goes away.

We've had all of five minutes to ourselves when Blaire arrives, phone in hand, listening to an update through her headset. Her face remains calm, but the line between her brows deepens. It's less than two minutes later when she ends the call and points two fingers toward us.

"Briefing room. Now."

The hallway to the briefing room is narrower, more official. Less festival glitter, more laminated signs and security guards. An Eon representative meets us at the door. He's a man in a sleek suit with a company pin, and a smile polished to a mirror shine.

"Midnight Halo," he says warmly. "Thank you for your quick cooperation. I'm Devin Park, talent relations. The Council is inside."

Jules leans toward Mina and whispers, "Talent relations sounds like a job where you say 'we value you' while actively not valuing you."

Mina whispers back, "Shh."

But she smiles softly again, which has Jules grinning.

I ignore them and step into the room.

The conference room is small and windowless. Someone has tried to make it friendly—there's a tray of fruit, a plate of pastries, a carafe of coffee—but the air feels thick.

Three people are already seated at the table when we walk in. They have that particular stillness of people who believe the world runs on rules and that they are the ones holding the rulebook.

One is Director Han. Another is an older man in signature council gray clothes, hair shaved close, eyes sharp behind thin-framed glasses. Eric Cohen, one of the leaders at the Council. I've seen him twice before, both times when something went very, very wrong. The last is clearly a Council Handler.

"Kaia Rhee. Midnight Halo. Thank you for coming promptly."

"Of course," I say, voice steady. "Thank you for having us again, Mr. Cohen."

"We'll be brief. But please, sit," he says.

We sit. I keep my back straight and my hands folded, the way I've been trained to look calm even when my pulse is climbing.

Blaire takes the seat closest to Mina. Not between us and them, but near enough to intervene if needed. Blaire's good like that. Even though she works for Eon, she genuinely has our backs too.

"First, allow me to say what an honor it is to have Midnight Halo perform at Harbor's Edge," Devin says as he takes a seat beside the Handler. "This is a special event—for Eon, for the town, for your fans."

"And for the Council," Eric Cohen adds. "Given the... patterns we have observed."

There it is.

I lace my fingers together under the table.

Mr. Cohen continues, "Demon activity has increased in the Harbor's Edge region in the last three weeks. Not isolated incidents—patterned."

"We're confident your kickoff concert will address the buildup," Devin cuts in smoothly. Annoyance flashes across Mr. Cohen's face at being cut off, but Devin continues. "Tonight's show is designed to be both a celebration and a containment measure. You've done this before."

Containment.

Eric Cohen, ever the serious Councilman, nods. "As you know, your concert is not simply entertainment. It is your job. Harbor Lights draws emotion. Tonight's performance is meant to address the issue and prevent manifestation before the festival begins."

"We've prepared a brief," Director Han says, sliding her tablet onto the table and tapping the screen. The wall behind her lights up with a projection: a map of Harbor's Edge, dots of red scattered around the bay and city center.

"You all know Harbor Lights is a high-emotion event," she says. "Wishes, nostalgia, community. For as long as anyone can remember, that festival has been a beacon."

"For demons," Remy says dryly.

Han doesn't deny it. "Yes. Historically, we saw sporadic manifestations—small, localized, easy to disperse. But in the last year, we've tracked a new pattern."

She taps again. Some of the red dots swell into nodes, connected by faint lines.

"We're calling it the Chorus," she says. "An echo that keeps coming back. This manifestation forms around repetition—chants, songs, jingles. Think of it as... the town's nostalgia growing a mouth."

Mina makes a face. "Gross."

Jules leans forward, frowning. "We've fought manifestations like that before."

"Yes. You encountered one in Seoul last year. So as you know, the Chorus is not a single entity in the way a typical demon is," Director Han continues. "And this variation seems particularly attached to nostalgia."

My stomach drops a fraction.

Because Harbor's Edge is the perfect buffet for it, if that's the case. People come back here to feel like they're sixteen again. Like nothing bad ever happened. Like love didn't leave.

Like leaving wasn't *necessary*...

"Now it's here," Director Han says, bringing up another slide. This one is a timeline, spikes in red clustered more and more tightly around recent dates. "In the last three months, we've seen a significant uptick in minor incidents across Harbor's Edge. Whispering static in the lighthouse. Unexplained feedback at the local station. A near-stampede at a community concert when the PA system glitched into a loop."

The image shifts again: security camera footage, grainy, of a busy street crossing. For half a second, the silhouettes of pedestrians blur, all their heads turning in the same direction, mouths open as if singing.

Then it's gone.

That's how it usually looks to civilians, *if* it looks like anything at all. Most fans can't actually *see* the demons. Not the way we do. If you don't have a Spark, if you haven't been trained to tune your senses to the frequency, the supernatural slides past your brain like a skipped frame. You register it as static, nausea, or a bad feeling you can't quite place... Or you don't register it at all—until something gets close enough to leave a scar in your nervous system, and then you start seeing shadows where there shouldn't be shadows.

"Harbor Lights is in three days," Devin adds. "That amount of focused emotional energy will draw the Chorus like a magnet. We would prefer not to cancel the event, for obvious reasons."

The obvious reasons being ticket sales, tourism revenue, good PR for both Eon and the council.

"And the less obvious reasons," Eric Cohen says, shooting him a look, "being that even if we cancel the festival, residents will still gather. The Chorus will still feed. This time we will stop it once and for all during your performance tonight."

Jules is the first to speak. Of course she is. "How?"

Eric Cohen's eyes stay steady. "Tonight's homecoming concert is a controlled release. The back to your roots energy should draw it's attention. The wards will trap it. They have been updated by Mr. Bane here."

For the first time, all of us actually look at the man sitting beside Cohen.

A Council Handler.

Handlers are a specialized unit inside the Council, Resonants whose Sparks don't flare into song or movement or light—whose resonance is tuned to one thing: containment. Hard lines. Seals. Circles that hold. When they're near, magic doesn't *wake* so much as it... obeys.

Like the world remembers there are rules and gets scared of breaking them.

Mr. Bane looks like someone pressed flat by years of quiet work. Tall, narrow, dressed in a dark, unwrinkled coat. His hands are gloved, fingers long and precise. His eyes don't catch the light the way ours do; they drink it in, dull and unreadable.

My skin always crawls around Handlers.

Even Jules—who never misses an opportunity to run her mouth—goes quiet, like she's suddenly remembered what predators are.

Mr. Bane doesn't speak.

He only inclines his head once, a minimal acknowledgment

Blaire's voice cuts in, polite and firm. "We had a report on stage. Mina saw something in the rafters. Could this be the Chorus?" "

Both Mr. Cohen and Mr. Bane's gazes turn towards Mina immediately. Devin's smile tightens by a degree.

Mina flushes. "It was only a second. A shadow. It was... *big*."

Mr. Cohen writes something down. "We will increase the sweep teams. But understand: the Chorus often does not appear as a single figure. It is a phenomenon. A pattern. It can gather in places where memory is thick."

Harbor's Edge has memory thick enough to drown in.

Suddenly, the receipt in my pocket feels like a hot coal.

"The scanners didn't show any entities in the arena," Director Han adds.

"Residual stress from the tour," Devin says dismissively to Director Han. "They have been working non-stop." His attention turns to Mina. "I'm sure once you've had a proper rest, Miss Mina, your... impressions will settle."

Mina slumps in her chair, cheeks flushing. Jules shoots me a look that clearly says *she is not making this up.*

Remy doesn't speak, but her eyes are cold. She gets like that, trusts very few people.

Director Han's gaze settles on me. "Kaia. You will lead the mission. You will keep your team grounded. Your setlist—"

"—Is already approved," Devin cuts in quickly, as if to reassure everyone that paperwork exists to keep the universe orderly.

Han's mouth tightens, like she dislikes being cut off, but she continues. "Your setlist must emphasize forward motion. Renewal. Release. Avoid songs that fixate on regret."

Jules makes a face. "So... no sad bangers."

I keep my expression neutral, but my throat tightens.

Avoid songs that fixate on regret.

If the universe had a sense of humor, it would be cruel enough to put me in my hometown and tell me not to sing about regret and longing.

Instead, I nod. Leader smile, leader composure.

"Understood," I say.

"Good," she says. "Then let's talk optics."

Of course.

She brings up a slide with our faces on it, overlaid with Harbor Lights branding. "Publicly, this is a nostalgic 'back to roots' special. Hometown girl returns as conquering hero. We want warmth, authenticity, community."

She looks at me when she says *hometown girl*, like I'm supposed to feel special instead of vaguely nauseous.

"We've lined up a pre-show interview with the local station," she continues. "Kaia, they'll ask about growing up here, your memories of Harbor Lights. Play up the sense of longing, but not regret. You made good. Everyone loves you. You owe it all to the support of the town. That sort of thing."

My fingers twitch toward my pocket again, toward the folded receipt with Evie's handwriting on it.

I don't owe it all to the town.

I owe it to one girl who kissed me on a pier and accidentally lit up the harbor.

"Any questions?" Director Han asks.

Surprisingly, Blaire asks, "And if Mina Sees anything again?"

Mr. Cohen answers, "If something manifests, you will act. That is why you exist."

The words are meant as reassurance.

They land like a weight.

Director Han regains control by standing. She says with a bright smile, "Rest up, then. Rehearsals at ten, soundcheck at two. Showtime at eight."

We file out of the room in silence that feels too tight.

The hallway outside is colder. Or maybe that's just my skin.

Mina's voice is small. "What if I see it again?"

I stop walking.

They all stop with me, instinctively. A little cluster in the sterile corridor, four women with too much power and not enough certainty.

I look at Mina—really look.

Mina is brave in a quiet way. She feels things before they have names. That doesn't make her fragile. It makes her a warning bell. Unfortunately, outside of us and Blaire, Eon and the Council rarely take it seriously unless their machines go off too.

"If you see it again," I say, low and steady, "you tell us immediately. You don't talk yourself out of it. I don't care if no one else sees it. We trust each other."

I glance at Remy and Jules, before looking at Mina again.

Mina's eyes shine a little. "Okay."

Jules nods hard, as if agreeing with her whole body. "Yeah. Mina sees weird stuff. That's literally her brand."

Remy adds, barely audible, "And we believe you."

I keep my face calm, but inside my chest something shifts.

"Alright," I say. "We do what we always do. Warmups. Rest. Dinner. Then we burn it clean."

Jules lifts her hands like she's presenting a prayer. "Burn it clean."

Mina repeats softly, "Burn it clean."

Remy's voice is a low promise. "Burn it."

Blaire's voice drifts from a few steps behind, already back in manager mode. "And stay hydrated," she calls. "If any of you get possessed because you refused electrolytes, I will be beyond annoyed."

Jules laughs despite everything. "Not the electrolyte de-mon—"

We move again.

As we pass another window, the town flashes by outside—wet streets, festival banners, a glimpse of the boardwalk.

And, in the distance, that diner sign again.

The Lighthouse Diner.

My fingers press the receipt through the fabric of my pocket until the paper creases.

A thought rises anyway, uninvited: *What if she's there? What if she's grown into someone I don't recognize? What if she sees my face on every poster and hates me for it?*

I shut it down the way I've practiced shutting down pain onstage.

Clean. Fast. Brutal.

Evie is better off without me reopening anything.

Tonight is about the show.

Tonight is about protecting this town.

Tonight is about being the global pop star group Midnight Halo.

THE DINER SIGN BUZZES like a dying insect, flickering in and out as if it can't decide whether it wants to be seen tonight.

THE LIGHTHO—

THE LIGHTHOUSE DINER

THE LIGHTHO—

I flip my hood up against the wind anyway and shoulder the door open with the same elbow I've been using for years, because the handle sticks when it's cold and Harbor's Edge is always cold when it wants to be mean.

A bell jingles overhead. The heat hits my face, fogging my lashes for half a second.

Grease, coffee, bleach. *Home.*

The Lighthouse Diner doesn't look anything like a lighthouse. It's a squat little building two streets off the boardwalk, painted white once upon a time and now mostly beige with time and salt stains.

But the tourists like the name, and the locals like the cheap eggs.

Behind the counter, Gus is counting out the till like he's personally offended by the concept of money existing.

He's in his sixties, built like a barrel, with an unruly mustache. His hair is a heroic gray. His expression is his usual: *I've never loved anything in my life and certainly not you.*

He sees me, and snorts. "You're late."

"I know." I slide behind the counter, shrugging out of my jacket. "Sorry. My grandma decided her afternoon pills were a personal insult to her freedom."

Gus doesn't look up. "Tell her to take 'em anyway."

"I did."

"And?"

"She told me she survived the eighties without being told what to do by a teenager."

I bite the inside of my cheek. I'm twenty-four, not sixteen—old enough to pay bills, file taxes, and keep another human being alive through sheer stubbornness and a pill organizer. But to my grandma, I'm permanently seventeen years old with an attitude problem.

Gus grunts. "Clock in."

From the far booth, Mr. Alvarez lifts his hand in greeting without looking up from his newspaper. Like he's been here since the earth cooled. Speaking of, his coffee looks mostly full and I know it's already cold.

Mr. Alvarez likes to sip on coffee, not actually drink it.

"Evening, Evie," he calls, voice warm.

"Evening," I answer automatically. "Your coffee is going to get cold if you let it sit any longer."

"It already is," he says, pleasantly.

He's been coming here every day for as long as I've been working. He reads the paper like it's a sacred text and eats pie like it's his job. His hands are spotted with age, and he remembers things most people pretend not to.

Which is why I like him.

And why I also sometimes want to hide under the fryer.

I tie my apron and step behind the counter, reaching for the coffee pot out of muscle memory. Might as well get him a fresh cup.

That's when I hear it.

A squeal, sharp enough to pierce the air.

"Oh my GOD, Evie, you're here! Did you see it? Did you see the clip?! They're so close, they're literally—"

Tasha bursts out of the back like she's been launched by a cannon.

Tasha is barely eighteen and looks like she has never had a single un-fun thought in her life. Tonight she's wearing Midnight Halo merch under her apron: an official tour hoodie with the sleeves pushed up and a glittery sticker of Kaia's face slapped on her phone case like a blessing.

I don't know why the universe gave me her. Some kind of cosmic joke.

Tasha's phone is already up, screen glowing in her palm. She looks like she's about to start squealing. *Again.*

I take one look at her face and know, in my bones, that tonight is going to be one of *those* shifts.

"What clip?" I ask, already regretting the words.

Tasha's eyes go bright with the feverish joy of someone who has never been emotionally betrayed by a pop star.

"The Kaia interview!" she says, as if there's only one Kaia and only one interview worth seeing. "They're doing promo in the arena, and she's like, 'It means everything to come home,' and she's wearing this jacket that makes her shoulders look illegal and—"

"Tasha," I warn.

She barrels over my warning like it's a traffic cone.

"They're literally ten blocks away tonight," she says, voice vibrating. "Ten. Blocks. Like, I could *walk* there. I could just walk there right now and—"

"Your shift starts in three minutes," Gus calls without looking up, deadpan.

Tasha spins toward him. "Gus, it's *Midnight Halo*."

Gus snorts. "It's a band."

"It's not *a band*," Tasha says, affronted. "They're an icon. A cultural movement! And they're doing the swords tonight—like, *obviously*—but it's the *homecoming* version. With big, dramatic choreography where they just—" she mimes yanking something out of thin air, eyes shining, "—and everyone loses their minds."

Gus squints at her like she's grown another head. "You're a cultural movement. Go fill the sugar caddies."

Tasha looks like she might combust. Then she looks back at me, pleading. "*Evie*. Tell him."

I pour Mr. Alvarez fresh coffee to buy myself time. "Tell him what?"

"That Kaia Rhee is a local hero," Tasha says, breathless. "Like, *our* local hero. She grew up here. She sang at Harbor Lights when she was, like, sixteen and then she got discovered and now she's coming back and it's like... *destiny*."

My hand tightens around the coffee pot handle.

Local hero.

Destiny.

A beat too sharp passes through my chest, like the snap of a rubber band against skin.

I set the pot down with controlled care. "She's a person," I say.

Tasha blinks. "Yes, obviously. But—"

"And this is a diner," I add, voice flat. "Not a fan club."

Tasha opens her mouth, closes it, then tries again. "Okay, but you have to admit it's kind of exciting. The whole town is buzzing. Like, even the gas station had a Midnight Halo poster and—oh! Look!"

She points.

The TV mounted over the counter is on, volume low, running a loop of local news. The screen is bright enough to cut through the diner's warm gloom. The anchor is smiling too hard, the kind of smile people use when they're trying to make commerce feel like community.

And there, flashing across the screen, is a promo package:

MIDNIGHT HALO RETURNS HOME

The camera cuts to the arena. Then to the crowd already gathering outside even though the show isn't for hours. Then to a close-up of a woman with perfect hair and perfect teeth holding a mic.

And then—

Kaia Rhee.

Her face fills the screen like she owns it.

She's different than the last time I saw her in person. We'd just been teenagers then. Now, she's older and time has carved her down into something sleek and bright and untouchable. Her hair is darker than it used to be, pulled back. But her eyes are the same.

God. Her eyes are the same...

The anchor's voice chirps about "record ticket sales" and "unprecedented excitement."

Kaia's mouth moves, saying something I can't hear over the diner's sounds, but the caption flashes:

"COMING HOME FEELS... SURREAL."

Tasha makes a sound of awe. "Look at her."

And I do look, because my body is stupid and my eyes have always been worse.

Kaia smiles on-screen—polished, practiced, the kind of smile you give when you're trained to be adored. It's not the smile she used to give me, back when her face would soften and she'd grin with her whole face.

Back when her laugh was loud and real and she didn't know what it meant to be watched by millions of people.

Back when she'd stand on the pier at Harbor Lights with cold wind in her hair, looking at me like I was the only thing keeping her from floating away.

I feel the memory hit before I can stop it.

The pier boards under our sneakers, wet with sea spray. Lanterns swaying overhead. Her fingers brushing mine like an accident. That second where she leaned in and I leaned in and—

My throat tightens like it's trying to swallow my heart.

"Nope," I say out loud.

Tasha turns. "Nope?"

I reach up and click the TV off mid-sentence.

The screen goes black. The diner seems to exhale.

Tasha stares at me like I've committed a crime. "Evie!"

"Diner's not a fan club," I repeat, leaning closer so my voice stays low and mean enough to end the conversation. "We serve breakfast and shakes and fries. We don't worship celebrities."

"She's not a celebrity," Tasha says instantly. "She's *Kaia*."

"She's literally a celebrity," I say.

Mr. Alvarez folds his newspaper with excruciating slowness. "That Rhee kid," he says, voice thoughtful. "Used to sing at the festival. Always had a set of pipes on her."

My hands still.

Gus grunts without looking up, like he's been waiting years to drop the line. "And you two used to sit in that booth like you paid rent." His tone stays flat, but there's something almost smug under it. "You two in there, heads together, giggling."

Tasha's eyes go wide like I've betrayed her and her attention doubles on me. "You were friends with her?!"

I keep my face neutral. I keep my hands moving.

"I *knew* her," I say, stressing the word like it matters. Like it fixes anything. "It's Harbor's Edge. Everyone knows everyone."

I turn away before my face can do something stupid.

"Okay," I say, too brisk. "We have work to do. Tasha, sugar caddies and wipe down booth three, someone spilled syrup last shift and it's turning into a science experiment. Mr. Alvarez, pie or are you doing that thing where you pretend you're not hungry until midnight?"

"Pie," he says immediately.

Gus slides a plate toward me with a short stack of order slips. "Tourists are already crawling in," he says. "Festival week. You ready to be miserable?"

"I was born ready," I say.

Tasha bounces on her heels, still vibrating with excitement she hasn't gotten to unload. "Evie," she says softly, like she's trying a different approach. "You're not... excited at all? You sat in the same booth as Kaia Rhee!"

I don't answer right away.

Because outside, through the front windows, I can see the street.

Harbor's Edge doesn't usually look like this. Not on a random weekday night. Not even the week before Harbor Lights. But people in Midnight Halo merch move in little packs, phones out, laughter too loud. Cars creep by like they're hunting for parking.

Even the air looks busier—headlights cutting through it, neon reflecting off windshields, a constant churn of bodies that don't belong to this town.

The concert's ten blocks away, and you can feel it anyway. Like gravity. Like the whole place is tilted toward the arena.

Everything feels... wired.

Not bad. Not *dangerous*, exactly.

Just tight.

Like the town is holding its breath and waiting for something to happen.

Tourist season, I tell myself. Harbor Lights. Money. Hype. Whatever.

Still.

My skin prickles.

Tasha keeps watching me like she thinks I'm going to break and admit something.

I don't.

"She's coming to do a job," I say, voice cool. "People come back for work all the time."

Tasha frowns. "It's her *homecoming*."

I laugh once, sharp. "Yeah. Sure."

Mr. Alvarez makes a small sound.

Gus, blessedly, slams down a stack of clean mugs and breaks the moment. "Less talking," he growls. "More moving. We're not getting swallowed by the dinner rush because you two are having feelings at the counter."

Tasha turns beet red. "We're not—"

I cut in, "We're not."

Gus grunts like he doesn't believe either of us.

The bell over the door jingles again as the first wave comes in: two college girls wrapped in scarves, laughing, Midnight Halo pins on their backpacks. A middle-aged couple with a guidebook already open. A guy in a hoodie who looks like he hasn't slept in three days and is holding a souvenir lantern like it's a holy relic even though Harbor Lights is days away.

I plaster on my customer face and grab my notepad.

"Hi," I say, voice sweet enough to rot teeth. "Welcome to the Lighthouse Diner. Coffee?"

As I move down the line of booths, taking orders, refilling mugs, and dodging Tasha's starry-eyed chatter, I keep catching myself listening for something I shouldn't be listening for.

A name.

Kaia Rhee.

Our hometown girl.

Local hero.

Every time I hear it, something in me snaps a little, like a wire being pulled too tight.

I keep working anyway.

Because that's what you do in Harbor's Edge.

You keep your head down. You serve the coffee. You pretend the past isn't sitting ten blocks away in an arena, smiling for cameras like she didn't leave you standing on a pier with your heart in your hands.

And when the TV stays dark behind the counter, the diner feels safer.

Or at least quieter.

Which is as close to safe as this town ever gets.

THE INTERVIEW LIGHTS STILL burn behind my eyes when Devin finally lets me step off the little media platform in the arena's press corridor.

"Perfect," he says, like I've just landed a plane, not answered the same questions I've been prepped for.

How does it feel to be back?

Are you excited for Harbor Lights?

Any surprises for the fans tonight?

Kaia, what do you love most about your hometown?

Hometown.

The word had sat in my mouth like a shard of glass.

I smiled anyway. I softened my voice the way I've trained myself to. I said the right things: *surreal, grateful, honored, can't wait to share this moment with everyone.*

I stayed on script. Mina had given me a thumbs up from behind the producers.

Now, Devin's hand hovers at the small of my back, guiding me as if the cameras might catch me getting lost in a hallway. He wears his sleek suit and his polished Eon pin and his smile that never quite reaches his eyes. He looks like someone who's been raised by PR.

What's his title again?

Oh, yeah. *Talent relations.*

Blaire intercepts us the second we clear the media area.

She doesn't raise her voice. She doesn't need to. She just appears in front of Devin like a door clicking shut.

"Soundcheck," Blaire says, headset tucked around her neck. "Now. No more interviews."

Devin's smile tightens. "We have one more local spot—"

"No," Blaire says pleasantly. "I need the whole lineup. Including Kaia."

The phrasing shouldn't make my chest tighten, but it does. Blaire doesn't draw lines like that often, and when she does, it means she's annoyed enough to let it bleed through her professionalism, and protective enough to claim us anyway.

Devin blinks once.

Behind her, Jules lifts her phone like she's filming a nature documentary. "Observe," she whispers to Mina. "The wild Blaire protecting her pack."

Mina smothers a laugh into her sleeve.

Remy doesn't bother hiding her amusement. She leans against the wall with her arms folded, looking like she'd pay money to watch Devin get told no for sport.

Devin's gaze flicks over the three of them, then back to Blaire, recalibrating. "Fine," he says. "Soundcheck. But the Council will want another confirmation of the plan after rehearsal."

"They can have it," Blaire replies. "After the girls have had water and fifteen minutes without someone shoving a mic in their faces. Vocal cords aren't a renewable resource."

Devin backs off with the smooth grace of someone who hates losing but prefers to lose quietly. He turns on his heel and disappears down the corridor.

Blaire watches him go, then exhales through her nose.

"Okay," Jules says brightly. "Now that the corporate serpent is gone—"

"Don't start," Blaire warns, but her mouth twitches.

Jules puts a hand over her heart. "I respect serpents."

Remy rolls her eyes.

Mina slips her fingers into mine for half a second as we start walking. A grounding touch—quick and secret—like she's sensed my pulse spiking during the interview and decided to anchor me before I float away.

I squeeze back once, grateful.

Then I let go, because I don't get to cling to softness when there's work to do.

The stage looks different in the afternoon.

This morning, it had felt like a mouth—empty, waiting, too quiet.

Now it's alive with crew. Work lights blaze hot and white. Screens cycle through visuals. Technicians move like ants along the catwalks. The air smells like warmed metal and faint incense from the Council's wardwork, layered over the ever-present coffee.

The festival-style set dressing has gone up even more since the morning: lantern frames hang above the stage like a cage of glowing ribs, unlit for now. A lighthouse silhouette is built into the main screen design, and the floor is painted with pale spiraling lines that look decorative if you don't know how to see spells hiding in aesthetics.

I know.

I see the seams.

"Alright," I say as we step onto the stage. "Mics in-ears. One clean run of the first three songs. No full output."

Jules groans theatrically. "Kaia, I'm going to start charging you for emotional damage."

"You'll survive," Remy says.

Mina tilts her head, listening to the room. "The wards are louder today."

"Council reinforced them after your report," Blaire calls from the wings.

Mina's shoulders lift a fraction, then drop. "Oh. Okay."

I force myself not to look up toward the rafters.

I've done it three times already since breakfast.

I've seen nothing every time.

Which doesn't help.

Remy glances at me—just a flash of attention. She's been watching me more than usual since we got into town. Not like Jules, who watches because she wants to poke. Not like Mina, who watches because she cares.

Remy watches like she's waiting for me to crack and will have to do damage control.

Remy's responsible like that.

I give her my calm face. My leader face.

"Positions," I say. "Let's work."

We take our places.

The earset mics come alive with soft pops and hums as the packs power on. The stage monitors feed back our breaths. The arena beyond is still empty, but the space holds sound differently now, like it's practicing being full.

I angle the thin wire closer to the corner of my mouth and let my voice drop into my chest.

"Check," I say, and the word comes out steady.

The magic in my bones stirs, familiar as a heartbeat.

"Kaia levels are good," someone calls from the board.

The other girls run through their checks—Jules snapping a quick riff that makes a tech laugh, Mina's "one-two" coming out softer than usual, Remy's low hum steady enough to level a room.

Then Blaire's voice cuts across the stage again, crisp as a cue light. "Alright. Lights and track. Treat it like a show, but keep it at thirty percent. We're testing timing"

Jules salutes with two fingers. "Copy that."

We run the first number.

Even restrained, the harmonies fill the empty arena with a pulse that makes my skin hum. Jules' voice lifts bright and fierce, Mina threads through with that bell-clear tone, Remy anchors with a low line that makes the melody feel inevitable.

My voice holds the center.

It always does.

I let my magic bloom only enough to taste it—heat rising like a sunrise under my ribs, a faint shimmer flickering above the stage before I pull it back in.

Controlled. Professional. Safe.

We stop after the third song.

The silence that follows is thick.

Jules flops onto the floor dramatically. "I'm starving."

"You are always starving," Remy says.

"For applause," Mina offers.

"For violence," Jules corrects. "It's different."

Blaire's voice comes through my in-ear. "Hydrate. Five minutes."

Jules rolls onto her back like she's been slain. "Tell my fans I died doing what I loved."

Remy steps around her like Jules is a stage hazard. "I'll tell them you died doing what you were told not to do."

Mina laughs softly, then glances out into the seats.

Her smile fades.

The motion is subtle enough that no one else would catch it if they aren't looking.

I'm looking.

"Mina," I say quietly, stepping closer. "You okay?"

Mina blinks, then forces brightness into her face. "Yeah. Just... vibes."

Jules sits up, hair falling in her face. "Are we vibing weird again?"

Mina's mouth twitches. "No."

Jules squints at her. "That's the 'yes' no."

"It's fine," Mina insists.

Blaire appears at the edge of the stage holding a water bottle like a weapon. "Drink," she commands, and hands it to Mina first.

Mina takes it with a small, grateful nod.

I drink too, because leadership means modeling behavior even when you want to chew through the walls.

The water tastes like plastic and minerals.

It doesn't wash the town out of my throat.

The private combat rehearsal happens after the crew clears the stage for lighting tests.

Council requires it now—ever since some idiot in a different city tried to fight a manifestation without rehearsing inside the wards and nearly blew a hole through a venue wall. The world pretends it's a freak pyrotechnic accident. We all know the truth.

Demons love crowds.

Crowds love spectacle.

Eon loves plausible deniability.

So we train. We practice. We keep the violence neat.

Mr. Bane, the Council Handler, meets us onstage. He traces a sigil in the air with two fingers. The wards click into a different configuration.

I feel it in my bones: the net tightening. The air changing. A pressure shift like the room exhales and decides to become a cage.

Jules shivers—then beams, like she's been handed a gift. "Oh, hell yes. Zip me in. Let's go."

"It's containment," Mr. Bane says evenly. "If anything manifests, it will be confined to the stage."

Jules bounces on the balls of her feet, practically vibrating. "Say less."

Blaire stays offstage with Devin and Director Han.

"Alright," I say, stepping into the center of the warded circle. "Same plan as always. We run the sim, we identify the hook, we kill it neatly."

We don't do this for every little prowler demon or straggler. Most nights, we can feel the shape of a threat from the first wrong note and cut it down on instinct. But when something this much mass? The Council makes us rehearse inside a tightened cage.

I continue, "Then tonight, we'll perform, let the Chorus surface inside the wards, and destroy it before the crowd disperses."

Mina adds, "Before the energy spreads."

"Exactly," I say.

Jules cracks her neck. "Before the tourists start texting each other 'I felt something weird at the show lol.'"

Remy's voice is low. "Before it learns new mouths to sing through."

A chill crawls up my spine.

I hate the way Remy can make anything sound like prophecy.

"Stay on me," I say, pushing the unease back into its box. "Jules, you're flank and bait. Mina, you're shield and sight. Remy, you're strike and sever. We keep it in the circle. We don't let it touch the wings."

Mina swallows, fingers flexing at her sides. "And you?"

"I anchor, like always," I say. "And I end it if it gets past you."

At the edge of the stage, Mr. Bane raises his hand.

The ward lines painted into the floor answer—thin sigils along the spiral brightening like someone has just traced them in molten gold. The air thickens. Pressure settles. The containment circle closes with a soft, inaudible click my bones can feel.

Then the house speakers come alive.

Not for us—for the sim.

One of our tracks kicks in on a clean loop: heavy beat, bright hook, the kind of chorus that makes stadiums jump in unison.

The sound hits the wards and the wards catch it, shaping it into a consistent pulse—music as metronome, metronome as bait.

Jules' grin flashes. "Oh, we're doing it pretty."

"Pretty gets you killed," Remy mutters.

"Pretty gets you *paid*," Jules shoots back.

Mina doesn't laugh. Her gaze fixes on the air above center stage, as if she can already see the seam opening.

And she's right.

As our chorus hits, the space above the stage shimmers—heat distortion at first, light bending like it doesn't want to tell the truth. The shimmer thickens, darkens, and congeals into something almost human, if you don't look too hard.

The sim construct isn't the real thing. It's a baited imprint: a training manifestation built to mimic the pattern and test our response.

The Chorus doesn't have a face.

It doesn't need one.

"Contact," I say, and the word snaps us into the choreography we've practiced a hundred times.

To any human watching—crew on a security feed, a stagehand peeking in—this looks like rehearsal.

Like dance.

Like four women hitting marks to music.

They don't see the war layered underneath.

She sprints into the downbeat and spins, feet carving a tight arc across the ward circle—movement so crisp it could be tour choreo. Her momentum builds fast, *faster*, her body a fuse—

—and then she snaps both hands up like she's catching something thrown from the rigging.

On cue, the stage lights strobe—one sharp white flash, then a wash of gold—like it's a planned beat drop. Like this is the part the crowd would scream for.

Nothing is there.

Until it is.

Light cracks into her palms like twin lightning strikes, solidifying into two short swords that hum with kinetic charge. Their edges spark with the energy of her movement, electricity crawling in disciplined, deliberate arcs—pretty enough to pass for an effect, dangerous enough to carve a demon in half.

Voltstep.

Jules flashes a grin and whips both blades through a cross-cut on the beat. The sparks don't fly randomly; they leap in neat, purposeful ribbons, as if even the electricity knows the choreography.

"Hey, ugly!" she calls, bright enough to read as banter for an unseen camera. "Miss me?"

The construct shudders, attention locking onto her the way attention always locks onto Jules—like she's a magnet and the world is metal.

It turns toward her—

And then the sound comes.

Not from its mouth. It doesn't have one.

From the air itself, slipping between the beats of our song like an invasive refrain.

A tinny melody, faint and warped, like it's playing through a broken speaker.

A jingle.

A familiar four-note hook that makes something in my chest jerk.

Harbor Lights.

The stupid festival ads that play on local radio stations every year.

Come back, come back, the lanterns will light your way—

My stomach drops.

Jules falters for half a heartbeat, eyebrows shooting up. "Oh my god," she breathes. "It's doing the tourism jingle."

Remy's face goes unreadable. "It's not random."

Mina's breath hitches. "It's using what people already know."

The construct lunges.

Mina moves like the next count of the routine—one smooth step, a turn, her arm sweeping up as if she's reaching for a partner.

Her hand closes on empty air.

The air answers.

A blade forms in her grip, translucent as ice and glass, catching the stage lights and throwing back a clean, merciless reflection.

Heartglass.

Not a shield—a truth. When she raises it, the reflection in its surface sharpens the world, stripping away illusion. The construct's edges flicker, briefly revealing wrongness beneath the sim's skin: threads of compulsion, stitched loops of familiarity, the pattern trying to wear the shape of something comforting.

Mina angles her sword like a mirror and the jingle warps, suddenly exposed—less sweet, more hungry.

She pivots again, and the movement completes the defense: a refracted plane of light snaps into place, a barrier born out of the sword's reflection.

The construct hits it and ripples, its dark body smearing like ink in water.

It doesn't stop the sound.

The jingle deepens, trying to turn lullaby-sweet again.

Like a hand on the back of your neck guiding you toward something you miss.

My mind flickers—uninvited—to the pier. Lanterns swaying. Evie's laugh on the wind. Her hand brushing mine like it's inevitable.

Pain sparks behind my eyes.

"Focus on me," I tell the girls.

Remy moves next.

Not fast like Jules—inevitable.

She steps into the beat, fingers tracing a shape in the air like she's writing with invisible ink. The air brightens where her fingertips pass—thin lines of glowing script, runes unfurling midair.

Then she pulls.

The glowing script tightens, twists, and hardens into a blade in her hand—black as fresh ink, etched with elegant, dangerous lettering that continues to crawl along its length.

Inkthorn.

When Remy swings, it isn't just a cut—it's a sentence.

The blade carves through the space between notes, leaving glowing runes hanging behind it like trailing lyrics. Her songs are encoded spellwork. Her strikes are punctuation.

She slashes on the downbeat.

The jingle stutters, as if the pattern itself is corrected mid-line.

The construct reels—hit not in flesh, but in structure.

"Remy," I breathe, impressed despite myself.

She doesn't look at me. "It's woven in," she says, voice low. "Festival ads. Hooks. Memory triggers."

Mina's eyes widen as Heartglass reflects the construct's threads more clearly now. "Woven in for years."

"Yeah," Remy says. "That's why it keeps coming back. Everyone knows the tune. They've been humming it their whole lives."

Jules kicks into a new combo, and her twin blades spark brighter—because she isn't just moving, she's charging. Each step feeds Voltstep more kinetic energy. Each spin loads the blades with heat.

She darts in, crosses her swords, then snaps them apart in a flourish that would be pure showmanship if it weren't aimed at a demon.

"Okay! Cool!" she shouts. "So the demon is basically an annoying commercial."

The construct surges again, hungry for attention, hungry for familiarity. The jingle twists into something older, slower.

A fairground melody.

A cheap keyboard version of a song I haven't heard in years.

The same one I sang on a rickety town stage at Harbor Lights when I was sixteen, hands shaking so badly I can barely hold the mic.

My breath catches.

No. Not this.

But my body remembers anyway—cheap lemonade, lanterns trembling, the crowd a dark ocean beyond the stage.

Evie's voice cutting through it all, loud, fearless, unapologetic.

Kaia! Kaia, you've got this!

Pain flashes behind my eyes.

Something in my chest tries to lurch backward toward that moment like it's a lifeline.

"Kaia," Mina says, and the word hooks me back. "Kaia, stay with us."

I swallow hard. "I'm good."

The construct lunges toward me, drawn by the spike in my emotion like it can smell it.

Fine.

If it wants me, it can have me.

I step into center on the chorus drop, feet hitting the mark like it's choreography—because it is. Because routine keeps me focused.

My hands lift—empty.

Then I reach upward like I can catch the light itself and pull it down into something solid.

Light answers.

It ribbons around my hand in a tight spiral—warm, prismatic, almost liquid—then snaps into shape with the finality of a locked chord: a broad winged sword, heavy in my grip. The metal isn't metal so much as condensed radiance—holographic sheen shifting with every angle, as if it holds a whole spectrum inside it.

Aurora.

It thrums the moment it forms, recognizing the music, recognizing me. Aurora is built for performance—made to take whatever lives in my throat and turn it into something the world can't ignore.

Magic surges up—not into words, not into lyrics, but into the blade itself—Aurora drinking it in and amplifying it until the air tastes like ozone.

I sing one note.

Just one.

Low. Controlled. Anchored to the beat.

The sound hits the construct as a shockwave, visible as a ripple in the air—a clean ring that slams into the thing and makes its edges shiver.

And this—this is the part no civilian ever understands.

To a normal eye, it's lights and smoke and four women dancing with swords that "appear" right on the beat.

To anyone with resonance—or anyone who's been unlucky enough to survive the wrong kind of night—it's a war in plain sight.

I lift Aurora and draw it down in a smooth arc.

The blade doesn't just cut; it translates—voice into force, force into barrier.

A protective plane flares in front of us for a heartbeat, catching the construct's lunge and throwing it back as if the air itself becomes armor.

The jingle sputters. The pattern buckles.

Remy is already moving, Inkthorn poised to sever the weakened thread. Mina angles Heartglass so the construct's true form is fully exposed in its reflection—threads and bindings laid bare. Jules darts along the edge, charging her blades with every step, laughing too loudly to keep fear from sticking.

"Sorry!" Jules calls, bright and vicious. "We don't do reruns!"

Remy strikes on the final beat of the loop.

Inkthorn carves a glowing rune through the air—an ending mark.

The pattern splits.

The construct shudders, collapses, and evaporates against the ward lines like ash caught in wind.

Silence drops.

My pulse hammers.

Aurora thrums in my hand, satisfied—like it just remembered exactly what it's made for.

For a moment, I stand there breathing hard, staring at the empty spot where the thing had been, trying not to think about how quickly my mind had jumped to Evie.

At the edge of the circle, the Handler gives a single approving nod. Director Han's mouth tightens in that way that means *good, contained,* and Eric Cohen offers one spare clap like he's signing off on a report. Blaire nods once from the wings, eyes on us, not the suits.

Voltstep vanishes as Jules flicks her wrists and throws up jazz hands. "We're amazing."

Inkthorn disappears next as Remy says, "We're practiced."

Mina doesn't laugh. She's staring—too still—past us into the arena bowl. I follow her gaze without meaning to.

"What?" I ask, already knowing I won't like the answer.

"There," Mina whispers, pointing with Heartglass.

My breath stops on instinct, my body bracing for impact—

—but when I follow her line of sight, I get... nothing. Empty seats. Shadow. The normal dark mouth of an arena waiting to be filled.

"I don't—" Jules squints hard, head tilting. "I don't see any-thing."

Remy's gaze narrows, not at the seats—at Mina. Like she's tracking Mina's pulse instead of a target.

Mina's grip tightens on Heartglass until her knuckles go pale. "It's up there. Back rows. It's—" She swallows. "It's clapping."

Jules's face changes. That quick, bright confidence flickers into something unsettled. "Clapping," she repeats, like the word tastes wrong. "Like... applause?"

Mina nods once, sharp. "No sound. Just—" Her shoulders rise, a tiny flinch. "Hands. And it's doing it like it's... enjoying this."

A cold thread slides down my spine. I don't need to see it to hate the shape of that.

Jules's mouth twists. "Great. Love that. Love a non-audible horror clap."

I force my eyes to cut the darkness into sections, trying to find it. Still nothing. Still emptiness. And that's the worst part—knowing something can be watching and your senses are just... shut out.

Blaire's voice crackles in my in-ear, brisk and controlled. "Nice work. Hydrate. We're holding schedule."

I don't answer with the automatic *copy*.

I say, "Blaire. Mina's seeing it again."

A beat. I can practically hear Blaire's brain shift gears.

"Where," she asks, clipped.

"Back rows," I say, gaze locked on the dark. "She says it's clapping."

Jules makes a strangled sound that is halfway between a laugh and a swear. "Yeah. Like we're entertaining."

Mina's voice is tight. "I'm not joking."

"I know," I say immediately.

I can't hear what happens on Blaire's end, but out of the corner of my eye I see her straighten in the wings. She turns toward Director Han and Devin—head angled, hand lifting in that subtle *come here* motion she does when she's about to apply pressure.

They step in closer to her. Blaire speaks without her mic picking up in my in-ears, which means she's deliberately keeping it off our channel.

Great.

Devin steps onto the stage edge a moment later with a strained smile, palms out like he's calming children. "Alright. Let's not panic. This is a controlled environment. Wards are up. Council is present. Mina, sometimes heightened sensitivity—"

Mina's face flushes, anger and embarrassment colliding. "I really saw something, Mr. Park."

"I didn't say you didn't," Devin says quickly, but his tone tries to. Smooth, dismissive around the edges.

Remy's stare stays flat. "You implied it."

My gaze cuts to Devin like a blade. "We need to take this seriously. Mina's never wrong."

Devin's smile tightens. "Of course. But we need to keep the team focused. If Mina fixates on—"

"Fixates," Remy repeats softly, like she's tasting the word. "You sure you want to use that one?"

Devin blinks, thrown off balance.

Before it can turn into a full-on argument, Director Han steps forward. She's all calm polish and practiced authority, like she's smoothing a wrinkle out of a suit.

"Enough," Han says, mild. "Mina, thank you for flagging it. We'll run an additional sweep and cross-check the monitors." Her eyes flick, briefly, to the handler and then to Eric Cohen.

The exchange is fast—too fast to be anything but communication.

And there's something in it I don't like. A shared look.

Han turns back to us with the same calm. "Nothing unusual is currently registering on the wards. That doesn't mean you didn't feel something. It means, at this moment, we don't have corroboration."

Devin seizes the opening like oxygen. "Tonight's show needs to proceed," he says, as if that's the only real sentence in the room. "We can't spiral over shadows."

Han gives a small nod, like she's agreeing with inevitability, not desire. "The performance proceeds. We increase monitoring."

Because it has to.

Because the alternative is letting the Chorus roam free through Harbor's Edge with no containment.

"Great," Devin said, relief slipping through his professionalism. "Perfect. That's what I needed to hear."

I nod once, even though my skin still feels too tight.

Aurora dissolves from my grip, light unwinding into nothing, and I force my hands not to shake as I step off my mark—already hearing that silent clap in my head, whether I saw it or not.

In the dressing room corridor, the festival posters have multiplied again.

Midnight Halo faces stare down from every wall—perfect skin, fierce eyes, glittering costumes that make us look like angels instead of women.

There's an old Council superstition about that, too—whispered in training halls and pinned into glossy recruitment language when they think you need a myth to survive the work. *Resonants are touched. Part angel, built to carry light without burning up.*

I've never bought it.

Jules stops in front of a poster and squints at her own face. "Do you think they'd notice if I drew little mustaches on these?"

Remy doesn't break stride. "I would."

Mina hugs her hoodie tighter. "Please don't get in trouble before the show."

Jules leans closer to Mina, voice turning syrupy. "For you, my moonbeam, I will behave."

Mina rolls her eyes, but it softens her expression, just a fraction.

I watch them, grateful for the banter, for the normalcy they manufacture out of habit.

Then my chest tightens as a memory slams into me anyway: open mic night at Harbor Lights a lifetime ago. The rickety town stage. My hands shaking. The mic too big in my grip.

Evie in the front row, eyes bright, laughing like the world can't touch her.

Cheering the loudest.

Believing in me before anyone else does.

Believing in me so fiercely it feels like a blessing.

And then I left her with nothing but the echo...

My fingers drift toward my pocket automatically.

Receipt.

The list.

    1. *breathe (yes you have lungs. use them.)*

So I do. I swallow hard, breathe, and keep walking.

My dressing room is small and too clean, like all arenas try to scrub the humanity out of their backstage spaces.

There's a long mirror rimmed with bulbs. A counter already crowded with glossy promo photos Eon has placed there—my face, Jules', Mina's, Remy's, all in high-definition perfection. A rack of costumes hangs to one side, garment bags labeled with Sharpie.

The air smells faintly of hairspray and lemons.

Someone has put a bowl of fruit on the counter like we're going to eat grapes between killing demons.

I shut the door behind me and lean my forehead against it for one long breath.

The quiet presses in.

My pulse slows.

A different kind of ache rises in my throat: the one that comes when I stop moving long enough to feel.

I cross to the counter and stare at the idol photos.

Kaia Rhee, Midnight Halo. The girl who burns demons. The hometown hero. The one who comes back with lights and glory.

The one who leaves and never looks back, my own traitorous mind reminds me.

My hand slides into my bag and finds what I packed before we left the hotel.

A photo.

Faded at the edges, creased down the middle, colors softened by time. Two teenagers on the Harbor Lights pier, lanterns glowing behind us. Evie with wind-tossed hair and a grin too sharp for her own good, leaning into me like she belongs there. Me with my arm half-raised like I don't know what to do with my body, smiling like I've just been handed the sun.

We look... happy.

We look like we don't know how much life could change.

My throat tightens until it hurts.

"Idiot," I whisper—not to her. To myself.

I lift the photo and stare at it, letting the pain have its moment.

Then I reach up and slide it behind the mirror.

Not fully hidden.

Just tucked behind the glossy idol shots Eon arranged, buried under layers of curated perfection.

A secret pressed flat against glass.

Something real in a room built for performance.

I stare at my own reflection—my eyes, my mouth, the practiced calm I wear like armor.

Then, very carefully, I touch the edge of the mirror where the photo hides, as if I can feel Evie through it.

"I'm not looking you up," I say softly, as if saying it out loud will make it true. "I'm not dragging you back into this. Especially not now. I can't."

My reflection doesn't answer.

The arena lights outside hum. Somewhere down the hall, Jules shouts something dramatic and Remy tells her to shut up. Mina laughs—small, bright, grateful for the sound.

Blaire's voice echoes faintly in the corridor, scheduling our lives into neat lines.

And somewhere in the back rows of an empty stadium, something enormous clapped for us like it enjoyed the show.

I straighten, smoothing my hair back, forcing my breath into steadiness.

Leader. Pop star. Weapon.

Tonight, we sing.

Tonight, we lure the Chorus into the cage.

Tonight, we kill it before it can slip its hooks into Harbor's Edge's hungry nostalgia.

And I keep my eyes forward.

Even if my past is less than ten blocks away.

THE LIGHTHOUSE DINER IS ten blocks from the arena, which is just close enough to make it everyone's personality as the night drags on.

The bell over the door doesn't stop ringing.

In. Out. In. Out.

Every time it jingles, another blast of cold air rushes in, carrying damp ocean wind and the smell of wool coats and cheap cologne and anticipation. The place is packed—every booth full, counter stools taken, a line forming near the front even though we don't technically have a hostess. It's just me, Tasha, Gus, and Sam the cook.

Gus is behind the grill with Sam, shoulders hunched like he's personally wrestling every burger into submission.

"Tasha!" he barks.

"I'm here!" Tasha yells back from the dish pit.

I slide between tables with my coffee pot like a weapon. At booth six, a couple in matching Midnight Halo scarves lean toward each other like they're planning a heist.

"Do you think they'll do 'Halo Burn' tonight?" the girl whispers.

"They have to," the other girl whispers back, like this is a sacred matter.

At the counter, a group of college kids argue loudly about which member is "most lethal."

"Jules," one says. "Jules is chaos. Chaos is lethal."

"Remy," another insists. "Remy is like... poetry with a knife."

"Kaia," a third says, dreamy. "Kaia is the moment."

Kaia.

The name bounces around the diner, ricocheting off plates and people and my skull. I pretend I don't hear it, because I'm very good at pretending.

"Evie!" Tasha pops up at my elbow like a sprite. "Table twelve needs ketchup, and they asked if you know where Kaia went to high school."

I don't even stop walking. "Tell them she went to Hell High and graduated with honors."

Tasha giggles, delighted and scandalized. "Evie!"

"Tell them we don't do trivia here."

"They're just excited!"

"They can be excited at home," I say to Tasha, before sliding ketchup toward table twelve with a smile that could cut glass. To them, I say, "There's only one high school in Harbor's Edge."

Harbor's Edge High: one long, low building that always smelled like floor wax and old fries. Pep rally banners that never fully came down. The same cracked trophy case by the office where Kaia's name had ended up printed on glossy plaques: Choir Soloist, Festival Showcase, "Most Likely to Make It Big."

At least they weren't wrong.

The woman at twelve takes it like I'm handing her a relic. "Thank you! Oh, are you going to the show?"

"Nope," I say.

Her face falls. "But it's Midnight Halo."

"I gathered," I say, and turn away before my mouth gets mean enough to be a problem.

The pre-show rush has a particular rhythm—frenetic and impatient, people shoveling fries like its fuel for worship. They keep checking their phones. They keep glancing at the windows like they expect to see Midnight Halo walk by.

Outside, festival lanterns sway on wires over the street, unlit but waiting. The air feels charged, like a storm is coming.

Tourist season in Harbor's Edge, which is mainly the week leading up to the Harbor Lights Festival is usually busy anyway.

Tourist season, I tell myself as I slide plates down, refill coffee, dodge elbows.

Tourist season, I repeat when someone asks if "Kaia Rhee ever came in here."

No. No, she didn't.

Not anymore.

Half an hour before the concert doors open, the diner is a boiling pot.

Then, like a switch flipped, the crowd empties. The bell over the door jingles and jingles and jingles: people flowing out in a wave of glitter and merch and breathless energy.

"See you after!" someone calls.

"Wish me luck!" a teen girl says, clutching her ticket like it's a passport to heaven.

"Tasha, come on!" one of her friends yells through the window, waving a lanyard. "Just ditch!"

Tasha's face presses against the glass for half a second, longing written all over it.

Gus catches her staring and barks, "Eyes on the dishes!"

Tasha jumps. "Sorry!"

I watch the last cluster of fans hurry down the sidewalk toward the arena, their laughter already half swallowed by the night.

Then the diner... exhales.

It doesn't go dead quiet—we still have a few regulars, a couple tourists who missed the memo about the world's largest pop group performing nearby, and Mr. Alvarez with his second slice of pie—but the frantic energy bleeds out of the room.

The town's attention shifts. Ten blocks away, a stadium fills.

I lean on the counter and take my first full breath in two hours.

Tasha wanders over, wiping her hands on her apron, eyes bright like she's about to launch herself through the ceiling.

"They're starting soon," she whispers, like saying it loudly might jinx it.

"Yep," I say.

Tasha squints at me. "You're being weird."

"I'm being employed," I correct.

She opens her mouth to argue, then the bell jingles again and a couple stumbles in, cheeks flushed, hair damp with fog.

"Is it too late for pancakes?" the woman asks.

"It's never too late for pancakes," I tell her, because that's the one thing I believe in without complicated feelings.

I slide them menus, take their order, and keep moving.

When I pass the TV mounted above the counter, my eyes snag on it.

Black screen. Remote sitting right there under the register.

I bet the local news station is having a field day with Midnight Halo.

I can picture it too easily: the livestream, Kaia onstage in a spotlight, voice filling the arena.

My chest tightens like a fist.

Yeah, nope.

Instead, I go to the old jukebox, the one Gus claims is "vintage," and click it on.

The jukebox crackles to life, neon lights buzzing softly. I select the first thing that comes up that isn't a power ballad and isn't likely to send me into a spiral.

Some old rock song. Loud guitars. Nothing soft. Nothing sweet.

Tasha makes a wounded noise. "Evie!"

"What?" I snap automatically.

"That's, like, dad music."

"Good," I say. "Let the dads have something."

Tasha huffs, then drifts toward the kitchen as if she's carrying her disappointment like a flag.

I hear her a minute later—her phone speaker muffled behind the swing door, then the unmistakable opening of a Midnight Halo track.

My shoulders go rigid.

The worst part isn't that I recognize it.

The worst part is that I recognize it *immediately*.

I don't want to know the beat drop.

I don't want to know the harmony line.

I don't want to know the exact point in the chorus where Kaia's voice will cut through like a blade wrapped in honey.

I know anyway.

I walk into the kitchen with the kind of calm that scares teenagers.

Tasha jumps, phone in hand like she's been caught stealing. "Oh! Hi!"

"Turn it down," I say.

She blinks. "Why?"

"Because I said so."

"That's not a reason," she argues, bravely, because she's eighteen and thinks the world is negotiable.

I stare at her until she remembers I am older, meaner, and currently holding a tray like I could become violent.

Tasha's voice softens. "Evie... it's the kickoff. Everybody's there. I can't go. This is the closest I'll get."

I shouldn't care.

I do.

That's the problem.

I exhale, sharp. "This is a kitchen, not a concert venue."

Tasha's jaw juts out. "You *hate* them."

"I don't hate them," I say too quickly.

Tasha's eyes widen, as if realizing it just now. "You totally hate them."

"I don't like their music."

Tasha blinks. "*What?*"

As if that is somehow less believable than me hating them.

"It's... glossy." I gesture vaguely at the air, as if the concept of pop production is floating above the fryers. "Overproduced. Like it was assembled in a lab by a committee of people who hate joy."

Tasha looks personally attacked. "That's—Evie, it's literally art."

"It's literally trashy," I argue. "All that glitter and—what—*swords* and smoke and everyone screaming like they're being exorcised. It's too much."

Tasha's mouth falls open. "They're iconic."

"They're loud," I correct, sliding a plate onto the pass with more force than necessary. "There's a difference."

She looks like she wants to argue again, then she hesitates, eyes searching my face like she might actually see the bruise under my annoyance.

Her voice drops. "Is it... because of Kaia?"

The name lands like a slap.

My throat tightens so fast it's almost embarrassing.

Tasha, oblivious, continues. "Because earlier Gus did say that you *knew* Kaia." Her eyes brighten. "Were you friends? Were you enemies? Were you like... rivals? Because—oh my god—what if you were in a band together—"

"Tasha." I don't look at her. If I look at her, I'll give myself away.

But Tasha is already vibrating with excitement, words tumbling out faster. "I'm just saying, it would explain why you're acting like her name is—"

"Don't," I repeat, and my tone comes out sharper than it should.

Tasha recoils slightly, stung.

I immediately regret it.

Because she's a kid. Because she's not trying to hurt me. Because I'm the one who keeps stepping on the same landmine and acting surprised when it explodes.

I drag a hand down my face. "Look. Play whatever you want," I say, forcing my voice into something less angry. "Just... quieter. Okay?"

Tasha hesitates, then nods. "Okay."

She turns the volume down until the music becomes background sound, a heartbeat under the kitchen noise, not the whole room.

I step back into the dining area and feel the shift again.

I can hear the arena from here, faint through the night: a low rumble like distant thunder.

Crowd noise.

A roar, muffled by buildings and fog and ten blocks of street, but still there.

Someone screams. Thousands answer.

The sound crawls under my skin.

Mr. Alvarez looks up from his newspaper. "They've started."

"Yep," I say, too casual.

One of the tourists at booth three laughs. "Wow. You can hear them from here."

"Yeah," Gus says from behind the counter, wiping a mug with a rag that's seen war. "Town gets loud when it wants something."

Tasha drifts out of the kitchen, hands clasped in front of her like she's trying to behave. Her eyes are shining. "Do you think they're opening with 'Halo Burn'?"

Gus grunts. "I think you should be sweeping."

Tasha sighs, dramatic. "You don't understand art."

Gus points the rag at her like a gun. "I understand rent."

His gaze flicks to me, then he jerks his chin once, almost grudging.

"At least *one* of you knows how to keep your head on straight," he mutters. "Evie doesn't let all this noise get to her head. She clocks in and works hard."

I don't react. I don't let my face do anything.

Instead I wipe down the counter that is already clean and say, "I can't go anyway."

Tasha frowns. "Why not?"

I keep my eyes on the cloth moving in circles. "I need to go home after this. Check on my grandma."

It's not even a lie.

Not fully.

Grandma is asleep more than she's awake these days, and she forgets where she is when she wakes up at night. If I'm not there, she wanders. She panics. Or, worse, she tries to make tea and forgets the stove.

Tasha's expression softens. "Oh."

Gus doesn't say anything. He just sets a slice of pie in the pass window.

I swallow hard and carry it to Mr. Alvarez's booth.

He looks up at me. "Your grandmother doing alright?"

"She's fine," I say, because that's my favorite lie. "Just... needs watching."

He nods, accepting it. "Family's family."

"Yeah," I mutter.

At the booth near the window, a trio of teen girls are whispering over milkshakes they're barely touching.

One of them says dreamily, "Kaia's voice sounds like first love."

I freeze mid-step.

The phrase sinks in under my skin like a splinter.

First love.

The second girl sighs. "Like the kind that ruins you."

The third giggles. "Shut up. You're so dramatic."

My chest aches in a place I don't have a name for anymore. I force myself to keep walking, coffee pot steady in my hand, expression flat.

Teenagers say stupid things, I tell myself.

Teenagers romanticize everything.

Teenagers don't know what it feels like to have your first love leave town and turn into a billboard.

I pour their refills without looking at them.

One of them smiles. "Thank you!"

I nod. I don't trust my mouth.

Behind the counter, the remote for the TV still sits there.

I glance at it once.

Just once.

My hand twitches.

Because ten blocks away, Kaia is singing. The whole town is hearing it. Feeling it. Letting it fill their ribs like a hymn.

And I'm here, pretending I don't care, wiping down the same clean counter, refusing to turn on a screen like it's a moral victory.

The crowd roars again, louder this time, a wave cresting and breaking.

My breath catches.

Tasha's phone in the kitchen shifts to another Midnight Halo song, quieter now but still unmistakable.

I close my eyes for half a second, then open them and go to the jukebox again. I punch the button for the loudest, dumbest song I can find.

The diner fills with guitars and drums and something deliberately un-romantic.

Tasha makes a small, offended sound from the kitchen.

The roar from the arena fades into the background for a moment, swallowed by our own noise.

I tell myself it helps.

I tell myself I'm fine.

I tell myself the past is just an echo, and echoes can't hurt you if you don't listen.

But the night keeps breathing through the windows—fog and salt and sound.

And ten blocks away, the world's loudest echo is singing like she owns the sky.

The lights hit like a confession.

For a second, I can't see anything beyond the stage lip—just white blaze, the haze of fog machines, the glitter of pyrotechnic dust still hanging in the air from the last number. The arena is a living thing around us, roaring, chanting, swallowing sound and spitting it back louder.

MID-NIGHT!

HA-LO!

MID-NIGHT!

HA-LO!

My skin hums with it.

Makeup tightens on my cheekbones when I smile. Sweat slicks the back of my neck under the collar of my costume. The outfit is all deep blue, especially designed for Harbor's Edge, with each of our signature colors woven into the details. For me, that's a deep purple.

This is the version of me Eon sells in posters and promo clips.

I stretch out my hands, and the crowd surges again, like they're physically leaning towards me.

"Harbor's Edge," I say, breathless on purpose, like I'm moved. "Are you still with us?"

The scream that answers could crack concrete.

Jules is to my left, glitter-smeared and feral. She bounces on her toes like she's plugged into the arena itself. Mina stands a step back, shoulders lifted in that poised way of hers, eyes bright and steady. Remy is calm on the other side, chin tilted like she's listening to something under the noise no one else can hear.

In my in-ear, Blaire's voice is a low thread. "Encore in sixty. We're running 'Firefly Night.' You're clean. You're perfect. Breathe."

Breathe.

I swallow down a laugh that would sound like a sob.

Jules steps forward, voice all heat. "Y'all want one more?"

The arena answers like it's a single creature.

Remy's lips quirk. Mina's smile turns shy for half a second, like she's startled to be adored this hard.

I watch them and feel the familiar ache: this is my family. This is what I protect. Even when my heart is full of old ghosts.

We regroup at center stage. The screen behind us cycles through Harbor Lights visuals—lanterns, ocean spray, a stylized lighthouse, our faces superimposed in shimmering gold. The festival branding makes it look like we're not just performers, but part of the town's mythology.

But the encore is one of our ballads.

The one that makes people cry in stadiums and swear it changed their lives. The one that Eon calls "transformative" because it spikes engagement and keeps fans looping it at night.

The first chord strikes through the air, and the arena quiets, almost obediently, like the crowd knows they're about to be allowed to feel.

The intro is soft. Piano, a slow swell of notes like tidewater. The lights drop into blues and purples. Phones and glowsticks rise like fireflies. The audience becomes a field of tiny stars.

I breathe in.

On the inhale, I feel the wards.

This is the last clean shot we get tonight. Our last chance to lure in the Chorus. So far, it hasn't taken any of the bait.

This song *has* to count, which is probably why they chose the most regret-filled, longing song we have for the encore.

Let's give the Chorus something tasty to feed on.

My voice slides out smooth, practiced, and still real enough that it hurts.

"We were wildfire in a paper town, chasing summer down the pier..."

The crowd sighs, a collective exhale. Somewhere someone starts crying immediately, which is impressive.

Jules takes the second line, voice brightened with sweetness for once.

"You said, *don't look back,* like that fixes it, like love can disappear..."

Mina harmonizes, her tone clear as glass. Remy's lower line anchors us like gravity.

My chest tightens as the song builds. This one always builds slow, like a bruise blooming. My eyes sweep the front rows out of habit—security, barricade, hands reaching, faces upturned.

And for half a heartbeat, my mind betrays me.

I see *her.*

Evie, the same girl I remember... Except, she's standing there in the crowd with her arms crossed, unimpressed, like she's only here to prove she doesn't care.

The image is so vivid it steals my breath.

Then it's gone, because she's not here.

She would never be here.

I keep singing anyway, voice steady, because that's what I do when my heart tries to fall out of my ribs.

The song's chorus hits, and the arena rises with it, people singing words like they've lived them too.

"If I could split the sky in two, I'd pull you through, I'd pull you through, but I'm just a song on somebody's lips, a light that leaves too soon..."

The crowd's emotion spikes like a wave cresting. It hits the wards. The wards hold. The sound becomes pressure. Heat.

The Chorus likes pressure.

Blaire's voice brushes my ear. "Kaia, eyes up. Rafters."

I don't move my head. I don't let the crowd see anything change in my posture. I keep my face soft, my voice warm.

But my attention snaps upward like a leash pulled tight. The rafters are a lattice of steel and shadow above the stage lights. And in that darkness... something starts to move.

At first it looks like haze. Like smoke catching wrong light. Then it swirls, thickens, and the air itself becomes a knot of sound and memory as it drops into the warded area.

The Chorus.

Not one body. Not one mouth.

A mass.

A rotating storm of half-heard melodies—Harbor Lights jingles, fairground keyboard loops, old radio hooks that have lived in this town for decades. It doesn't speak; it *sings* in fragments, trying to find our rhythm.

Trying to join.

Trying to harmonize with us like a parasite slipping into a choir.

The screen behind us flickers, lantern visuals glitching in quick bursts. For half a second, the lighthouse graphic becomes something else: a mouth. A spiral. A tunnel.

My stomach drops.

The wards hum louder. The Chorus presses against the net like it wants to break it.

"Here we go," Jules murmurs into her mic, still smiling for the crowd. To human ears it's a playful aside, part of the performance.

The second verse begins, and Remy takes lead. The one that always catches in my throat when we rehearse, even when I pretend it doesn't.

"I left a girl behind in salt-air light, and I told myself she'd be fine..."

The line lands like a punch to the ribs. Remy wrote it, but it still finds the soft part of me like it was written with my blood.

For a breath, my voice almost falters.

The crowd *feels* it—because the crowd always feels the crack—and their emotion spikes again, eager and hungry for something true.

The Chorus shudders in the rafters like it's being fed.

I force my next line out smooth, my smile intact, my body still in performance posture.

"But the truth is, love doesn't die, it just learns to hide..."

Above us, the Chorus swells, and the jingles twist into something sweeter, trying to wrap itself around our melody. It mimics us badly at first—off-key, too tinny—then it adjusts, learning fast, trying to slide into our harmony like it belongs there.

It doesn't.

It never will.

Blaire's voice is a calm knife. "Halo protocol. On my mark."

Behind the stage lights, the illusion layer activates. To the crowd, the lantern visuals intensify—gold light spilling across the stage like magic. A pyro rig fires in a controlled bloom at stage left, a harmless flourish timed to the bridge.

To us, it's cover.

I shift one step back on the next beat, exactly as the choreography calls for.

Jules mirrors me. Mina glides to the opposite diagonal. Remy pivots into her mark.

We look like we're dancing.

We are.

But it's the kind of dance that kills.

"Mark," Blaire says.

We draw.

To human eyes, there's nothing in our hands until there is, until the lights hit just right and the movement is so clean it reads as choreography flourish, not summoning.

Jules reaches down mid-spin like she's grabbing the air by the ankles.

Voltstep snaps into her grip, twin short swords sparking bright with kinetic charge. She's already moving, and the movement feeds the weapons; each step loads them hotter, brighter.

Mina turns her wrist outward like she's presenting her palm to the crowd.

Heartglass forms—translucent, merciless, catching the stage lights and reflecting the world back sharper. In its surface, the Chorus stops looking like "cool smoke." It becomes what it is: threads trying to latch onto every screaming mouth in the audience.

Remy lifts her hand as if tracing a lyric in the air.

Inkthorn arrives like a sentence finishing itself—black blade, script-etched, leaving glowing runes trailing behind it when she moves.

I step forward into the bridge, still singing, and reach as if catching light.

Aurora blooms into my grip. It's prismatic under the stage lights, like dawn trapped in metal. It hums in resonance with my throat, an amplifier tuned to my voice.

The bridge swells. The crowd is drowning in feeling.

"If you hear me in the dark, if my echo finds your name—"

Just like in the sim, Mina's Heartglass flashes, and she cuts. Jules launches into a charged combo, feet striking the stage in time with the beat. Every step pumps Voltstep brighter. She slashes in twin arcs that crackle like lightning, carving the Chorus's mass into smaller pieces the wards can contain.

"Follow every flicker, baby, I'm still the same," Jules breathes into her mic.

Remy moves like she's writing on the air. Inkthorn leaves glowing runes behind each strike, glittering sigils that hang for a second, then sink into the ward lines painted on the stage, reinforcing them.

I sing one low note threaded under the music, hidden inside the performance. Aurora drinks it and throws it forward as a sound-shock, invisible to the crowd but felt in the bones of the Chorus.

The mass buckles.

The arena lights strobe—planned. The pyro pops—planned.

Our violence disappears inside the spectacle.

To the audience, it looks like an insane, perfect dance break in the middle of a power ballad. They scream louder, thinking we're giving them art.

We are.

Just not the kind they think.

The Chorus writhes, trying to slip around the ward boundaries. It throws nostalgia like a net—old fair melodies, the Harbor Lights jingle, half-remembered radio choruses.

My throat tightens again, the pier flashing in my mind—Evie's laugh, Evie's hand, Evie's mouth just a breath from mine—

"No," I whisper into the next lyric, and turn it into a weapon.

"But I'm not the girl who runs, I'm the flame that learned to stay..."

Aurora flares.

The note becomes a barrier—a curved plane of shimmering force that catches the Chorus's push and rebounds it into Mina's reflection, where Heartglass reveals the seam, the weak point, the knot holding the pattern together.

The core thread.

We hit the thread together, moving as one.

Jules' charged blades slam in first, breaking the outer mass into fragments.

Mina slices through the binding contracts, stripping the Chorus of its borrowed sweetness.

Remy strikes last, Inkthorn carving a glowing rune.

I bring Aurora down in a clean arc and pour my voice into it, one sharp sustained note that becomes impact.

The Chorus collapses inward like a song choking on its own hook.

It evaporates against the ward lines in a burst of glittering ash that looks, from the audience's perspective, like a perfectly planned visual effect.

They lose their minds.

The final chorus hits, and the crowd sings with us, unaware they're cheering their own rescue.

"So sing me back, don't let me fade, I'm the echo you can't outrun..."

Phones wave. People sob. The arena is pure feeling: raw, holy, dangerous.

And we are still working.

Still scanning.

Still listening.

Because even as the main mass dies, I feel it...

A wrongness.

A tiny note out of tune.

A *drop* in the pit of my stomach, like something slipped through my fingers.

My eyes snap to the main screen behind us. It glitches, just for a heartbeat. Lanterns smear. The lighthouse graphic tears like wet paper.

A thin thread of sound—high, sharp, almost inaudible—slides toward the glitch, compressing itself into something small enough to escape.

A splinter of the Chorus breaking off.

No.

I tap my mic, switching to our internal channel only so my voice doesn't broadcast across the entire arena.

"Blaire," I breathe, still smiling for the crowd. "We have a leak."

"What?" Blaire's voice snaps, suddenly not calm.

Onstage, the others feel it too. They reach up, tapping their in-ear mics.

Mina's head jerks toward the screen, Heartglass reflecting the seam. "It's slipping."

Remy's voice goes flat. "It found an exit."

Jules takes a step like she's going to chase, then catches herself because the music is still fading and the crowd is still watching. "Oh, that's—bad."

The splinter threads itself through the glitching pixels like water through cracked glass.

Then it's gone.

The screen stabilizes.

The crowd screams, thinking the flicker was part of the show.

Confetti cannons fire. The arena becomes a snowstorm of glitter and paper and joy. The sound is so loud it turns into pressure.

And under all of it, I feel that splinter moving away from the wards like a cold finger tracing my spine. It's headed somewhere.

Somewhere *familiar.*

Somewhere it can hook into nostalgia and feed.

My mouth keeps smiling while my mind runs ahead ten blocks.

A diner.

A buzzing sign.

A girl with sharp eyes, who knows every Harbor Lights jingle because she grew up drowning in them.

Evie.

I don't know why my brain goes straight for her, but I know I'm not being paranoid. I know what the Chorus wants.

My breath catches so hard it almost breaks the smile.

No. No, not her.

Not *there.*

The others are still taking bows, waving, blowing kisses into the adoring crowd.

I can't.

I pivot on the next scream and bolt off stage, dismissing Aurora.

Backstage is a blur—curtains, cables, crew shouting congratulations.

"Kaia—!" someone calls.

Mr. Cohen steps into my path with a hand up. "Where are you going? We're not clear—"

"I'm clear," I snap, voice raw through the in-ear feed. "*Move.*"

His eyes widen at my tone. "Kaia—"

I don't stop. I slip past him like he's part of the set.

Blaire's voice is in my ear, suddenly fierce. "Kaia, do not—"

"I felt it drop," I say, already running. My boots hit concrete. My heart hits my ribs like it wants out. "It's out."

"Council will handle it—"

"No," I cut in. "No, it's heading into town."

My hand lifts as I run, fingers flexing.

Aurora half-summons, light curling around my wrist, the blade not fully formed, just the weight of it promising to become real. I don't want a full draw in a corridor full of humans and cameras.

But I need it close.

I need it ready.

I push through a side exit and the night hits me like a slap—fog, salt, cold.

The crowd's roar is behind me now, muffled by concrete and distance, but still huge—still feeding the town with noise.

Streetlights smear in the mist. Lantern frames sway overhead. Fans spill onto sidewalks, laughing, crying, singing pieces of our ballad back to each other like they're holding onto something holy.

They don't know what just almost ate them.

I run anyway, cutting through the human tide, ignoring the calls behind me, ignoring the way my lungs burn.

Because I can feel the splinter now—faint, sharp, a needle of sound moving through the streets.

A hook looking for a throat...

A memory looking for somewhere soft to bite.

And I know *exactly* where it's going.

I know, because it's going where *I* left something.

Where the past is still alive, to the girl I left behind and can't stop thinking about.

"Evie," I whisper into the fog, like it's a plea.

Then I run faster.

Evie

THE LAST CUSTOMER DRIFTS out at 11:47 p.m. with a paper cup of coffee and a dazed smile. For the first time all night, I can hear the neon sign buzzing in the front window—its usual angry little insect whine.

THE LIGHTHO—
THE LIGHTHOUSE DINER
THE LIGHTHO—

"Finally," I mutter, flipping the lock.

The street outside is damp and fog-soft, lantern frames already hanging over the road like skeleton ribs. Ten blocks away, the arena still throbs faintly—bass echoing through concrete, the kind of distant rumble you feel more than hear. The show must be in the finale. Or maybe it's already over and the crowd is just... refusing to stop existing.

I turn the sign to CLOSED and walk back behind the counter.

Gus is already there, wiping down the grill with grim determination.

Tasha stands at the register, counting the tip jar like she's doing sacred math. Her hoodie sleeves are pushed up, and the glitter on her cheeks has migrated into her pores. She looks exhausted in the way only teenagers can, like they've been awake for thirty hours and are still somehow functioning.

She glances at her phone and makes a tiny sound. "They're doing the encore."

"Good for them," I say, because it's my favorite phrase tonight.

Tasha frowns at me like I'm a puzzle she can't solve. "You didn't... you didn't watch *any* of it?"

"Nope."

Her eyes narrow. "Not even a little?"

"No."

Gus snorts. "She's got a stubborn streak."

"I do not," I say automatically.

Gus gestures with the rag. "That's it. That's the streak."

Tasha looks between us, her phone, then sighs dramatically. "Okay. I'm gonna go. My friend's mom is picking me up."

"Wear your hood," Gus grunts.

"I always wear my hood."

Gus slides a hand over the counter and drops something in front of her: a large cup of leftover fries. "Here, for you and your friend."

Tasha's face brightens. "Thanks, Gus!"

"Go on," he says.

"Okay. Goodnight, you two."

"Night," I say.

She bolts for the door, yanks her hood up, then disappears into the fog.

Gus grabs his coat and keys off the hook, then pauses like he's remembering he's technically the owner and should probably act like one.

"You sure you're good?" he asks, voice rough.

"I've closed alone a hundred times," I say.

Gus looks at me like he wants to argue, then grunts. "Lock both bolts. Don't leave the back door propped."

"I know."

He points one thick finger at me anyway. "And don't fall asleep at the counter."

"God forbid."

He almost smiles. Almost. Then he shoves his hands into his pockets and heads out the back, shoulders hunched against the cold.

The bell jingles. The door shuts.

And suddenly it's just me and the diner.

Me and the buzzing neon and the faint echo of a stadium ten blocks away.

I flip the second lock on the front door, then walk back behind the counter and finish closing out the drawer, because numbers are soothing and paper doesn't have feelings.

I can still hear Tasha's phone music from earlier in my head like an earworm, and I hate it. I hate that Kaia's voice lives in my memory like she paid rent to be there.

I finish counting, jot the total, and tuck the cash into the envelope Gus keeps in the safe.

Then the jukebox clicks on. A tiny mechanical sound, like someone flicking a switch. The machine lights up. Neon strips glow. The display sputters like it's waking from a long sleep.

And then music starts.

Not the rock I put on earlier.

Not anything I've *ever* heard from that machine.

A tinny, bright little melody spills into the diner—too cheerful, too familiar, like a commercial. Four familiar notes. Then the sing-song line that follows, warped slightly like it's coming through an old speaker:

Come back, come back, the lanterns will light your way—

My blood goes cold and goosebumps rise on my arms.

"What the hell?" I snap

The song keeps going.

A stupid Harbor Lights jingle. One of the old ones. The kind that used to play on the local radio every fifteen minutes during festival season until you wanted to drive into the ocean.

Except, this version is... wrong.

It's too slow by half a beat.

And my brain does the thing it does when it wants to torture me: it plays a memory on top of the sound...

Kaia at sixteen, sitting on the pier with her knees pulled up, mocking the jingle in a ridiculous falsetto just to make me laugh. Taking the dumbest, brightest part of the town and turning it into a joke we could share.

I swallow hard.

I hate the way my chest aches at the memory.

I hate that I still remember the exact way she sang it. The stupid little flourish she added at the end to make me groan.

The way she sang it a half beat too slow too...

"Hell no," I say out loud, as if the jukebox might respect consent.

I look around the empty diner like I'm going to catch someone crouched behind a booth, laughing into their sleeve. Like Gus is going to pop up with a camera and tell me I've been punked by small-town America.

But there's nobody.

Just the neon sign's faint buzz, the hum of the fridge, and that jingle crawling through the air like it owns the place.

The hair on the back of my neck rises.

I stalk to the jukebox and jab at the buttons. Nothing happens. I hit STOP. I hit POWER. I hit the side of it with the flat of my hand like it's an old TV that needs intimidation.

The song doesn't even hiccup.

"Of course," I mutter, because why would anything in my life ever be normal?

I crouch and find the power cord. My fingers close around it. Then I rip it out of the wall.

The jukebox dies instantly—lights out, screen dark, the whole thing finally shutting up.

Silence drops so hard it feels like pressure in my ears. My heart pounds and the air in the diner doesn't relax with the silence.

It gets thicker.

Like fog inside a building.

Like the diner is holding its breath.

I stand and step back slowly.

"Okay," I say, voice low. "Cool. Great. Awesome."

I glance at the windows. Dark glass. My reflection. Empty street beyond. Except my reflection looks... smeared. Like the glass is damp from the inside. I blink hard. It clears.

Probably just fatigue.

Probably just festival weirdness.

Probably—

I stop. Breathe. Re-center before I lose my shit entirely.

This is a diner. Jukeboxes glitch. Neon signs buzz. Everything is *fine*.

I need noise that's neutral, that isn't lanterns and longing and Kaia Rhee worming her way into my skull through a commercial. I turn away from the jukebox and head for the TV behind the counter. My hand finds the remote like it's a lifeline.

"Fine," I tell the room. "We're doing normal television."

I click it on.

The screen flares to life.

A cooking show. Some man smiling too hard while he whisks eggs. Bless him.

I exhale. "Thank you."

For half a second, it works. The bright, stupid normalcy fills the diner. The cooking host says something about *perfectly fluffy* like he's never suffered a day in his life.

Then the TV glitches too.

The picture tears—horizontal lines rolling, the image bending like wet paper.

The cooking show stutters, freezes, and the audio warps into—

—into a roar.

A crowd.

My stomach drops.

The TV snaps into a shaky fan-cam video, vertical, pixelated, overexposed. The arena. The stage. The lights.

Midnight Halo in full glittered perfection.

Kaia at the center.

Her face is huge on-screen, not the polished local-news clip but raw footage—eyes bright, mouth open in song like the world is pouring out of her.

The sound that hits me isn't just audio.

It's *pressure.*

It's like someone opened a door and shoved the stadium into my skull.

I gasp, sharp, and my hands fly up instinctively, palms pressing hard against my temples like I can physically hold my brain in place.

"What—" My voice comes out thin.

My stomach flips. My vision swims for half a second, the edges of the diner going a little too soft. The crowd's screams flood the diner, too loud for the little speakers, distorting into something that feels... *infinitely wrong*.

And underneath it, twined into the noise like a second melody—*the jingle*.

Not from the jukebox now.

From *everywhere*.

The windows smear again, and this time they don't clear when I blink. The glass reflects the diner, yes, but the reflections multiply.

Too many shapes.

Too many silhouettes.

A crowd where there shouldn't be one.

Open mouths. Heads thrown back. Singing.

Off-key. Hungry.

My breath catches.

"Oh shit," I whisper, and my body moves on instinct—back, away, like distance will fix it. Like I can just step out of the range of whatever this is the way you step away from a spill.

My heel hits the edge of a floor mat. I stumble.

The air shifts.

Something moves through it, something I can't see but can *feel* as cold air wafts towards me.

And it finds me.

Invisible pressure slams down on my shoulders, my spine, my chest—pinning me in place like I'm suddenly under a car. My knees buckle and I grab the counter, fingers scrabbling on laminate.

The sound surges.

The fan-cam Kaia sings on the TV, her voice distorted, looping, layered with the jingle until it becomes something else entirely: a chorus of echoes trying to crawl into my throat.

My ears ring. My vision blurs. Something claws at my neck—not nails, not hands—sound. A vibrating chokehold.

I try to scream.

Nothing comes out.

My mouth opens, my throat strains, but the noise jams there, stuffing me full of someone else's song.

Tears sting my eyes from the pressure. My fingers slip on the counter edge.

Come back, come back—

The jukebox. The TV. The windows. The air.

Everything is singing at me.

And the memories start to rise, dragged up like bodies from deep water.

The pier. Lanterns swaying. Kaia's laugh. Kaia's hand in mine. Her mouth close... And my heart pounding because I have never loved someone like I love Kaia—

Then the memory twists.

I'm sixteen again and furious, standing on wet boards with lantern smoke in my hair, trying to make words out of a thing that's bigger than my chest.

"Are you going to pretend it didn't happen?" I snap. "I don't want to spend the rest of my life acting like you're just my—my friend who accidentally kissed me!"

Kaia's face looks panicked.

"We were hyped on Harbor Lights," she says.

My stomach turns—same as it did then.

"And you've been hiding this whole other path from me!" I snap at her. "Why am I the last to know?"

A flash—Gus's counter, coffee smell, Kaia's mom laughing too bright, bragging about a "special program," a "big opportunity," like it's harmless gossip.

"I had to find out from your mom."

The sound in the diner swells, the jingle trying to lace itself through the argument like it's seasoning. Like it wants the hurt.

My throat tightens harder. My vision blurs. I can't breathe.

The memory keeps coming anyway, relentless.

My voice—smaller now, broken at the edges. "So what, I'm just a mistake you have to erase before you go chase your big dream?"

Kaia replies, "Maybe I don't want my whole life decided by one stupid kiss and one girl who never wants to leave this place!"

Stupid kiss.

One girl.

Never wants to leave.

No—no, no—

The jingle purrs come back like it's offering comfort. Like it didn't just drag a knife through my ribs for fun.

My fingers scrabble on the counter again, desperate. I try to suck in air. I can't. The sound packs into my throat, choking me.

In the memory, I'm shaking, lantern light blurring, tears welling in my eyes even as I glare at her.

"Fine," I hear myself say, voice vicious with pain. "Go be special somewhere else, Kaia. When you're done pretending this place and everyone in it doesn't exist, don't bother coming back."

And then—nothing.

Kaia going quiet. Pride like a locked door.

In the diner, the invisible pressure bears down harder, pleased, finding the exact bruise to press. My body gives up. I slide down the side of the counter, hitting the floor.

The sound presses tighter, forcing my head to tilt back, forcing my gaze to the TV.

Kaia's face fills the screen, mouth forming lyrics I can't hear clearly over the jingle, over the crowd, over the wrongness.

She looks like first love, some teenager said earlier.

The phrase hits like a cruelty.

Because first love is supposed to be soft. Safe. A memory you keep in a shoebox.

Not a weapon someone can use to choke you.

My throat tries to swallow around it. The pressure tightens. My ears pop. My vision tunnels. The windows reflect a crowd that isn't there, all of them singing at me with empty mouths.

I can't move.

I can't breathe.

I *can't*—

Tears spill anyway, hot tracks down my cheeks, my body leaking panic because it can't leak sound.

My fingers twitch uselessly against the floor.

And then—

The back door explodes inwards.

The sound of it is violent: wood slamming concrete, the bolt snapping, cold fog rolling in like a living thing.

Light *floods* the diner.

Something brighter and sharper than the warm, overhead bulbs. Gold-white. The air pressure *breaks* for half a heartbeat, as if whatever has me pinned flinches.

A woman strides in through the fog like she belongs to a different world...

Her back is to me but there's clearly a *sword* in her hand—the blade blazingly prismatic, throwing rainbows across the walls as it moves, white wings flaring at the hilt. A strangely *familiar* sword, but my brain can't place it.

She looks unreal. Like a myth... Or an *angel.*

For one terrifying second, my brain refuses to connect that image to anything human.

Then she moves.

Not toward me—toward *it.*

"Get *away* from her!" she snarls.

She swings the sword in a clean, brutal arc, and the air answers like it's been waiting. A gust slams through the diner, sharp and bright, as if the space itself is being shoved back.

The pressure on my chest breaks just enough for me to gasp, air tearing into my lungs like I've been underwater.

The windows rattle. The jukebox sputters. The TV picture tears. The crowd-reflections in the glass jerk backward as if slapped.

I suck in air like it's the first breath I've taken in years.

The thing—*whatever it is*—shrieks without sound. The reflections smear violently, and the jukebox jingle speeds up, pitch warping into something frantic.

My savior moves.

It's too fast to be real.

She slides across the floor in a motion that could be a dance if it weren't aimed with killing intent—boots skimming wet tile, sword carving light through fog.

A stool levitates off the floor and hurtles toward her.

"No!" she snaps.

She turns her shoulder, and the air *hardens*—a barrier blooms from her voice and sword together, catching the stool midair and smashing it aside in splinters.

Coffee cups explode off the counter, shattering like gunshots. Glass rains down.

Then she's moving again, chasing something I can't *see*, but definitely feel.

I instinctively throw my arms over my head and crawl, half blind, under the nearest booth table like an animal.

From under there, I see it in flashes:

The angel's sword arcing in bright crescents, cutting through something that isn't solid.

The air rippling with each shouted command.

The TV flickering between fan cams and static.

The windows reflecting a crowd that twists and collapses as if the reflections are being peeled off the glass.

The thing tries to get to me again, I *feel* it—sound reaching, tugging at my throat and mind, trying to hook into the place where my memories live—

And the angel throws herself into the path like she's made of stubbornness and light. A blow hits her, something invisible slamming her sideways into the counter. She grunts, knees skidding, but she doesn't go down.

She plants the sword tip into the tile like an anchor, and her voice goes sharp.

"Not *her*," she snarls, and the words land like a threat carved into stone. "Try me."

The words become force.

The air shoves back.

The diner shakes.

For one insane second, it looks like choreography—like this is a planned stunt in a music video: the perfect lighting, the fog, the warrior angel spinning through flying debris.

Except nothing about the sound of shattering glass is planned.

Nothing about the fear in my bones is scripted.

The thing lashes again, desperate now. The jukebox plays the jingle at double speed, a maddened loop. The TV shows Kaia's face in close-up, eyes shining, mouth open—then the image twists, her voice layering into the wrong chorus until it feels like the diner itself is singing.

The angelic warrior turns her head slightly, as if she can hear the thread the thing is using to anchor itself.

She steps forward, sword raised.

And then she shouts.

Not a lyric.

Not a song.

A raw, brutal sound, ripped from somewhere deep in her chest.

Her sword seems to amplify it into a blast—sound made solid, a shockwave that slams into the air.

The diner erupts with it.

The jukebox goes dead mid-note.

The TV explodes into static.

The window reflections shatter—not the glass, but the *images*—the crowd-mouths collapsing into nothing like smoke sucked into a vacuum.

The pressure releases so suddenly I almost throw up.

Silence drops like a curtain. I sit there under the booth, shaking so hard my teeth click, breathing in sharp, ugly gulps.

The angel stands amid overturned stools and broken cups and glass, chest heaving. The sword in her hand dims slightly, still humming, like it's satisfied.

She lowers it, turns slowly, scanning.

Then her gaze lands on me.

I blink up at her, still half convinced I'm hallucinating.

The light on her face fades just enough, and the angle shifts.

And suddenly I see her.

Not my savior.

Not an angel.

Her.

Kaia Rhee.

My chest goes hollow and hot at the same time.

"*You*," I say. The word comes out flat with disbelief, like my throat can't decide whether to laugh or scream.

And because my life has no mercy, my brain chooses *now* to register details.

She's still in the stage look—midnight-blue glitter and sharp gold seams, the kind of structured, lethal little outfit designed to make her look untouchable. High ponytail swinging, earrings catching the diner lights, boots that look like they were made for kicking doors in. And her sword is humming like it wants a second round.

But worse? Tasha was right. Which is the worst possible thing to realize mid-trauma.

Her shoulders really are 'illegal,' my traitor brain supplies, furious and helpless.

Fuck you, Tasha, for putting that word in my head.

"You have got to be *kidding* me," I say, because if I say anything else my heart might actually rip.

Kaia swallows, sword still in her hand like she forgot how to put it down.

"Hi, Evie," she breathes, voice breaking.

Kaia

"Hi, Evie."

Evie doesn't answer.

At first I think she's frozen.

She's still under the table, half-crouched in the wreckage, and her expression is pure disbelief, like her brain is trying to reject what her eyes are reporting.

And underneath it... something that looks *a lot* like revulsion.

Like I'm the nightmare that followed the demon in...

My stomach drops.

Her hair is a mess, her apron twisted, and there's a dark smear under her eye that might be mascara—*please let it be mascara.*

Her eyes lock on mine.

She looks exactly like my memory and nothing like it. Older, obviously, grown into herself in a way that makes my chest ache. Her face has sharper lines now, less soft teenage roundness, and there's a steadiness to her that wasn't there at sixteen, a hardness earned.

She takes one look at me—at the blade, the costume, the glitter, the light still humming around my wrist—and her mouth twists again.

"What the *hell*?" she snaps.

For a second, I don't know what to do with my hands.

Aurora is still half-present as light curled around my wrist, ready to be summoned again quickly. I'm still in stage makeup. I'm in costume.

I take a step forward anyway, because my body runs on instinct and instinct says *get closer, check her, make sure she's real.*

"Evie—" I start.

I hold out my hand, palm up... an offer, a question, a *stupid* reflex.

Evie scoffs like my hand is an insult.

She ignores it and scrambles out from under the table on her own, movement sharp and angry. She stands too fast, swaying for a half second.

"Don't touch me," she says.

My throat pinches.

I deserve that. I deserve worse.

So, I withdraw my hand.

"I won't. I'm—" I start, then stop, the apology sticking in my throat. I swallow it and ask the only thing that matters. "Are you hurt?"

Evie laughs once. The sound is sharp, humorless. "No."

But then her hand flies to her throat anyway, fingers pressing like she's checking that it still belongs to her.

My chest goes tight.

I want to touch her. I want to check the skin, make sure there's no bruising, make sure she really isn't hurt... I want to make sure my world didn't leave marks on her.

I don't.

I keep my hands to myself because she told me not to touch her.

Evie's eyes meet mine again, blazing. "You're not real," she says, like she's trying to make it true. "This isn't real."

I hold still, breathing hard, forcing my face into neutral. "I promise it is."

Behind her, the TV is nothing but gray static. The jukebox is dark again, but the air still tastes wrong, like ozone and old pennies. Broken glass crunches under my boot when I shift my weight.

Evie's gaze flicks down—Aurora's light, my half-summon—and back up to my face with fresh disgust.

"What is that?" she says.

"It's—" I swallow. "It's done."

I let the breath out and release Aurora. The prismatic light unwinds from my wrist like a ribbon cut loose, dissolving into nothing but a faint afterimage that fades fast.

"That wasn't my question."

I take a slow breath, the kind Blaire drilled into me for interviews. "A weapon. Mine."

Evie's eyes narrow. "A *real* weapon?" Her voice spikes. "I thought those were... props. For the shows. For the stupid sword choreography."

Her gaze snaps to the shattered glass, the overturned stools, the dead TV spitting static. "And what was that—*thing*? What attacked me?"

My stomach turns. There's no gentle way to hand someone the truth.

"A demon," I say simply.

Evie goes still like the word hit her in the sternum.

Then her face tightens, anger rushing in to cover the fear. "You're kidding."

"I'm not," I say.

I set my jaw. I don't move closer. Her whole body is saying *do not touch me.*

"Evie," I say carefully, "there might be more. I can explain more, but for your safety—"

"Oh my god," she snaps, voice climbing. "You're still as bossy as ever. Don't you walk in here after—after years and start giving me instructions like you're—like you're still—"

Her voice breaks on something she refuses to finish. My breath catches.

"Okay," I say softly. "No instructions."

It isn't fair—*bossy* was never the word for me. Evie was the one who was bossy. Who told me to breathe, and eat, and to keep singing even if I was scared. I was the one who followed her light.

But this isn't the moment to argue semantics.

She stares at me, breathing hard, eyes bright with adrenaline and fury. She's still shaking. Not dramatic shaking—her hands tremble just slightly, like the aftershock of a near car crash.

My instincts scream to reach for her, to *steady* her.

My instincts are useless. Her glare would burn my hand off.

So I do the only other thing I know how to do.

I put myself between her and the doors.

I turn my head slowly, scanning the windows, the reflections, the corners where sound can hide. My skin still remembers the pressure of the splinter trying to crawl into her throat. The diner is quiet now.

Evie follows my gaze. "What, are you expecting round two?"

"Maybe," I say honestly.

She opens her mouth, then closes it. Her anger flickers into something else for a heartbeat. Fear, maybe, or the raw memory of being pinned to the floor by invisible weight.

And the worst part is, I can't lie to her about it.

I didn't *kill* it.

Not really.

I drove it off. I severed its grip long enough for the room to breathe again, blasted it into static and silence, but a splinter like that doesn't always die clean. It slips. It hides. It looks for another seam.

It could come back.

I press my tongue to my teeth, swallow down everything that wants to spill out, and turn it into something usable.

"I need to call this in," I say.

Evie's eyes sharpen. "To *who*?"

"To—" I hesitate, because the truth is ugly. "To Eon. And the Council."

My fingers twitch toward my ear out of habit, and I re-member—too late—that my in-ear went dead the second I cleared the ward perimeter. Once I was out of range, the comms cut like a severed thread. No Blaire in my head. No calm voice telling me what to do next. Just the empty hiss of nothing.

"Ah," she says, and the sarcasm returns like armor. "Your people."

"My people," I repeat, quietly.

She gestures at the wrecked booth, the shattered cups, the smear of coffee across tile. "Tell them to bring a mop."

Something in my chest almost loosens because that's Evie. Sarcastic and kind of huffy. It's so familiar... I almost smile.

It would be easier if I could smile.

"My comms are dead in here," I say. "Out of range. Can I use your phone?"

Evie stares at me like I've asked to borrow her spine.

Then she jerks her chin toward the counter. "Diner phone. If it's still alive."

Miraculously, it is.

The cord is twisted, the receiver slightly off-hook, but the dial tone is steady, like this place refuses to stop functioning out of spite.

I grab it and punch in the number from memory. Blaire's direct line. The one I'm not supposed to need unless something is on fire.

It rings once.

Twice.

Then—

"Kaia?" Blaire's voice snaps in, sharp with contained fury. "Where are you? You ran—"

"I'm at the Lighthouse Diner," I cut in. "A splinter of the Chorus made contact with—a civilian. It's neutralized, but we need a cleanup crew. Now."

There's a silence so sharp I can hear her inhale.

"Kaia," Blaire says, voice suddenly all ice. "Are you hurt?"

"I'm fine."

"And the civilian?"

I glance at Evie. She's watching me like she might throw something.

"Fine," I say.

Blaire's answer is immediate. "Stay put. Don't leave the site, and don't let anyone touch anything. Cohen is already mobilizing. Council's en route."

"Understood."

I slowly hang up.

Evie's jaw clenches. "Jesus."

"I'm sorry," I say.

"Are your people at least going to fix this? Because Gus will literally kill me if he walks in tomorrow and sees his diner looks like it got robbed by a tornado."

"Yes," I say immediately. "They'll clean it. It'll look exactly as it was before." My gaze sweeps the broken glass and overturned stools, cataloging the damage.

Evie's mouth twists. "Great. So I get a magical assault and a corporate cleaning service. What a night."

She's taking it in stride. Or she's pretending she is. Or shock is holding her upright like a splint.

Evie has always been like that though: adaptable in the way people get when they've had to be. When the world keeps changing the rules and you learn to keep moving anyway.

I should be relieved she isn't screaming.

I am, a little.

But the relief curdles fast, because underneath it is the truth I don't say out loud:

It came here because of me.

Because the Chorus—whatever it is, however it listens—caught my thoughts running ten blocks ahead. Felt the pull in my chest. Noticed the shape of my attachment like blood in water...

Evie in my mind's eye.

Evie as a weakness I've tried to pretend isn't one.

And then it followed that thread straight to her throat.

My stomach twists hard.

I keep my face neutral anyway, because if I let the guilt show, it becomes real in a way Evie can see.

We stand in the wreckage, ten feet apart, but separated by more than distance. The neon sign buzzes in the front window like it's laughing at both of us. Outside, the town is still awake, still drunk on the concert. I can hear it faintly—shouts, laughter, distant honking, the lingering bass pulse from the arena.

Evie moves behind the counter, side-stepping glass, to pick a shattered tip jar from the debris with hands that are still shaking.

"What are you doing?" I ask because I can't help it.

"Closing," she snaps, not looking up. "Because I have a job. Because I live in reality."

I absorb it. "Okay."

She stacks the bills with aggressive precision. "Also," she adds, voice tight, "because I'm not leaving my tips on the ground for your—your demon friends."

"They're not—Never mind." I swallow. "Evie... you should sit down."

She shoots me an incredulous look. "Why? I'm fine. And what did we say about instructions?"

"I'm not telling you what to do," I blurt. "I'm... *suggesting*."

Her nostrils flare. "No."

I nod once. "Okay."

The silence stretches.

I hate it.

I clear my throat, then immediately regret it. "Don't you have... questions?"

Evie's laugh is sharp. "Oh, I have questions."

I brace without meaning to.

She looks straight at me, eyes flat. "For *you?* No."

The words land clean. Surgical.

Then she adds, still looking past me like she's making sure the distance stays in place, "For your people? Yeah. I've got a whole list."

I swallow hard. Of course she does. And it's painfully clear she's not putting *me* on the list of things she's willing to deal with tonight.

Even a demon attack can't drag us into some dramatic reconciliation. Not when the last time we talked ended in barbed words and silence that lasted years.

I don't push.

Instead, I keep scanning the windows. The reflections look normal now, but normal doesn't mean safe.

Evie lets out a harsh breath. "They need to hurry up," she says. "I need to go."

My attention snaps to her. "Where?"

She glares. "Home. I have to make sure my grandma took her meds. And check the locks. And—" Her voice wobbles, and she hardens it instantly. "And I'm not leaving her alone because some—some *demon* decided to—"

Guilt detonates in my gut so fast it makes me dizzy.

"You can't leave yet," I say, too fast.

Evie's eyes flash. "That's rich coming from you."

The words aren't about tonight.

I start to reply, but headlights wash across the diner windows. A van pulls up. Then another. Doors slam. Footsteps.

Evie stiffens, eyes snapping to the front.

"They're here," I say.

"Great," she mutters.

The back door is the one that swings open, because that's the one I came through.

Eric Cohen steps in first. His gaze lands on me and hardens with clear disapproval. To be fair, I did sprint right past him after the show.

"Kaia," he says, clipped.

"Mr. Cohen," I answer automatically, respectful.

Behind him comes Devin, looking like someone just handed him a liability nightmare wrapped in a bow. His suit is too crisp for midnight fog. His smile is already on, but it's brittle at the edges.

And behind Devin—

Mr. Bane.

The Council Handler moves into the diner, gaze taking in the wreckage slowly. He carries a slim black briefcase in one gloved hand. The air tightens around him as he crosses the threshold.

Evie's shoulders stiffen, and her chin lifts a fraction, defensive. Like her body can smell *predator* even if her brain doesn't have the vocabulary yet.

Mr. Bane sets the briefcase on the counter—careful, precise—then opens it with the quiet ritual of someone unpacking tools.

He finally looks at Evie.

Not unkindly. Not warmly either. Just… assessing.

"Ma'am," he says, voice level. "I'm Mortimer Bane. Handler."

Evie's head whips toward me. "Handler?"

I feel myself snap into my on-switch: leader posture, smooth voice.

"Yes," I say, controlled. "He's with the Council."

Then, to Mr. Bane, because this is a disaster and gratitude is also protocol, I say, "Thank you for coming quickly."

Mr. Bane inclines his head once. That's all he gives anyone.

He raises two fingers and draws a short sigil in the air. The mark doesn't glow the way my resonance glows; it darkens, like ink soaking into invisible paper. The temperature in the diner drops half a degree.

The sigil turns slowly, then snaps toward Evie like a compass finding north.

"Exposure confirmed," Mr. Bane says, calm as a form being stamped.

Evie's mouth tightens. "Exposure to what, exactly? The *demon*?"

Devin clears his throat, jumping in like he can PR his way out of this. "Eon will handle the property damage," he says brightly. "We'll replace anything that's—ah—irreparably damaged."

Mr. Bane doesn't look at him. His gaze stays on Evie.

"The civilian witnessed an uncontained manifestation," he says. "Standard protocol requires memory sanitation."

Evie goes very still.

"Memory *what*?" she says.

"Wipe," Devin supplies quickly, smiling like he's softening the word. "Oh, don't worry. It sounds scarier than it is."

Evie's laugh is sharp. "Oh, perfect. Just delete my brain. That's not scary at all."

The Handler nods as if she's confirmed a checkbox. "I'll prepare the sanitation."

"What?" Evie's voice snaps up, all bite and disbelief. "No. Absolutely not. You don't get to come into *my* diner and—what—wipe me like a whiteboard!"

Mr. Bane doesn't react like a normal person would react to being yelled at. He doesn't flinch. He doesn't argue. He just opens his case another inch, calm as paperwork.

Devin's attention is already sliding away, like Evie is an inconvenience he can file under *civilian agitation*. And Mr. Cohen watches her the way you watch a storm—impersonal, measuring.

They barely look at her.

And something in my chest goes hot and sharp, because this is *Evie*. Not a data point, not an "exposure," not a problem to mop up. She's standing in her own ruined diner, throat still red from the thing that tried to crawl inside her, and they're treating her like she's a problem they've already resolved.

My heart slams once, hard.

"Wait," I say.

The word comes out louder than I mean it to.

Then I move.

I take one step—just one—so I'm between her and them. I don't touch her. I don't crowd her. I just… place myself like a barricade.

Evie stops speaking. She looks startled for half a second, like she didn't expect that from me.

It hurts, how surprised she is that I would protect her.

"Wait a moment," I say.

Mr. Bane looks up, expressionless. "Ms. Rhee. You understand the security implications and protocols."

"I understand," I say, voice even. "And I'm invoking my veto."

Silence.

Even the neon sign seems to hesitate, buzzing softer for half a heartbeat.

Evie's head snaps toward me. "Your *what?*"

Devin's smile drops into something annoyed. "You can't just—"

"Yes, I actually can," I say, and for once I don't care how I sound. "Contact Blaire if you need to. I am using my veto. On her."

Evie stares at me like she can't decide whether to be furious or suspicious or both.

"Kaia," Devin says, tone warning now. "This is going to complicate things."

"Good," I say, without looking at him.

This isn't like me. I don't like complicated things. I like contained outcomes and following protocol. But Devin is pissing me off, and Evie is standing behind me, about to be erased, and my patience for anyone's convenience is gone.

Mr. Bane's gaze flicks to the wreckage again, then back to Evie. "You're certain?"

No, but it's Evie. I left her. I don't get to erase her night because it's convenient.

I don't say any of that. I say the truth that fits in their language.

"Yes, besides, her diner is now marked," I say. "You wipe her and it doesn't change what happened here. It doesn't change that the Chorus can find this place again. It just makes her blind."

Evie's breathing goes shallow. She looks down at the broken stools, the shattered mugs, like she's seeing the room differently now.

"She's involved," I add, voice steady. "Whether you like it or not."

Mr. Cohen shifts his weight, arms folded. He's watching the Handler, not me.

Finally, he says, "Very well. Minimal briefing. Secrecy binding. NDA. Warding reinforcement on the structure. And this place becomes a monitoring point."

Evie's head snaps up. "A *monitoring* point? What's that mean?"

I glance at her, and the words are gentler than my posture. "*Evie—*"

"No," she says again. "No. I'm not signing a—an NDA with— with people who walked in here and tried to erase me like I'm a messy problem!"

Mr. Bane tilts his head, unreadable. "You are not a problem."

Evie's laugh is bitter. "Then why were you about to wipe me?"

Devin steps forward, palms up like he's calming a crowd. "Evie, right? We understand you're upset, but this is for your safety."

"My safety was under a table while *she*—" Evie's gaze snaps to me, "—almost got thrown through a counter!"

Devin's smile tightens. "Kaia is trained. That's why she handled it."

"Yeah," Evie says, and her eyes flick to me again. "Trained."

My throat tightens.

Mr. Bane raises a hand slightly. "The binding will not erase anything. It will prevent disclosure. If you attempt to speak of what you witnessed to an unauthorized party, the words will not form. You will be... redirected."

Evie's mouth twists. "Redirected."

"Prevented," Bane corrects, tone unchanged.

Evie's hands curl into fists. "So you're going to—what? Magically gag me?"

"No," I cut in, too fast. "It won't hurt you."

Evie's voice shakes. "This is *insane*."

"It is," I say quietly. "And I'm sorry. But it's real."

Her glare says she hates that I'm the one saying it.

Bane removes a thin strip of pale material from his suitcase. It looks like a ribbon at first glance, but when it moves it wafts cold through the air. Fine runes shimmer along its length when the fluorescent lights catch them.

Evie recoils, but doesn't object. She looks at the ribbon, then at me, then away again, jaw working like she's chewing through rage.

Devin clears his throat, eyes flicking between my face and Cohen's like he's watching a budget line item catch fire.

"Kaia," he says carefully, "are you certain you want to veto here?"

I don't hesitate. "Yes."

Because I can't stand the idea of Evie losing this night, even the ugly parts.

Bane steps toward Evie with the ribbon, unhurried. Unemotional. Like he's approaching a form that needs signing, not a person.

"Fine," Evie spits. "Fine. Whatever. Just—make it quick."

Bane lifts his eyes. "Name."

Evie snaps, "You know my name."

Bane's voice stays calm. "Speak it. Binding requires consent through declaration."

Evie glares at the ribbon. "Evelyn Calder."

The ribbon lifts from the tech's hands and delicately curls through the air. It circles Evie's wrist without touching at first, hovering like a question.

Evie's throat bobs.

"Do you consent to secrecy binding?" Bane asks.

Evie's eyes cut to me. "Like I have a choice."

"Yes or no," Bane says.

Her lips press tight. Then, through her teeth, she says, "Yes."

The ribbon settles.

A faint shimmer—like glass cooling—wraps around her wrist. The runes dim until they're invisible.

Evie flexes her fingers as if expecting pain.

"Great," she says, brittle. "So now I'm contractually gagged by magic. Awesome."

Devin brightens with relief. "Thank you for cooperating. This will remain confidential."

Evie's smile is sharp. "Yeah. I gathered."

Mr. Bane turns to me. "Brief her."

Evie's eyes narrow again. "*You're* briefing me?"

"I'm the one who dragged this into your diner," I say. My voice stays steady, but my stomach twists. "So yes."

Cohen checks his watch as if time itself is a weapon. "We'll begin containment cleanup."

Mr. Bane doesn't waste a second. He steps into the wreckage with the same calm he brought through the door and begins drawing sigils into the air, murmuring something I can't quite catch. Each is drawn with two fingers and a soft, final motion, locking a door only he can see.

Devin is already on his phone, back in his "this is fine" voice. "Yes. Yes, Lighthouse Diner. Minor property damage. No injuries. I need a discrete overnight crew. Yes, cleaning and replacement. No uniforms. No signage." He glances toward Evie, smile strained. "Thank you."

Evie's eyes narrow at him like she'd like to throw his phone into the fryer.

Cohen watches all of it with clipped approval, clearly satisfied the mess is being handled, then looks at me. "Brief her *quickly*."

As if Evie is a file that can be summarized.

And I'm tasked with figuring out how to tell her the world is bigger and uglier than she ever asked it to be.

I gesture toward the least-destroyed booth: one corner still upright, table only slightly shifted, like the diner itself tried to preserve a small pocket of normal.

Evie moves first, stiff and wary. I follow, careful not to crowd her.

We sit across from each other. And for a moment, the sight of her in a booth again hits me so hard it feels like I've fallen through time.

It reminds me of old nights: fries between us, receipts covered in scribbles, laughter that felt like home.

Another life.

I swallow and force my voice into something simple.

"Okay," I say. "Here's what's real. Demons exist," I say. "Not in the metaphorical sense. In the literal sense. They take many different forms, but they all feed on *emotion*. The one that attacked you tonight's favorite is nostalgia, longing, anything that loops."

Evie's eyes flick to the jukebox, then the TV static. "So... that thing was—what?"

"A splinter," I say. "A fragment of the main demonic presence."

"The Chorus," Evie says, as if the words taste like rust. "That's what you called it earlier."

I nod. "Yeah, that's what they named it. Demons like the Chorus form in places like this... festivals, traditions, anything that makes people cling to the past. It piggybacks on familiar hooks. Jingles. Songs everyone knows. The Council tracked it here... to Harbor's Edge."

Evie's voice is low. "It used the Harbor Lights commercial."

My stomach twists. "Yeah. It's attracted to the festival..."

"And it..." Her throat tightens. She swallows hard. "It tried to—"

"Get into you," I say, blunt because softness would break her. "It wanted your voice. Your memories."

Evie looks away like she might gag.

I keep going. "We perform inside warded venues because music is bait. Our shows pull it in. The wards trap it. We kill it before it spreads."

Evie's laugh is hollow. "So you're demon hunters with fancy lighting?"

"Yes," I say. "Basically."

Her gaze snaps back. "And you do this... all the time?"

I don't flinch. "Yes."

"And people just—go home after? Like nothing happened?"

"They don't know," I say. "The wards keep the demons from touching them... Well. Most of the time."

Evie points at the diner, at the destruction. "Most of the time."

I nod once. "Most of the time."

There's a beat where the only sound is the neon buzzing and the distant town noise outside.

Then Evie says, voice quiet and vicious, "So when you left... when you were recruited... You left and joined... *this*?"

The word *joined* hurts, because it implies I ran toward it with open arms.

"I got recruited," I say, and the sentence tastes like old panic. I force the next part out carefully, plain. "Some people are born with a Spark. Most of them never know it's there—they just have weird luck, or lights flicker when they're upset, or their dreams feel too real. The Council calls them Resonants. People whose bodies... are capable of magic."

Evie doesn't blink.

"So yeah. The Council trained me on how to control it, and Eon recruited me to be part of Midnight Halo."

Evie's brows raise, and she simply says, "Congrats."

Nothing else. She doesn't ask how they found me, what it was like, or anything.

She doesn't *care*.

Somehow, that stings worse than anything.

Behind her, Devin and Mr. Bane speak in low voices.

"...crowd readings were off the charts," Devin says.

"Patron yields," Mr. Bane murmurs back, quietly, "are higher when..."

Patron.

The word hooks behind my ribs.

I keep my face still. My heart rate ticks up.

Patron yields?

I don't know what it means, not really, but it doesn't sound like typical Council and Eon talk.

I file it away for later though, because Evie is staring at Bane now like she can smell the same wrongness.

"Can I go?" she asks abruptly. "I need to get home."

Mr. Bane's gaze slides to her wrist, to the place the binding sits invisible. "Not unescorted," he says, calm as a policy. "You're a fresh exposure. The first hours are the most unpredictable."

Evie's breathing goes faster. "I *have* to go. I need to check on my grandma."

The guilt spikes so hard it nearly knocks the wind out of me.

Cohen seems to register the word *grandma* in the way bureaucrats register liability. He steps closer, voice smoothing into something almost humane. "We can escort you," he says. "Just to the door. No fuss."

"I can walk her," I cut in before I can overthink it.

Devin's head snaps toward me, alarmed. Cohen's gaze sharpens like he's about to remind me of a hundred rules.

Evie's eyes slide to mine, unimpressed. "Bad idea," she says flatly. "You'd be recognized in a heartbeat. I'm fine."

I take a slow breath. "I want to make sure you get there safe."

Her shoulders lift, defensive. "I can take care of myself."

"I know," I say, and I mean it. "You've been doing it for years."

The words land wrong. They always do when I admit anything that sounds like regret.

Evie's face flickers—hurt, then anger again—and she gives me a thin, bitter smile. "Wow. Thanks for the reminder."

"I'm not—" I start.

"Don't," she cuts in, and the word is sharp enough to end the sentence.

She looks away first.

Devin clears his throat as if he's desperate to get back to a script. "The diner will be in perfect condition before we leave tonight," he says. "Restored. Sanitized. No... evidence."

Evie glances around at the wreckage—broken glass, overturned stools, coffee smeared like blood—and for a second, disbelief cracks her expression.

Then she nods once, tightly. "How generous."

She reaches for her purse and fumbles with her keys and phone.

I step slightly closer, but not close enough to touch. Just close enough to be heard without Devin and the Council to catch every syllable and turning it into a liability report. I've already made myself a problem tonight. I don't need to hand them another reason to pull me aside and lecture me later.

Or worse, label me as incompetent.

"Evie," I say quietly. "I'm going to walk you to your door."

Her head snaps up. "No."

"Yes," I say, calm. "You can hate me the entire way. But you're not walking through Harbor's Edge alone right after a demon tried to crawl down your throat."

Her lips part with a retort.

I beat her to it. "If you want to yell at me, you'll have more opportunities. If it tries to attack you again, it won't get the chance."

Evie stares at me, chest rising and falling fast.

Then she shakes her head and says, "Fine."

Cohen glances toward the door. "We can keep it low-profile," he says. "No vans. Just a walk. We'll follow behind."

Evie looks like she wants to refuse out of principle. But her hand tightens around her keys until her knuckles go pale.

She exhales, sharp. "Fine. Whatever. Walk me. But if anyone tries to step into my house, I will hit you with a pan. My grandma can't know about any of this."

I nod once. "Understood."

Evie grabs her coat and shrugs it on with jerky movements. She doesn't look at the wreckage again. She doesn't look at me.

She walks toward the door like she's walking out of a fire.

I follow two steps behind, Aurora fully dismissed now—just a faint warmth under my skin. I keep my hand near my side anyway, ready to summon if I have to. Everything about me is painfully human again.

Devin appears at my shoulder with the kind of brisk efficiency he uses when he wants a problem to look smaller. He shoves a beanie into my hand, then a plain dark coat. "Cover up," he mutters.

"Thanks," I say, even though he's likely more worried about the PR scandal this could cause than me being cold.

Still, I pull the beanie down and shrug into the long coat, letting them swallow any part of me that reads like *pop star* from ten feet away.

At the threshold, Evie pauses and looks back at the diner.

Her voice drops to something raw. "This is insane."

"I know," I say again

She turns her head just enough to look at me out of the corner of her eye. "Don't think saving me buys you anything."

The words hit hard because a part of me—*some pathetic part*—wants it to buy me forgiveness. A reset. A hug. A do-over.

Instead, all I can do is tell the truth.

"It doesn't," I say quietly. "I didn't do it for that."

Evie's mouth tightens like she hates that answer more than any excuse.

Outside, fog curls around the streetlights. The town still hums with leftover show energy—some people drifting home in little groups, laughter too loud, voices snagging on half-remembered choruses.

Behind us, Devin heads to a nearby van, and Cohen focuses on the diner like it's a scene to be managed and filed away. Like broken glass and terror can be reduced to paperwork.

Evie steps into the night.

I step after her.

And for the first time in years, I'm walking beside the life I abandoned, close enough to feel the heat of it, close enough to hear her breathing.

Close enough to know that whatever I just did, whatever "terms and conditions" I signed with my veto and my voice...

I'm not leaving this time.

Fog makes Harbor's Edge look like it's trying to forget itself. Streetlights blur into soft halos. The festival lantern frames sway overhead. Confetti from the arena—silver and black and gold—sticks to wet pavement and gutters like the town tried to dress up for a night out and ended up looking hungover.

Kaia walks beside me like she belongs here.

That's the first insult.

The second is that she's quiet.

Not the onstage quiet. Not the interview quiet. A different kind—like she's holding her breath so she doesn't say the wrong thing and make me swing.

Or maybe she just has nothing to say.

Maybe she's thinking the same thing I've been trying not to think since the moment she walked back into my life: that I'm in the way. That I always was.

She's not clutching her sword anymore, thank god. If she'd kept that whole "angel-with-a-weapon" situation while we walked through town, I would've thrown her into the harbor out of civic duty.

She still looks... wrong for the sidewalk, though. Sparkly costume under a coat someone shoved at her. Stage makeup intact. Face perfect in a way that doesn't belong in mist and street grime.

And I'm in clothes that smell like coffee and fear.

We make a pair.

Kaia breaks the silence first.

"I need you to listen," she says, and there it is again, that tone she probably uses to get people to listen to her. "For your safety—"

"Okay," I cut in. "Rule number one."

Kaia glances at me, cautious. "Yeah?"

"You do not talk to me like you're giving a briefing."

"I—" She exhales, slow. "Okay. No briefing voice."

I keep walking, keys digging into my palm hard enough to hurt.

"Rule number two," I add, because if I stop talking I might start shaking again. "If you say 'for your safety' one more time, I'm going to walk into traffic."

Kaia almost smiles, then thinks better of it. "Noted."

"Rule number three," I say. "You don't get to act like this is normal."

Kaia's footsteps slow by half a beat. "It isn't."

"Okay, good," I say, and it comes out meaner than I mean it to. "Because I'm having a really bad night, and I'm running out of what little patience I started with."

Kaia doesn't argue. She just walks beside me, shoulders tense under that borrowed coat, like she's absorbing every word and letting it hit.

Which somehow makes it worse, because if she fought back, I could stay angry. And anger is easier than anything else.

I stop walking long enough to look at her properly.

Kaia *immediately* stops too, like her body is trained to respond to cues. Her eyes meet mine. There's no stage light in them now, just exhaustion and something that looks like it's been living under her ribs for years, waiting to be punished.

Good.

Kaia's voice is careful. "You look like you have more to say."

I let out a short, humorless laugh. "You came back with a magical sword and demons and magical contracts and—who knows what else. And of course, out of *everywhere* in Harbor's Edge, that *thing* attacked the diner?"

Kaia swallows hard. The fog beads on her lashes, making her look almost unreal again, but her expression is painfully human.

"I didn't bring them *to you*. I didn't come here looking for you." Then she adds, quieter, like she can't help it, "I didn't want you anywhere near this."

She says it like it's protection.

I hear it like it's distance...

Because the last time we talked, we were shouting on a pier, words sharp enough to leave scars. We never fixed it. We just... stopped. And the silence has been sitting between us for years like a rusted fence neither of us dared climb.

I shake my head once, trying to shake the feeling loose, and start walking again. Kaia falls into step beside me without crowding.

We pass the corner where the diner sign is visible through fog if you squint. It buzzes faintly, stubborn as ever.

I don't look at it.

If I look at it, I'll see the broken window reflections and the table I crawled under and the way my throat wouldn't work.

If I look at it, I'll think about her standing there in my life like an avenging angel.

And I don't know what to do with that yet. So I keep my eyes on the wet sidewalk. Kaia keeps her hands in her pockets, clearly trying to look normal.

It's not working.

A group of fans stumbles past us, laughing too loud, cheeks flushed with cold and joy. One girl is crying into her friend's shoulder and still smiling.

Kaia turns her head slightly, keeping her face angled away. I watch her do it. Even now, she's trained. *Even now,* she's hiding in plain sight.

And some stupid, traitorous part of my brain supplies the memory of teen Kaia doing the exact same thing in the diner when tourists wandered in and recognized her from the Harbor Lights stage.

Not famous then. Just... bright.

Too bright for this town.

She'd tug her hoodie up and duck behind the counter and grin at me like we had a secret.

The memory hits without permission, sharp as a flashbulb.

Gus in the kitchen. Kaia in the booth across from me, knees tucked up, hair falling in her face as she scribbles on a napkin like it's a sacred text.

"You can't put 'burn the world down' in a set list," I tell her.

Kaia looks up, eyes gleaming. "Why not?"

"Because we're trying to get you on the Harbor Lights stage, not exiled."

She grins, then pushes a basket of leftover fries toward me like she's bribing me into being on her side. "Okay. Fine. What do you think I should open with?"

I steal a fry. "Something that makes them tip."

Kaia snorts. "You're such a capitalist."

"You're singing for tourists," I say, deadpan. "You're literally the capitalist."

Kaia leans over the napkin, writing song titles and little notes. Her handwriting is messy and alive.

I feel warm watching her. Like I'm sitting too close to a heater.

"What about that new one?" I ask, trying to sound casual. "The one you wrote after the storm?"

Kaia's fingers pause. "That one's... not for them."

"For who, then?" I ask, still casual, still pretending I don't know.

Her gaze flicks up to my face, and something in it goes soft.

"You," she says, like it's obvious.

A car honks somewhere nearby, and I blink myself back into the present so hard my eyes sting.

Kaia is still beside me.

"Stop looking at me like that," I say, because I can't stand the weight in her gaze.

Kaia's head snaps slightly. "Like what?"

"Like you're surprised I'm still... standing."

She stops walking this time. I take two more steps before I realize and stop too, because I'm not letting her control the pace of this conversation. Not again.

Kaia stands in the fog with her shoulders tense, eyes fixed on me like she's holding something back so hard it might crack her teeth.

Then, like clockwork, she reaches for the version of herself that knows how to sound calm.

"Look," she says carefully, voice smoothing into something practiced, "I know we didn't part on great terms. But we need to work together. Just until the festival's over. For your safety."

My jaw tightens. "There it is again. 'For your safety.'"

"That's not—" She exhales, frustrated. "Evie. I saw what it tried to do to you."

"I'm fine," I snap.

Kaia's eyes darken. "You weren't."

Silence swells between us, thick as the fog.

Kaia's gaze flicks toward the pier, and for a second I see teen Kaia in her face—the kind of look she'd get when she was about to do something stupid and brave.

I hate that I can still recognize her tells.

I hate that my brain still catalogs her like she's mine.

Before she can say anything, a thought hits me, practical and sharp, the way I keep myself from falling apart. "Does your mom know about any of this?"

Kaia blinks. "What?"

"The demons," I say. "The *real* swords. The Council. The fact you're apparently a... magical girl demon-fighting pop star."

Something flickers over her face, annoyance, regret, exhaustion. "No."

"No?" I repeat. "She doesn't know her daughter fights invisible monsters for a living?"

Kaia's jaw tightens. "She could," she admits, voice low. "Immediate family can be briefed. Bound. NDA'd." A pause. "I didn't."

"Why?" I demand, even though I already know the answer is going to make me mad.

Kaia looks away for half a second. "Because there was no point in worrying her," she says quietly. "It's easier if she doesn't know."

Easier.

That's just like her.

I swallow the bitterness. "Right. Well. Congrats on keeping things easy."

I start walking again before the quiet can trap me.

Kaia's footsteps catch up, two quick strides.

"You're doing the same thing," she blurts. "With your grandma! It's not as if you want her involved either!"

My stomach drops so hard it feels like gravity changes.

I turn on her. "That's different."

Kaia's eyes flare. "Is it?"

"Yes," I spit. "Because my grandma was diagnosed with dementia five years ago."

The word lands between us like broken glass.

"Oh," she says, and the sound is small. "Evie. I—"

She swallows hard. Her face changes—shock first, then guilt so immediate it's almost painful to watch.

"I'm sorry," she says, voice rough. "I didn't know."

I laugh once, bitter and hollow. "You wouldn't."

Kaia flinches like I hit her. She opens her mouth, closes it. Doesn't argue.

I look away first, because if I look at her too long I'll remember the girl she used to be. And I can't afford that tonight.

"Look," I say. "we're fine. You went on and became a pop star and a demon hunter—*great*. You don't need to pretend like you regret any of it. We were dumb kids."

Kaia's mouth tightens. "I'm not pretending."

"You are," I insist. "And it's gross."

Then her gaze drops—briefly—to my wrist. The place where the Council ribbon settled. It's invisible, but I can feel it. A faint cold itch under the surface, like someone drew a line in ink I can't wash off.

Kaia's face tightens. "Evie, I—"

"It's fine," I say, cutting her off. "I won't tell anyone. I can't. I agreed to the whole NDA thing, didn't I? Mostly because that creepy guy was two seconds from wiping my brain like a whiteboard, but hey."

Kaia's voice goes sharp, protective. "I stopped that."

"You used some veto," I say. "You made sure everyone knew you were in charge."

Kaia's eyes flash. "That's not why."

"Then why?" I demand, and my voice cracks on the edge of it.

Kaia opens her mouth.

And closes it.

Her jaw works. She swallows.

"I didn't want them to erase... this," she says finally, voice rough. "I—" She stops. Starts again. "I didn't want you to *forget.*"

That word hits something in me, sharp and specific.

Forget.

Because that's what it felt like when she left, like I was something she could set down and walk away from, easy to *forget* once the world got loud enough.

Like I was small enough to be *forgotten* the second a bigger stage opened its arms.

My chest tightens until breathing hurts. So I turn and start walking again, because if I stand still, I'm going to say something that will scorch the air.

Kaia follows, a step behind now, like she's learned the shape of my rage and is trying not to step into it. The fog thickens as we head toward my street. The houses here are older with salt-worn siding, small yards, and fences that lean like they're tired.

My house sits at the end of a narrow lane, porch light off because my grandmother hates "wasting electricity."

I fish my keys out and pause at the gate.

Kaia stops at the sidewalk, like she's waiting for me to tell her to come inside too.

The idea makes my stomach twist.

"You're not coming in," I say immediately.

Kaia nods. "Okay."

No argument. No push. No charm.

It throws me off balance anyway.

I unlock the gate and push it open with my shoulder. The hinges squeal.

Kaia stays put.

The porch steps creak under my shoes. The house smells like damp wood and the faintest hint of menthol rub, like my grandmother's medicine has seeped into the walls over time.

I get the key into the lock and—

My wrist tingles.

Not a pain. A warning. A cold, tight flicker under my skin, right where the invisible ribbon sits.

The sensation hits the exact second my brain forms the thought: *What if they don't restore the diner? I should tell Gus what happened. I should—*

My mouth goes dry.

I shove the key in harder than necessary and unlock the door.

Before I go inside, I turn my head slightly and aim a glare at Kaia. She looks closer than where I left her.

"Don't follow me," I say.

Kaia holds both hands up in surrender. "I'm not."

"Don't... stand there like a sad statue either. You walked me home. Mission accomplished," I add, because I hate the way my chest tightens at the thought of her alone in the fog.

Kaia's mouth twitches. "What would you prefer?"

"Go be famous somewhere else," I snap, and immediately taste how old that line is.

Kaia goes very still. The air between us shifts, turning more raw.

I realize, a beat later, that was pretty much what I said all those years ago in our fight: *Fine. Go be special somewhere else.*

Kaia's face does something small and awful, pride and shame tangling.

My stomach flips. I turn away before I can see more.

Inside, I lock the door behind me out of habit. My coat goes on the hook. My keys land on the counter with a soft clink. The kitchen is dim except for the light over the stove. The clock ticks loud. The house feels like it's holding its breath.

"Gran?" I call softly.

No answer.

I walk down the short hallway toward her room, careful with my footsteps because she startles easily at night. The floorboards creak anyway, traitors.

Her bedroom door is cracked open. A faint nightlight glows inside. She's curled in bed under a quilt, hair white and thin against the pillow. Her face looks smaller than it used to when I was a teenager, and softer in a way that feels like theft.

I swallow around the ache in my throat and step in.

"Hey," I whisper, approaching the bed. "Gran. It's me."

Her eyelids flutter. She makes a small sound like a question.

I reach for the pill organizer on the bedside table. Of course she didn't take the ones she was supposed to take earlier... I then reach for the glass of water. My hands move with the practiced choreography of caregiving: open, shake, place, coax.

I touch her shoulder lightly. "Time for your meds."

Her eyes open halfway, bleary. She stares at me like she's trying to place me in the dark.

"Evie?" she rasps.

"Yeah," I say softly. "It's me."

She blinks. "It's... late."

"I know," I murmur. "Festival week. Everything's weird."

She makes a little disapproving noise. "Too much noise."

"Yep," I agree.

I help her sit up enough to swallow the pills. She takes them with the seriousness of someone signing a treaty.

Then she squints at me. Her gaze sharpens strangely, like a flare of old awareness.

"Did the Rhee girl sing?" she asks.

The question hits me like a fist. My chest goes tight, and for a second I'm back in the diner after hours, fries on table, Kaia humming while she scribbles song lists and steals my pencil.

Back on the pier with lanterns swaying, Kaia leaning in like the world was going to hold still for us.

Back in the fight—her voice sharp, mine sharper, both of us saying things we could never take back.

One stupid kiss.

You're scared to leave.

You're too good for me.

Back to us, tonight, to the mean things I'd said to her. Years of hurt and resentment and anger bubbling up.

My fingers tighten around the water glass until it squeaks.

"No," I say, too fast. Too bright. "Didn't see her."

Gran hums, sleepy again. "Shame. She has... a pretty voice."

I swallow hard. "Yeah."

She sinks back into the pillow, eyelids drooping. "You always liked her."

My heart stutters.

"I did not," I lie on reflex.

I stare at her in the dim light, throat tight, and let the lie sit there anyway because the alternative is too messy to explain to a woman whose memory slips like tidewater.

Gran's mouth twitches, half smile. "You used to say it," she murmurs, voice drifting. "Said you and that Rhee girl were gonna be friends forever. Like you'd already decided."

My chest aches.

"Go back to sleep," I whisper.

She does, breathing evening out. The moment of lucidity fades like it never happened.

I adjust her quilt and stand there for a second longer, hand hovering over her shoulder. Then I slip out of the room and close the door quietly.

In the hallway, I press the heel of my hand to my forehead and breathe.

The house is so quiet compared to the diner. Compared to the arena. Compared to the way Kaia's voice must still be echoing through town in people's heads...

I walk back into the kitchen and flick on the light. The window over the sink reflects the kitchen behind me—counter clutter, dish rack, my face pale in harsh light.

But for a heartbeat, the reflection looks... off. Like the air behind my shoulder is thicker than it should be. Like there's a shadow where there shouldn't be one.

My skin prickles.

I whip around.

Nothing.

Just the kitchen. The hum of the fridge. The ticking clock.

I let out a shaky breath.

"Okay," I mutter to myself. "We are not doing this. I don't have time for paranoia."

Kaia's voice drifts in from outside, faint through the front door, like she's speaking to someone on the porch.

"—I'm staying here," she murmurs. "At least until she's settled."

Then quieter, as if the fog might listen, "No. I don't care what Devin wants."

There's a pause.

Then, "Because I already did."

I don't know who she's talking to. Maybe Blaire. Maybe Bane.

My throat tightens, and I press my lips together until the feeling has nowhere to go.

A soft knock sounds at the front door. I walk to it, silent, and open it a crack. Kaia stands on the porch, fog curling around her like a stage effect the world didn't ask for. Her face is stripped down now—no glow, no power—just Kaia, breathing cold air, eyes careful.

"I'm not coming in," she says immediately. "I just—wanted to make sure your gran was okay. That she got her meds... and..."

My fingers tighten on the door edge. "Congratulations. You witnessed me being a functional adult."

Kaia's mouth twitches, then stills.

We stare at each other through a doorframe like it's a border treaty. Kaia's gaze dips—briefly—to my wrist again. As if to check that the NDA is still there.

"I'm still leashed, don't worry."

Kaia's voice is low. "It's not a leash."

"It's literally a magical gag order."

Kaia flinches. "It's... for your safety."

I glare. "*Traffic.*"

A small, exhausted breath slips out of her that might almost be a laugh if it didn't sound like it hurt. "Right. Sorry."

I wait for her to say more. She doesn't. She just stands there, hands open at her sides, like she's trying to show me she's not holding anything. Not a sword. Not a contract. Not a lie.

It doesn't work.

My heart doesn't care about my logic. My heart remembers.

So I do what I always do when my heart misbehaves.

I get mean.

"You don't get to stand on my porch like you belong here," I say, voice flat.

Kaia's eyes flicker. "I'm not."

"You are," I snap.

Her face tightens, and for a moment I see that old fight in the set of her jaw, pride bracing against shame. Then she nods, once.

"I'll be nearby," she says quietly. "Not here. Just... nearby."

Kaia hesitates, then turns.

She steps off my porch into the fog, disappearing into the blur of streetlights like a ghost who doesn't know she's unwelcome.

I close the door.

I lock it again.

Then I stand with my back to it.

Outside, Harbor's Edge is still humming with leftover music and lantern-light fantasies.

Inside, the kitchen smells like medicine and old wood and the sharp, bitter taste of a past that just walked back into my life with a sword.

Kaia

MORNING IN THE HOTEL tastes like stale coffee and consequences.

The blackout curtains in the common area of our shared suit are fighting for their lives, but sunlight still finds the seams and stabs through in thin, accusing lines. My head throbs in that post-show way: too much adrenaline, not enough sleep, nerves still buzzing like a live wire under my skin.

Somewhere down the hall, someone laughs too loudly. A cart rattles. The building hums with the soft chaos of a tour morning.

I'm sitting on the edge of the sofa in yesterday's sweatpants and a hoodie that says MIDNIGHT HALO—TOUR CREW, and I'm trying to drink hotel coffee like it's medicine.

It isn't working.

Mina sits cross-legged on the carpet with a bowl of cereal balanced in her lap, eating like she's still half asleep. Her eyes keep drifting toward me in little sideways glances, thoughtful and quiet in the way that always makes me nervous.

Remy is at the vanity, carefully lining her eyes like she's preparing for war. Her posture is calm, her movements precise. She's the only one who looks like she got more than three hours of sleep, which is rude.

Jules is sprawled across the armchair like she fell out of a music video and didn't bother to get up. Her hair is in a messy bun again, her face scrubbed clean for the phone that is held in front of it. Onscreen: a tiny dog.

Blaire is due in twenty minutes for the debrief. Council. Devin. The whole bit. And Jules is FaceTiming her dog.

"Hi, my baby!" Jules wails, voice cracking like she's in a tragic drama. "Hi, my perfect angel! Do you remember me? Do you remember your mother??"

The dog sneezes directly into the camera and immediately tries to eat it.

"YES," Jules sobs. "Yes, eat the phone, show them who's boss!"

Mina glares up at her. "Jules," she croaks. "It's... eight-thirty."

"It's dog o'clock," Jules says with the ferocity of someone defending a sacred ritual. She tips her phone toward us. "LOOK. Look at Kiki. She's literally aging without me."

The dog's temporary caretaker—Jules's sister—laughs from the other side of the call. "She's fine. She just destroyed her stuffed kitty and is now emotionally blackmailing you for treats."

"She takes after me," Jules says proudly. "My chaotic daughter."

The dog barks—high and sharp—like it's agreeing.

Jules makes a strangled noise. "She's talking to me! She's literally saying, 'Mother, where have you been? I've been abandoned in this cruel world.'"

"Jules," Mina says gently, voice still sleepy, "she's barking because she wants the treat bag."

The dog launches itself at the caretaker's shoulder, trying to climb into the phone. Chaos, affection, and teeth in a tiny package.

Jules clutches the phone closer to her chest like she's about to weep into it. "I miss youuu. I'm going to come home and give you lots of treats."

I should find it funny. I do, a little. It's absurd and normal and so *Jules* it hurts.

But my chest is still tight.

My mind is still ten blocks away in a diner with a shattered booth and a girl whose throat wouldn't work. My guilt keeps trying to crawl up the back of my spine and take control of my face.

Jules keeps talking to her dog as if nothing in the world is wrong.

"Okay, listen," Jules says, stern now, like she's giving a mission briefing. "No biting anyone you love. That is a rule. And no eating socks. And—"

The dog barks again, sharp and defiant.

"That's my girl," Jules says, immediately proud of the rebellion. "Mama's going to come get you soon, okay?"

Another happy yip from the dog, and Jules ends the call.

Meanwhile, my mind keeps replaying last night in ugly little flashes: Evie under the table, the taste of ozone, the way my veto sounded out loud. Blaire barely spoke to me after. Beyond a clipped *Are you alright?* and a sharper *We'll discuss this in the morning,* she didn't ask for details about my post-concert solo mission.

I should be using this time to rehearse my "I take full responsibility" speech.

Instead, I'm watching a coffee stir stick spin in a paper cup and wondering if Evie slept at all.

I hate that I'm wondering.

"Okay," Jules says, suddenly sitting up like she's had a revelation. "I'm sorry, but I'm not letting this go."

I keep my eyes on my coffee. "Letting what go?"

"The fact," she says, leaning forward with both elbows on her knees, "that Kaia Rhee—our fearless captain, professional mission-first, 'everyone hydrate and hit your marks' leader of the century—ran out of a stadium like she was in a *romance drama* and then heroically rescued a mysterious diner girl at midnight."

Mina's spoon pauses halfway to her mouth. Remy's eyeliner wing stops mid-flick.

I close my eyes for one long second.

"I did not," I say.

Jules grins like she can taste blood. "Oh, I think you did."

"It wasn't heroic," I mutter. "It was... damage control."

"Damage control?" Mina repeats softly, starry-eyed. "You crashed into a diner to save her. I overheard Blaire say it was *trashed.*"

Remy's eyes flick to mine in the mirror. "And then you didn't come back."

"I did come back."

Jules makes a sound like a buzzer. "Not right away, babe. You were out for a while~"

I glare at her. "Can we not?"

"No," Jules says immediately. "We can't."

Mina tilts her head. "Was she pretty?"

I choke on my coffee.

Remy's mouth twitches. Jules cackles.

"I'm not answering that," I say, wiping my mouth on my sleeve.

Jules points at me like she's caught a criminal. "That is a yes. That is absolutely a yes."

"It's not—" I inhale sharply. "She was a civilian. She was in danger. That's it."

"Mm-hmm," Jules says, utterly unconvinced. "And your jaw is doing the thing again."

Mina's brows knit as she studies me.

"The Kaia Jaw Thing," Jules adds, breezy. "Which means I'm hitting a nerve. It's very cute."

"I'm going to throw you off this balcony," I say.

Jules beams. "That's the affection talking."

Remy caps her eyeliner and finally turns, gaze sharp. "Kaia."

I sigh. "What?"

Remy's voice is calm. "Who was she?"

Silence drops into the room like a curtain. Mina's spoon lowers slowly. Jules's grin fades just a notch, not gone, but attentive now.

Leave it to Remy to piece things together. Remy is perceptive like that.

I stare at my coffee like it might give me a new past.

It doesn't.

My fingers tighten around the paper cup until it creases. I can still feel last night in my bones—the sprint, the fog, the diner door giving way, Evie's eyes when she realized it was me.

If I say her name out loud, it makes it real in a way I can't take back. I force the word through anyway.

"Evie," I say, carefully.

Jules goes still for half a second, then her mouth opens in delighted horror. "Oh my *god*."

Remy's expression doesn't change, but something in her gaze sharpens. "*That* Evie?"

Heat climbs up my neck.

"It's not a big deal," I say too fast, which is how everyone in this room knows it's a huge deal.

Mina leans forward, eyes bright like she's looking at a storybook illustration. "The same Evie you told us stories about?"

"I didn't tell stories," I snap, sharper than I mean to.

Jules blinks. Mina's expression flickers, hurt and surprised. I regret it immediately. Jules' eyes narrow at me, protective of Mina on instinct.

"Hey," she snaps back, "she's not attacking you."

I exhale and force my voice back down into something controlled as I drag a hand down my face, exhausted.

"Sorry." I look at Mina, apologetically, "I—didn't sleep well."

Jules, because she is allergic to solemnity, pounces on the opening. "No kidding, but Mina's right. You told stories. You *absolutely* told stories."

Remy's tone is dry. "You once described her laugh as 'a match striking in a dark room.'"

My heart drops straight through the floor.

Jules' eyes go huge. "You *did not.*"

I look at Remy like she betrayed me.

Remy shrugs. "Well, you did."

Mina whispers, reverent, "That's so romantic."

"It's not romantic," I say, voice strangled. "She hates me."

Jules tilts her head, grin returning slowly. "Oh, she hates you? That's even more romantic."

"It's not," I repeat.

Mina's gaze is soft. "Why would she hate you?"

Because I broke her heart, I think. Because I said our kiss was stupid. Because I made our friendship sound like a joke. Because I left without a goodbye and then showed up again with a sword and a contract and literal demons.

I shrug instead, the motion too tight. "Because I left."

Remy watches me for a beat, then says quietly, "You chased the splinter because you knew where it would go."

I don't answer, but it's true. I felt the drop and the direction and the pull like the universe was pointing at one person on purpose.

Jules whistles. "Okay, wow."

Mina's voice is tentative. "Is she okay?"

My throat tightens in a way that has nothing to do with sleep deprivation. "Yeah, she's fine now. She's alive."

Mina nods slowly. "Good. I'm glad."

Jules is quiet for a second—*genuinely* quiet, which is alarming. Then she says, softer, "So... she saw everything?"

I nod once.

Remy's gaze sharpens, and my stomach clenches because I *know* that look. Remy always asks the questions I'm hoping to avoid.

"And they wiped her memory," she says calmly, "so now she doesn't even know you saved her?"

My stomach drops. Jules' head snaps toward me. Mina's eyes widen. I look away, because my face always betrays me around them.

"Kaia," Remy says, voice still calm but edged. "They didn't wipe her?"

I exhale. "No."

Jules sits up straighter. "How?"

Mina sets her bowl down carefully like she's about to be sick. "Wait. Kaia—*how?*"

I rub my forehead, and the next words come out small. "I used my veto."

Silence. The kind that feels like being underwater.

Jules' mouth opens. Closes. Opens again. "You—*Kaia?!*"

Mina stares at me like I've sprouted wings. "You used your *one* veto?"

Remy's gaze doesn't waver. "On Evie."

I nod, jaw tight, as my gaze jumps between them sheepishly. "Yes."

Jules stands up so fast the chair squeaks. "Are you *insane?*"

"It was necessary," I say, defensive.

"Necessary?" Jules repeats, incredulous. "We get one veto each."

"I know," I snap back.

Mina's voice is small. "Only one."

"I know," I repeat, softer.

Remy crosses her arms. "And you used yours in the first twenty-four hours back in your hometown."

I glare at her. "It wasn't like I had time to workshop my decision."

Jules paces a step, then points at me. "You could have let them wipe her and spared yourself the complication."

My chest tightens. "No, I couldn't."

Mina's voice is gentle. "Kaia... why?"

I swallow.

Because I couldn't let them erase our reunion, no matter how messy and incredibly unideal it was. I couldn't let her wake up tomorrow with bruises on her body and no explanation in her head. Because I've already taken so much from her...

I shrug again, because I'm a coward and also because I don't know how to say the truth out loud without breaking down completely.

"She deserved to know," I say finally.

Jules goes quiet. Mina's eyes go glassy. Remy's gaze softens just a fraction, like she understands more than she's saying.

"Okay," Jules says, voice different now, more serious. "Okay. That means she's... in it."

"Yes," I say. "The diner is warded. It's a monitoring post now."

Mina murmurs, "That's... huge."

"It's terrible," I say. "But it's—" I stop. "It's the best option."

Jules exhales. "She must really hate you."

"Yes," I say immediately, because that part is easy.

Mina's voice is soft. "And you still did it."

I look away. "She was almost wiped. I wasn't letting them do that."

Remy taps a black nail against her arm thoughtfully. "She's exposed now. Splinters will circle back."

I nod. "Mr. Bane said the same. Blaire assured me that the NDA also protects her though... at least a little. It makes it harder for the Chorus to get in her head and latch onto her again. But..."

My gaze cuts to the door without meaning to.

I should be there. At the diner. Outside Evie's home. Anywhere close enough that I can intercept the next wrong note before it finds her throat again. She's not truly safe, not until we burn the demon clean for good.

Jules stops pacing. Her grin tries to return, but it doesn't fully stick. "So... we're going to a diner."

"Not we," I say quickly.

Jules' brows lift. "Kaia."

I exhale. "We're not making it worse."

Mina's eyes brighten again, worry and fascination mixing. "But what if she—what if she's in danger again?"

"She is," I say bluntly.

They all stare at me.

I meet their eyes. "She is. That's why the monitoring post exists. And the wards. And the binding."

The room goes quiet again, heavier this time. A knock lands on the hotel door. Sharp. Professional.

"Debrief in five," Blaire calls from the other side.

My shoulders tense automatically.

Jules flops back into the chair like she's trying to look casual again, but her eyes are still too sharp. Mina gets up and stretches a little. Remy turns back toward the vanity, as if we can paint our faces into something invincible.

I stand, smoothing my pants like I can press my life into place.

And that's when Mina's rummaging starts. She's always tidying, always organizing. It's one of her tells—when she's anxious, she makes the world neat. Her attention drifts to my opened, and clearly messy, duffel by the dresser.

"Your bag is stressing me out," she murmurs, half to herself.

"It's a bag," Jules interjects. "Let it alone."

Mina ignores her. Of course she does. She kneels, unzips my duffel, and starts pulling things into order—garment tape, Blaire pins, throat spray, a charger, the emergency sewing kit, some candies, spare lip gloss, and so on.

Then a photo slips out.

It flutters to the carpet like a leaf.

Mina scoops it up before I can.

I see it in her hands and my heart does something humiliating.

It's a candid, grainy shot from Harbor Lights many years ago. There are lanterns strung overhead, a crowd blurred into soft smears of light. And off to the side, half-caught by accident, two teenagers are kissing on the pier.

Me.

And Evie.

At the time, we didn't know the camera caught us. I didn't know *anything*... except that her mouth was warm and the lanterns were swaying and for one reckless second, it felt like the town itself was blessing us.

Except the photo is wrong in a way that still makes my skin prickle. Every lantern near us isn't an orb of light like the rest of the frame—it's distorted into tiny heart-shapes and halos, as if the brightness is literally reshaping itself around us. The blur around our bodies isn't just grain. It's patterned. If you look too long, you can almost make out faint sigils hidden in the noise.

And there's a flare around my head that shouldn't be there: a soft halo of light, focused and impossible, like the camera decided I was a star and the world agreed.

It's the photo that the Council flagged as high-resonance. It's the whole reason they scouted me to begin with.

Mina's eyes go wide, soft. "Kaia..."

Jules peers over and makes a strangled noise. "Oh my god. You took this on tour?"

I snatch the photo out of Mina's hand so fast it almost tears.

Heat floods my face. "It was... in the bag already."

Jules grins, back to being a menace again. "In the *bag*. Sure."

"It's nothing," I say, stuffing it back into my duffel bag and burying it under my clothes.

Remy's tone is mild. "Nothing that's been with you for years."

I glare at her. "Can we please not?"

Jules throws both hands up in surrender. "Fine. We'll not. For now."

The door opens before I can recover.

Blaire steps in first, wearing that same black blazer like it's fused to her bones, hair pulled back, headset already hooked around her neck. Her expression is all business, but her eyes flick to me like she's checking for cracks and deciding whether to cover for me or scold me.

Behind her comes Devin, smiling already, holding a tablet, hair perfectly styled like he slept eight hours and drank lemon water.

Mr. Bane and Mr. Cohen follow. Their gaze sweeps the room like they're counting exits.

"Morning," Devin chirps, too bright. "Big night last night."

Jules mutters, "Understatement."

Blaire's mouth twitches, brief, almost a smile, then she looks at us like she's trying to keep four disasters upright with nothing but tone.

"Let's sit." She gestures toward the small conference table by the window.

We sit.

I fold my hands under the table so no one can see them shake.

Bane speaks first, like he's reading from a template. "The meeting schedule is this: Debrief. Incident report. Consequence mitigation."

Devin nods along like he loves consequences.

However, Mr. Cohen is serious. He leans in slightly. "Kaia, you ran off stage."

"I did," I say.

"You left the team," Mr. Cohen continues. "You left security. You left the agreed perimeter."

"I did," I repeat, jaw tight.

Devin leans in, smiling like he's delivering feedback in a staff meeting. "We understand you were acting on instinct. But instinct can be... expensive."

I stare at him. "Someone almost died."

Devin's smile doesn't flicker. "And you saved her. Excellent. But the splinter escape—"

Remy's voice is quiet. "We saw the glitch. Our job is to ensure civilian safety."

Mina nods quickly, as if to back us both up.

Mr. Cohen says, "A monitoring post has been established at the Lighthouse Diner. Wards will be reinforced. The civilian—Evelyn Calder—has been bound by secrecy."

Devin smiles, like it's a fun announcement, as he adds, "Which opens an *opportunity*."

I already know I'm going to hate whatever he says next.

He continues, "A low-key, authentic group appearance at the diner tonight. Nothing too official. Just a drop-in. Bane will strengthen the wards, and it gives us *controlled visibility*. Fans love 'hometown vibes.'"

My stomach twists. "Is that... necessary?"

Devin's smile turns sympathetic. "Yes, it's already in motion."

I glance between Devin and Blaire. Blaire simply nods, and shoots me a look that tells me to *behave*. It's normally the look she saves for Jules. Not me.

Jules notices immediately. Of course she does. Jules sees everything that shifts.

She leans forward, tone bright but edged. "Why are we turning a civilian's workplace into a 'vibe'?"

Devin's smile doesn't move. "It's not a vibe. It's a mitigation step."

"That's not what you just called it," Jules says, sweet as poison. "You said 'controlled visibility' and 'hometown vibes.' Which sounds like 'content.'"

Her eyes flick to me, quick, protective.

Jules loves to tease. She lives to get a rise out of people. But when it matters, she goes protective in a way that's almost feral—pack instinct, no questions asked. All of us do. We fight for each other because we have to, because nobody else is going to put themselves between us and the worst parts of this job.

I register it, grateful and embarrassed all at once.

Devin's gaze slides over her. "Jules," he says, smooth and patronizing, "I appreciate your passion, but this is not a democracy."

Blaire's voice cuts in, calm but firm, before it can escalate. "It's happening. We keep it short. We keep it quiet. We do not make a spectacle."

Devin nods like he agrees, even though he's the one who brought the word *visibility* into the room. "Exactly."

Jules's jaw tightens. Mine does too.

We share a look, then Jules mutters under her breath, only for me, "Don't worry. He's going to die someday."

I shake my head at her a little.

Mr. Cohen's eyes slide back to his tablet. "We must assume the civilian's location is now a recurring attractor for the Chorus. As long as the demon remains active, it may test the wards."

The words hit like a slap. I hate how they say 'civilian.' My jaw tightens so hard it aches.

I keep my voice even. "She is a person."

Mr. Cohen doesn't react. "Yes. And she is now involved. You may have destroyed the Chorus's main body, but we have evidence multiple splinters broke off."

Jules sits forward. "Multiple?"

Blaire nods once, grim. "Not just the one Kaia chased."

My skin goes cold.

Not just the one that found Evie.

Remy's eyes narrow. "Where?"

Bane lifts a device with readout lines and ward graphs. Fancy Council tech. "Unknown. Traces in multiple directions."

Mina clears her throat softly. "I saw... something."

Everyone turns to her.

Mina's cheeks color, but she forces herself to keep going. "During the concert. When we killed the main mass of the Chorus. There was... something outside of the wards. Bigger. Like, like a shadow watching. The same one I saw yesterday."

Devin sighs like he's about to explain a spreadsheet to a child. "Mina, you've been overextended. Anxiety can—"

Mina's eyes flash, hurt. "I'm not making it up."

Mr. Cohen's gaze is flat. "Perception distortions occur under high resonance."

Blaire says, "We'll note it," and this time her voice doesn't sound dismissive. It sounds like she's storing it. Filing it. Keeping it. "Mina, if you see it again, you tell us immediately. Understood?"

Mina nods, small and grateful.

Devin pivots back to me like a heat-seeking missile. "And Kaia, no repeats of last night," he says, crisp. "Running off-script is dangerous, and if more civilians see anything, it's not just a containment issue. It's a PR nightmare."

"I stopped a demon from killing someone," I say, voice tight. "Isn't that our job?"

"You stopped *one*," Devin counters. "You also escalated civilian exposure. You invoked a veto." His smile turns thin. "Which is... dramatic."

I glare at him.

Blaire's voice snaps, sharp enough to cut. "We do not shame veto use. It's in place for a reason."

Devin lifts both hands in surrender, all charm and faux humility. "Of course. No shame. Just consequences we now have to manage."

I hate him so much.

I swallow. "I accept responsibility for the escape."

Mr. Cohen inclines his head once, satisfied. "Good. You will be present for the monitoring post calibration tonight."

Meaning: you will see Evie again. On our terms.

My chest does a painful, stupid thing at the thought.

Jules leans toward me and whispers, barely moving her lips, "Told you we're *so* going to the diner."

Mina whispers, earnest, "We should bring her pie."

Remy murmurs, deadpan, "We should bring her Kaia's dignity in a box."

"Stop," I hiss, and it comes out like a plea.

Blaire stands, signaling the end. "Our next chance to eliminate the Chorus is Harbor Lights. The Council wants you on the main stage, and the festival committee wholeheartedly agreed." Her eyes flick to me. "Which means we do this by the book. No freelancing."

I nod once. "Understood."

Blaire nods, satisfied. "We'll reconvene at three for practice."

Devin stands too, smoothing his suit. "And Kaia? Try to smile. We're going for 'homecoming warmth'."

I incline my head, even as my cheeks burn.

Jules mutters, "I'm going to commit a crime."

Devin walks out like he can't hear her. Cohen follows. Bane goes with them, silent.

Blaire lingers at the door. Her gaze flicks to me, sharp but not unkind. "You alright?"

I should say yes.

I should say I'm fine.

I should say anything that doesn't sound like my life is unraveling.

Instead I say, quiet, "She was supposed to be safe."

Blaire's expression tightens, and for once she looks older than she really is. "You don't get perfect control over 'safe,'" she says softly. "Not in this job." A beat. "But you did the right thing last night."

Then she's gone too.

The door shuts.

The room feels smaller.

Jules lets out a long breath. "Well. That was fun."

Mina looks at me with soft intensity. "You're really worried about her."

"I'm worried about—" I stop, because lying is exhausting. "Yes. Okay. I'm worried about Evie."

I rub my face. "She really does hate me though."

Jules waves a hand. "That's a solvable problem."

"It's not," I say.

Remy's voice is quiet, deadly accurate. "It is if you stop trying to solve it like a mission."

I stare at her.

She holds my gaze. "She's not an objective, Kaia. She's a person you hurt."

The words land deep.

I nod once because there's nothing to argue. I haven't told them all the details—everything I'm ashamed of—but Remy knows enough. She always does.

Remy's gaze softens slightly. "You should tell her you used your veto."

"She was there when I did it," I say.

"Yeah," Jules murmurs, gentler than usual. "But does she know what it means? What you chose?"

My throat tightens. "I don't want it to trap her," I say quietly. "I don't want her to feel like she owes me anything because I burned my one veto."

Jules nods, then grins mischievous again. "Well, I, for one, can't wait to meet her."

Mina nods, earnest. "We'll be careful. We won't overwhelm her."

I stare at them—the three women who fight beside me, who know me in ways the audience never will, who just found out my past is ten blocks away and still bleeding.

Remy's voice is quiet. "And Kaia? If you're relieved she's alive…"

I freeze.

Remy's eyes hold mine. "You're allowed to be relieved. Even if everything is not fine."

My chest aches. I look away before they can see how much.

"It is fine," I lie.

Jules snorts. Mina's smile goes sad. Remy doesn't argue.

Outside the window, Harbor's Edge wakes up under fog and lantern frames, the festival already building toward its next peak.

And somewhere in that town, I imagine that Evie is pretending her life isn't tethered to mine by magic and monsters.

Tonight, we go to her diner.

Tonight, Eon calls it 'controlled visibility.'
But I know what it really is.
A second chance I didn't earn.
And a danger I can't afford to ignore.

THE SIGN ON THE door captures my attention first.

CLOSED — PRIVATE EVENT *(Reopening tomorrow)*

It's handwritten on cardstock and taped crooked, like whoever put it up was annoyed. I'd know that handwriting anywhere. Gus. Of course.

I stop on the sidewalk, keys still in my fist, and stare through the glass.

The Lighthouse Diner looks... too clean. Not "wipe the counter and call it good" clean, which is usually where I end up at the end of my shift.

Corporate clean.

Chairs stacked with military precision. Booths wiped until they shine. Floor dry, no coffee smears, no broken glass, and definitely no sign that last night tried to kill me in here. Like Kaia's people came through with a mop and a mandate and scrubbed the fear right out of the tile.

No tourists. No late-night pie hunters like Mr. Alvarez. No Tasha doing that thing where she pretends she's not checking her phone every three seconds.

Just Gus behind the counter with his arms crossed like he's guarding the gates of hell.

He sees me, sighs like *I'm* the problem, and unlocks the door.

"Come on," he grunts.

I step in. The bell jingles. It sounds wrong in the quiet.

"Private event?" I ask, pulling my hood down. My hair is still damp from the fog. My nerves are still damp from everything else. "Since when do we do private events?"

Gus locks the door again with a heavy click. "Since tonight."

"I'm scheduled," I say, because I am, and because routine is the only thing keeping my brain from replaying last night's demon karaoke.

"You're still working."

I blink. "Then why is the diner closed?"

Gus scratches his jaw. "Because I'm not having a bunch of screaming idiots in here."

"Gus," I say slowly, "that is... most of our business model."

He grunts. "Not tonight."

I set my bag down behind the counter, eyes narrowing. "What's going on?"

He looks at me for a long second too long. Then he says, like it's no big deal, "We got a call."

My stomach drops. A cold tingle flicks under my skin at my wrist, where the invisible ribbon of magical binding now lives. It's not pain. It's a *reminder*.

Don't talk. Don't name it. *Don't—*

I keep my voice level through my teeth. "A call from who?"

Gus's eyes flick to my face, then away. He clears his throat. "Someone from Eon Entertainment. Blair? Blaine? Whatever."

My pulse kicks.

"Blaire," I correct automatically, like my mouth is ahead of my brain. Like I don't hate that I know that. "That's Midnight Halo's manager."

"Yeah, her." He gestures vaguely, annoyed at the concept of explaining anything. "Said they needed a place to sit for a minute. Quiet. Private. A bite to eat. Something about a 'homecoming' photo. In and out. No wait staff except—"

Except.

I stare at him. "Except *who*?"

Gus jerks his chin at me. "You."

The air in my lungs goes cold.

"They asked for *me*?" I echo.

Gus's gaze sharpens, knowing creeping in. "Yeah. The girl group."

My heart does that stupid stutter thing it does when my past shows up uninvited.

"No," I say. "Nope. That's not happening. If anyone's waiting on them, it should be Tasha—she actually *likes* them."

Gus lifts his brows like he's daring me to make it his problem. "Sit down and breathe, Evie."

"I am breathing," I hiss.

Gus points at the private event sign. "They're coming in through the back. They want to be discreet. They're eating, doing some meeting, doing a quick photo shoot, then they're leaving. That's the deal."

My wrist tingles again, like the world is amused by my fury. I clamp my hand around it.

"And you want me to *serve* them?"

Gus looks at me like I'm missing the obvious. "You *are* a server."

"I am not *their* server."

"You are tonight."

Panic floods through me, followed closely by annoyance. I lean closer across the counter and lower my voice. "Gus. I am begging you to be a gruff little wall of stubbornness right now and tell them I'm not available."

Gus's expression softens a fraction, which is always terrifying because it means he cares.

"Evie," he says, quieter. "Is this about Kaia?"

He doesn't say her name like a celebrity. He says it like a kid he watched grow up.

"I remember you two," he adds, gruffly. "Always in that booth. Like you were—"

"It's not about Kaia," I cut in too fast.

My wrist flares hot under my sleeve, an abrupt sting, like the air itself just snapped a rubber band against my skin. I shut my mouth instantly, anger swallowing itself.

Gus studies me for a beat. He doesn't push. He just resets his expression into his usual armor and grunts, like feelings are a health hazard. "Alright, well," he says, louder now, "you're the only one who won't lose her damn mind and ask for an autograph."

"I will lose my damn mind," I say.

Gus squints. "Not like Tasha would."

That's true, and I hate it. I can already picture her exploding through the roof when she figures out Midnight Halo ate here and she missed it.

I exhale hard and straighten. "Fine. Where's Tasha anyway?"

"Sent her home," Gus says. "Told her the fryer needed maintenance."

I snort. "She's going to be so upset when she finds out they were here."

Gus grunts like that's between Tasha and God.

His gaze sharpens, and his voice drops. "Evie."

"What?"

"You okay?"

I want to say yes.

I want to say no.

Instead I say, "I'm working."

Gus grunts again, accepting it as the closest I'll get to honesty. Then he jerks his chin toward the spotless counter, the stacked chairs, the floor that looks like it's never seen spilled coffee in its life.

"You sure worked hard last night," he mutters. "Haven't seen this place so clean in years."

Heat crawls up my neck. I don't answer.

Gus jerks his chin toward the back hallway. "Put your apron on. And try not to start a war."

"No promises."

Gus's mouth twitches. "That's my girl."

I hate that my throat tightens at that, too.

I tie my apron on with hands that are steadier than I feel. I stack coffee mugs, wipe down the already spotless counter, and try to pretend this is just a weird private party.

Outside, the town is still buzzing from last night. Between festival week and Midnight Halo, the energy is high. On my way here, I passed a group of girls, maybe sixteen, walking shoulder to shoulder and loudly singing a Midnight Halo hit. After that, a car that passed me was blasting the same song.

Everyone's got leftover music in their bones.

The back door clicks. Not the loud front-door bell. A controlled, quiet sound. My body goes rigid anyway. I turn before I mean to.

A woman steps in first. She's maybe early forties and dressed like she could walk onto a red carpet or into a courtroom and win over either one. Dark blazer, clean lines, hair pulled back with the kind of precision that says she doesn't tolerate problems. There's a headset tucked around her neck and a phone in her hand, screen lit up.

She scans the diner in one sweep—windows, corners, exits—then her gaze lands on me with quick, professional assessment.

Not a fan. Not a tourist. Definitely not someone here for pancakes.

Behind her comes Mr. Bane. The creepshow from last night. Same calm, same gloves, same briefcase as if he keeps nightmares filed alphabetically.

And then—

Then the world's biggest girl group walks into the diner.

Jules first, looking like she woke up and decided chaos was a lifestyle: her hair is pulled up into a messy bun, big hoodie, ripped jeans, yellow-tinted sunglasses even though we're indoors and it's getting late. She pauses, takes in the empty diner, and grins like she's delighted to be somewhere unglamorous.

Mina follows, small and soft-eyed, hair loose, hands tucked into her sleeves like she's trying not to touch anything without permission. Her gaze lands on me and sticks, surprisingly curious.

Remy comes in next. She's in all black with a beanie pulled low and an expression that says she's already ten steps ahead of everyone else. Her eyes sweep the diner like she's reading it.

Then Kaia walks in.

Not glowing. Not armed. Not unreal.

Just the famous Kaia Rhee in a plain coat, hair down, face softer without the colorful stage makeup but still unmistakably her. Still too bright for this room. Still the kind of person who draws the eye even when she's trying not to.

Her gaze pierces me, and my pulse jumps.

Kaia stops when she sees me, as if she didn't expect me to be real after last night. Maybe she expected last night to be a nightmare too.

I lift my chin, because if I don't, I'll do something stupid like show emotion.

"Welcome to the Lighthouse Diner," I say, voice flat and professionally pleasant.

The woman in the dark blazer steps forward before anyone answers.

"Hi," she says, brisk but not unkind. "I'm Blaire. I manage the group. Thank you for accommodating us on short notice."

I'm forced to drag my eyes off Kaia and look at Blaire properly.

"It was all Gus," I say, because I refuse to sound like I'm hosting. "I just work here."

She offers her hand anyway, professional, polite. I shake it because I'm not an animal.

"Thanks for making it work," Blaire says.

I give her a tight little smile. "Sure."

Gus appears from the kitchen like a bear emerging from a cave. He wipes his hands on a rag and grunts, "Yeah. Welcome." Then his eyes land on Kaia. His voice shifts half a degree. Still gruff, but real. "Good to see you, Rhee."

Kaia hesitates, then offers a small smile. "Gus," she says quietly. "Good to see you too."

Gus jerks his chin toward a few booths tucked deeper inside, away from the windows, private. "Go on, sit here."

Jules salutes him. "Yes, sir."

Mina whispers, "Hi," as if she can't help it.

Remy nods once.

Kaia doesn't speak again. She just watches me like she's trying to figure out how close she can stand without setting off a bomb.

I turn away first. Not because I'm weaker, but because I refuse to give her the satisfaction of seeing my face do anything except a customer-service smile.

They slide into the back booths.

I grab menus, and I approach the booth containing the girl group first.

Jules pulls her sunglasses down and grins at me. "Hi."

I stare. "Hi."

Mina's eyes are huge, like she's looking at a celebrity, except I'm not the celebrity; I'm the civilian who almost got eaten by a demon. *She's* the celebrity.

Remy's gaze is sharp, assessing.

Kaia sits rigid, hands clasped under the table.

I set the menus down with a soft smack. "Can I get you something to drink?"

Kaia speaks first, voice low. "Coffee. If that's okay. Cream, no sugar."

My fingers tighten around my notepad. I write it down, the pen digging a little too hard into the paper.

I look her dead in the eye and say, clearly, "Of course, Ms. Rhee."

The formality lands like a blade.

Kaia flinches, just a fraction. Jules literally chokes on her attempt to hold in her laughter.

Mina's eyes go even wider, and she whispers something inaudible. Remy's elbow drives gently into Mina's side. Mina squeaks.

"What," Jules whispers, delighted. "What is happening?"

"Nothing," I say, still staring at Kaia. "Anything else?"

I look at the others.

Mina says quickly, "Tea, please. If you have chamomile? Or anything warm?"

"We have black tea. Is that okay?"

"Of course!" Mina lights up like I've given her a puppy.

Remy says, "Black coffee."

Jules says, "Coffee, but with, like, extra sugar."

I write their orders down with exaggerated professionalism, pen scratching a little too loud. "Extra sugar. Got it."

Blaire orders black, of course—efficient and sleepless. Mr. Bane doesn't even look at the menu.

"Water," he says.

At the other booth, Jules whispers to Mina, "Look. She's doing the Kaia Thing again. The jaw. The tragic ocean-girl stare."

Kaia's head snaps toward them, eyes blazing. "*Jules.*"

I turn away before my expression can betray me, and I disappear behind the counter. I move on autopilot—pots, mugs, sugar caddies, cream. My hands know this work even when my head is still back in last night's static.

When I come back with the drinks, I set them down with careful, controlled clinks. Mina beams at me like I'm the nicest person she's met all week, which is... unfortunate for her.

I still don't look at Kaia. If I look at Kaia, I'll start measuring the distance between us in inches and mistakes.

Jules, on the other hand, seems determined to treat this like a normal diner outing with friends.

"Are you ready to order?" I ask.

At the nods, I look at Jules first.

"So," she says brightly, leaning in like we're best friends. "Whatever's best."

I hate when people do that.

I keep my voice neutral. "We do a decent cheeseburger."

Jules blinks, delighted. "Perfect. However it comes is great."

Mina points at the menu with cautious politeness. "Um... is the blueberry pancake special good?"

"If you like sweet."

"I like sweet," Mina says. "I'll take that."

Remy doesn't look up from the laminated menu. "Patty melt. No pickles."

"Of course," I say, still not looking at Kaia.

Blaire orders with the brisk competence of someone who's had meetings in worse places. "Two eggs, toast, hash browns."

Mr. Bane doesn't waver. "Nothing."

Of course.

I wait one extra beat before I finally force my eyes to the side, just enough to catch Kaia's order without really seeing her.

Kaia's voice is careful. "Just... fries. Please."

My pen pauses for half a second.

Fries. That's it. Just like when we were teenagers and had to save up for a basket, unless Gus took pity on us. The difference now is that she could probably buy the entire diner with a snap of her fingers. Still, she orders 'just fries.'

I write it down anyway.

"Anything else?" I ask, because my job is my armor.

Jules grins. "Can we get milkshakes?"

Gus's voice booms from behind the counter. "No shakes. Machine's down."

Jules clutches her chest like she's been shot. "You're kidding. This is, like... McDonald's-core tragedy."

"Welcome to life," I say, and turn on my heel before Kaia can say anything that makes my chest do something stupid.

I take the ticket back to Gus and the cook, slap it on the rail, and call it out.

Gus's grunt is his version of approval.

Blaire types away on her phone, and Mr. Bane has taken to wandering the diner. Whenever Gus isn't eying him suspiciously, he's drawing those creepy sigils into the air again. My skin prickles.

Mina watches the handler, then looks back at me with wide, earnest eyes, like she wants to apologize for him existing in my workplace. But Kaia's gaze keeps flicking to my hands.

Has she noticed them trembling?

I'm not trembling because I'm scared of her.

I'm trembling because my body remembers loving her and my brain is trying to murder that memory with a brick.

Mina whispers, audible only because the diner is too quiet, "Oh my god, she's exactly how you described her when we were trainees."

Another elbow from Remy. Mina squeaks again.

Jules laughs into her hand. "I cannot believe this is real."

It doesn't take long for Sam to complete the order. Once everything is ready, Gus shoves the plates toward me. I pick everything up, balance it, then walk over. I set the plates down one by one, efficient, clean.

And when I set down Kaia's fries, my fingers brush hers. Just a graze. Nothing. Yet, electricity crackles down my spine, causing me to straighten. I pull my hand back first, too fast, like I touched a hot pan.

"Anything else?" I ask, voice sharp to cover the fact my pulse just spiked.

Jules brightens instantly, "A therapy session?"

My brain stutters.

Therapy.

Session.

My face heats so fast I almost hate myself for being capable of blushing.

So they *know*.

Of course, they know.

Did Kaia really tell them about me? When? When they were trainees, like Mina whispered? How? Like it was a funny story? Like I was a character in her origin myth? Had she *bragged* about breaking my heart? Laughed about it?

Kaia's head snaps toward Jules with a glare that could crack glass. Jules's grin only gets wider until Kaia shifts in her seat, and Jules makes a small, surprised "oof" sound like she just got kicked under the table.

Mina's eyes go round with secondhand panic. "Jules," she hisses.

Remy doesn't even look up. She just takes a bite like this is none of her business, which somehow makes it worse.

Mina says softly, to me, sincere as a prayer, "Thank you."

Remy nods once, respectful.

Kaia's voice is quiet. "Thank you."

I finally look at her then, just to make sure she hears me. "Of course," I say. "Ms. Rhee."

Her eyes flicker. Hurt flashes there, quick and unwanted.

Good, I think viciously. Now she knows what it feels like.

Except the good feeling doesn't last. Because the hurt on her face looks real. And part of me—some stupid, soft part—hates that I caused it even when she deserves worse.

I turn away before my expression can betray me and look at Blaire and Mr. Bane. I set their food down, well... Blaire's plate and Bane's water refill, because of course he's still on water. They murmur thanks without really looking up.

They're too busy murmuring about 'ward integrity.'

I retreat, embarrassed and pissed, and disappear into the kitchen.

Sam is wiping down the grill, humming under his breath like nothing in the world is wrong. I grab a towel and start helping him because my hands need something to do before I explode.

For a few minutes, it works.

Then Gus barks my name from the front like I'm a dog he regrets owning.

"Evie. Front."

Of course.

I leave the kitchen and walk out just in time to see Gus carrying dessert plates, pie and something chocolatey he definitely didn't make for tourists. And because the universe is determined to humiliate everyone in this diner, he's not alone.

Sam traipses out behind him with the last plate, eyes wide like he's staring at living mythology.

He sets the plate down in front of Jules, clears his throat, and then says, "Could I... maybe... get a quick autograph?"

Jules, of course, lights up. "Oh my god, yes."

Sam pulls a receipt book out like he's been carrying it for this exact moment.

Gus presses his fingers to his forehead in a full-body facepalm. "Sam."

Sam whispers, "For my niece."

"*Sam*," Gus repeats, warning.

Jules grabs the receipt book anyway, grinning. "What's her name?"

Sam beams. "Sierra. She's twelve. Loves your music!"

Jules scribbles something fast and dramatic and slides it to the other girls to sign too. "Tell Sierra that Jules says hi and to eat her veggies."

Kaia hands him the receipt paper, now fully autographed.

Sam looks like he might ascend. "Thank you. Thank you so much."

He scuttles back to the kitchen like he's afraid someone will take it away.

Gus mutters, "I'm surrounded by idiots," and storms off.

Jules watches him go, delighted. "I love him."

I roll my eyes. "Do not encourage him."

Jules puts a hand over her heart. "Yes, ma'am."

I don't laugh. I refuse.

But Mina does—soft, surprised—and it makes the booth feel less like a battlefield for half a second. Then my wrist tingles again, and my brain reminds me I'm in a cage with velvet walls.

I step back, forcing distance. "Let me know if you need anything else."

"Evie—" Kaia starts, then stops, eyes flicking briefly to Blaire and the others. "Thank you," she says, quieter.

I finally look at her, and I hate myself because I see it... she's trying. She's actually *trying* not to make it worse.

It doesn't matter.

Trying doesn't undo years.

Trying doesn't un-say "stupid kiss."

Trying doesn't un-leave without a word.

I keep my voice cold because it's the only thing holding me up.

"Enjoy your meal." I turn away before my eyes can do anything traitorous.

I retreat to the counter and start wiping something that doesn't need wiping. The rag moves in angry circles. I pretend I'm not listening.

I listen anyway, and let their voices fill my head.

Jules talking in low bursts, like she can't help filling silence. Mina's soft laughter. Remy's dry comments. Kaia barely speaking at all.

But I feel Kaia's gaze on me like heat. Every time I move, she tracks me. I don't look at her because I refuse to let her win my attention like she wins everything else.

I want to throw the rag through the window.

Somewhere in the booth, Mina whispers again, soft and awed, "She *really* is exactly—"

Remy murmurs, "Eat your food, Mina."

Jules says, delighted, "Kaia, you are *so* doomed."

Kaia's voice is barely audible. "Stop."

Jules laughs. "No."

I set the coffee pot down with a little too much force. I take a breath, force my shoulders to loosen, and force my face into neutral. Because I can't afford to be the emotional buffet anymore.

Not for demons.

Not for Midnight Halo.

And definitely not for *Kaia Rhee*.

Still... When I glance at the booth again, Kaia's eyes are on me.

Not hungry. Not triumphant.

Just... relieved.

Before I can spiral, Blaire stands and claps her hands once, quiet and efficient.

"Okay," she says, the way you say *we're wrapping this up.* "Quick homecoming shots. Then we're gone."

She walks over to the booth where the girls are and lifts her phone. "Alright, Midnight Halo, positions. Jules, do the thing."

Jules lights up like she's been waiting her whole life for permission. She throws up a peace sign and leans into Mina. Mina tries to look composed and fails adorably when she ends up grinning. Remy doesn't move much, she just tilts her head and gives the camera a calm look like it's a skill she was born with. Kaia sits still and flashes a perfect smile. It's identical to her poster shots.

Blaire snaps a few photos. "Perfect."

I keep my eyes on the counter and pretend my job is not currently being turned into content.

Then Blaire pivots—phone still up—and her gaze lands on poor Gus.

"Now," she says, "can I get you and Kaia with the diner? Under the Lighthouse sign."

Gus grunts like he hates everyone equally and shuffles out from behind the counter. Kaia stands too, following him. She steps to the counter beneath the *LIGHTHOUSE DINER* sign inside, the one with the painted lighthouse and the little wave flourish. The sign I've looked at a thousand times without thinking.

Now it feels like a target.

Blaire frames the shot. "Gus, look alive."

"Impossible," Gus mutters.

Kaia's mouth twitches.

Blaire lifts her phone. "Kaia, just a little more warmth. Hometown, you know?"

Kaia's face shifts into something practiced and gentle. My chest does something stupid. Blaire is about to snap the photo when her eyes flick to the side... straight to *me*. And my blood goes cold, because I recognize that look.

"Evie," Blaire calls. "Can you step in? Just for a second. Staff with Kaia. It'll be great."

"I'm just a waitress," I say, too flat to be polite.

Blaire's smile stays on, but it sharpens. "You're staff, come on."

Gus glares at me like I'm the one about to cause trouble. "*Evie.*"

My wrist itches under my sleeve, cold and insistent, like the binding is listening for me to say the wrong thing.

I swallow hard... and I step out from behind the counter, because apparently today's theme is *humiliation, with a side of trauma.*

Kaia's eyes meet mine.

I walk to the counter and stop at the edge of the frame, keeping as much distance as I can without making it obvious.

Blaire tilts her phone. "Closer."

My jaw tightens. I take one more step. Kaia shifts closer too—not touching me, not crowding, just... closing the gap because Blaire demands it.

Now I'm close enough that Kaia's warmth reaches me. Close enough that I can smell her expensive perfume and something clean that doesn't belong in a greasy diner.

Close enough that my body remembers what it's like to be sixteen and stupid and laughing in booth three like we had forever.

I stare straight ahead, chin lifted, refusing to look at her again.

Blaire lifts the phone. "Perfect. Hold."

The shutter clicks.

For a heartbeat, the flash leaves a ghost behind my eyes.

Then it's done.

I step away from Kaia immediately.

Blaire beams at her screen. "Great. Thank you."

Gus grunts and goes back behind the counter to reclaim his territory. Kaia stays still for half a second longer, as if she's reluctant to break the moment. Then she returns to the booth with her girls.

I retreat behind the counter, back into my side of the world, and grip the edge of it until my fingers stop wanting to shake.

Because this does not feel like a homecoming reunion. This feels like a war zone.

And somehow, I'm standing in the middle of it—close enough to smell her, close enough to remember, close enough to get hurt.

Again.

BY THE TIME WE step out of the diner, Harbor's Edge has cooled into that late-night quiet that makes everything feel staged.

The fog is thicker now, rolling low along the curb like it's trying to seep into every crack in the town. The lantern frames still hang overhead, skeletal and patient.

Blaire walks ahead of us toward the parked car with sheer managerial purpose. Mr. Bane trails a few steps behind her, briefcase in hand.

I keep my gaze forward.

I don't look back.

If I look back, I'll see Evie behind the counter. Cold. Professional. Calling me *Ms. Rhee* like she's filing me under *stranger*. It hurts worse than yelling would have.

Blaire's phone lights up and she lifts it to her ear automatically. Her whole posture tightens like a leash just snapped taut.

"Yes," she says, voice low. "I hear you."

A pause.

Her jaw clenches. "No, I understand what you want."

Another pause, longer.

She exhales through her nose like she's trying not to swear. "With respect, it's not 'routine' when you've got splinters slipping out through screens and a civilian exposure on the record."

Jules whispers loudly, "Ooooh, Blaire's doing the 'with respect.' Someone's in trouble. I hope it's Devin!"

Mina elbows her, hissing, "Shh."

Remy doesn't look up, but I feel the way she's listening with her whole body.

Blaire's eyes flick back toward us without turning her head. "Yes. I'm aware it's festival week. That's why I'm saying—"

She cuts herself off mid-sentence, listening. Then her shoulders drop an inch, resignation settling in like a cloak.

"Fine," she says. "We'll do the sweep."

She lowers the phone, stops by the car, and turns to face us, expression flat.

"You're going on patrol," she says.

Jules' face lights up like it's Christmas. "Yay!"

Mina's eyes widen. "Now?"

Remy's voice is calm. "Council order?"

Blaire nods once. "Council order."

She points at Jules first, because of course she does. "No shouting."

Jules puts a hand over her heart. "I never shout."

Blaire's gaze slides to Mina. "Stay close."

Mina nods quickly. "Okay."

Her eyes land on Remy. "You're my brain tonight. You feel something, you call it."

Remy inclines her head.

Then Blaire looks at me. Her stare is a loaded gun.

"Kaia," she says. "No freelancing."

My jaw tightens. "Understood."

Blaire gestures vaguely at the sleeping town. "Low-level sweep. Boardwalk first. Then main street. Then loop back. Don't get seen by civvies. If you get seen, you smile and pretend you're four exhausted tourists who can't read signs."

Jules beams. "Perfect. I can't read signs."

Blaire's mouth twitches despite herself. "That's the only believable part."

Mr. Bane steps forward, calm as a diagnosis. "There is residual cluster frequency detected near the boardwalk. Minor but unstable."

Mina swallows. "So it's... close."

"Testing," Remy murmurs.

Blaire lifts a hand, palm down. "Okay. Here's how this works. I'm not babysitting you down every alley. You're going as a unit. Clear whatever you can, then meet us at the intersection of fourth and Bass." She jerks her chin toward Mr. Bane and the car. "I'm taking him the other way to check the secondary trace. Different street. We are *not* circling back to the diner."

Her eyes flick to me like she knows exactly where my mind just tried to go.

"You check. You clear. We regroup. In and out."

Jules bounces on her heels. "Blaire. Babe. You trust us."

Blaire stares at her. "I trust Remy."

Remy doesn't react.

Jules gasps, offended. "Wow."

Blaire points again, sharp. "And if you sense anything bigger than a splinter, you retreat and call it. We are not having another diner situation."

My stomach twists at the words.

I nod anyway. "Understood," I repeat.

Blaire looks us each in the eye. "Good. Then go."

So we go.

It's late enough that Harbor's Edge feels like it's been put away for the night—shops dark, booths shuttered, the occasional straggler drifting home after a long day. Outside of festival season, Harbor's Edge doesn't have much of a night life. Just a few silhouettes in the distance and the hush of a town trying to settle.

The boardwalk is a long strip of wet wood disappearing into fog, lit in patches by streetlamps that turn the fog into floating halos. The ocean is invisible, but I can hear it breathing—low, patient, endless.

I inhale, and my chest tightens with something old. Lantern night memories try to crawl up my throat.

I shove them down hard.

"Stay on me," I murmur, letting my voice drop into the cadence that makes the team align without thinking. "We keep it quiet. We keep it clean."

Jules grins. "Captain Kaia is back."

"Jules," Mina whispers.

Jules mimes zipping her lips.

We walk. At first, it's just fog and salt and the creak of boards underfoot. Then my skin prickles. It starts as a thin pressure in my ears, like altitude change. A faint hum in the air that doesn't belong to wind or ocean.

Remy slows. "There," she says softly.

Mina's eyes widen. "I see it."

Jules' grin sharpens into something hungry. "Finally."

Then I see it too. The air ahead shivers—heat distortion, light bending. A smear forms near the railing, stretching upward like ink pulled through water.

Not a full Chorus body.

A splinter that broke off.

It doesn't have a face. It never does. But as it coalesces, the first notes leak into the air—tinny, warped, and sickeningly sweet.

Come back, come back—

Jules makes a gagging noise. "Ew. Tourism jingle demon. *Again.*"

Mina's breath catches, but she steadies. "It's trying to hook into us."

But her eyes dart to me. I'm the only one that grew up on that jingle.

Remy's eyes narrow. "It's weak."

Weak means we do this fast.

"Formation," I murmur.

We don't need to discuss. We've done this in arenas and backstage corridors and hotel hallways when the world thought we were just girls in glittery costumes.

Jules moves first, because she always does. She steps forward, and in the same motion, her hands flick outward as if she's snapping open invisible fans.

Voltstep answers. Two short swords flash into existence, sparking with kinetic energy like they're hungry for movement.

Jules grins. "Miss me?"

Mina draws next, more careful, more precise. Her hand rises like she's lifting an invisible ribbon, and the air condenses into her translucent sword, Heartglass. Its blade catches the fog and splits it into prismatic fragments, reflection shimmering along its length like a mirror that tells the truth.

Remy's draw is almost silent. Her fingers curl as if gripping a pen, and then the black blade appears—Inkthorn—script-etched, leaving faint glowing runes in the air as she shifts her wrist. Spellwork encoded in her grip, her breath, her focus.

Then me.

I reach, not upward now, but forward, like I'm grabbing the shape of a note before it escapes. Light blooms. Aurora forms in my hand.

To the splinter, we are four frequencies it can't swallow without choking.

It lunges.

Mina shifts, Heartglass angled, not just to block, but to reveal. The splinter's smear sharpens for a heartbeat in the blade's reflection, its true edges showing like a secret dragged into light.

"There," Mina breathes. "Thread is exposed."

Remy slides in, Inkthorn carving a rune in the air with a flick, the glowing script that hooks into the splinter's pattern like a snagged sweater.

The jingle stutters.

Jules is already moving, Voltstep charging with each step she takes. She darts in and out like a dancer hitting beats only she can hear, blades sparking brighter as her momentum feeds them.

"Sorry," she chirps, and slashes.

The splinter recoils, pattern fraying.

I step into the center, Aurora humming. I don't sing a lyric. I sing a note, low, controlled, weaponized. The sound becomes force as I bring my blade down.

It hits the splinter like a wall, compressing the smear into a tighter knot.

"Now, Remy," I say.

Remy's already moving. She strikes. Inkthorn slices through the tightened thread, severing the pattern cleanly.

The splinter collapses in on itself. Static. Then nothing.

Fog rushes into the empty space, reclaiming the air. Silence drops so fast my ears ring.

Jules lowers her blades, grinning like she just finished a dance break. "That's it? That's all you had? Embarrassing."

Mina exhales shakily, then steadies. "It's gone."

Remy watches the air for a beat longer, then nods. "Clean."

I dismiss Aurora with a flick of my wrist. Light folds in on itself, vanishing into nothing. The others do the same—swords gone, bodies relaxed, posture returning to "normal girls on a foggy boardwalk" in the blink of an eye.

Jules stretches her arms above her head. "Okay, patrol was fun. Can we go back and tell Blaire we did a crime?"

"We didn't do a crime," Mina scoffs.

Jules winks. "We did a *righteous* crime."

Remy glances back toward town, eyes sharp. "We should move. Before anyone recognizes us."

"Back to Blaire," I agree.

We head off the boardwalk in a tight cluster, boots quiet on wet wood, hoodies up, faces angled down.

Just four women in fog.

Nothing to see here.

Except the way my throat still hums with the aftermath of that note, and the way, even after killing a splinter cleanly, my mind is already drifting back toward one place.

The diner.

Evie.

The person I can't stop orbiting, no matter how hard I try to walk straight.

But more than that, I'm worried.

Not in the abstract, mission-report way. In the ugly, personal way. Because splinters don't stop being hungry just because you destroy one. The other splinters will test. They circle. They come back to whatever felt *easy*.

And last night, Evie became easy. She's marked by proximity, by exposure, by my own stupid attachment lighting her up in whatever language demons can taste.

I swallow hard and force my gaze forward. Because I didn't just feel the splinter there last night. I felt something else. A thin ripple behind it. Like a shadow behind a shadow.

And Mina saw something bigger in the rafters. She said it clapped.

The Council dismissed it with smooth voices and tidy words, the way they dismiss anything that isn't on a monitor.

I didn't.

By the time we loop back toward Fourth Street, the town is nearly asleep. The only people out now are drunks and fisher-men. We turn onto the street behind the diner—narrow, wet, lined with dumpsters and utility doors.

The alley behind the Lighthouse Diner is darker than it should be, as if the fog itself avoids it.

I know we should keep walking. The sweep route doesn't include *this*. Blaire said regroup at the intersection.

But the diner lights are on. A thin, stubborn glow behind the back windows. Fluorescents, harsh and familiar.

Somehow, I get the horrible feeling that Evie's still there, alone.

My chest tightens with something hot and sick—admiration, worry, guilt, all stacked on top of each other. After last night, after being pinned and choked and almost swallowed by sound, she's still here closing up like the world didn't try to take her.

Brave or furious enough to pretend she isn't afraid.

My pace slows.

Jules notices immediately. Of course she does. She doesn't say anything yet, but I feel her attention slide to me. Mina glances up at the diner's glow and then back at me, eyes wide with a quiet *don't.*

And then my skin prickles. Not from wind. Not from cold. From that faint, wrong pressure in the air, like a note vibrating just under hearing range.

Remy's gaze is fixed ahead. "There. You See anything, Mina?"

Mina's fingers curl in her sleeves. "No. But I feel it…"

Of course the town chooses *this* moment to get interesting.

We stop at the mouth of the alley behind the diner, the fog pooled thick between dumpsters and service doors. The air shivers. We look to Mina.

Mina shakes her head. "I don't think it's a full manifestation."

Just… a ripple. A testing touch along something invisible, like fingers brushing a fence to see how solid it really is. Except the fence in this case are the wards surrounding the diner.

My gaze drifts to the diner's back door—metal, painted, familiar. The same one I crashed through last night.

Evie is inside.

"We should tell Blaire," Mina whispers.

"We will," I say. My voice stays steady because that's my job. "But first—"

Jules tilts her head. "But first you're going to do something stupid."

"It's not stupid," I say, and immediately regret it because it sounds exactly like something stupid people say right before they do something stupid.

Remy's mouth twitches. "Sure."

I exhale slowly and force the truth out in a version they can accept. "This is a hotspot. If it's probing here, we should check the wards."

Mina's eyes widen. "Right now?"

"Yes."

Jules crosses her arms. "Bane just checked them."

I meet her gaze. "I'll only be five minutes. In and out."

Remy's eyes flick toward the diner door, then back to me. "Alone?"

I hesitate for half a heartbeat.

Because if they come with me, Evie will feel cornered in her own space. If they come with me, the world's loudest girl group walks into her kitchen like an invasion.

And because—if I'm honest—I don't want witnesses for whatever happens between us.

"Yes," I say. "Alone. Just a ward check. What if Bane missed something?"

Jules' eyebrows shoot up. "If *Bane* missed something, Captain, what exactly do you think you're going to do? Wave your sparkly sword at the doorframe until it feels safer?"

"We're not ward-trained," Mina adds quickly, anxious. "Handlers do that."

"I know," I say, keeping my tone even.

Remy's gaze stays on the fog. "So why risk it?"

Because Evie is in there, my body answers before my mouth can. I swallow it down and give them the part that makes sense on a mission report.

"I'm not going to rewrite his work," I say. "But I can feel if there's a gap. If the threshold's wrong. If something is using it as an easy seam." My eyes flick to the back door again. "And if there *is* a seam, I'd rather find it before it finds her."

Jules' expression sharpens. She hears the *her* even if I don't say the name.

I keep my voice calm. "You three wait here. Watch the alley. If that ripple strengthens, you pull me out. If anything manifests, you call Blaire."

Jules' eyes narrow. "And if Evie throws a coffee pot at you?"

"I'll dodge," I deadpan.

Jules snorts despite herself. "Okay, fair."

Remy's voice is soft but firm. "Five minutes. Not six."

I nod once. "Five."

Mina reaches out and catches my sleeve lightly, just for a second. "Be careful," she whispers.

I look at her, and there's too much in that request. *Be careful with demons, with the Council, with Evie, with your own stupid heart.*

"I will," I say, and mean it.

Then I step into the alley alone. Fog clings to my coat. The hum under my skin sharpens as I get closer to the back door. The wardlines here are threaded through brick and metal, tightened by our visit earlier. Their geometry lays under my feet like an invisible grid.

I stop at the door.

My hand lifts then pauses. I knock before I can talk myself out of it. A beat. Then the metal clicks. A chain scrapes. The door opens a crack, and fluorescent light spills into the alley like a confession.

Evie's face appears in the gap. Her eyes land on me and go flat.

"Absolutely not," she says.

I swallow. "Hi."

Her gaze flicks past me toward the alley, suspicious. "What are you doing here?"

"I felt a ripple," I say quietly, keeping my voice low so it won't carry to the street. "Behind the diner. *It's* testing. I'm here to check the wards."

Evie's laugh is sharp. "We just had a private event, remember? Isn't that what Mr. Tall, Dark, and Creepy was doing? I've had enough excitement to last the rest of my life."

"I know," I say, softer than I mean to. "That's why I'm here."

Her eyes narrow, like softness from me is a language she refuses to speak. "No, actually. That's why you should leave."

She looks exhausted—rag in hand, sleeves pushed up, the kind of tired that lives in the bones.

I hate that my first instinct is to step closer.

Even more than that, I hate that I *don't.*

"I'm not bringing the others," I add quickly. "They're waiting down the alley. It's just me. Five minutes."

Evie stares at me like she's weighing whether letting me in is worse than whatever's outside.

"It might come back," I say, and immediately regret the phrasing when her face tightens.

She holds my gaze—furious, shaken, stubborn. Then she exhales sharply, like she's swallowing a scream.

"Fine," she says. "Five minutes. Then you go away and I go home."

Relief flickers through me, unwanted and sharp.

I nod once. "Okay."

Evie unchains the door with aggressive movements and steps back just enough to let me in.

The diner smells like coffee, lemon cleaner, and something faintly metallic underneath—the residue of magic that never fully leaves.

Evie's gaze flicks to my hands, then my face. "Where are your... your cosplay weapons?"

"Aurora is dismissed," I say. "But I can summon if needed."

Evie grimaces. "Please don't summon anything in the kitchen. I just finished cleaning it."

"I won't," I promise.

I walk toward the back corridor, where the threshold wards were reinforced earlier by Mr. Bane. I can feel the lines under the floor, in the walls. I may not be able to place them, but anyone with high resonance can sense them.

My fingertips hover near the doorframe, not touching.

"So. Aurora," she says, skeptical. "You... named it *Aurora?*"

"It's the weapon's name," I answer. "I didn't pick it."

Evie's mouth twitches. "Sure. The sword comes pre-branded."

"It does." I glance at her. "They're manifestations that match your resonance—sorry, *magic*. The name is... part of the imprint."

Evie's eyes narrow, trying to keep up without letting me see how much she's listening. "Okay, so. How do you summon it?" She gestures vaguely at my empty hands. "Is it... invisible?"

"It's not invisibility," I say carefully, choosing plain words. "It's... compression."

Her brow furrows. "Compression?"

"Magic is... emotion and attention," I say. "Most people generate it without meaning to. Some people—*Resonants*—can *shape* it. When I dismiss Aurora, I'm not throwing it away or turning it invisible. I'm pulling it back into myself. Into the part of me that holds the magic." I tap two fingers lightly against my sternum. "It stays here."

Evie's expression shifts, disbelief wrestling with reluctant comprehension. "So it's inside you."

"In a way," I say. "When I summon it, I give it a path out. I focus, I pull, and it manifests in my hand because my resonance recognizes the shape." I glance at the doorway, at the quiet hum in the wood. "Onstage, with lights and smoke, it looks like choreography. Like a prop. But it's real. It's just... arriving."

Evie stares at my empty hand like she's trying to see the outline of something that isn't there.

Her eyes flick to my face, sharp again. "And that demon the other night... It could hear you. Through—what—feelings?"

I hesitate, because the answer is dangerous.

"Patterns like that," I say slowly, "follow emotion. They follow repetition. They follow... the places where... thoughts keeps looping." My fingertips hover a fraction closer to the doorframe, still not touching.

Evie's jaw tightens. "So how did it find me?"

"I don't know," I cut in quickly, because I can't say *I thought of you and it followed the thought like a thread.* Not to her. Not yet.

I swallow and focus on the ward line instead. Safer. I hum one low note under my breath. Just a resonance test. The ward lines respond with a faint shimmer, like glass catching light.

Evie's eyes narrow. "Did you just... hum at the wall?"

"Yes," I say, because there's no point lying about something that ridiculous.

Then my gaze catches the neon sign's reflection in the window, buzzing faintly, flickering on the edge.

A memory rises uninvited.

Evie at sixteen, glaring at the sign like it personally offended her.

The diner's haunted, she'd said. That buzzing is the ghost trying to get out.

The thought slips out before I can stop it.

"Maybe it's just the lighthouse ghost again," I mutter, mostly to the doorframe.

Evie freezes like I just said a slur.

Her head snaps toward me. "Excuse me?"

I immediately regret having a mouth. "Nothing."

"No, no," she says, stepping closer to the counter like she's about to interrogate me. "You don't get to walk into my diner and start talking about ghosts."

I swallow. "We used to joke about it," I say, quiet. "You and me. The 'ghost' that supposedly haunts this place. You used to blame it for everything."

Evie's eyes narrow. "So it's the ghost's fault you're here?"

"That," I say carefully, "and the demon ripple in the alley."

She scoffs, but her mouth betrays her. One corner twitches like it's trying to remember how to smile without permission.

"You're unbelievable," she mutters, and for half a heartbeat the words sound like they used to. Like banter. Like an eye-roll instead of a wall.

My chest tightens.

I force myself to keep it light, because if I push, she'll snap shut. "You're the one who insisted the neon sign buzz was 'a dead fisherman trying to order pancakes.'"

Evie blinks.

"I said *maybe*," she corrects automatically, voice less sharp. "And it wasn't a fisherman. It was a lighthouse keeper."

I can't help it. "Oh, right. Sorry. My mistake. That's a very different haunting demographic."

Evie lets out a short huff, almost a laugh.

It's tiny. It's reluctant. It's real.

And it hits me harder than any scream could.

Her shoulders loosen for a second. Her gaze drops to the counter like she's suddenly embarrassed she almost... warmed.

"You're not allowed to use my stupid ghost theory against me," she says, quieter now.

"Why not?" I ask softly. "It was one of your better ones."

Evie's eyes lift to mine, and for a moment her face is unguarded—tired, raw, and achingly familiar.

"You really remember that, huh?" she says.

"Yeah," I admit. "Of course, I remember. How could I forget?"

Evie's grip tightens on the rag. The softness in her eyes tries to retreat, as if she's realizing she stepped too close to the edge. She gives a short, bitter laugh that isn't really a laugh.

"Funny," she says. "Because you seemed like you *forgot* about everyone in this town pretty fast after you left."

The words land and stay there, heavy.

My instinct is to defend myself—to say it wasn't like that, to say I was trapped, to say *you don't know what they told me.*

Instead, I say something stupid.

"Not everyone... I remember you ordering coffee for it. For the ghost," I blurt, softer than I mean to. "You'd hide it right by the window. Gus used to get so annoyed."

Evie clears her throat hard, scrubbing the counter again like she can erase the moment.

"For the record," she adds, voice snapping back into place, "the ghost coffee was for Gus."

"You labeled it 'FOR GHOST,'" I remind her.

Evie's glare returns, familiar and sharp and safer than tenderness. "I was making a point."

"What point?"

"That Gus is gullible," she says immediately. Then, after a beat, she adds, quieter, "And that if the place was haunted, at least the ghost deserved a hot drink."

My chest aches.

There's so much *Evie* in that sentence. Sharp edges and secret kindness.

I swallow it down.

"Noted," I say, voice steadying. "If the ripple comes back, I'll offer it coffee and see if it leaves."

Evie's lips twitch again, this time she smothers it faster.

"Just check your stupid wards," she says, brisk. "No more ghost talk."

I turn back to the ward line, because it's safer to touch magic than the past. I move to the window by the back door, where the ward sigils were etched into the glass in a pattern only visible to someone with resonance.

The lines are clean. The geometry is precise.

But the shapes—

My stomach tightens.

The sigil pattern echoes *Eon* branding...

Not the literal logo. But the same design language: clean curves, mirrored angles, a stylized halo-like arc embedded in the containment lattice.

It's subtle enough that most people would call it a coincidence. Maybe it is a coincidence. Maybe my brain is just looking for something to blame besides myself.

But Council-grade warding doesn't accidentally borrow corporate aesthetics. Not this clean. Not this consistent.

I don't have proof. Just a crawling feeling under my skin and a pattern that looks too familiar.

I push the thought down and file it where I file everything that makes my skin crawl: *later. Investigate later. Ask Blaire later.*

Evie watches me from behind the counter, arms folded now, rag hanging from her hand like she forgot what she was doing.

"What?" she demands, catching my pause.

"Nothing," I lie automatically.

Evie's eyes narrow. "Are you lying?"

I exhale slowly. "No. The wards are fine."

Evie nods. "Great."

I turn slightly, keeping my voice low. "Evie... I wasn't sure you'd still be here."

The sentence is out before I can soften it. Evie stills. I push forward because if I stop now, I'll retreat into professionalism and never say anything real again.

"My mom moved," I add, voice rougher. "Once I started making money, she left Harbor's Edge and... bought a house. Everything shifted. People shift. I—" I swallow. "I didn't know if you'd... stay."

Evie's eyes flash, something sharp and old. "I didn't have a golden ticket."

I shouldn't have said anything.

"Evie—"

"No," she snaps, stepping out from behind the counter now. Not toward me, just into the open, like she refuses to be cornered in her own diner. "Don't do that. Don't come in here and act like you're surprised I'm still... still holding everything together with duct tape."

"I wasn't judging," I say quickly. "I was—"

"You were what?" she demands. "Missing the small-town ghost? Nostalgic?"

I flinch. "I—"

Evie's voice drops into something dangerous. "You left. You got to be *special somewhere else.* And now you're standing here acting like this is some tragic little museum exhibit you can visit when you're feeling sentimental."

I feel shame flare so hot it makes my eyes sting.

"That's not—" I start.

Evie cuts me off like she's been practicing. "No. We're not doing this."

The old rhythm tries to surface... argument lines we know by heart, the way we used to push and parry and then soften, the way we used to end up laughing after because we couldn't stay mad at each other forever.

For a heartbeat, I see it: Evie's mouth twisting, my chest loosening.

But then Evie's face goes hard. She slams the door shut emotionally with a single sentence.

"Whatever you came here to check, check it," she says coldly. "Then leave. Because you don't get to talk about the past like it's a cute story. You can do that for the news stations, but not me."

My throat tightens so hard that it hurts.

"Okay," I manage.

Evie's gaze flicks to my face, and for half a second, I see something under the anger—pain, raw and bright. Then she buries it. She turns away and goes back to wiping the counter like she can scrub away years.

I stand there, useless and full of words I don't deserve to say.

I force myself to be professional. Useful. Controlled. Anything but begging. I step back to the window, let the ward line hum settle against my senses, and take a slow breath.

"Wards are strong," I repeat. "It'll hold."

Evie's laugh is brittle. "Amazing. Great. I love living in a horror movie."

I swallow, because I want to say *I'm sorry I dragged you into this.*

But apology is cheap in a place this broken.

Evie's voice cuts through my thoughts. "You done, aren't you?"

I look at her. She's still wiping counters, but her hands have slowed. Her shoulders are tense. She looks like she's keeping herself upright by sheer spite.

I nod once. "Yeah."

Evie doesn't look at me. "Good."

I hesitate.

The girls are waiting in the alley. Blaire's clock is ticking in my ear even when my comms aren't. I should leave. I should take the win—no breach, no manifestation—and walk away before I make it worse. But my chest doesn't listen to strategy.

It's stupid. I know it's stupid. But my mouth moves anyway.

"Evie," I say softly.

She stills. I don't push. I don't reach. I just say the smallest true thing I'm allowed.

"I'm... glad you're still here," I whisper.

Then I step back out through the diner's rear door into the foggy alley, and the cold hits my face like a reset button.

Jules is exactly where I left her, leaning against the dumpster like this is a photoshoot backdrop instead of a demon corridor. Mina hovers a few feet away, hands tucked into her sleeves, eyes wide with the kind of worry she pretends is curiosity. Remy stands slightly apart, head tilted, listening to the dark like it's speaking in punctuation.

Jules' grin goes wicked the second she sees me. "Oooh. There she is. Five minutes later. Totally normal."

"It's been, like, two," I lie.

Remy doesn't even look at me. "It's been seven."

Jules laughs. "*Doomed.*"

Mina steps forward a fraction. "Is she—" She stops herself, then tries again in a smaller voice. "Is Evie okay?"

"She's fine," I say. It comes out too quick. Too defensive.

Jules makes a soft sound like *aw.* "Captain Kaia is emotionally stable."

"Shut up," I mutter, but there's no real heat in it.

Mina studies my face like she's trying to read what I'm not saying. "Is she... mad?"

I exhale. "Yes."

Mina nods, as if that's actually reassuring.

Jules pushes off the dumpster, bouncing on her heels. "Did she throw anything at you?"

"No."

Jules looks disappointed. "Not even a spoon?"

"Not even a spoon."

Remy's gaze flicks to the diner door, then to the alley mouth. "And the wards?"

I feel my shoulders tighten again. The banter drains out of me like someone pulled a plug.

"They were fine," I say quietly. "Though they looked different."

Remy's interest perks immediately. "Different how?"

"Cleaner," I say, searching for the right words. "Too clean. The geometry's Council-grade, but the design language..." I shake my head once. "It echoed Eon. Same curves. Same mirrored angles. Like someone couldn't help stamping a signature into the lattice."

Mina's arms wrap tighter around herself. "Is that normal?"

"No," Remy says before I can. Flat certainty.

I don't argue. "I'm going to ask Blaire," I say. "Later."

Remy nods once, but I can tell that she's filing it away, the same way she files everything that might become a knife.

I glance down the alley. The fog looks thicker toward the street, like it's gathering.

"Let's head back," I say.

I glance back at the diner door one more time.

Jules watches me for a beat, then her voice softens. It's rare, and it's only when she's trying to be kind without admitting it. "Hey."

I glance at her.

She jerks her chin toward the alley mouth. "You did the ward check. You did the responsible thing. Now you come with us before you get any more ideas."

A laugh threatens in my throat, small, tired. I swallow it.

"Okay," I say.

Mina steps closer, relieved. Remy turns first, already scanning the shadows as we start back toward the street.

Jules falls into place at my side and whispers, gleeful and horrible, "So... *Ms. Rhee.*"

I shoot her a look.

She grins wider. "That one stung, huh?"

"Walk," I mutter.

We move out of the alley, fog swallowing our footsteps. Behind us, the diner stays lit and stubborn, a warm square of fluorescents in a town that feels too eager to turn everything into a stage.

For now, the wards hold.

And somewhere in the seams of Harbor's Edge, something hums with familiar hunger—testing the fence, tasting the air, and learning the shape of what we fight to protect.

Gran's bedroom smells like lavender and old paper and the faint medicinal sweetness of the hand lotion I keep buying because it's the only one she'll tolerate.

She's half-sitting in bed when I come in, hair flattened on one side, eyes bright in that way that means she's awake but not necessarily *here*.

"Morning," I say gently.

She stares at me for a beat, then her face relaxes. "Oh. There you are."

"I'm right here," I tell her, because I've learned that reassurance is a tool, not a feeling.

She frowns at the window. "It's still dark."

"It's morning," I say. "Fog makes everything look dark this time of year."

That earns me a small, suspicious hum, like she's filing it under *possible*.

I cross to her dresser and pick up the pill organizer. Monday, Tuesday, Wednesday—bright plastic boxes that try to make time behave. I shake out the morning dose into my palm and grab the water glass I left by her bed last night.

"Okay," I say, upbeat the way nurses are upbeat. "Meds first. Then breakfast."

Her mouth tightens immediately "I don't need those."

"Yes, you do."

She narrows her eyes like I've challenged her authority. "You're very bossy."

"I'm efficient," I correct, because it's safer to joke than to beg.

She huffs. "Your mother never talked to me like this."

"I'm not my mother," I say, and it comes out too sharp. I soften fast. "I'm Evie."

She blinks.

For a terrifying second, her gaze goes distant, like she's looking for me on a shelf where I used to be.

Then she finds me again. "Evie," she repeats, relieved. "That's right."

My throat tightens anyway.

I sit on the edge of her bed and hold out the pills. "C'mon. We do this every day."

She looks at them like I'm offering poison. I wait her out.

Finally she takes them, one at a time, with exaggerated suffering. When she's done, she hands the cup back and wipes her mouth with the back of her hand like she's just survived a war.

"There," she says, proud. "Happy?"

"Thrilled. I'll make breakfast. Come out when you're ready."

I head for the kitchen, because if I don't move quickly, the day gets away from me. I crack eggs into a bowl, put a pan on the stove, start the coffee. Routine. Anchors.

The house is quiet in that hollow way it's been since her good days ended... quiet the way a room is quiet after everyone you love has left it. Then her footsteps shuffle in behind me, slow and careful.

I turn and find her in the doorway in her robe, one hand braced on the frame. She looks smaller than she used to. Some days she looks like herself. Some days she looks like a stranger wearing her face. Today, she looks... oddly alert.

Her eyes flick over the counters. The stove. The mixing bowl.

Then she says, clear as a bell, "Is Kaia coming for pancakes?"

My hands still mid-motion. For a second I can't even *breathe*.

She hasn't said Kaia's name in years. Not once since the dementia got bad. Not once since I learned how to lock my heart like a deadbolt.

Hearing Kaia's name from Gran's lips is unsettling.

"What?" I manage, because I'm brilliant.

Gran's brows knit, impatient with my stupidity. "Kaia. Your friend." She squints at me like I'm being dramatic for no reason. "She likes pancakes. You always make a fuss. Didn't you say she'd eat syrup with a spoon if you let her?"

My eyes sting so fast it's like someone threw salt in them.

Because I remember.

I remember a Saturday morning years ago—sunlight pouring in, no fog, no pills.

Gran stands at the stove in a floral apron, humming while she flips pancakes like it's an art form. Teenage me on a stool, hair still damp from a shower, arguing with Kaia across the counter.

"You can't just drink the syrup," I say, scandalized.

Kaia grins, all teeth and teasing. "Watch me."

Gran laughs—full-bodied, healthy, real—and swats Kaia's shoulder with a dish towel. "Don't tease my girl," she says. "Eat your food."

Kaia ducks her head, but the mischievous smile lingers. "Okay, okay."

And then, softer, to me, Kaia whispers, "Your grandma likes me. That means I'm basically family."

I blink hard, and the kitchen wobbles. The memory is so clear that it hurts.

Gran is still watching, waiting for an answer as if she expects it to be simple.

"No," I say, and my voice comes out too thin. I clear it. Try again. "No, Gran. Kaia's not coming."

Gran's face falls, just slightly. "Oh."

Then, like a wave washing it away, her expression resets. She glances toward the window. "It's foggy."

"Yeah," I whisper.

She shifts her weight, restless. "We should make pancakes anyway."

My hands tighten on the spatula until my knuckles hurt.

"Okay," I say, because I can give her pancakes. I can give her syrup and warmth and something easy. I can't give her time back.

As the eggs cook, I turn to the cabinet and pull down the pancake mix we keep for weekends and bad mornings. Behind me, Gran wanders to the table and sits. I measure the mix into a bowl, add milk, stir. My vision blurs and I blink again, furious with myself.

Of course seeing Kaia's face plastered all over town would shake loose old memories. And now even my grandma is dragging Kaia out of the past.

I get the batter into a second pan and watch the edges bubble. The first pancake flips imperfectly.

Gran taps her fingers on the table. "You're late," she says, suddenly stern.

My stomach drops. "Late for what?"

"For school," she says, matter-of-fact, as if I'm sixteen again. "You'll miss the bell. And you'll make that poor girl wait."

I freeze.

"Which girl?" I ask, even though I already know.

Gran looks at me like I'm being ridiculous. "*Kaia.*"

My throat tightens so hard it aches. I set a pancake on a plate with hands that want to shake, coupling it with some eggs and put it in front of her.

"I'm not in school anymore," I say gently. "And Kaia's... she's busy."

Gran frowns, processing. "Busy where?"

I should lie. I should say anywhere else.

But the truth is, her face is everywhere. The town is screaming it. Even Gran can feel the shift in the air.

I keep my voice careful. "In town."

Gran's eyes brighten, that dangerous, hopeful brightness. "Oh." She leans forward. "Then she can come. Tell her to come. We have plenty of pancakes, don't we?"

My eyes burn. I turn back to the stove so she won't see my face break.

"Eat," I say softly. "Eat first."

When I look back, she's already forgotten the question.

She's staring at the pancake like it's a puzzle. "Is this mine?"

"Yes," I say, swallowing the lump in my throat. "That one's yours."

She nods, satisfied, and starts eating with slow, careful bites.

I stand there for a moment in the quiet kitchen, listening to her chew, listening to the coffee drip, listening to my own heartbeat. I wipe my eyes with the back of my wrist like it's just steam. Like I'm *fine.*

Then I rinse the bowl, sit down with my own plate and make a to-do list in my head—locks, meds, trash, laundry—anything but *Kaia.*

The day goes by like it's trying to pretend nothing happened.

I get Gran settled with her shows and a blanket she insists she doesn't need. I double-check the back door chain. I leave a sticky note on the counter that says MEDS AT 6 even though I know there's at least a fifty percent chance she'll ignore it. Then I go to the diner and put on my apron, like I can clock into a version of my life that makes sense.

And, somehow, the shift is almost normal.

Almost.

Tasha finds out about last night five minutes into clocking in, because of course she does. It's all over the news. The media is having a field day with the photos and the idea of the famous Kaia coming back to her roots.

Tasha is scandalized. "You're telling me Midnight Halo was *here*? In *this* diner? And I wasn't here?!"

Gus grunts from the register. "Fryer maintenance."

Tasha whips toward him like he's personally ruined her life. "That was a lie, Gus!"

Gus doesn't blink. "Yep."

Tasha clutches her chest. "This is the betrayal of the century."

"Go bring table two their food," Gus says, deadpan.

"I can't believe you deprived me of my destiny," she moans, but she goes anyway, dragging her feet like a tragic heroine.

After that, it's just... work. Coffee refills. Orders. Mr. Alvarez complaining about the weather. A couple tourists asking if Harbor Lights is "worth it this year" like festivals come with guarantees. The NDA on my wrist itches and I keep smiling.

Then night creeps in. The kitchen closes. Gus counts the till like he's mad at money for existing. He leaves with a grunt that means *clean up and lock up.*

An hour goes by.

Tonight is supposed to be quiet. It's past midnight. The last customers have stumbled out. I'm alone at the counter with a rag and the stubborn feeling that if I keep wiping, I can scrub the last few nights out of the place.

It's not working.

Outside, fog presses against the windows like a curious mouth. The neon lighthouse sign buzzes, flickers, buzzes again—persistent as an old habit.

I catch myself listening for footsteps that aren't there. For the metallic click of the back door. For a voice I told to leave.

I hate myself for that. I wipe harder.

The bell over the front door doesn't ring. No customers. No tourists. No late-night pie emergencies.

Good.

Then—

A sound hits from outside, sharp and wrong. Not a car backfiring. Not drunks laughing. Not the ocean. A thud. A scrape. A strained shout. Then another sound.

My wrist tingles. Not the binding warning, not the "don't talk about demons" leash. Something else. A prickle under my skin like the world is shifting a fraction sideways.

I freeze with the rag in my hand.

"Absolutely not," I tell the empty diner.

The sound comes again, closer. Behind the building. I stare at the back door like it's a dare.

I should stay inside. Lock it. Pretend I didn't hear anything. I'm a waitress with an invisible NDA tattoo and a grandmother asleep at home.

I am not whatever *this* has turned me into.

But my brain is already trying to invent excuses because that's what I do when fear shows up—I rename it until it's manageable.

What if Tasha left her phone again? Or her purse? She always leaves her stuff behind. What if she's outside and something happened and she needs help?

What if it's a drunk? Harbor's Edge collects drunks during festival week like the ocean collects trash. What if someone stumbled into the alley and cracked their head and I'm in here pretending not to hear because it's easier?

Or...

What if it's a demon?

Another crash.

Something slams into the dumpster outside hard enough that the metal rattles.

My body moves before my brain finishes arguing.

"Goddamn it," I hiss, throwing the rag down and grabbing the heavy flashlight from under the counter like it's a weapon. It isn't. But it makes me feel slightly less like prey.

I shove through the back door into the foggy alley. Cold hits my face. The smell hits next, salt, garbage, and something sweet-rot underneath, like burnt sugar and old perfume.

The alley is a smear of shadow and mist. And then I see *it*. A shape skittering near the dumpster, low to the ground, half-formed like it can't decide what it wants to be. In the fog, it looks like a stray dog made of shadow.

Except it moves *wrong*.

It jerks toward a sound that isn't there. A thin, warped melody leaks out of it like a dying radio: a festival jingle, but pitched down and stretched.

Hell no.

My stomach turns.

And there—two steps away, body half-hidden behind the dumpster—*Kaia*. Not glowing. No sword in sight. Just Kaia in a dark hoodie, breath fogging in short bursts. Her stance is wide, protective, weight on the balls of her feet like she's ready to launch.

She's alone.

My pulse spikes with anger so fast it almost feels like *relief*.

"Are you kidding me?" I snap, voice too loud.

Kaia's head whips toward me. Her eyes widen like she didn't expect me to be real.

"Evie—" she starts.

The smaller entity lunges—fast and hungry—aiming for her leg like it's trying to latch on.

Kaia pivots. Her hand flicks, and light answers. Aurora flashes into existence, blade gleaming pale-gold and prismatic. She moves with that impossible grace that looks like choreography even in the dark, even in an alley behind my diner.

One slash.

The entity screeches and splits into a smear that evaporates against the wet air like it was never fully here.

Silence slams down.

Kaia exhales hard and dismisses the sword. The light folds away, gone.

I stand there with my flashlight raised like a useless torch. My heart hammers.

Kaia turns toward me, shoulders still tense, and that's when I see the blood.

Not pouring. Not dramatic. Just a shallow cut at her hairline, dark and glossy where it's started to run down her temple and into her eyebrow.

It's small. It makes my throat go tight anyway.

Kaia reaches up, touches it, then looks at her fingers like she's surprised they're red.

"It's fine," she says automatically.

I take one step forward before I realize I'm doing it.

"Don't," I snap. "Don't say that. You're bleeding. Outside the diner. Because of—whatever the fuck that thing was!"

"It's shallow."

"Still blood," I say. My voice cracks on the edges. "And you're alone?"

Kaia's gaze flicks past me toward the street like she's listening for another shadow, shoulders still keyed up like she expects the air to lunge.

"Yeah..." she says.

Something in my chest tightens, less anger now, more that sinking, resigned anxiety that's been living in me since the first time a TV glitched and tried to eat my memories.

"Are you... allowed to be out here by yourself? Is this part of the plan? Or did you just decide to—what—stalk this alley?"

Kaia turns her head slightly, eyes scanning the fog. "Evie—"

"No," I cut in, because my brain is spiraling and I need answers to grab onto. "I'm serious. Where are the other girls? Where's your manager? Blaire, or whatever? Aren't you supposed to be... in a unit? Aren't there rules? Because last time you were alone, you crashed through my door glowing and almost got yourself killed in the booths."

Kaia's mouth tightens. "I didn't almost—"

"You did," I snap.

Kaia's gaze finally comes back to me. "We were together. We were sweeping. There was a disturbance near the harbor."

"So you got separated," I say, and the way I say it makes it sound like I already know the ending and I hate it.

Kaia shakes her head once. "We split the perimeter."

I stare at her. "You split."

"It's standard," she says quickly, like she's repeating training material. "Two and two. Cover more ground. Clear faster."

"And you ended up here," I say. My voice goes too tight. "Behind my diner. Alone. Where's your *partner* then?"

Kaia's mouth opens, then closes. Just that half-second hitch, enough to make my stomach sink.

"We... split," she says, too fast. "It made sense."

"Mm," I murmur, unimpressed.

Kaia exhales through her nose, frustration flickering. "It's standard perimeter coverage. We felt a residual spike earlier and this corridor has been... active. So I swung by to check it."

"Swung by," I repeat, deadpan. "Like you're picking up milk."

Kaia's jaw tightens. "Evie."

"*Where*. Is. Your. Partner?" I press, each word clipped because my anxiety needs something solid to grab.

She hesitates, then finally gives, voice tight. "Jules is a few streets over."

My stomach drops anyway. "So you *are* alone."

"Temporarily," Kaia says quickly, like she can patch it with a word. "She's close. Remy and Mina are on the opposite side. If anything spikes, we converge."

"And Blaire is fine with you playing night watch behind my diner?" I say, flat.

Kaia's eyes flick away. "She doesn't know I'm *here* specifically."

Of course.

I stare at her, the anger in me turning into something colder and more exhausted. "Kaia—"

"I know," she cuts in, and her voice is sharp for a second, defensive. Then it softens immediately, like she regrets the edge. She drags a hand through her hair and winces when it pulls near the cut. "But if something surfaces near here..." Her eyes flick to mine. "...it's more dangerous for you."

The words wrap around my ribs and tighten until I can barely breathe. I laugh once, bitter and disbelieving, because what else am I supposed to do with that?

"Oh," I say. "So you're doing this whole... guardian angel routine now?"

Kaia flinches. "No, that's not—"

"It is," I insist, even as my throat tightens in a way that scares me. "You're here. Alone. Bleeding. In an alley. Because you've decided I'm... what? Your responsibility?"

Kaia's voice goes rough. "You're a target."

"And you think standing near me makes me less of one?" I snap. "That's not how danger works. That's not how *anything* works."

Kaia holds my gaze, quiet and stubborn. "It's how it works for me."

My chest aches, sharp and stupid.

I hate her for making me feel things I don't want.

I hate myself more for the tiny part of me that hears that sentence and remembers what it used to mean when she said things like that.

I swallow it down hard.

It shouldn't. It shouldn't matter. It shouldn't make my chest ache in that familiar way.

But it does.

I hate it.

I step closer again, because my body keeps betraying me.

"Inside," I say, sharp. "Now."

Kaia doesn't move.

"Inside," I repeat, pointing at the door with the flashlight like I'm directing traffic. "Before you drip blood on yourself. Come on."

Kaia's lips twitch like she almost smiles. "Okay."

I hate that, too.

I grab her hand without thinking and yank her through the back door into the diner. Kaia follows easily, letting me pull her like I'm still allowed.

The fluorescent lights make everything look too real. Her face is pale from adrenaline, hair slightly damp from fog, blood smeared at her hairline in a line that looks like an ugly accent mark.

I let go and nudge her toward the counter. "Sit."

Kaia hesitates. "I really am fine."

"Sit," I repeat, already opening the cabinet under the register. "Or I'll make you."

Kaia settles onto the counter with a soft hop, hands braced behind her. She looks absurdly out of place perched there like a wounded angel in a hoodie.

I yank out the first aid kit—red plastic, faded sticker, more used for burns and knife nicks than demon-slaying injuries—and slam it onto the counter like I'm filing a complaint with the universe.

Kaia watches it land, then lets out a soft, breathy sound that's dangerously close to a laugh.

"What?" I snap, already peeling open the latch.

Kaia's mouth twitches. "Nothing. It's just... it's kind of nostalgic."

I pause with the kit open. "Nostalgic?"

"Yeah," she says, and there's something gentle in her voice that I don't want to hear. "You always had that thing. The kit. The wipes. The... 'sit down and let me handle it' routine."

I glare up at her. "It's called basic first aid."

Kaia tilts her head, eyes warm for one reckless second. "It's called you mothering me."

"I did *not* mother you."

"You did," she insists softly. "You don't look bossy at first glance, but you are. Secretly."

I scoff, but it comes out weaker than I mean. "I'm not bossy."

Kaia's smile turns faintly smug. "You made Mrs. Harlan move my seat in tenth grade because you said the sun glare was 'sabotaging my future.'"

My throat tightens.

Because she remembered that.

Because for a heartbeat, I can see it too—*teenage Kaia in that stupid classroom, squinting into a blade of sunlight every day, and me marching up to Mrs. Harlan's desk with righteous fury.*

"She can't see the board. She can't see the notes. She's going to fail because of glare. This is sabotage."

Mrs. Harlan stares at me like I'm insane.

Kaia stares at me with unbearable fondness.

I remember her scraped knee from the fair when she tried to climb the stage supports like an idiot, and I made her sit on a milk crate while I cleaned it, glaring the whole time. I remember her laughing and calling me "mean," and me muttering "you're welcome," and the way she let me fuss because she liked that I cared. She liked that I cared about *her.*

I miss that so suddenly it feels like I swallow a shard of glass.

I hate that I miss it.

I hate that it's her face that makes me miss it.

I step closer, lifting the wipe toward her hairline. Kaia holds still, eyes on mine. We're close enough that her breath fans over my cheek when she exhales.

The diner hums quietly. The neon sign buzzes. The world narrows down to this stupid, small distance between us.

"Hold still," I say.

Kaia murmurs, "I am."

I dab the wipe against the cut, careful despite myself. Kaia flinches slightly.

"Sorry," I mutter.

"It's okay," she says, voice low. "I've honestly had worse."

"Yeah," I say. "I figured. You fight demons for a living."

I keep cleaning, because if I stop, I'll say something crueler than I mean. Then my mouth betrays me anyway.

"You're supposed to be on magazine covers," I blurt, "not bleeding in some shitty diner."

Kaia goes still.

Her voice is quiet when she answers. "I'd rather bleed here than anywhere else."

The words hang in the diner like smoke.

My hand pauses at her hairline. Kaia goes strangely still beneath my touch, and I hate how instantly my body notices her skin, her breath, the stupid closeness of her mouth. My chest goes tight. For half a second, the world tilts dangerously toward something soft.

Then we both do the same thing at once—

We look away.

Like eye contact would turn that sentence into a confession neither of us can survive.

"Okay," I say too briskly, like I'm returning to a shift schedule. "Well, you're not dying. Congratulations."

Kaia's mouth twitches. "Thanks."

I press gauze gently to the cut. "Hold this."

Kaia takes it, fingers careful not to touch mine, which somehow feels worse than if she had. Silence stretches, thick with everything we're pretending isn't here.

Then the front lock unlatches and the bell jingles.

I jolt so hard I nearly drop the tape.

"Hello?" Tasha's voice calls from the front, muffled. "Evie? I forgot my vape."

Oh no.

No no *no*.

Tasha comes around the corner, still smelling like smoke and cheap vanilla body spray, eyes bright from whatever she was doing outside.

Then she sees Kaia. Her entire body stops. Her mouth opens. Nothing comes out for two full seconds, like her brain is trying to buffer.

Then—

A noise. High-pitched. Unholy.

"*OH MY GOD*," she shrieks.

Kaia's eyes widen. "Hi."

Tasha claps both hands over her mouth. She's vibrating like a cartoon character. "Oh my god. Oh my god. You're—*You're*—"

"Inside voice," I hiss.

Tasha drops her hands just enough to whisper-shout, "*YOU'RE KAIA RHEE!*"

Kaia gives a small smile. "Yeah. Nice to meet you."

Tasha's eyes go huge as she sees the gauze. Then the blood. Then the cut.

Her expression flips instantly from fangirl to panic. "Why are you bleeding?!"

Kaia's posture stiffens. I can feel her preparing to give a lie that sounds official. I beat her to it.

"She hit her head," I say quickly.

Kaia blinks at me.

Tasha stares. "Here?! How?!"

"On the—" I glance around wildly. "On the freezer door."

There is no freezer door near her. That doesn't matter.

Tasha looks ready to cry. "Why were you near the freezer door?!"

Kaia and I exchange a glance. Brief. Communal. The kind we used to share across a crowded diner when Gus yelled at us and we had to decide whether to lie or laugh.

For one second, we're on the same side.

Kaia slides in smoothly. "I was... touring the diner," she says, dead serious.

Tasha's face crumples with joy. "You toured the diner?"

"Yes," Kaia says with the sincerity of a diplomat. "I didn't get the opportunity to do so last night. It's very... historic. I used to come here as a teenager. Evie was kind enough to show me the changes."

I choke, half laugh, half cough.

Kaia's eyes flick to mine, warning.

I swallow it down.

Tasha steps closer, hands clasped like she's praying. "Can I—can I—"

"No," I say immediately.

Tasha blinks. "What?"

"You can't ask for an autograph," I say, pointing at Kaia's cut like it's evidence in court. "She's injured."

Kaia murmurs to me, "It's shallow."

Then, to Tasha, Kaia says, gently, "I'm okay. I'll sign anything you like."

Tasha looks at me like she still needs *my* permission. "Evie. Please. *Please.* Just a small one. For me. For my soul."

Kaia gives a helpless little shrug, like she's resigned to fandom being a natural disaster.

I exhale hard. "Fine. One. Quietly. And then you leave."

Tasha fumbles in her pocket so violently she drops her lighter. She produces a receipt and a pen like she's been carrying them at all times, which, she probably has.

Kaia signs with her non-gauze hand, quick and neat.

Tasha stares at it like it's scripture. "I'm going to frame this."

"Great," I mutter. "Go frame it at home."

Tasha finally looks up at Kaia again, dazed. "So you... came to the diner this late alone? Is that safe?"

My wrist tingles, warning.

Don't say it.

Don't explain it.

Don't—

Kaia answers before I can, voice smooth in a careful way. "I wasn't alone," she says. "I was checking on Evie. We... knew each other. Before. We were catching up."

Tasha's eyes flick between us, suspicious for the first time tonight. Like she can smell a story. Like she remembers me calling Midnight Halo trashy and overproduced days ago.

Heat climbs up my neck, so I double down like an idiot.

"Yeah," I cut in too fast, too flat. "I invited her. For—" I gesture vaguely at the air, at the coffee pot, at the entire concept of normalcy. "Coffee."

Tasha's stare deepens into full detective mode. "Uh-huh."

My wrist tingles again, like the binding is laughing at me. I ignore it. I turn back to Kaia, who's still perched on my counter like she belongs there. She doesn't. She never will again.

I tape the gauze gently into place and step back.

"You're done," I say, brisk.

Kaia's eyes meet mine, soft again. "Thank you."

I nod once, because if I speak, my voice will do something stupid.

The TV flickers on by itself.

All three of us freeze. Tasha reacts first.

"Oh my god," she groans, rolling her eyes. "This TV is such a piece of junk. Gus keeps saying he's going to replace it and then he buys, like, seventeen new coffee scoops instead."

She lunges for the remote on the shelf under the counter, muttering about "ancient wiring."

Kaia and I share a look. Not a soft one. A sharp one. A *did you feel that* look. The screen glitches—static, then a bright, polished local commercial. Colorful. Cheerful.

HARBOR LIGHTS FESTIVAL — THIS WEEKEND!

Confetti graphics. Smiling families. Lanterns. Fireworks. And at the bottom, in crisp sponsor text:

Presented by Eon Entertainment.

My stomach drops.

Kaia's gaze snaps to the screen, jaw tightening.

Tasha beams. "Oh my god! Eon is sponsoring!? I didn't know that! That's huge!"

Kaia's voice is low, barely audible. "Yeah."

On the TV, the old jingle plays, clean and bright, not warped like the demon version. But now that I've heard it twisted, I can't un-hear the hunger hidden inside it.

I look at Kaia.

"Okay," I say, too loud, too brisk. "Tasha. Go home."

Tasha blinks. "But—"

"Home," I repeat, pointing toward the door. "Now."

She hesitates, then sees my face and nods quickly. "Okay. Okay. I'm going. I'm going."

She backs away, clutching the autograph like a holy relic even as she grabs her forgotten vape. "Goodnight. Thank you."

Kaia manages a smile. "Of course, any time!"

The front bell jingles as Tasha leaves. Silence settles again. The TV keeps playing. Lanterns. Smiles. Music.

Eon.

I scramble to turn the TV off, and finally we're blessed with silence.

And for a second, I miss how things were—when the biggest problem in my world was whether Gus would let us stay after hours, whether Kaia's set list had too many sad songs, whether we'd ever have the courage to finish that kiss properly.

Before demons.

Before contracts.

Before she *left*.

Kaia's phone buzzes in her pocket. She checks it and her expression tightens the tiniest bit, caught between duty and... whatever this is.

"Jules," she says quietly, like it explains everything. "She's waiting. Blaire wants us back."

Kaia slides off the counter and pauses at the back door, looking at me like she wants to say something.

She just says, quietly, "Goodnight, Evie. Be careful on your way home."

I don't answer. But I stand there until the back door closes, and the neon sign buzzes, and the Harbor Lights commercial loops again in my head like the town is trying to sell me a dream that already died once.

EON'S "TEMPORARY OFFICES" IN Harbor's Edge are exactly what you'd expect from a corporation that wants to look local while swallowing the town whole.

They've rented out the old maritime museum annex—the one that used to host school field trips and dusty model ships—and transformed it into something sleek and sterile overnight. Everything smells faintly of citrus cleaner and printer ink.

Blaire flashes a badge and gets us waved through. "Heads down," she murmurs. "No selfies, no fans, no headlines."

Jules makes a face. "You're no fun."

"I'm plenty fun," she says without missing a beat. "In private."

I keep walking.

The cut at my hairline tugs slightly when I tighten my ponytail, and my brain does something traitorous. It replays Evie's hands at my temple, the antiseptic smell, the way her voice went sharp to hide the softness underneath.

I shut it down. Not now.

Conference room three is at the end of a hallway lined with framed photos of Harbor's Edge "heritage" landmarks.

Inside, the room is surprisingly packed. Mr. Bane and another handler sit along one side of the table with devices and folders. Mr. Cohen sits nearby. Across from them are Eon executives in tailored jackets and polite smiles, including Devin and Director Hans. There's some other people I don't recognize, and a wall screen shows a color-coded festival map with blinking nodes.

Wards.

Routes.

Crowd density projections.

Since failing to kill the Chorus at our show, we need to be prepared for anything at Harbor Lights.

Devin gives us a bright, fake-friendly wave. "Morning, Halo."

Jules mutters something under her breath.

Blaire steers us to seats. "Sit. Listen. Don't talk unless I say."

Jules whispers, "Do I ever listen?"

Blaire looks at her.

Jules sits immediately.

I take the chair nearest the screen so I can see everything. My phone vibrates in my pocket. Not a message. Just a calendar notification: **HARBOR LIGHTS— LAUNCH SCHEDULE POSTED.**

I open it. A neat list. Times. Segments. Closures. Sponsor blocks. "Hometown Heroes" featurettes.

Then my thumb drifts and I open my texts. Evie's contact sits near the top like it belongs there. Like my phone thinks I have a normal life and a normal past and a normal reason to keep someone's number saved for years.

Her name is just... there.

No thread. No history. No *hey* or *sorry* or *are you alive.* Just empty space beneath it, like an open wound.

I stare at the number and my brain does that stupid thing where it checks the digits even though I've memorized them years ago. Wonders if it's still the same as it was in high school.

Wonders if she ever changed it and I just never noticed because I never tried.

I could send her the schedule.

I could warn her about the crowd surges and the road closures.

I could even—*God help me*—say hi.

My thumb hovers over the keyboard, but I don't type. Instead, I lock the screen and shove the phone back into my pocket like it burned me.

Across the table, Mina watches me for half a second, then looks away like she's being polite. Remy doesn't look, but I know she noticed. Remy notices everything.

Jules, however, leans in, voice barely above a whisper. "Text her, coward."

I keep my eyes forward. "I don't know what you're talking about."

Jules grins. "Uh huh. That's convenient."

I glance at her just long enough to deliver a warning with my eyes.

She mouths, exaggerated: *text her.*

"Enough," Blaire murmurs without turning her head.

The meeting starts.

Mr. Cohen stands and taps the table once. "Let's begin."

The wall screen changes. A clean, animated graphic fills it: Harbor's Edge from above, dotted with glowing points.

"The Chorus's pattern remains consistent," Cohen says, voice calm. "It feeds on nostalgia. It gathers around repeat rituals and we predict that it will be lured by Harbor Lights. This is why we're proposing a controlled convergence."

One of the Eon executives—tall, silver hair, name tag that reads MARROWSON—nods along like we're in a boardroom, not planning a monster trap. "Harbor Lights is a gift," she says.

"The town is already primed. The emotional output is unprecedented. It is the perfect trap for the Chorus."

Output.

My stomach tightens.

She clicks a remote. Another graphic appears: **Projected Attendance**, **Engagement Spikes**, **Emotional Yield**.

Yield.

There it is again.

"Midnight Halo's presence increases emotional stability and concentrates the pattern," Mr. Cohen continues. "Our plan is to encourage reformation at the main stage."

Marrowson gestures to a highlighted zone on the map: the festival's central performance platform near the pier.

"Eon has handled the performance logistics. The performance," she says, "will be positioned at peak lantern hour. Maximum crowd density. Maximum emotional output. We want the Chorus to think it's found a feast."

Jules whispers, "Gross."

I elbow her under the table without looking.

Marrowson smiles wider. "And then—because our wards will be strongest there—we trap it. Collapse it. Neutralize it. Mortimer Bane has updated the warding. Mr. Bane?"

Mr. Bane slowly stands. He's quiet a long moment before saying, "Containment will be reinforced by the Council's new lattice design."

He slowly gestures to the screen.

My gaze catches on the ward schematics. The curves. The mirrored angles. That subtle halo-arc embedded in the geometry. The same design language I saw in the diner's sigils.

New warding design, huh?

A little shiver slides down my spine.

Remy's voice is quiet, precise. "Your lattice is… branded by Eon?"

The room goes very still for half a second.

Marrowson smiles like she's made a joke. "It's a standardized design."

Remy doesn't back down though. She's staring at the warding design. "By who?"

Marrowson's smile doesn't slip, but her eyes sharpen. "By the Council. Joint safety initiative. Same templates across venues. It keeps things consistent."

Mr. Bane doesn't react. Cohen doesn't correct her. Which is its own kind of answer.

Remy's gaze holds steady for another beat, then she gives the tiniest nod like she's filing it away instead of arguing in a room designed to make arguing useless.

Marrowson takes that as an answer and says, "Great. Moving on."

A different exec—young, sharp suit, eyes too bright—leans forward. "To be clear, this also significantly elevates Harbor Lights' profile," he says. "Midnight Halo appearing as a 'surprise performance' drives press, boosts streams, creates a narrative. It's… mutually beneficial."

Devin beams, chiming in, "Yes, exactly. Local authenticity with global reach."

I keep my hands folded on the table, nails digging into my palms to keep myself still.

"And the civilians?" I ask. "The streets? If splinters do break through the wards again—"

"We'll have increased roaming suppression," Marrowson says quickly. "Low-level patrols. Increased ward checks."

"Low-level patrols," Jules repeats under her breath. "Like the one where Kaia got hurt?"

I cut her a look.

She doesn't care. "What? It's relevant."

For a moment, no one speaks. Devin glances at my hairline like he's noticing the small cut for the first time, and is the first to break the silence. "A minor injury does not indicate plan failure."

Mina inhales like she's about to jump off a cliff. "Actually. I'd like to add something."

Blaire's face does something between a wince and a prayer, like she wants to crawl under the table but also like she's proud Mina is brave enough to speak.

Everyone turns to her.

Mina straightens a little, voice still gentle but firm. "There was something bigger behind the Chorus last time."

The room shifts, subtle tension.

Devin sighs like she's bringing up an inconvenient rumor again. "Mina, as discussed, perception distortions are common during high resonance."

Remy's voice cuts in, calm and sharpened. She doesn't raise her volume. She doesn't need to. "Mina isn't prone to theatrics. If she says she saw an observer, we treat it as data. Stop dismissing her."

Silence.

For a moment, even Devin doesn't have a neat line.

Then the silver-haired exec speaks again, voice softer now, the way people speak when they're about to invoke something bigger than all of us.

"Regardless," Marrowson says, "this performance is non-negotiable. Harbor Lights is a keystone event. The town's emotional output peaks here." Her eyes flick, briefly, to Cohen and then back to us. "We need a strong showing."

I keep my face blank because I can't afford to show fear in a room like this. But inside, something tightens. A bad feeling settling into my gut like a stone.

Devin clears his throat, forcing brightness back into the air. "So. Operationally: Midnight Halo will remain 'off-duty' publicly until the surprise set. Social media will be throttled. Location leaks will be controlled. We'll push the festival narrative through official channels."

He clicks to the next slide: **SURPRISE SETLIST — PROPOSED**.

The meeting drags on—routes, protocols, "acceptable collateral," words that make my skin crawl. The Eon execs smile through it like they're planning a product launch.

When it finally ends, Blaire is the first to stand. "We're done."

Devin beams. "Great synergy, everyone!"

My phone vibrates again in my pocket.

I don't take it out.

But my brain fills in the schedule anyway—lantern launch, pier stage, surge in the diner district after closing...

My thumb aches with the urge to warn her, to talk to her. I don't.

I can feel Jules watching me, reading my mind, seeing the way I glance at my phone.

She leans in again, whispering like she can't help herself. "Text her, coward."

I snap before I can stop it.

"Shut up," I hiss, sharper than I mean to.

Jules blinks, grin fading. Mina goes still. Remy's gaze flicks to me, assessing. The room is loud enough that I'm not sure if anyone else heard, but Blaire's head turns slightly.

I force my voice back down. "I'm focused."

Jules' expression shifts into something more serious under the humor. "Right," she murmurs. "Because this is... you focused on work and not waitresses, right?"

My face burns. I don't answer. Because if I do, I'll say her name. And if I say her name in this room, I'm afraid the walls will learn it.

Blaire claps her hands once. "Okay. That's enough. Girls, *up*. We're done here."

We file out into the hallway, fluorescent lights buzzing overhead. The maritime photos stare down at us like the town is watching its own takeover.

My phone is heavy in my pocket.

Jules walks beside me in silence for a whole ten steps, which is how I know she's about to do something dangerous.

Then she says quietly, "You can face demons but not one irritated waitress?"

I stop.

Blaire keeps walking, assuming we're following. Mina and Remy slow, sensing the shift.

I turn to Jules, jaw tight. "For once, don't *start*, Jules."

Jules' eyes are sharp now, playful mask gone. "Kaia. You snapped at me in there."

"I said I'm *focused*."

"You're not," Jules says, blunt. "You're terrified."

I scoff. "Of *what*?"

Jules gestures vaguely back toward the conference room. "Of *them*. Of messing up again." Her voice drops. "And of her."

I stare at her.

Jules softens, just a fraction. "I thought it was a crush," she says. "I thought it was—cute. Hometown angst."

Mina's voice is barely audible. "It's not."

Remy's gaze stays on me, unreadable.

Jules nods, like she's arriving at the same conclusion in real time. "It's deeper," she says quietly. "That's why you won't text her. Because if you do, it becomes real."

My chest aches.

I want to deny it.

I can't.

So I do what I always do when I can't deny something: I go cold.

"Drop it," I say.

Jules' eyes narrow. "No."

I flinch. Jules may whine and argue, but she never says *no* to me unless she thinks I'm about to implode.

She steps closer, voice low enough only we can hear. "Kaia, you don't get to punish yourself into silence and call it strategy."

My pulse jumps. "You don't understand."

Jules laughs once, sharp. "I understand plenty. You're brave with monsters because monsters don't remember what you said to them when you were sixteen."

My throat closes, and I glare at her.

Jules' voice softens immediately. "Sorry. That was…" She trails off, then shrugs.

Mina's eyes go sad. Remy's gaze drops for a beat, giving me privacy even while standing there.

I exhale slowly, forcing myself to move again because if I stand still, I'll crack.

"We have a job here, a plan," I say, voice flat. "We follow it."

Jules watches me for a long second, then nods once, reluctant.

"Fine. We follow the plan." Then she adds, softer, like a warning and a promise, "But after this? You're going to talk to her. Or I'm going to drag you to that diner by your collar."

I huff and turn away from her. Because in my pocket, my phone feels like a loaded weapon.

And I can't shake the feeling that the worst part isn't the demon.

It's how much I still want to run to *her*.

My MORNING OFF IS not a real morning off. It's just a morning where the diner can't claim me first.

The sun is out, which feels like a lie after nights that keep trying to eat me. Fog still clings low to the street, but it's thinner now, pulled apart by the bustle—people hauling folding tables, stringing lantern frames, taping posters to windows like the town is dressing itself up for a date.

Harbor Lights is tomorrow.

I carry a laundry basket of towels down the hallway and find Grandma in her chair by the front window, squinting at the porch like she's supervising the world into behaving.

Her hair is loose, silver and soft, and she's wearing her favorite cardigan.

"Morning," I say, setting the basket down.

She blinks at me like she has to bring me into focus. Then her face brightens. "There you are."

"Here I am," I reply, leaning down to kiss the top of her head. It smells like lavender shampoo and the powder she's used since I was little.

She squints. "You look tired."

"I'm fine," I lie automatically.

She makes a sound of disbelief. "Mm."

She seems more coherent today—eyes clearer, voice steadier. Some days are like this. Little pockets of lucidity, or close enough that it feels like I've been handed her back for a minute and I'm supposed to pretend I'm not terrified of losing her again.

I grab her brush from the side table and stand behind her chair. "Want me to fix your hair?"

She lifts her chin. "If you do it the way I like."

I snort softly. "Yes, ma'am."

As I brush through her hair, she hums under her breath an old tune that used to be a hymn and now is just something her body remembers. Her shoulders relax a little as I gather the strands, twist them gently, pin them into place the way she's taught me a thousand times.

There's something soothing about it. The simplicity. The care. The fact that some things still make sense.

When I'm done, I tilt a hand mirror up so she can see.

"Alright." I keep my voice light. "Verdict?"

She leans forward and squints at her reflection as if she's grading me. Then her mouth softens.

"Pretty," she murmurs.

"You're always pretty," I say.

Grandma pats my hand.

Outside, a hammer thunks. Someone laughs on the sidewalk. A truck rumbles past hauling booth panels.

Grandma turns her head slightly toward the sound. "They're busy."

"They're always busy before Harbor Lights," I say.

"Yes," she agrees, and then adds, casually, as if she's asking about the weather, "Did the Rhee girl sing last night?"

My stomach does that stupid drop.

I keep my face neutral. I keep brushing a nonexistent strand like it matters. "No."

Grandma nods slowly. "Shame. She always had a nice voice."

I swallow. "Yeah."

Grandma studies me through the window reflection. She's not as sharp as she used to be, but she has her moments—little flashes where the woman who raised me looks right through my skin.

"You should go enjoy the festival," she says abruptly.

I blink. "I have enough to do—"

Grandma lifts a finger. "Evie."

I stop because that tone still works on me at any age.

She looks toward the porch again where lantern frames are stacked, waiting. "Help me hang these. Then you should go for a walk."

"Gran—"

"Walk," she repeats. "Pier. Fresh air. The town's pretty too when it's trying."

I huff, but I'm already helping her outside and reaching for the lantern frames because arguing with her is like arguing with the tide.

"Fine," I mutter. "But be careful. Remember the porch steps are crooked and the railing is basically decorative. Don't you dare fall."

She laughs, delighted. "Bossy girl."

I freeze for half a second.

Bossy.

Kaia used to say that too—laughing, eyes bright, like it was a compliment.

I shake it off.

The porch smells like sun-warmed wood and salt. Grandma shuffles out behind me, slow but stubborn.

The lanterns are cheap paper lanterns—cream-colored with little gold flecks, because Grandma likes anything that sparkles. I hook one to the porch rail, then another, then another, spacing them evenly like I'm building a tiny altar.

Grandma watches with approving hums. "Higher," she directs. "No, not like that. Like you want the wind to see it."

"The wind does not have eyes," I mutter.

Grandma ignores that. "Tie it tighter."

I tie it tighter.

She pats my shoulder when I'm done. "There. Lovely."

I step back, hands on my hips, looking at the line of lanterns. They sway faintly in the breeze, catching the morning light like little captured suns. For a second, it's... nice.

Then Grandma points at me as if she's sentencing me. "Now. Go enjoy the festival."

"It's tomorrow," I remind her.

She waves a hand. "Go enjoy the *build-up*. That's half the magic."

Magic.

I flinch internally. The word rings different now.

Grandma's gaze softens. "You look like you've been carrying something heavy."

"I'm fine," I say again, because it's my favorite lie. I'm like Kaia in that way.

Grandma huffs. "Then go."

I roll my eyes and grab my jacket. "Okay, okay."

As I head down the porch steps, she calls after me, voice suddenly bright with mischief, "And if you see that Rhee girl, tell her to come over for pancakes!"

My foot catches on the step.

I don't turn around. "Sure," I lie.

Grandma hums to herself and goes back inside, blissfully unaware that she just twisted the knife in my ribs.

I walk.

Harbor's Edge is dressed up and loud even in daylight. Booths line the main street like ribs of some enormous creature being assembled. Kids run with armfuls of glittery paper. Vendors argue about placement. Someone is already selling festival pins, because capitalism never sleeps.

And everywhere—*everywhere*—are the posters. They're on telephone poles, shop windows, the side of the florist's cooler. They've been layered over old posters as if the town is burying itself in fresh ink.

MIDNIGHT HALO — SPECIAL HARBOR LIGHTS APPEARANCE

Kaia's face is at the center. Perfect skin. Fierce eyes. Glittering costume. Haloed lighting.

She looks like an angel... or like a product.

Like someone who never tripped on a pier and laughed until she cried. I stop in front of one without meaning to. The paper is glossy under my fingertips. Kaia's face stares down at me with a confidence so polished it feels like a weapon.

As stupid as it is, it feels like the town took our private memories and replaced them with propaganda.

A version of her that belongs to everyone.

A version that doesn't get to be *mine*.

Good, I tell myself bitterly. She chose that.

I keep walking, faster now, as if speed can outrun memory.

But it doesn't. It never does.

The pier road comes into view, lined with lantern frames waiting to be lit tomorrow night. The water is bright today, sun glinting off it in sharp flashes.

I step onto it.

The wood boards creak under my boots in the same old rhythm.

Halfway down, the air shifts. Not demon-shift. Not danger. Just... time.

My brain does what it always does here. It rewinds.

I'm sixteen again with a cheap paper lantern crinkling in my hands, sneaking down the pier late at night. Kaia beside me, breathless with laughter, carrying one of her own. We carry those lanterns like they're contraband. We wrote wishes on them with cheap markers that bled through the paper.

I can't remember what I wrote any more, but whatever it was... it must not have come true.

The pier boards under my feet now are the same boards. The air smells the same. The ocean sounds the same.

But Kaia is not here.

And now more than ever, her absence is a physical thing, like a missing limb.

I keep walking anyway, hands shoved deep in my jacket pockets, until the pier opens up and I can see it in the distance—the festival grounds half-built, the little Harbor Lights stage. Even from here, I can make out the rickety platform and the crooked mic stand. The string lights are up early, flickering in the fog like nervous stars.

Kaia's first amateur performance was on that stage. Her hands shook so badly she had to grip the mic with both of them.

She looked like she might run.

I'd shoved my way through the crowd and planted myself front and center like a barricade.

"Kaia!" I'd yelled. "KAIA!"

People around me had laughed and shushed me.

I'd ignored them.

Kaia's eyes had found mine, wide and panicked—

And then, because I was there, she'd steadied. Like my belief in her could hold her up.

She'd opened her mouth and sang. And the whole town had gone quiet.

She'd always had that power, even then. That *resonance.* I just didn't know what to call it.

In the present, a shop radio on the pier blares cheerfully from the bait shack.

A jingle floats out on the breeze:

Come back, come back, the lanterns will light your way—

My skin prickles.

It's the same melody. Cleaner than the demon version, but the bones are identical. The tune the Chorus used. The one that tried to shove its way down my throat like a hook.

I stop mid-step. My heart beats faster.

A couple walking past me hums along without thinking.

A kid on a bench swings his legs and sings it softly to himself.

Two elderly women argue about booth placement while the radio plays in the background, and one of them taps her fingers to the beat unconsciously.

The entire town is humming the demon's song without knowing it.

A chill crawls up my spine. My wrist warms. Not burning, just a sudden heat under the skin, like a hand pressed there. A warning.

Don't say it.
Don't tell them.
Don't spread it.

I stare at my wrist like it might glow. The binding is invisible, but I feel it. The NDA woven into my life like a leash disguised as jewelry. I clench my fist hard enough my nails bite my palm.

"Great," I mutter. "Even my wrist is bossy now."

A laugh threatens—hysterical, sharp—and I swallow it down.

I keep walking to the end of the pier, where the water opens wide, sunlight flickering like shattered glass. I rest my hands on the railing and stare out, breathing salt and trying to convince myself I don't care.

But I *do*. That's the problem.

I care so much it made me angry enough to survive without her.

I care so much that seeing her face on every poster feels like someone stole my memories and sold them back to me with a sponsor logo.

I care so much that when she bleeds, my body moves before my pride can stop it.

I care so much that I want to warn the whole town about the song in their mouths... and I can't.

Because I signed an invisible contract.

Because demons listen.

Because Kaia came back into my life carrying a sword.

The radio keeps playing, bright and cheerful.

Come back, come back—

The words snag under my ribs. I close my eyes.

For half a second, I let myself remember what it felt like when "come back" was a wish, not a threat.

The breeze catches the radio and warps it for a heartbeat. Just enough that I could swear something ugly rides under the melody, soft as breath against my ear.

Stupid kiss.

My eyes fly open, pulse kicking hard, but the song is bright again by the time I look back. I turn back to watch the water, because tomorrow night the lanterns will rise.

And something in the dark is already humming along.

Kaia

THE FESTIVAL GROUNDS LOOK innocent in daylight.

That's the trick.

In the afternoon sun, Harbor Lights is just a half-built maze of booths and lantern frames and string lights waiting to be plugged in. Workers move like ants, hauling crates, taping down cords, arguing about where the "authentic" clam chowder stand should go. Kids weave between metal barricades.

They don't see the ward lines.

They don't see the speaker towers wrapped in containment sigils like a second skin. They don't see the light rigs etched with runes that make the air feel slightly tighter, slightly safer.

Blaire's rule for today is simple: training only when the grounds are "empty."

Thanks to Eon, a large part of the pier is "temporarily closed for safety upgrades," which means we get the actual Harbor Lights stage to ourselves—cordoned off, fenced in, and guarded by polite Council personnel holding clipboards like shields. Two hours between vendor setup and the first rehearsal sound checks. "Construction zone" signs go up. Civilians get redirected with smiles that don't quite reach anyone's eyes.

Jules swings her arms as we cross the cleared boards. "Nothing says small-town charm like barricades and a Council-sponsored vibe kill."

I don't answer.

Blaire's voice crackles in our in-ears. "You have ninety minutes."

Jules groans. "Blaire, why do you hate art?"

Blaire doesn't dignify that with an answer.

I step to center stage and look out over the empty rows of folding chairs waiting to become an ocean of people tomorrow.

The air here is different than the arena.

Looser.

More exposed.

More... *hungry*.

"Focus," I murmur.

My voice shifts automatically into the cadence that makes the team align. I hate that it comes so easily, but I love that it works.

Jules salutes. "Yes, Captain."

Remy rolls her shoulders. "Formation?"

"Warmup first," I say.

Jules makes a face. "Ugh."

Mina smiles faintly and starts stretching anyway.

Remy's gaze flicks over the stage perimeter where Eon's new lattice warding has been integrated into the rigging. The ward lines shimmer faintly in the corner of my vision.

She murmurs, "Brand consistency," with so much contempt it could be a weapon.

I pretend I didn't hear.

We move through a basic sequence first—footwork, breath, timing. If someone were watching from far away, it would look like choreography practice: a girl group hitting clean counts under lantern frames, the kind of behind-the-scenes clip fans would eat alive.

We keep it that way on purpose. Demons aren't the only things that watch.

By the time sweat starts to gather at the back of my neck, the sun has shifted lower. The string lights overhead flicker on as the Eon sound crews test circuits.

"Okay," I say. "Draw on my count."

Jules' grin goes sharp. "Finally."

Remy's gaze narrows, calm and ready. Mina inhales slowly like she's centering herself.

"One," I say.

We step together.

"Two."

Hands rise together.

"Three."

The swords appear.

To human eyes, it would be a flourish. A prop trick. A dance move that catches light just right.

To us, it's resonance snapping into shape.

Aurora forms in my grip, blade gleaming pale-gold and prismatic at the edge.

Jules' Voltstep flashes into existence, twin short blades sparking with kinetic energy, brighter as she bounces lightly on the balls of her feet.

Remy's Inkthorn appears like a thought made solid, black blade etched with script, leaving faint glowing runes in the air when she shifts her wrist.

Mina's Heartglass blooms into being, translucent and prismatic, its reflective surface catching the lantern light and splitting it into fragments.

We hold for one beat—swords up, bodies aligned—then move.

"Sequence A," I call.

Jules darts first, Voltstep buzzing with potential. She spins, blades carving arcs that look like dance lines.

Remy glides through the center, Inkthorn leaving rune trails that hang in the air for half a second before fading, spellwork written in motion.

Mina anchors the back line, Heartglass angled in a way that would look like a dancer's pose, but to my eyes it's a mirror turned toward the unseen, ready to reveal anything hiding behind glamour.

I step forward and let my voice hum, low and controlled, not lyrics, not performance, just a resonance note that feeds into Aurora. The blade answers with a soft flare, sound-shock contained tight to the warded perimeter.

"Clean," Remy murmurs.

"Pretty," Jules says, because she can't help herself.

"Again," I order.

We repeat.

And *repeat*.

Sweat. Breath. The soft hum of ward lines. Lantern light that feels like an omen.

We practice the fight the way we always do: like it's choreography, like our bodies are instruments, like every slash is a beat and every parry is a harmony. It has to look flawless. Tomorrow, the crowd will be ten feet away, screaming, crying, and humming along without knowing they're feeding a monster.

We have to be perfect.

Perfection is what keeps civilians alive.

Perfection is what will keep *Evie* alive.

But the thought lands wrong in my chest. Fragile. Like the second I let myself want her safety too much, the dark under this town turns its head and notices.

After the sequence, Jules flops onto the stage floor dramatically, Voltstep dismissed in a glittering snap. "I'm dying."

"You're sweaty," Mina corrects.

Jules points at me. "Captain Kaia is in a mood."

"I'm focused," I say automatically. "You should be too."

Remy sits cross-legged with eerie grace, Inkthorn gone, hands resting on her knees like she's meditating. "She's been in a mood since the diner."

Mina's cheeks pink slightly. "Since... Evie."

My stomach tightens.

Jules pops up on her elbows, eyes gleaming. "Evie," she sings softly, like she's tasting the name.

"Can we stop making everything about Evie?" I ask. "It's childish."

She grins. "Text her, coward."

"I am not texting her," I snap, sharper than I mean to.

The words ring under the lantern frames.

Mina blinks. Remy's gaze flicks up. Jules' grin fades into something more serious.

I exhale slowly. "Sorry."

Jules sits up fully now, expression unreadable for once. "Okay. So it's like that."

"It's not—" I start.

Remy cuts in, calm as a blade. "It is."

I clench my jaw. "We have a schedule. We have a plan. We cannot afford distractions. We've been over this already."

Jules points at me as if she's calling me on stage. "You're part of a company that schedules your entire life. And if you want anything with her, you can't keep letting them decide when you breathe."

The words hit too close to the truth, because they've already decided the surprise set time. They've decided where we stand. They've decided what we say. They've decided what we feel is useful. And somewhere inside that machine is Evie—collateral I keep pretending I can protect.

"I don't want anything with Evie," I say immediately, too fast, like speed makes it believable. "Who said I did?"

One of the lantern bulbs overhead buzzes and spits a brief flare of light. My pulse jumps. It feels absurdly, horribly like being caught in a lie.

Jules just smiles wider, like she loves watching me lie. "Sure, Captain."

Mina makes a small, pained sound. Remy's expression doesn't change, which is worse.

Jules adds, "Remy. You're the 'tell Kaia she's being an idiot' person now."

Remy's mouth twitches. "I've been doing that."

"Fair," Jules says.

My throat tightens. I stare down at the stage floor, at the faint chalk marks we've used to map movement.

"I can't," I say quietly. "I can't—just—show up and act like nothing happened."

Mina's voice is gentle. "It doesn't need to be like nothing happened."

I swallow.

Remy's gaze is steady. "It would be honest."

Jules leans forward. "When we were trainees, you told us stories about her like she was... home."

Mina nods quickly, eyes bright. "You did. You talked about her like she was... a lighthouse."

I flinch at the word.

Lighthouse.

Of course.

Jules' voice is softer now, no teasing. "So how does she seem to you *now*?"

My chest tightens. I try to make my voice casual. "You met her. You tell me."

Mina thinks for a beat, then says with blunt sweetness, "Like someone who still looks at you like you hung the moon..."

Jules snorts. "Aw."

"...and wants to throw it at your head," Mina finishes.

Jules laughs. Remy's mouth twitches.

I swallow hard, because it's too accurate, and it makes me ache in a way I don't have time for.

"She hates me," I say.

Mina shakes her head slightly. "She's... hurt."

Remy adds, quiet, "Those are different."

Jules points at me. "And you did mess it up."

I flinch.

Jules doesn't let me escape. "Like. Completely."

"I know," I say, voice rough.

The three of them go still.

It's the first time I've said it like that. No minimization. No *it's fine*. No pretending I'm over it.

Just the truth.

"I messed it up," I repeat, because if I don't keep saying it, my shame will turn it into something else—self-pity, anger, denial. "I said cruel things. I left. I didn't explain. I didn't... come back."

Mina's eyes soften. Jules looks oddly pleased. Not happy, but relieved. Remy inclines her head once, like she's acknowledging the truth as a tactical asset.

"Okay," Jules says quietly. "Good. Because step one is admitting you were an idiot."

I glare weakly. "Thank you."

"You're welcome," she says sweetly.

Mina hesitates, then says softly, "You can still... make it right. Maybe not all the way. But... some."

Remy's gaze shifts toward the festival map taped to a nearby rigging tower "Eon's meeting at the diner later," she says, voice neutral. "Talk to her then."

My stomach tightens.

Right. Tonight.

The Council want to do their little "check." Their readings. Their anchor assessments. Their polite invasion of Evie's space. And the Harbor Lights committee wants to make sure everything is in place for the festival tomorrow.

Jules watches my face. "You can't keep pretending it's fine," she says, softer.

I nod once, throat tight.

Blaire's voice crackles in our in-ear headsets. "Time's up. Pack it in."

Jules groans. "Nooo. We were having character development."

"Do it on your own time," Blaire says.

We stand. Lantern light flickers overhead like a warning.

Tonight, Eon goes to the diner again.

Evie will be there.

And for the first time since I came home, I can stop pretending that means nothing.

Evie

By the time the Harbor Lights logistics meeting starts, the booths are full of clipboards and binders instead of regulars. The counter has a stack of printed agendas where the tip jar usually sits. Gus put a little sign on the front door that says:

CLOSED — PRIVATE EVENT *(Reopening tomorrow)*

Every year the Harbor Lights committee meets at The Lighthouse Diner. The town officials show up first. Festival planners follow with tote bags full of lanyards and laminated schedules. Then the Eon liaison arrives with a tablet and a smile that looks practiced in a mirror.

Her nametag reads Marrowson.

"Evie," Gus mutters as he passes me behind the counter, low enough no one else can hear. "Smile. Pour coffee. Don't stab anybody."

"I make no promises," I mutter back, grabbing the pot.

Gus gives me a look that says *I may have basically raised you, but I cannot save you from yourself.*

I grab mugs and start my circuit.

They're all talking over each other in that familiar meeting way of people who love hearing themselves speak.

"Booth spacing needs to meet fire code—"

"Lantern release timing has to coordinate with tide—"

"Security barriers are a must this year, we're expecting un-precedented turnout—"

"Eon's sponsorship includes upgraded stage equipment, which means—"

Marrowson cuts in smoothly, voice warm. "Which *means* Harbor Lights can be bigger, safer, and more accessible than ever."

My jaw tightens as I pour coffee into the mayor's mug. "Cream?"

He startles like he forgot workers exist. "Oh, yes. Thank you."

I keep moving.

A festival planner with glitter on her cheeks turns to Marrowson. "We loved the draft for the memorial reel, by the way."

Memorial reel.

I pause just long enough that my coffee pot drips onto a saucer.

Marrowson beams. "It's important we honor the town's story."

The planner nods vigorously. "Exactly! We want something... emotional. The kind of thing that makes people cry in a good way."

Marrowson's eyes glitter. "Emotion is what brings people together."

My wrist warms faintly.

Not the binding warning exactly, more like a low simmer under the skin, like the sigil is reacting to the word *emotion* the way a dog reacts to thunder.

I swallow hard.

A man in a festival polo says, "And we'll have the 'Hometown Heroes' montage between sets."

"Montage?" someone repeats, delighted.

Marrowson swipes on her tablet, projecting a mockup onto a small portable screen they've propped at the end of the counter. A polished graphic appears: sepia photos, lantern glow overlays, sentimental fonts.

HOMETOWN HEROES, FEATURING KAIA RHEE

My stomach drops.

A councilwoman claps her hands. "Oh, that's perfect."

I pour another cup of coffee and pretend my hands aren't shaking.

Marrowson continues, sweet as poison. "We'll include a commemorative segment honoring those we've lost, a reel of old Harbor Lights footage, then—"

She pauses, smile widening.

"—the guest appearance and star of the show: Midnight Halo."

Laughter. Gasps. Excited whispers.

I stare at the coffee pot as if it personally betrayed me. Of course Eon would turn the festival into a giant nostalgia battery and then plug Kaia directly into it.

A man near the end says, "This will be the biggest Harbor Lights in decades."

Another adds, "Record ticket sales already—"

"Unprecedented excitement—"

My wrist warms again, sharper.

I grit my teeth.

The meeting drones on. I keep serving. Coffee, refills, sugar packets, polite nods. I do my job while a corporation scripts my town's emotions like a product demo. I refill mugs and listen anyway, because being in the room means being warned. It means knowing what's coming.

And what's coming feels... dangerous.

Not in a "fireworks safety" way.

In a "this is exactly what a demon would order off the menu" way.

The meeting finally starts to break apart—people stacking binders, gathering their coats, congratulating themselves for "collaboration."

Marrowson stays seated, tapping on her tablet.

Gus leans in close to me as I collect empty mugs. "They're leaving."

"Thank god," I mutter.

Then the front door bell jingles.

I freeze.

The diner door swings open and the air changes instantly, like the room just got a little more charged. Blaire walks in first.

Behind her—

Kaia.

Jules.

Mina.

Remy.

All in regular clothes—hoodies, jeans, jackets. But the way they move together, the way the room subtly orients toward them, is unmistakable.

Marrowson's face lights up like she's been waiting for this cue.

"Perfect timing," she says brightly, rising. "Ladies."

Town officials immediately go into polite chaos. Whispering. Smiling too hard. Pretending they're not fans.

I hold my tray against my hip and keep my face blank.

Kaia's gaze finds me instantly. Her eyes flick to my hands. To my face. To the coffee pot like she's checking whether I'm about to throw it.

Blaire clears her throat. "We were told to stop by."

Marrowson beams. "We're just wrapping up. I thought it would be... meaningful for the group to connect with the local organizers."

Meaningful.

Sure.

Jules smiles brightly. "Happy to be meaningful."

Remy gives a polite nod. Mina offers a small wave that looks genuinely shy. Kaia stands still, gaze still locked to me for a fraction too long, then she looks away like it cost her and greets the coordinators.

One of the festival planners—young, starstruck—leans forward toward the pop group. "We are so honored to have Midnight Halo perform at Harbor Lights."

Kaia inclines her head and answers easily. "The honor is ours."

The planner squeals.

Then Mina, wide-eyed and sincere, looks right at me and asks, "Are you gonna be there?"

The question is casual, but Kaia's head snaps toward me so fast it's almost comical.

Way too interested.

Way too tense.

Like my answer is going to decide whether she can breathe.

My throat tightens. I shrug like I don't care. Like the idea of the festival doesn't make my stomach twist. "Maybe."

Kaia's gaze stays on me. Jules notices and immediately looks entertained. Remy's expression stays neutral, but her eyes flick between us. Mina looks confused and earnest, like she doesn't understand why the air just got sharp.

Marrowson laughs lightly, smoothing the moment. "We'd love for everyone in town to attend. It's going to be a once-in-a-lifetime Harbor Lights."

Once-in-a-lifetime,

Marrowson smiles. "We're done. Thank you so much, Gus."

Gus grunts.

As the town officials file out, one of them pauses near Kaia, eyes bright. "It's an honor," he says. "To have you back."

Kaia smiles politely. "Thank you so much."

I want to scream.

Because back is not what she is. She's not back. She's a visitor with a badge and a sword and a corporation attached to her like a parasite.

The last of the officials leave. The door bell jingles. The diner quiets in the aftermath.

Marrowson gathers her tablet. "We'll be in touch about to-morrow's segment timing," she says to Blaire, all business now. "I'll send the revised run-of-show tonight."

Blaire nods, jaw tight. "Great."

Marrowson glances at the girls. "Rest up. Tomorrow is big."

Then she leaves too, heels clicking like punctuation. The moment the door closes, the diner feels smaller.

Too small for all the unsaid things.

Blaire checks her phone, then gestures at the girls. "Two min-utes. Then we go."

Kaia looks like she might be vibrating with restraint.

"Evie," she says quietly. "Can we talk?"

I should refuse. I should go refill sugar caddies or hide in the kitchen or fake a dishwasher emergency.

Instead, I say, "Sure."

My feet carry me toward booth three—the booth Gus always complained we "lived in" when we were teenagers. It's tucked deeper inside, away from the windows, half-shadowed by a rack of old posters.

I slide in first, back to the wall. Control. Exit in sight.

Kaia hesitates, then sits across from me.

"What do you want to talk about?" I ask, crossing my arms.

Kaia's gaze drops to the tabletop, then lifts again like it takes effort. Her voice comes out quieter than I expect—almost shy, which should be impossible coming from someone who fills stadiums.

"Us," she says.

My stomach flips, furious at itself.

I let out a short, ugly laugh. "There is no *'us.'*"

Kaia flinches. "Evie—"

"No," I repeat, sharper. "You don't get to drag out 'us' like a first aid kit because you feel guilty that a demon attacked me."

Something hard flashes across her face, hurt, then resolve. "It's not just that."

"Then what is it?" I snap.

Kaia inhales, controlled. "I mean—yes. The demons *are* getting worse. The Chorus—"

"I know," I cut in. "I'm the one with the demon magnet diner and the wrist leash, remember?"

Something flashes across her face, guilt so fast it looks like pain.

"I didn't want that for you," she says.

"But you brought it anyway," I shoot back.

Kaia's eyes sharpen. "No. That's not—"

"It is," I insist. "You left, Kaia. You left and then you came back with a corporation and a Council and a plan that uses my town like bait."

Kaia's breath catches. "We're trying to protect people."

"By turning the festival into a nostalgia bomb?" I hiss. "Do you hear yourself?"

Kaia's voice goes rough, "Do you hear *yourself?* You're acting like I want any of this."

I stare at her, anger and something else twisting together.

"Don't you?" I whisper. "Don't you want the big stage? Don't you want the lights and the screaming and the—"

I stop because my throat tightens.

Because what I'm really saying is: *Didn't you choose that over us?*

Kaia's eyes soften for a fraction too long. "Evie..."

Then her face hardens, like she's forcing herself into honesty instead of apology. "I messed up," she says, voice low. "Back then. I know I did."

My chest tightens like it always does when she gets too close to the past. The fight is still hanging between us, unfinished and rotting.

Kaia leans forward—still careful, still not crowding me, like she's learned at least that lesson. "But that doesn't mean I'm going to mess up again."

The words are too close to what I've wanted for years. Too close to an apology.

And I can't... I *can't* handle what it would mean if she actually said it properly. If she looked at me and told me she was sorry without excuses. If she gave me something to hold that wasn't anger.

Because then I'd have to decide what to do with it.

And I don't trust myself.

So I slam the door shut before she can open it.

"Don't," I say, voice sharp. "Don't do that."

Kaia freezes. "Do what?"

"Try to fix it," I snap. "Like this. Because you're feeling guilty."

Kaia's eyes flash with hurt. "It's not just guilt. I missed you. I've been missing you for years, and being back here is making it impossible to pretend otherwise."

My breath catches. I hate that part of me still knows when Kaia's telling the truth. My anger slips for half a second, and that's all it takes for panic to rush in after it.

Before I can spit something cruel enough to push her back where I need her, a voice pops into our space like a grenade tossed with a grin.

"Evie, don't—" Jules starts, then pivots, pointing at Kaia like she's presenting evidence. "She literally used her one veto on you. Like, the *only* one. So maybe don't bite her head off?"

Kaia's head snaps to Jules, horrified. "*Jules.*"

Jules freezes, grin faltering as the words land in the air and she realizes what she just did.

Across the booth, Kaia goes rigid—eyes wide, throat working, like Jules just ripped off the bandage and exposed something raw.

The diner tilts.

My heart stops so hard it feels like it drops out of my chest.

Because I remember it—Kaia stepping between me and Mr. Bane, voice like a blade: *No.* The way the room went silent when she said *veto.* The way she looked at me afterward like she'd made a choice she couldn't take back.

I didn't know it was *one.*

My eyes snap to Jules. "Her *what?*"

Jules' face drains of color. "Oh." She swallows. "Oh, shit."

I look back at Kaia. My voice comes out low, careful, deadly. "One?"

Kaia's face is tight with a kind of dread I recognize too well.

"You have one," I say, each word coming out like it's being pulled through barbed wire. "You get *one?*"

Kaia swallows, "Evie—"

"Don't," I snap, and the wrist-leash flares hot like it disapproves of the word. I ignore it. "So when you stopped them from wiping me, that wasn't just you being noble. That was... what? A *finite resource?!*"

"It's not—" Kaia starts.

"Is that why you didn't tell me?" My voice rises despite me. "Because you didn't want to say it out loud? Because you didn't want me to know there was a real price?"

Kaia's eyes widen. "I didn't want you to feel trapped."

I laugh, sharp and humorless. "Trapped? Kaia, I'm already trapped. I have an invisible sigil on my wrist that burns when I try to talk. I have demons sniffing around my workplace. I'm standing in a diner while your company plans Harbor Lights like a stage set."

My hands shake. I hate it. I shove them under the table.

"And you did it *again*," I say, voice cracking on the edge of it. "You made a huge decision, and I'm the last to know. Again."

Kaia flinches like I slapped her.

"That's not fair," she says, and there's desperation in it. "You were there when—"

"I didn't know what it meant!"

Kaia doesn't look away from me.

"I didn't tell you because I didn't want it to become... transactional," she says, voice rough. "I didn't want you to feel like you owed me."

"I *always* find out last," I say, voice shaking now. "That's what you do. You make a choice. You keep it in your pocket. And then I find out from—" I flick my gaze briefly toward Jules. "From *someone else*."

Kaia's mouth opens. No sound comes out. The silence is loud enough to hear the refrigerator hum.

I stand so fast the booth squeaks. "You don't get to decide what I can handle," I say. "You don't get to decide what information I deserve. You don't get to keep treating me like a side character in your—" my voice breaks, ugly, "—in your mission."

Kaia rises too, just enough to keep eye level. "Evie, I was trying to protect you."

"That's what you always say," I spit. "And it always means you're hiding something."

Kaia's face goes pale.

There it is—the old fight's shadow, snapping back into place like it never left. *You didn't tell me. I was the last to know.* The same wound, reopened with a new blade. And that's when I realize that Kaia and I will *never* be okay.

Kaia grips the table hard enough her knuckles pale. "I didn't have a choice."

The words hit something ancient and ugly inside me. I go very still.

Then I say, low and clean, "You always had a choice."

Kaia's breath catches.

I keep going anyway, because if I stop, I'll break. "You just didn't choose me."

Kaia's eyes water. My glare holds.

Kaia's voice drops, ragged. "I couldn't—I was *recruited.*"

"And you didn't *tell* me," I snap, and the old fight rises like smoke. "I had to find out from *someone else*. And it's the same with the veto. So what else is new?"

Kaia's face pinches like she's making a decision she's terrified of. Then she says it. Quiet. Plain. Like ripping off a bandage.

"It was us," she admits.

I freeze. "What?"

Kaia's gaze holds mine, steady, miserable. "That night. The pier... The kiss. Someone took that photo... of us."

My stomach drops so fast I feel sick.

Kaia continues, voice low. "The Council monitors for Sparks. For resonance. Big emotional spikes." Her throat works. "That kiss lit up something in me. In the air. In the lanterns. In—everything. That cool light effect? That was my Spark... and they saw it."

The booth feels too small. My skin prickles.

"So you're telling me," I say slowly, "that the Council found you because of me?"

Kaia flinches. "They found me because of my *Spark*. Because I have resonance... But... yes. That moment flagged me."

My mouth goes dry.

All the old betrayal twists into something even crueler.

Not just *you left me and never even called*.

But *you left because of us*.

And *you still didn't tell me*...

My voice comes out sharp with pain. "And you didn't think I deserved to know that either?"

Blaire's voice again, sharper. "Kaia. Time."

Kaia doesn't move. Her eyes stay on mine, wrecked. "Does it matter? I'm here now," she says, like it's a promise.

I laugh, bitter. "You're always here when there's an audience."

Kaia flinches like I hit her.

Good.

Bad.

I don't know.

My wrist warms faintly again, like a reminder: rules, consequences. Or maybe it's my own fear warning me.

I step back. "Just—go," I say, and it comes out like a command because if it sounds like a plea I'll collapse. "Go back to your plan. Go back to your schedule. Go back to being... that."

Kaia's throat works. "*Evie*, listen—Please."

"I am listening," I whisper harshly. "And all I hear is the same thing. The big machine. The big stage. And me finding out last."

Kaia's breath shakes. "Tomorrow... if something hits the festival..."

I don't answer.

She continues anyway. "Your grandma. Your regulars. Half the town. They'll all be there."

My stomach drops, because she put the fear into words.

I imagine Mr. Alvarez under lantern light. I imagine Tasha screaming with her friends. I imagine Gus pretending not to care while he absolutely does. I imagine Gran insisting she wants to walk to the pier because it's "pretty when it's trying."

And I imagine something wearing a song sliding through them like smoke.

My breath catches.

Kaia's voice is softer. "That's why we're doing this."

I swallow hard.

When I finally speak, my voice is flat because it's the only way I can keep it together. "Then do it," I say. "Protect them."

Kaia's voice breaks slightly. "And you."

I look at her for half a second too long.

She looks... tired. Not idol tired. Not camera tired.

Real tired.

For a moment, my anger shifts into something like grief. Something like missing. I crush it down.

"I have to go," I say, and this time it's quieter.

Kaia hesitates like she wants to say more.

Then Blaire appears at the end of the aisle, expression set. "Kaia. *Now*."

Kaia nods once—small, defeated—and backs away like she's leaving a wild animal alone in a trap. Mina hovers, stricken. Jules looks like she wants to say something and, for once, doesn't. Remy's eyes linger on me like she's memorizing the shape of the damage.

The front door bell jingles when they leave. Silence settles too quickly, like the diner is holding its breath again. I stare at my wrist, at the place the invisible sigil lives under my skin.

Tomorrow, the festival happens.

Tomorrow, the town will hum the demon's tune like it's tradition.

Tomorrow, my grandma and my regulars will be there.

And no matter how much I want to pretend Kaia is just a poster face, she's right about one awful thing: If something hits Harbor Lights, I don't get to opt out.

I'M NOT SUPPOSED TO leave the hotel.

Blaire's rules are simple tonight: rest, hydrate, don't wander, don't get photographed doing anything that can be turned into a headline.

Which means I lie in bed with my eyes open, listening to the hum of the mini fridge and the distant bass of festival setup down by the pier like Harbor's Edge is already rehearsing for tomorrow.

Sleep doesn't come.

Every time I close my eyes, I see Evie in the diner—shoulders rigid, voice like a door slamming shut.

Just go.

And every time I open them, the ceiling feels too close, like the hotel room is a box I can't breathe inside.

I slip out quietly. The hallway carpet swallows my footsteps. The security outside our floor barely glances up. I'm wearing a hoodie and cap. Anonymous enough. A ghost of myself.

Outside, Harbor's Edge is damp and dark and awake in that pre-festival way. Lantern frames sway faintly in the wind, unlit. Posters rustle against poles. Someone left a radio playing too soft in a booth on main street, the jingle looping like a spell.

I keep walking anyway.

I tell myself I'm doing a ward check.

I tell myself I'm checking for Chorus residue.

I tell myself anything that sounds responsible.

My feet take me where they've always taken me when I don't know what else to do here: the pier. It's colder out here. The ocean breathes against the pilings, slow and endless. The boards creak under my weight in the same familiar rhythm, and my chest tightens like muscle memory is grabbing me by the throat.

Halfway down, I see someone sitting at the edge with their feet hanging over the water. A hood. A jacket. Even before she turns her head, I know. My heart drops into my stomach.

Evie.

She looks up when she hears the boards creak, and for a second her face is unreadable—shadowed, guarded, tired. Then recognition washes over her face.

"Oh my god," she says flatly. "*You.*"

I stop like I've walked into a wall.

"Hi," I manage, because I'm pathetic.

Evie's gaze flicks over me the way it did the first night in the diner—fast, assessing, looking for danger. Then it lands on my face.

"What are you doing here?" she asks, voice low.

"I—" I start, then stop because any answer is going to sound like a lie.

Her eyes narrow. "Are you stalking me?"

My spine goes straight with reflexive indignation. "No!"

Evie's mouth twitches like she doesn't believe me for a second. She turns her head back toward the water, voice dry. "Sure."

"I'm not," I insist, quieter this time. "I didn't—I *didn't* know you'd be here."

She snorts softly, still looking out at the dark bay. "Let me guess. Wards. Demons. Corporate community partnerships."

The bitterness in her voice stings because it's accurate.

"I couldn't sleep," I say instead.

Evie's shoulders lift in a small, unimpressed shrug. "Yeah. Same."

The quiet stretches. The ocean keeps moving, entirely uncaring of what's broken between us.

I swallow and force myself to breathe. "Can I... sit?"

Evie doesn't look at me. For a moment I think she's going to tell me to leave again.

Then she exhales slowly and says, "Sure."

It's not warm.

But it's not a *no*.

I move carefully, like sudden motion might spook her. I sit a few feet away, close enough to feel the heat of her presence, far enough to pretend we're not one wrong breath away from falling back into something dangerous or another fight.

Evie keeps her gaze on the water. I keep mine on the boards, because looking at her feels like stepping into a flame.

After a long beat, Evie says, "Does Blaire know you're out here?"

"No," I admit.

Evie laughs once, sharp. "Of course."

"I'm not doing anything wrong," I say quickly.

Evie's head turns just enough that I catch her profile. She says nothing, which is worse than her arguing with me or telling me off.

I can argue. I can defend. I can make this about rules and patrols and safety.

But I don't know what to do with silence.

So I stare at my hands and say the truest thing I have. "I didn't come here to start trouble."

Evie's voice is quiet, almost rough. "Well, trouble seems to find you."

We lapse into silence. I don't have a defense for that.

I think about the Eon office. The diagrams. The word *yield* and the strange Eon logo etched into the new warding.

I think about tomorrow night—lanterns rising, the town humming, the Chorus licking its lips.

I think about Evie's wrist warming under an invisible binding.

And I think about how none of this would've touched her if I hadn't been flagged, recruited, and shaped into a weapon.

I pull my sleeves lower onto my hands.

"I'm scared," I admit.

Evie's head turns fully now, eyes narrowing like she's trying to decide if I'm manipulating her or finally being honest.

"Of what?" she asks.

I let out a breath that fogs in the air. I keep my gaze on the water because if I look straight at her, I might lose the thread of bravery I'm clinging to.

"Of tomorrow night," I say. "Of the festival. Of the Chorus breaking into splinters again and—" My throat tightens. "—and people getting hurt because we thought we had it contained..."

Evie's expression doesn't soften. It sharpens. "You mean like how you had it contained when it came for me?"

The words sting because they're fair.

I swallow. "Yes."

A beat.

"And," I add quietly, because I can't stop myself, "I'm scared things are never going to be... even remotely okay between us again."

Evie lets out a short laugh with no humor in it. "How could they be?"

I flinch.

Her voice cuts colder. "You didn't even tell me about the veto."

The pier suddenly feels too narrow, like the boards are trying to squeeze us closer than we can survive.

"I know," I say. "I'm sorry. I should have told you."

Evie's eyes hold mine, bright with anger and something underneath it. "So why didn't you?"

I hesitate, hating myself. "Because I was scared to."

"Scared of *what*?" she snaps.

"Of you hearing it as a price tag," I say, the truth spilling out ugly. "Of you thinking you owed me anything. Of you—" I swallow hard. "—of you hating me more."

Evie's jaw tightens and she looks away for a moment.

God, she really does hate me...

I deserve that too.

Slowly, her deep brown eyes slide back to me and stare at me for a long second, then her voice drops, quieter. "Why did you use it on me?"

The question lands heavy. She isn't asking about policy. She's asking why I chose *her*.

Her eyes flick away and back like she hates how much it matters. "If that's your *one* mind-wipe pass—your one override—why spend it on me? Why not save it for someone else? *Anyone* else?"

"Because..."

I open my mouth.

The truth comes out before I can dress it up.

"Because you're the only person I've never been able to forget, and when they tried to erase that night, something in me snapped... And, maybe, because I love you," I say.

It's out in the open now, and instead of freezing up and shutting down, the words suddenly *won't* stop.

"And that scares me too," I add, voice quiet. "It always has. I think I've always been scared of loving you, of what it would cost, of what it would mean, of how easy it is for the world to use it against me. Against *you*."

My breath catches. My throat tightens.

The silence that follows feels like someone sucked all the air off the pier.

Evie's face goes still. Then her mouth twists like she tasted something bitter.

"Don't," she says, low. Not soft. Not kind. A warning.

I flinch.

"You don't get to drop that on me like it's... like it fixes anything," she continues, voice tight with restraint. "You don't get to say *love* now, like that's a bandage you can slap over *years* of silence."

My chest aches. I deserve every syllable.

Evie's eyes shine with something sharp and furious. "If you loved me, you would've told me the truth. If you loved me, I wouldn't have been the last to know. *Again*." Her laugh is short and ugly. "So don't stand here and act like I'm supposed to be grateful you... what—*feel* something?"

"Evie, *please*." I look at her now, because I can't help it. "The Council tells us attachment is a vulnerability. They tell us clean breaks are easier and that the people we care about will be safer if we keep our distance."

Evie's eyes flash. "And you believed them."

"I did," I admit. "Because I wanted to believe I had a reason that wasn't just cowardice."

Evie looks away again, fast. Like looking at me too long makes her throat tighten.

I shouldn't push.

But I'm already here. I already shattered the rules by coming. I'm already sitting on this pier with the person I've been orbiting like a punishment.

So I push anyway.

"I didn't tell you," I say softly. "About the Council. About the recruiter when we were teens. About any of it. I was scared."

Evie's laugh is bitter. "You were always scared. About everything. And you haven't changed."

"That's not fair," I say automatically, then immediately regret it because it sounds defensive.

Evie's head snaps toward me. "Oh, I'm sorry. Was it not *scary* for you to tell me our kiss was *stupid* and then disappear?"

My throat closes.

Evie keeps going because anger is her armor and she knows how to wear it. "Was it not *scary* to let me think I was the problem? That I was too small-town for your big dreams of stardom?"

"Evie," I whisper.

"What?" she snaps, eyes bright with something that looks too close to tears. "You want to apologize now? You want to do it properly this time?"

I flinch.

Because yes.

Because I've wanted that sentence—*I'm sorry*—in my mouth for years and I've been too ashamed to let it out...

"I do," I say, voice raw.

She shakes her head hard, like she's physically rejecting it. "Well, don't."

My chest tightens. "Why?"

"Because if you do," Evie says, voice lower, shaking at the edges, "then I have to—" She swallows. "Then I have to decide what to do with it."

I stare at her. She keeps her eyes on the water like it's safer than looking at me.

"And I can't," she says, quieter. "Not right now."

The honesty in that hurts almost worse than the anger.

I nod slowly. "Okay."

Evie lets out a breath like she didn't realize she'd been holding it. She rubs her thumb over her fingertips, grounding herself.

We sit in silence again. The pier creaks. The water breathes. Somewhere back in town, a radio plays the Harbor Lights jingle faintly and my skin prickles as if the world is warning me we don't have long.

Evie breaks the quiet first.

"You know what's funny?" she says, voice flat.

"What?"

Evie's mouth twists. "I never asked you to stay."

My heart clenches.

Evie laughs once, humorless. "Everyone acts like I was begging you to pick me and Harbor's Edge over your big dream."

I don't speak. I don't dare.

Evie's voice softens, just a fraction. "But I would *never* have asked that of you."

I swallow. "Evie—"

"No," she cuts in automatically, but it's not as sharp as before. "Let me say it."

I shut my mouth.

Evie stares out over the water. "I knew you wanted more. I knew it even when we were pretending our plan was 'together.' I could feel it in you. Like... like the town was a jacket you were outgrowing."

My throat tightens because it's true and because she's saying it like she's been carrying it too.

"I didn't want you to resent me," Evie says. "And... I wanted your dreams to come true..." She swallows. "And... you couldn't even tell me yourself... Your mom told me... Your *mom*, Kaia. She didn't even tell me." A bitter laugh. "I *overhead.*"

A sharp ache blooms behind my ribs.

I picture it too clearly: Mom, proud and loud, letting the news spill like it belonged to everyone. Evie with a smile freezing on her face.

"I didn't mean for you to hear it like that," I say, and it comes out wrecked.

Evie's laugh is thin. "But I did."

"I know." I swallow hard. "And I hate that I let it happen, but I was—"

"Scared," Evie cuts in, exhausted. "Yeah. I know." There's no bite this time. Just resignation, like she's said the word so many times in her head it wore smooth.

She stares out at the water. Her voice drops. "You were my everything back then, Kaia." A beat. "And I didn't need you to stay small. I didn't need you to pick Harbor's Edge over... whatever you wanted."

My chest tightens.

"I just needed you to tell me," she says, and it sounds like a confession she hates. "To let me be part of it. To not make me the last to know like I was a *stranger*. To not—" Her throat works. "—to not make me feel like I was something you had to outgrow."

Her cheeks heat in the dark. I see it even with the fog, even with the weak pier lights. I see the way she hates that she's saying any of this out loud.

"And I needed that kiss to mean something," she adds, quieter, almost vicious with vulnerability. "I wanted it to be enough that you didn't regret it."

My own breath catches.

"I didn't," I say immediately.

Evie's head snaps toward me. "Then why did you act like you did?"

Because fear makes me cruel.

Because I panicked.

Because I thought choosing you meant losing myself.

And because I didn't know how to want both without breaking...

I swallow, throat burning. "Because I was terrified," I say, honest in the ugliest way. "And when I get terrified, I... I make things smaller. I cut them down until they can't hurt me."

Evie's eyes narrow, pained. "So you cut *us* down."

"Yes," I whisper. "And I hated myself for it the second I said it. But it was already out."

Her voice cracks, just slightly. "You called it a stupid kiss."

I flinch like the words are a slap.

"I know," I say. "And it wasn't. It wasn't stupid. It was—" My breath shakes. "It was the bravest thing I'd ever done. And I got scared of what it meant."

Evie looks away fast, jaw clenched like she's holding back a sound.

I keep my hands still at my sides.

"I didn't regret you. You were my best friend," I say, quieter. "I regretted that I wanted you so much I couldn't think straight."

Evie looks away again, jaw clenched. "And then you left. After our fight. You left without a goodbye. I woke up one day, and you were gone."

"I know," I say.

The simplest confession.

No excuses.

Evie's breath trembles. "You don't get to come back and act like—like you're just... here now."

"I'm not acting like that," I say softly.

Evie's head snaps toward me. "Aren't you? You show up with swords and suits. You bleed in the diner. You're everywhere and then you *start* to say something like an apology and then—"

"And then you told me not to," I finish quietly.

Evie goes still. The anger in her eyes flickers, briefly replaced by something vulnerable and startled, like she forgot she did that and now she has to face why.

She turns away fast. "Whatever."

I look at her profile—sharp nose, tight mouth, the faint line between her brows that's always been there when she's trying not to feel too much.

I want to touch her so badly it feels like hunger.

I don't.

Instead, I reach into the inside pocket of my jacket. The photo is warm from being against my ribs. I pull it out slowly, careful, like I'm presenting evidence in court.

Evie notices immediately. Her gaze snaps to my hand.

"What is that?" she asks, voice suspicious.

I hold it between us, the edges worn, the colors faded, but the moment still alive in it.

Evie goes very still.

Her breath catches.

And for one heartbeat, the walls in her face falter.

"Kaia," she says, quieter than I've heard her in days.

"I kept it," I admit. "I know I don't... deserve to have it. But I kept it."

Evie stares at the photo of our kiss like it might bite. Then her eyes lift to mine, and there's something raw there—grief and anger and longing all tangled together.

"You took that on tour with you," she says, and it sounds like an accusation and a question.

I nod. "Yes."

Evie swallows hard. "Why?"

Because even when I left, I really didn't stop loving you.

Because I couldn't.

Because the world can own my schedule but it can't rewrite what you were to me.

Because you were the first person who looked at me like I mattered before the rest of the world decided I was useful.

I can't say all of that without breaking open.

So I say the simplest truth again.

"Because it's you," I whisper. "Us."

Evie's eyes shine. She blinks hard, fast, like she's trying to keep herself from tipping into softness. But she doesn't look away from the photo.

She reaches out—slow, hesitant—and takes it from my hand. Her fingertips brush mine. Electric. Familiar. Wrong and right at the same time.

Evie studies the photo, jaw tight. Her thumb drags over the edge where the paper is worn.

Her voice is barely audible. "We looked happy."

I swallow. "We were."

Evie's eyes flick up to mine, anger returning like a shield. "You don't get points for keeping a picture."

"I'm not asking for points," I say quietly. "I'm asking for—" I stop. Because asking for anything feels like too much.

Evie's breath shakes. She shoves the photo back at me like it burns.

I catch it and tuck it back into my pocket quickly.

Evie's gaze drops to my mouth and then away again like she's mad at herself for noticing. The air between us feels charged, trembling at the edge of something we've been avoiding for years.

Evie clears her throat. "So what, you came out here to—what—be sentimental?"

"No," I say, then pause. "Yes. Maybe. I don't know."

Evie's laugh is short. "Wow. The great Kaia Rhee, reduced to 'maybe.'"

I glare weakly. "Don't use my name like that."

Evie's eyebrows lift. "Like what?"

"Like 'Kaia Rhee' is a stranger. Like... you don't know me anymore," I say, and my voice comes out too raw.

Evie goes quiet.

Then she says, softer, "I *don't* know who you are anymore."

The sentence hurts because it's true.

I swallow hard. "I don't either. Not all the way."

Evie's mouth twists. "That's comforting."

"I'm trying," I say.

Evie snorts. "You're trying now."

"Yes," I admit. "Because I'm here now. Because I can't—" My voice breaks slightly. I force it steady. "Because I *won't* lose you again..."

Evie's breath trembles. She looks away, jaw clenched, and I can see the fight in her—between wanting to hurt me and wanting to fall into something softer and hating herself for both.

I want to say I'm sorry.

A real apology.

The one she wouldn't let me give.

But her hands are shaking faintly on the pier edge, and I realize she's not just angry. She's terrified too. Evie never admits when she's scared, but she is.

So I don't push an apology into a place that might break her. I do the only thing I can.

I ask, quietly, "Evie... can I—"

She cuts in, voice sharp with panic. "If you say 'kiss,' I'm throwing you in the ocean."

A laugh bursts out of me before I can stop it—small, surprised, almost disbelieving. Evie's head snaps toward me, eyes wide like she hates that she made me laugh.

"You sound like Blaire," I blurt, and immediately regret it because it's such a stupid, normal thing to say here.

Evie squints at me. "Huh?"

"My manager," I explain, still catching my breath. "She has ocean-throwing energy too... as Mina would say."

Evie's expression does something complicated—confused first, then faintly offended on my behalf. "That's... healthy."

"It's terrifying," I admit, and the smile won't leave my mouth no matter how hard I try to shove it down. "But effective."

Evie's mouth twitches, betraying her. For half a heartbeat, we're almost sixteen again. Almost...

Then she hardens again. "Well, say whatever you were going to say."

My pulse pounds. My throat is dry. I look at her, really look. At the way her breath fogs. At the way her eyes keep flicking to my mouth like she's fighting her own body. At the way she's sitting here alone the night before the festival because the town feels too loud.

I take a slow breath. "Can I touch you?"

Evie freezes.

Then she exhales, shaky. "*What*?"

"Not—" I blush immediately, face flushing with heat. "Not like *that*! Just... can I touch your hand? *Hold* your hand, I mean..."

Evie stares at me for a long time, and she has the audacity to almost look amused, just a flicker at the corner of her mouth, like she can't believe *this* is what I'm tripping over after everything. Like she's watching me fumble through something simple and human and finding it ridiculous in the way she always did.

I don't dare rescind it now. If I pull back, I'll never ask again.

Evie exhales through her nose. Her eyes stay sharp, but her shoulders loosen a fraction. Then, like it costs her, she turns her palm upward between us.

For some reason, it feels like a dare.

My breath catches. I reach out slowly and slide my fingers into hers. Her hand is warm. Her grip is tight, like she's afraid I'll disappear if she doesn't hold on. The contact hits me like a punch to the chest. I don't move closer. I don't rush. I just hold her hand and let this new reality settle between us.

I'm holding Evie's hand.

And it really does feel like we're sixteen again... until she speaks.

Evie's eyes squeeze shut for a second. When she opens them, she's looking at me like she's standing on a cliff.

"I'm not forgiving you yet," she says.

"I'm not asking you to," I whisper.

Evie's gaze drops to our hands. "Then what are you asking?"

I take a shaky breath. The words feel stick in my throat, but I force them out anyway, because if I don't say them now, I'll spend the rest of my life choking on them.

"I'm asking to say it," I whisper. "Properly. Even if you don't... even if you never—"

Evie's eyes meet mine, wary. "Say what?"

"That I'm sorry," I say, and my voice breaks immediately, humiliating and honest. "Because I am. I'm sorry... I was a stupid kid. I was a coward. I got scared and I made you pay for it." I swallow hard, blinking fast. "I said things I didn't mean because I didn't know how to want you without panicking. And then I left like—like that was better than facing what I did."

The pier light blurs. Tears sting hot behind my eyes, and I hate that she can see them.

"I'm sorry," I repeat, quieter. "I'm so sorry, Evie."

Evie's face goes still. Then she leans forward as if she can't stand the sound of my apology in the air. Not fast. Not dramatic. Like she's testing whether the world will punish her for wanting. And she kisses me.

Her lips are soft, yet the kiss is pure heat and relief and anger and hunger tangled together, like we're biting back years of silence. A tear slips down my cheek as our mouths move, as if the grief has to go somewhere.

She makes a small sound against my mouth that goes straight through me. My hand tightens on hers. My other hand lifts—hesitates—then cups her jaw carefully, like she might shatter if I'm too rough. Evie grabs the front of my hoodie and yanks me closer like she's done being careful.

The pier disappears.

There's only *her*.

Her mouth. Her breath. The taste of salt and smoke and something achingly familiar that I tasted once years ago and never again.

We break for air, foreheads almost touching.

Evie's voice is rough. "This is a bad idea."

"Maybe," I whisper.

Evie's eyes squeeze shut. Then she kisses me again, harder, like she's trying to erase thought. It's desperate and real and it makes my whole body hum.

When we finally break, we're both breathing hard, the night air cold in my lungs, her warmth blazing against me anyway.

"I should go," she says, voice rough. "It's late. And my grandma... she gets restless at night sometimes. She'll wake up and decide it's 1998 and she needs to go to work. Or she'll go looking for me." Her jaw clenches. "I need to make sure she doesn't wander."

The word *wander* lands like a weight. I picture Grandma Calder alone in the dark, confused and stubborn, and my stomach turns.

"Okay," I say, because I'm not going to argue with that.

Evie shifts as if she expects me to let go. I don't. The idea of her walking home alone—after everything, after demons and schedules and my own stupid gravity toward her—feels intolerable.

"I'm walking you though," I say.

Evie's eyes narrow instantly. "You don't need to do that, Kaia."

"Yes," I say, gentler than I feel. "I do. Not to control you. Not to—" I swallow. "Just... to your gate. Your porch. Whatever you'll allow. *Please*."

Evie looks like she hates that word.

She looks away toward the dark water, toward the fog, toward anything except me.

"Fine," she says finally, resigned. "Walk me. But if someone recognizes you and freaks out, it's your own fault."

My mouth twitches. "Deal."

We stand and I make sure my long hair is still tucked into my jacket and covered. Then, we leave the pier together, hand in hand.

The town is quiet in that late-night way that makes everything feel too intimate. Fog blurs the streetlights into soft halos. The lantern frames overhead sway.

Evie's thumb drags once over my knuckles—absent, unconscious—then she seems to realize what she's doing and stiffens like she caught herself committing a crime.

I don't comment.

I don't squeeze back too hard.

I just keep my hand where it is, letting the contact be what it is: a thin bridge over a canyon.

We pass dark storefronts and closed booths. I keep scanning the shadows because my body refuses to trust silence anymore.

After a few minutes, Evie exhales through her nose. "Looking for monsters?"

I swallow. "It's hard to turn off."

Evie's hand tightens on mine for half a second. Then loosens again like she's reminding herself not to.

Her neighborhood comes into view—small houses, wet lawns, white fences, porch lights glowing faintly through the fog. We reach her house. Evie slows at the gate. Her keys jingle in her fist.

"This is fine," she says, and I can tell she means *you can stop here.*

I nod, because I'm trying to learn restraint. "Okay."

Then she swings the gate open and starts toward the porch. My feet follow without thinking.

Evie glances back sharply, then says an exasperated, "*Kaia.*"

"Porch," I say, soft. "Just... to your door? I want to make sure you get in."

She studies me, then shakes her head and mutters, "Fine."

Though she huffs a laugh right after and climbs the steps. The porch boards creak under our weight. I remember those creaks. I remember them under teenage feet, under laughter, under whispered plans that felt permanent.

Evie unlocks the door slowly, listening. The house is quiet.

She turns to me. "Thank you..."

"Of course."

I don't move.

I wait.

Evie exhales, sharp and frustrated with herself. "Can I—" she starts.

My breath catches. "Yes," I say, too fast.

Evie rolls her eyes like she wants to throw something at me. "I didn't even ask yet."

"Sorry," I whisper.

She stares at me for a beat, then her voice drops. "Can I kiss you again?"

It's not a demand. It's not a dare. It's a genuine question. The fact that she asks breaks something open in my chest.

"Yes," I say, and it comes out as a plea. "*Please.*"

Evie steps closer and kisses me on the porch. It's slower than the pier kiss. Less frantic. Still sharp with anger at the world, still hot with want, but steadier. Intentional. Her hands slide up to my hoodie, fist bunching the fabric.

My hands hover at her waist, then settle—careful, reverent. A silent question.

Evie answers by pulling me closer.

When we break, she rests her forehead against mine for half a heartbeat, eyes squeezed shut, like she hates how good it feels. Then she exhales, and the words come out like surrender.

"Come inside," she says.

My whole body goes still. "Evie—"

She glares up at me with bright brown eyes, cheeks flushed. "Don't make it weird."

"I'm not," I say, voice rough. "I just—are you sure?"

Evie's eyes flash. "No," she admits. "But I'd still like you to..."

My chest aches. I nod once. "Okay."

We step inside and close the door softly behind us, like we're trying not to wake the past.

Warmth washes over us, along with a mix of scents: old wood, laundry detergent, something faintly sweet like pancake syrup that never fully leaves a house once it's lived in. My throat tightens with nostalgia so sharp it almost makes me dizzy.

The living room is dim. There's a blanket folded on the couch and a little table crowded with pill bottles and sticky notes. A framed photo sits on the mantle—Evie and her grandma, both smiling. Evie looks younger. Happier.

My chest aches.

Evie sets her keys down with careful quiet. "I'm going to check on her," she whispers.

I nod and stop in the entryway, hands at my sides, trying not to touch anything.

Evie disappears down the hall. I stand there and listen to the house breathe. A floorboard creaks somewhere deeper in. A soft murmur—Evie's voice, too gentle for the person who snarls at me in public. A pause. Then another murmur, quieter. A door closes softly.

Evie comes back a minute later, expression tight but relieved. "She's asleep," she says.

"Good," I whisper, and I mean it.

Evie looks at me like she doesn't know what to do with the fact I'm standing in her house. Neither do I.

The silence stretches. I should leave. I should go back to my hotel. Back to schedule. Back to my girls and my weapons and the safety of distance.

Blaire is going to kill me if she finds out I'm here...

But my body is still buzzing from Evie's mouth. My hand still remembers her grip like it's branded.

Evie's gaze drops to my hand, then lifts back up. "You're still here," she says, as if surprised.

I nod.

"Come on," she says softly.

Evie leads me down the hallway. I recognize the framed family photos on the wall. The scuffed spot in the wood where someone dragged a chair too hard. The little hook by the bathroom where Kaia-from-years-ago used to hang her jacket when she came over drenched in pier fog.

Some things are the same in a way that hurts.

Some things are different in a way that hurts worse.

Evie's bedroom door is at the end of the hall. Her room is different from the one in my memory, but it's still hers. Different bedspread. Different lamp. A stack of books on the floor like she tried to be organized and failed. An old corkboard with receipts and schedules and reminders pinned up.

But on the windowsill, there's still that chipped little jar she used to fill with sea glass. And the curtains are still the same pale color. And the air still smells faintly of salt and soap.

Evie catches me looking. "What?"

"It just... looks like you."

Evie's throat works. She looks away first, then sits on the edge of the bed like she's bracing for impact.

"I'm sorry," I say quietly. Being in her room makes me want to just apologize all over again. "For everything. For—"

Evie's eyes snap up. "*Kaia*."

I stop mid-breath.

"Don't," she says, firm but not cruel. "Not right now."

My mouth opens anyway, a reflex. "I just—"

"It's okay," she cuts in, softer. "You're here. I'm here. That's enough for tonight, at least."

My chest aches with the relief of being allowed to stop trying to earn oxygen.

I nod once, throat tight. "Okay."

The word is small. The word is *huge*.

I step closer slowly, giving her all the room in the world to tell me to stop.

Evie doesn't.

She reaches for my hoodie and tugs me down until I'm standing between her knees, close enough to feel her breath. Evie grabs my shirt and kisses me again—messy, hungry, like the pier kiss broke the seal and now everything floods. Right there, in her room, with the door shut and the world held back.

I kiss her back with a desperation I've been starving on for years.

Her fingers slide into my hair, tugging just enough to make my breath catch. My hands settle at her waist and when she shivers, it sends a tremor through my whole body like my Spark is answering her touch.

We end up sitting on the bed together, knees brushing, close enough that every inhale feels shared.

Evie's hands hover at the hem of my hoodie like she's approaching a live wire. She looks up at me, jaw tight, eyes bright with the weight of asking.

"Is this okay?" she whispers.

My chest clenches. "Yes," I say immediately. "Yes. Only if you want it."

Evie swallows hard. "I do."

The words hit me like permission and grief at the same time.

She tugs again, gentler this time, and I help her—slow, deliberate—peeling the hoodie up and over my head like we're dismantling armor instead of clothing. I keep my movements careful, not because I'm scared of her, but because I'm scared of how precious this feels.

I don't want to rush. I don't want to spook her. I don't want to blink and find myself alone again.

Evie does the same to me—careful, stubborn—like she refuses to let this be frantic. Like if we go too fast we'll crash into the past and shatter.

The room is quiet except for breath and the soft creak of the mattress and the distant ocean hush through the window.

Evie's mouth finds mine again. I meet her there, and it's softer now—still hungry, still real, but steadier. She kisses like she's choosing it on purpose instead of falling.

When we break, her forehead rests against mine.

"Tell me what you want?" I request, meeting her gaze.

Her eyes flick to my mouth. "You," she says—furious and soft at once. "I want—" She swallows. "I want you to stop being careful like you're going to disappear."

Something in my chest breaks open—relief, guilt, love, all tangled.

I press my forehead to hers, breath shaking. "I'm not going anywhere."

Evie exhales like that's all she can handle, then nods once, small and certain. Her fingers hook into the hem of my shirt and tug me closer, impatient in a way that makes my stomach flip. My hands slide to her waist automatically.

Our shirts come off first, pulled over our heads in the kind of clumsy hurry that makes us both laugh under our breath. The air of the room feels cooler against my skin, but the space between us is warm enough to make up for it.

For a moment we just sit there.

Her bra is plain black—simple, practical, very Evie. Mine has lace along the edges, something I probably bought in a city halfway across the world without really thinking about it.

I reach for her again, tugging her closer until our bodies meet.

Her breasts brush mine through the thin layers of fabric.

The contact is light at first, almost accidental, but the second it happens we both go still. Then Evie exhales slowly.

The warmth between us deepens as I pull her flush against me. The lace of my bra grazes her chest; the soft cotton of hers presses back against mine. Our bodies fit together more naturally than they have any right to.

My hands rest at her waist, thumbs brushing the bare strip of skin where her shirt used to be.

I keep looking at her face. Her eyes. Her mouth. The way her shoulders move when she breathes. I'm checking without meaning to—making sure she's still here with me in this moment. And to make sure that this is still *okay*.

Evie notices. Instead of pulling back, she slides her hands up my sides and pulls me closer again, closing the last inch between us like she's answering the question without saying it out loud. Her forehead brushes mine.

"You always overthink everything," she murmurs.

"Occupational hazard."

Her mouth curves just a little.

But she doesn't move away. Her fingers tighten, holding me there. The heat of her body seeps through the thin layers still between us, and I can feel the steady rhythm of her breathing against my chest.

It feels like something we've both been walking toward for years without quite admitting it.

Evie tilts her head slightly, her nose brushing mine, and for a second neither of us moves.

Then she closes the space again.

And this time there's no hesitation left in the way she pulls me closer.

When her hands slip under my jaw and she whispers, "*Kaia*," like it hurts, I almost break.

I kiss her harder instead. The bed creaks beneath us.

The room is too warm and not warm enough.

Evie's mouth finds my throat and I gasp, fingers tightening in her hair, and she makes a small, wrecked sound like she hates how much she wants this too.

My pulse roars. The world narrows to skin and breath and the terrible, beautiful fact that we're done pretending this is nothing.

Evie's hands move over my ribs, my shoulders, steadying me the way she used to steady me in front of that rickety little stage years ago. But now her grip isn't about grounding nerves before a show—it's about holding on.

My hands slide up, palms hot against her bare skin. She shivers under the touch, breath hitching as my fingers trace upward along the lines of her back. We keep kissing—messy and hungry, mouths colliding again and again like we're afraid to pause.

I find the clasp of her bra by feel and undo it.

The second the fabric loosens, I cup her breasts through the thin material, thumbs brushing over her nipples. They tighten instantly beneath my touch. Evie sucks in a sharp breath and her fingers clamp down on my shoulders.

I pull back just enough to look at her.

Really look.

Her hair's a mess. Her lips are swollen from kissing. There's color high on her cheeks I don't remember seeing before.

She suddenly goes very still under my gaze, and the blush deepens.

"You've probably been with so many people who look like models," she mutters, voice rough with embarrassment.

I shake my head immediately, leaning in again, nuzzling her cheek before kissing slowly down her neck.

"No," I murmur against her skin. "You're the only one who ever knew me before I became... all of that. You're the only one that's ever mattered."

She makes a soft noise when my mouth reaches her chest. I pull the bra down and close my lips around her nipple, sucking gently. Evie's fingers tangle hard in my hair. Heat pools between my legs, little sparks of tension building low in my stomach, and *God*, I'm embarrassingly wet.

The mattress dips when I push her backward onto the bed. She lets out a surprised laugh that turns into a breathy sound when she lands against the pillows.

Her hands move quickly, tugging at my bra. I help her unhook it and shrug it off, letting it fall somewhere onto the floor. Evie's eyes drop to my chest. My breasts are smaller than hers, but her hands come up immediately, palms warm as she touches me.

My eyes flutter closed.

God.

"I used to touch myself thinking about this," I admit before I can stop myself.

The words land between us like a lit match.

Evie blinks up at me, stunned. "When?"

I laugh softly, a little breathless. "Always. Hotel rooms. Tour buses. Everywhere."

I lean down and kiss her again before she can respond.

This kiss is different. Slower at first, then suddenly deeper when Evie bites down on my lower lip. I gasp at the sharp little jolt of pain, grabbing her hair and tilting her head so I can kiss her harder.

Her body presses into mine.

My underwear is soaked now. I can feel it when my hips roll instinctively against her.

Evie's hands slide to my waist, tugging at my jeans. I kick them off, then we're both scrambling, half-laughing, half-gasping as the last of our clothes disappear.

When I settle back on top of her, the first brush of bare skin against bare skin makes both of us make helpless sounds.

My thigh ends up between her legs without either of us really planning it. Evie rocks against it immediately.

"God," I breathe, realizing what she's doing as I slide my hand between us. My fingers brush her slick heat. "You're so wet."

She cries out softly when I touch her clit, hips bucking upward to chase the pressure.

I circle my thumb over it experimentally.

Evie grabs my wrist suddenly, guiding my hand.

"Like this," she gasps, adjusting the angle. "Right there—"

I follow her lead, increasing the speed just enough. Her back arches off the bed. Her head presses into the pillow as a moan tears out of her, the sound raw and unfiltered. I keep going, watching the way her body tightens beneath me.

Her climax hits fast.

Evie goes rigid for a second before she shudders hard, breath breaking into a series of shaky sounds as she comes.

I slow my hand, letting her ride it out.

Then I shift.

I don't know if Evie has ever scissored before, but I'm *desperate* for that closeness.

Evie lets out a small protest when I move, but it turns into another soft sound when I slide my body down and tangle our legs together. Our hips line up. The moment our sexes press together, the friction makes both of us inhale sharply. Evie grips my thigh, pulling me closer, angling her hips to increase the contact.

Electricity shoots down my spine.

For a second we both freeze, eyes meeting, like she's realizing too that this is the first time we've ever been *this* close. No distance. No stage lights. No years between us. And definitely no panties.

Just skin and delicious heat.

I move first. A slow roll of my hips, tentative, testing the friction between us. The warmth there is dizzying, the sensation sending a shiver all the way up my spine.

Evie gasps.

"*Kaia—*"

Her voice breaks on my name, and I grab her hip to steady us as we start moving together. The slick heat between us makes every glide slow and dragging and impossibly good.

My thoughts start dissolving almost immediately.

My lips part. My breathing turns ragged.

The sounds in the room are wet and desperate—skin sliding against skin, our uneven breaths, the little whimpers I can't quite hold back.

Sweat gathers in the hollow of Evie's throat, lewdly sliding slowly between her breasts.

Fuck.

I grind down harder.

Evie meets me thrust for thrust, hips lifting, chasing the pressure the same way I am. The tension in my stomach tightens with every desperate movement. I shift slightly, just enough that my clit presses directly against hers.

We both cry out at the same time.

"Right there," Evie gasps, gripping my hips. "Don't stop."

I dig my nails into her hip.

I have absolutely no intention of stopping.

Our pace picks up, desperate now, chasing the building pressure that's swallowing every other thought.

My head falls back. "I'm so close."

The rhythm turns sloppy, frantic. And then the tension snaps.

The release hits like a sudden burst of light—sharp and bright and impossible to hold back. Somewhere in the blur of it I feel

Evie's body tense beneath me too, her breath catching as she shudders through her own wave of release.

For a few seconds the world disappears.

When it returns, we're still tangled together—breathing hard, foreheads nearly touching, both of us a little stunned by what just happened. And by the quiet realization that we're not pretending anymore.

For a few seconds neither of us moves. Our bodies are still pressed together, breaths uneven, hearts pounding hard enough that I can feel Evie's through the place where our chests touch.

Then the tension drains out of both of us at once.

I collapse forward with a quiet laugh, my forehead falling against her shoulder. Evie exhales beneath me, one arm sliding instinctively around my back as if catching me there.

"Wow," she murmurs, voice hoarse.

"Yeah," I breathe, the word muffled against her skin.

We're tangled in sheets and limbs, the room warm and dim, the air carrying the soft salt smell of sweat and the lingering electricity of everything that just happened.

I roll onto my side beside her, pulling her with me. The mattress dips as we settle together, legs still loosely tangled.

For a moment we just look at each other.

Evie's hair is a mess across the pillow. Her lips are swollen from kissing, and there's still color high in her cheeks that makes something warm bloom in my chest.

God, she's beautiful.

She notices the way I'm staring and lets out a small, real laugh. "What?"

There it is. The match in the dark room.

It's quieter now. Softer than I remember...

Still enough to light everything up anyway.

"Nothing," I say softly.

I reach out and tuck a piece of hair behind her ear. My fingers linger there, brushing the line of her jaw.

"I missed you," I say quietly.

Evie's expression shifts. "I missed you too."

The silence that follows isn't uncomfortable. It's soft, almost fragile, like we're both aware we're standing in the middle of something new and trying not to scare it away.

Evie pulls the blanket up over us, then tugs me closer until my head rests against her chest. Her hand slips into my hair automatically, fingers combing through it. The rhythm of it makes my eyes heavy almost immediately.

"Kaia," she murmurs after a moment.

"Mm?"

"You okay?"

I smile against her skin.

"More than okay."

Another quiet stretch of time passes. I can hear the slow steady beat of her heart beneath my ear, feel the rise and fall of her breathing.

The words come out again before I can reign them in. "I love you."

Evie's hand stills for just a second in my hair. Silent in return. For a moment, an old instinct flares up, a mix of panic and pride, the one that used to make me reach for the nearest exit when something mattered too much.

But Evie doesn't pull away. Her arm tightens around me and pulls me closer.

And that's enough.

Maybe it has to be enough, after the way I turned wanting her into something I swallowed down until it was just ache. I don't get to demand words from her when I spent years offering her none. I don't get to rush her into softness when I taught her that softness with me could be punished...

So I stay. I breathe with her. I listen to her heart like it's a metronome recalibrating my whole body.

There are so many versions of love I used to believe in, but this is the one that feels like truth: Her chin on my head. Her hand in my hair. The quiet weight of her choosing to hold me when she could have let me go.

If she never says it back, I'll still know what this is.

If it takes her weeks, months, years—if she needs to build the word from scratch because I smashed the old one—I can wait.

Evie is not a crowd I can move with a hook and a bridge.

She's a person who learned how to survive after I broke both our hearts.

And now she's letting me be here anyway.

My throat tightens with gratitude so deep it hurts. I press my mouth to her shoulder again, one soft kiss, a vow I don't say out loud.

I'm here.

I'm *staying*.

And I'm going to earn every quiet second she gives me.

The room grows quieter.

Our breathing evens out. The warmth between us sinks deeper into the mattress, into the soft tangle of blankets and limbs. Evie's thumb traces absent shapes against my shoulder as sleep begins to creep in around the edges of my thoughts.

The last thing I register is the way she presses a gentle kiss into my hair.

And how she doesn't let go of me when we both drift off.

I WAKE UP WARM.

Which is not normal for me.

My room is usually cold in the morning because the house is old and the ocean air finds every crack. My bed is usually mine alone, with one pillow stolen by Grandma at some point and never returned. My mornings are usually a checklist: meds, coffee, diner, survive.

This morning I wake up warm because there's a body pressed against mine and an arm draped over my waist like it belongs there.

My eyes crack open.

Kaia's hair is everywhere—dark strands across my collarbone, across the pillow, across my mouth. Her face is tucked into the space between my shoulder and my neck, breathing slow and soft.

For one dangerous second, my brain tries to pretend. It tries to rewrite the world into something simple.

We got our almost. We got our kiss. We got our—

My chest tightens.

Because this is not simple.

Because sex does not fix the way she left.

Because the festival is today.

Because demons don't care about afterglow.

Because Kaia is still going to leave eventually and I am still the girl standing on the pier watching her disappear.

My throat closes hard enough it wakes me more fully.

Kaia shifts. Her arm tightens around me, instinctive. Her mouth brushes my skin in a half-asleep kiss that makes my stomach flip despite myself.

"Mm," she murmurs, voice thick with sleep. "*Evie.*"

The way she says my name sends shivers down my spine. I squirm a little and she notices. Kaia's laugh is quiet, warm. She lifts her head just enough to blink at me, eyes soft and puffy and so unguarded it feels unfair.

"Good morning," she says.

I should be mean. I should be cold. I should roll out of bed and pretend last night was a hallucination induced by salt air and unresolved trauma.

Instead I say, "Morning," like I'm normal.

Kaia smiles like I just handed her a gift.

Not the stage smile. Not the interview smile. Not the careful, polite one she's been wearing around me like armor.

This one hits different.

It spreads like she can't keep it contained. Like it starts in her chest and climbs up into her eyes and takes over her entire face.

You smile with your whole face, I hear my own teenage voice in my head, smug and affectionate. *Not just your mouth.*

This is the first real smile I've seen in years. Which is insane, considering I've seen her face everywhere—posters, billboards, screens in the diner, commercials, fan-cams—Kaia Rhee turned into a product the world consumes for fun.

But none of those versions of her ever looked like *this.*

None of them ever looked like *Kaia.*

And suddenly, she feels real in a way that makes my chest go tight. Like if I blink too hard, she'll turn back into pixels.

Kaia pushes up onto her elbow, hair sliding over her shoulder in a dark curtain. The sheet slips down her arm. I look away on instinct, then immediately resent myself for it because I spent half the night with my mouth on her and now I'm acting shy.

Kaia catches my reaction anyway.

Her smile turns fond and soft in a way that feels illegal on her face. "You're gorgeous, Evie..."

My cheeks heat. "Stop looking at me like that."

"Like what?"

"Like you're—" I gesture vaguely, furious at words. "Happy."

Kaia's smile deepens. "I am."

That should make me feel warm.

It makes me nervous.

Kaia shifts a little closer, and when her eyes catch mine, something flashes in them—deep, vivid purple, like a bruise made of light.

Just for a second.

Then it's gone.

My hand moves before I can overthink it. I reach up and cup her face. Kaia leans into my palm like she's been waiting for permission.

And then she notices the way I'm staring—not at her mouth, not at the sheet, not at the obvious.

At her eyes.

Kaia blinks. "What?"

"Your eyes. They just did that thing where they glow. The 'Halo Glint'. I thought that was... reflective contacts and stage lights though?"

Kaia's expression goes blank for half a heartbeat, like she's scanning her mental list of *which lies do we tell civilians.*

"I saw it last night too," I add quickly. "A few times, while we were...'"

Kaia exhales, slow, and something in her shoulders eases like she's choosing truth with me instead of the script. "It's resonance. Magic. When we draw our weapons, our whole nervous system becomes the conduit. For a second, it... bleeds to the surface. Eyes, throat, palms. The glamour seals after, but there's a moment where the aura leaks..."

"So the purple isn't contacts," I say, stupidly, because my brain wants something simple.

Kaia's gaze holds mine. "No."

Something in my chest twists. "So the world literally sees you light up."

Kaia gives a short laugh. "For a second."

"And everyone just... buys that it's an effect?" I ask.

Kaia's voice goes smooth automatically, like she can't help it. "The Halo Glint. Signature contacts plus lighting cues. Sometimes AR overlays for the screens."

I stare at her.

She winces. "Sorry. That's the—" She clears her throat. "That's the cover."

"Uh-huh," I say flatly. "And if your eyes do it longer than a second?"

Kaia's expression tightens. "Then something's wrong," she admits. "Wards failing. Injury. Something pushing in."

"And last night? ...Now?"

Kaia's throat works. She looks at my hand still holding her face, and something tender flickers there, like she's trying to be careful with honesty.

"Last night was... a lot," she says. Her eyes lift back to mine. "And now—" she hesitates, then admits, "now it's just emotion. The glamour isn't built for... this. Not for being human. Not for feeling this much."

I hold her gaze for a beat, then—because I'm me—I mutter, "Hmm."

Kaia's brow lifts. "What?"

"They're pretty," I say, like it's a fact I'm annoyed about. "It's inconvenient."

Kaia laughs again, then shifts closer, pressing her weight into me. Her knee slides between my legs under the sheet and my brain short-circuits like it forgot it has a job besides panicking.

She kisses the corner of my mouth. "I missed you."

I go still. It hits too hard because it's honest and because I missed her too and I hate that.

My voice comes out rough. "I missed you too, Kaia..."

Kaia's whole face changes. Relief, grief, hunger—everything flickers through her like she can't decide what to do with being wanted.

She leans in and kisses me slowly, then nuzzles at my cheek, my jaw.

I don't really move. Not because I don't want her. But because my body is still catching up to the fact that wanting her doesn't automatically mean I'm about to be left.

Kaia notices immediately. Of course she does. She pulls back, just enough to see my face. Her gaze studies me like she's reading for fracture lines.

"Are you okay?" she asks quietly.

I laugh once, dry. "Define okay."

Kaia's mouth twists. "Fair."

Silence stretches. I can hear traffic outside, faint. The town already waking into festival day. The distant echo of someone testing speakers down near the pier—one bass note that vibrates the air like a heartbeat.

My wrist tingles faintly under the skin.

Reminder.

Rules.

Consequences.

Kaia notices my stare and shifts, propping her chin on her hand. "You're the one overthinking now."

"Unfortunately," I repeat.

Kaia's smile softens again. "Evie."

"What?"

She takes a slow breath like she's about to step onto a stage without armor.

Then she says, quietly, "Do you... forgive me?"

The words land like a dropped plate. My stomach twists.

That's the question, isn't it? The one I've been avoiding. The one I've been punishing her with instead of answering.

Kaia's eyes are wide and scared in a way I almost never see, like she can fight demons but not my silence.

I stare at her.

My brain flashes through everything at once: the pier, the kiss, the fight, the way she left, the way she came back with blood on her face, the way she stood in front of me like a shield in a hallway full of suits.

Sex did not fix our shit.

But it did strip away some of the distance I've been using as a weapon.

It did make me look at her like a person again.

And that is... terrifying.

I exhale slowly, and the truth comes out in pieces.

"I forgive you," I say, and the words hurt on the way out, like pulling a thorn from skin that's grown around it. "I do."

Kaia's whole face changes. Shock first. Then something like relief that she doesn't trust. I lift a hand before she can speak, because I can already feel her hope trying to make this into a miracle.

"But it still hurts," I add, voice rough. "It's not... magic. It's not like you say sorry and my chest stops hurting."

Kaia's expression tightens with pain. "Okay."

"And I'm not pretending it didn't happen," I continue, because if I don't say it plainly I'll backslide into anger again. "I'm not pretending you didn't leave. I'm not pretending you didn't say what you said."

Kaia flinches, guilt flickering over her face.

"But," I say, because there's still a but and I hate that there's a but, "I understand more than I did."

Her eyes flick up. Hope flashes—dangerous.

I glare at her reflexively. "Don't look at me like that."

"I'm sorry," she says immediately, but she's smiling now, like she can't help it.

I roll my eyes. "You were scared," I say, and it tastes bitter in my mouth. "And you were under pressure. And you were... young. We were both young."

Kaia's throat bobs. "Yeah."

"That doesn't excuse it," I snap, because I need that line to exist. "But it explains it."

Kaia nods quickly. "Yes."

I stare at the ceiling again because eye contact is too much. "And I—" My voice catches. I clear my throat and try again. "I'm sorry for... punishing you so much."

Kaia goes very still. Her breath hitches, and my own chest tightens because I can't believe I said that out loud.

"I had a right to be angry," I add quickly, defensive.

"You did," Kaia says, voice rough.

"I still do," I warn.

Kaia nods once, solemn. "Yeah."

I swallow. "But I've been... using it. Like a knife. Because if I keep you bleeding, I don't have to feel—" I cut myself off, jaw clenched.

Feel what?

Love?

Loss?

The fact that I never stopped wanting her?

"I just can't—" I say, voice rough. "I *can't* keep being the last to know. I can't keep finding out the important stuff from someone else, after the fact, like I'm—" I shake my head hard, angry at the sting in my eyes.

Kaia's breath catches. "Evie..."

"No," I cut in, sharp. "I'm serious. You can't decide what I can handle and what I can't. You can't do the 'I was protecting you' thing and leave me blind."

Kaia nods immediately, like she'll take any punishment I hand her if it keeps me talking. "Okay," she says, voice steady even though worry shadows her eyes. "You're right."

I blink at the lack of defense. It throws me off more than an excuse would.

Kaia continues, softer. "I won't do that again. I won't let you be the last to know. Not about anything that impacts you." Her throat works. "I promise."

The word *promise* should make me flinch. It doesn't. Not this time.

I let out a shaky breath through my nose. "Good."

Kaia's hand slides up my arm slowly, asking without words. She pauses. I don't pull away. So she cups my shoulder gently, thumb rubbing small circles like she's grounding me.

Her voice is soft. "Thank you."

I scoff. "Don't make this weird."

Kaia's smile turns more real. "You made it weird by being emotionally responsible."

"Shut up."

Kaia laughs—quiet, delighted—and leans in to kiss my jawline. The kiss is slow and warm and makes my skin buzz.

I hate that it works.

"Stop," I mutter, but there's no bite in it.

Kaia kisses my jaw again. "No."

"Kaia—"

She kisses the corner of my mouth. "*Evie*."

I try to hold onto my annoyance. I do.

But then she kisses me properly and my brain gives up.

Her mouth is warm. She tastes like toothpaste and sleep and last night. Her hair falls around us like a curtain, shutting out the room.

I kiss her back, harder, and she makes a soft noise that goes straight through me.

Kaia's laugh breaks against my mouth. "You're so mean."

"I'm not mean," I whisper, breathless.

"You are. Mean and secretly bossy," she murmurs, and the fondness in her voice makes my chest ache again.

"Stop saying that," I say, but I'm smiling. I hate that I'm smiling.

Kaia shifts and swings a leg over me, straddling my hips with casual confidence like she belongs here. The sheet tangles around her thighs. Her hair falls forward, dark and soft, framing her face like she's a painting someone forgot to finish.

She looks down at me, eyes bright, and for a second she looks… happy.

Not billboard happy.

Real happy.

My heart pounds. Kaia leans down and kisses me again, slow and deep, and my hands slide up her back under the sheet, fingers shaking.

We giggle like idiots between kisses, breathless and ridiculous, like the world isn't a disaster waiting outside the curtains.

Kaia whispers against my mouth, "I—"

Her phone buzzes.

We both freeze like teenagers who just heard a parent's footsteps in the hallway.

Kaia groans into my shoulder. "Oh my god."

I lift my head, blinking. "Is that—"

"Blaire," Kaia says, already half-laughing, but half-panicked.

The phone buzzes again, insistent.

Kaia exhales. "I should get that. Blaire is going to be so mad."

"Good," I say. "Tell her I'm mad too."

Kaia laughs, then kisses me once—quick and desperate, like she's trying to steal one more second.

Then she rolls off me reluctantly and scrambles for the sheet like she's suddenly remembered she's a public figure and not just a girl in my hands.

I sit up, hair a mess, heart pounding, and the cold air hits my skin like reality.

Kaia perches on the edge of the bed, sheet at her waist, phone in hand. Her shoulders tense as she types, thumbs moving fast like she's putting on armor made of words. It's crazy how quickly she switches. How easily her body remembers to be careful.

Something in my chest twists. I slide closer behind her without thinking and wrap my arms around her middle, pressing my cheek to her shoulder blade.

Kaia goes still, then melts into me.

She smells like soap and salt and the faint metallic heat of magic that hasn't fully cooled. Under that, she smells like herself, warm and familiar, the kind of scent my brain files under *home* even though I'm furious about it.

Her back is solid under my cheek. Real. Alive. I bury my face into her shoulder and inhale like I can anchor myself there.

Kaia's voice comes out soft. "Evie..."

"Shush," I mumble into her skin, because if she says anything tender I'm going to combust.

Kaia makes a quiet sound that might be a laugh.

I don't know why the next words come out of me. They just... do. Like my brain is still living in last night.

"Do you want to stay for pancakes?" I ask, muffled against her shoulder. "If you have time."

Kaia turns fully, like I just offered her oxygen.

"You're serious?" she whispers.

I pull back enough to glare at her, because I hate how exposed I feel. "It's... just pancakes."

Kaia's eyes shine. "I want to stay."

My chest does something stupid.

"But," Kaia adds quickly, holding up her phone like it's a weapon pointed at her, "I have to—"

"I know," I say, and it comes out gentler than I mean. "Do your little manager obedience ritual."

Kaia laughs, breathless. "Okay."

She takes a steadying breath and hits call.

I hear the ring. Then Blaire's voice, sharp even through the tiny speaker. "Kaia."

Kaia winces. "Hi."

"Do you have any idea what you just did?" Blaire snaps. No preamble. No soft entry. Pure manager fury. "You *disappeared.* You don't vanish on festival day. You don't go dark without comms. You don't make me hunt you like you're a missing teenager."

Kaia squeezes her eyes shut. "I know."

"I'm not joking," Blaire continues, voice tight with controlled panic. "If something happens and I can't account for you, I can't protect you. I can't protect the group. I can't protect the entire—" she cuts herself off, inhales hard, then comes back colder. "Irresponsible. I expected better from you."

Kaia's throat works. "I'm sorry."

"Are you safe?" Blaire demands, suddenly all business. "Right now. Answer me."

Kaia's voice steadies. "Yes. I'm safe."

A beat. Blaire's tone shifts, still irritated, but focused. "Where are you?"

Kaia hesitates for a fraction of a second.

Then she says it anyway, like she's jumping. "At Evie's."

Silence on the line. I can practically hear Blaire pinching the bridge of her nose.

"Of course you are," Blaire says finally, with the exhausted fury of someone who has lost a bet to the universe. "Kaia. We have press in three hours."

"I know," Kaia says, voice steady now. "I'll be there."

"Then why are you calling me," Blaire says flatly, "instead of getting your ass back to the hotel?"

Kaia's cheeks color. She clears her throat. "Because... Evie asked if I wanted pancakes."

I stare at her, horrified. "*Oh my god,*" I hiss, because I did not expect her to say it out loud like that.

Kaia keeps going anyway, gaze locked on the wall like she's bracing for impact. "And I want to stay. For a little bit."

Blaire makes a sound that is not a word. It's the sound of a person watching their schedule burst into flames.

Blaire exhales long and slow. "You're unbelievable."

Kaia's voice softens. "Please."

Another beat.

Then Blaire says, clipped, "You have forty-five minutes."

Kaia's face lights up so fast it's almost funny. "Thank you, Blaire!"

"Forty-five," Blaire repeats. "And you are not walking any-where alone. I'm sending a car. It will be waiting outside for you."

Kaia nods quickly. "Understood. Thank you."

She hangs up and turns toward me like she can't believe she got away with it.

I'm still staring, stunned.

"You told her about pancakes," I say, aghast.

Kaia's grin widens. "I did."

I drag a hand down my face. "You're insane."

Kaia leans in, kisses my cheek, and murmurs, smug, "You asked."

My stomach flips in a way that makes me furious.

"Okay," I say, voice too brisk, because if I let myself get soft I'll cry. "Then get dressed."

Kaia laughs. "Okay."

I throw a pillow at her.

She catches it easily, still smiling, and starts pulling on her clothes with quick, practiced movements. I do the same, yanking on a t-shirt and shorts and shoving my hair into a messy knot, even though bringing Kaia Rhee to breakfast feels like committing a crime.

Like the past didn't break both of us.

Like pancakes can hold the shape of something new.

Gran is awake when I get to her room, which is either good timing or the universe setting me up for maximum emotional damage. She's sitting on the edge of the bed in her robe, hair still pinned from yesterday, staring at her hands like she's trying to remember what they're for.

"Hey," I say softly. "Morning."

She looks up. Her eyes clear for a second, enough recognition to make my throat tighten.

"Morning," she echoes.

"I'm making pancakes," I tell her, practical on purpose. "Come sit at the table."

Her face brightens immediately, the way it does when food is involved and the world stops being confusing.

"Pancakes," she repeats, delighted. Then she frowns. "Do we have syrup?"

"We have syrup," I say. "We have enough syrup to kill a small animal."

She laughs—real laughter, thin but genuine. I help her into her slippers and guide her down the hall with a hand at her elbow.

The kitchen smells like coffee and batter and the faint sweetness of the syrup bottle I already set out. Normal smells. Safe smells.

Kaia is in the kitchen already, hoodie on, hair tamed, sitting at the table like she's trying to take up as little space as possible. She looks up the moment she hears us. Her expression is so open it makes my chest ache, like she's bracing to be thrown out but hoping she won't be anyway.

Gran sees her and stops dead in the doorway.

For a terrifying second, I think she won't know. That she'll look right through Kaia like she's just another stranger.

Then Gran's whole face changes.

"Oh!" she says, bright as morning. "There you are!"

Kaia goes still. "Hi," she says softly.

Gran strides forward with the confidence of a woman who, in her mind, is still in full command of the world. She stops in front of Kaia like she's inspecting her.

"You're late for pancakes," Gran informs her.

Kaia's mouth opens, startled. She glances at me like she doesn't know whether to laugh or cry.

"I'm sorry," Kaia says, voice gentle. "I got... held up."

Yeah, held up for years. I bite my tongue.

Gran hums, satisfied, like this is a normal excuse. Then she reaches out and pats Kaia's cheek.

My stomach flips.

Kaia's eyes close for a split second like she's absorbing the touch.

"You look tired," Gran says, matter-of-fact. "You been singing again?"

Kaia swallows. "Yes, ma'am."

Gran nods firmly. "Good. Use your gift. But you still have to make time to eat."

"My mom used to say that," Kaia adds, quieter, like it slips out before she can stop it. "When I came home hoarse, she'd make kimchi jeon and tell me it would scare bad spirits away."

Gran beams, delighted. "Pancakes that fight ghosts," she declares, as if this is the most sensible thing anyone's said all morning.

Kaia's smile flickers. "Exactly."

I turn back to the stove before my face can betray me. Batter into the pan. Bubbles forming. Flip.

My hands know what to do even when my heart doesn't.

Behind me, Gran keeps talking.

"You still like blueberries?" she asks Kaia.

Kaia's voice is careful. "Yes."

"Evie never puts enough in," Gran complains, like I'm not standing three feet away. "Stingy."

"I can hear you," I call, and my voice comes out rougher than I mean.

Gran waves a hand dismissively. "You can hear lots of things. Doesn't mean you listen."

Kaia huffs a quiet laugh—soft, delighted—and the sound hits me like a memory.

For a second, it really is like old times. Not perfect. Not healed. But... familiar.

I slide a plate in front of Gran first.

"Gran," I say gently, "that's yours."

She looks up, confused. "Oh."

Then she pushes the plate toward Kaia anyway. "Eat," she orders.

Kaia's eyes flick to mine. I nod once, because what am I going to do—argue with the tide? Kaia takes the plate like it's a sacred object.

"Thank you," she says softly.

Gran beams like she's solved something important. "There. Better."

I set another plate down in front of Gran and then a third in front of myself.

We eat.

It's quiet at first, though I keep catching Kaia's eyes and can't help but smile softly.

Gran breaks it by pointing her fork at Kaia. "You gonna sing at the festival?"

Kaia's posture tightens. "Tonight," she says carefully. "Yes."

Gran nods, pleased. "Good. Evie likes it."

I almost choke on my coffee.

"Gran," I say, warning.

Grandma looks at me like I'm being ridiculous. "You do," she insists. "You always did. You used to yell from the crowd like a seagull."

Kaia's mouth twitches. Her gaze drops to her plate like she's trying not to look directly at me and explode.

My face burns.

"I did not yell like a seagull," I mutter.

Kaia's voice is quiet, amused. "You did."

I shoot her a look that says *don't you start too.*

Kaia's eyes soften anyway, and for half a second the air between us goes warm and dangerous.

Gran watches us with vague satisfaction like she can sense something right even if she can't name it.

Then her attention drifts. Her gaze slides to the window, to the fog outside.

"Your mother's coming?" she asks suddenly.

My stomach drops.

"No," I say quickly. "No, Gran. It's just us."

She frowns, upset. "She said she'd come."

Gran has been doing this more lately—waiting for my mom the way you wait for a bus that stopped running years ago. My mom has been dead since I was little, long enough that the grief should've settled into something quiet and manageable. Gran raised me alone after that. She held the whole world up with her hands.

And now her brain keeps reaching for the easiest, safest story it can find: *She's coming home. She'll walk through the door. Everything will make sense again.*

Like loss is something you can undo with a knock on the porch.

Kaia's hand stills on her fork.

I force my voice gentle. "She's not coming today."

Gran's face tightens, confused and angry, emotion rising without a place to land. "Liar," she says, and it's not even aimed. It's just a word her fear picks.

I reach out and cover her hand with mine. "Hey," I say softly. "Hey. You're okay."

Her breathing quickens. Her eyes dart, searching for something she can trust.

Kaia moves without thinking.

She reaches out too—slow, careful—and places her hand lightly on Gran's other wrist, like she's offering steadiness without demanding anything.

Gran looks at her.

Kaia's voice is gentle. "It's okay," she says, like she's said it onstage to crowds and in quiet rooms to herself. "You're safe. You're home."

Gran's shoulders loosen a fraction. She blinks, then her eyes soften, and she pats Kaia's hand like she's grateful but doesn't know why.

"Good girl," Gran murmurs.

Kaia's throat works.

I have to look away.

I scrape my chair back and go to the sink under the excuse of rinsing a plate, because my eyes sting and I'm not giving either of them that.

When I turn back, Gran is humming again, calmer, eating syrup-soaked bites like the moment of fear never happened.

Kaia sits very still, like she's holding herself together by force.

I slide back into my chair and keep my voice casual because it's the only thing I can do.

"More coffee?" I ask.

Kaia nods. "Please."

Gran points her fork at me again. "Don't be stingy."

"Yes, ma'am," I mutter.

For a few minutes, it is almost normal.

Then there's a soft knock at the front door. Three knocks. Controlled. Polite. Kaia's whole body tenses.

She glances toward the hallway. "That'll be—"

"Your people," I say flatly.

Kaia winces. "Technically Blaire's people."

We both stand at the same time like we're being pulled by the same invisible string. Kaia wipes her hands on her jeans—pointless, nervous—then turns toward the kitchen doorway.

"Grandma Calder," she says, gentle, the way you speak to someone you actually respect. "It was really nice to see you again."

Gran looks up from her plate, syrup on her fork, pleased as a queen. "You ate," she says, approving. "Good."

Kaia smiles, soft and real. "Yes, ma'am."

"And you come back," Gran adds, like she's issuing a schedule. "Next weekend. Pancakes."

Kaia's voice catches just slightly. "Okay," she says. "I'll... try."

Gran nods, satisfied. "Good girl."

Kaia's eyes flick to me—quick, private—then she steps toward the front. I follow her to the door and open it.

Fog beads on the porch railing. The streetlight makes everything look softer than it is. A black SUV idles at the curb, engine whispering, windows tinted like secrets.

Jules and Remy stand nearby pretending to be casual civilians even though I'm pretty sure Jules is physically incapable of casual.

Jules lifts a hand. "Hi," she whispers too loudly. "Sorry to interrupt domestic bliss."

Kaia steps onto the porch. "What are you two doing here?"

Jules' grin goes wider. "Oh, I wasn't about to miss *this*." She jerks her thumb at Remy. "And she's only here because Blaire made her come with me."

Remy rolls her eyes like it physically pains her to be associated with Jules in daylight. "I'm here because you can't be trusted to stand near a sidewalk without causing a scene."

Jules gasps. "I can be trusted. I'm a professional."

"Professional menace," Remy replies, deadpan.

I glance at Kaia and see she's already got her hoodie zipped, hair tucked back, shoulders set—moving like she's putting the mask on.

Like the girl at my table is already being folded up and packed away.

Gran calls from the kitchen, cheerful. "Tell the singing girl to take leftovers!"

Kaia's face softens so fast it almost breaks me.

"I will," I call back.

Then she looks at me. Just me.

Kaia's voice drops. "Can I... text you later?"

My pulse kicks, stupidly.

She swallows. "Is your number still the same?"

For a second I just stare at her, because it's such a small question and it holds so much history I can taste it.

Then I nod once. "Yeah," I say, rough. "It's the same."

Relief flashes across her face—quick, bright, almost painful.

"Okay," she whispers, like she's anchoring it. Like she's afraid if she says it too loudly the world will steal it. "Okay."

She steps onto the porch, and I follow her out automatically, like my body refuses to let her leave without watching it happen.

The fog is colder now. The world feels too awake.

Kaia stops at the bottom step and turns back.

"I'll text you."

I nod once. "Okay."

Kaia's gaze lingers, like she wants to kiss me, like she's choosing not to because Jules is five feet away vibrating with curiosity.

Instead she reaches out and squeezes my hand once—quick, private.

Then she lets go.

She walks toward the SUV.

Jules opens the back door with exaggerated politeness, like she's chauffeuring royalty. "M'lady."

Kaia flips her off without looking, and Jules cackles. Remy's gaze flicks to me, unreadable, then she gives me the smallest nod—acknowledgment, not pity.

Kaia slides into the car. The door shuts with a soft, final thunk.

The SUV pulls away, taillights blurring into fog.

I stand on the porch in my pajama shorts and old hoodie like an idiot, watching it go until the street is empty again.

Behind me, Gran calls, "Evie! More pancakes!"

I swallow hard, turn back toward the warmth of the kitchen, and tell myself I'm fine.

Because the alternative is admitting that for a few minutes at my table, my life looked like a version of itself that never got the chance to happen.

And then it drove away.

I spend festival day pretending I'm fine at a professional level.

Really, I'm one breeze away from snapping in half.

Harbor's Edge looks like it's been dipped in glitter and set on fire. Lanterns everywhere. Booths packed tight. The boardwalk is a river of bodies and sugar and noise. Kids with glowing wands. Tourists with tote bags. Locals acting like they aren't impressed by the crowds while absolutely being impressed by the crowds.

And everywhere I turn, I catch pieces of Kaia like my brain is a magnet and she's the metal.

A flash of her hair on a stage monitor.

A soundcheck note that makes the air feel like it's bracing.

A poster. A banner. A giant LED screen looping promo footage where she smiles like she wasn't just in my bed last night, eating pancakes with me and Gran this morning.

I tell myself: Don't look. My eyes do it anyway.

I'm not working today. So today I do the festival the way I used to. I do it with Grandma.

She insists on lipstick because she's apparently decided Harbor Lights is a formal occasion. I help her into her cardigan, fix her hair, and take her down the street at a pace that makes the town blur by like a movie set.

She keeps stopping to admire things like they're miracles.

"Look at those lanterns," she says, delighted. "They're bigger this year."

"Because corporate sponsorship," I mutter.

Grandma pats my arm. "Because people still try."

I don't answer that.

We pass the main stage at the far end of the grounds and the crowd thickens like the air itself wants to lean closer. It's different than past Harbor Lights. There are more security barriers, and the big speaker towers have decorative wraps.

There's a rehearsal happening.

Not full concert, just camera blocking and press clips. But the stage lights are up, and the LED screens are live, and my stomach flips when I see her.

Kaia stands center, perfect posture, hair swept back like the wind knows better than to touch her without permission.

Matching outfits on all four girls—dark, sharp, glittering in a way that reads like armor pretending to be fashion.

Jules is laughing at something off-camera, bouncing on her toes like she's made of electricity. Mina stands close to Kaia with that gentle intensity she has, listening like she's catching echoes no one else hears. Remy looks almost bored.

Kaia turns her head—

And for half a heartbeat, her eyes are on the crowd, searching.

I duck behind a man holding a funnel cake the size of his head like I'm in an action movie and not a grown woman hiding behind fried dough.

Grandma squints up at the stage. "Is that the Rhee girl?"

I force my voice into neutral. "Yeah."

"She looks successful," Grandma says, pleased.

"Mm," I manage.

Kaia laughs onstage at something, bright and practiced. The sound goes through me anyway.

My wrist warms faintly, like the binding knows I'm looking.

Or maybe it's just my pulse.

We move on. I steer Grandma toward the calmer booths, toward the places where the noise isn't so sharp it feels like it's scraping my nerves. But even when we're buying candied nuts, even when Grandma is arguing with a vendor about the price of kettle corn like it's a moral issue, I keep catching Kaia in pieces.

A clip on a TV in a booth.

Her voice drifting over the festival speakers during a "local pride" promo.

A press photographer's camera shutter snapping rapid-fire as she steps offstage briefly, surrounded by handlers and security.

Every time I think our eyes might meet across the crowd, something interrupts.

A fan screams.

A security guard shifts.

A camera swings.

A child runs between us.

It's like the universe keeps slamming doors in my face and laughing.

By mid-afternoon, Grandma gets tired. Her energy burns bright and then drops all at once, like a lantern running out of oil.

I bring her home, settle her in her chair, make sure she takes her meds, and she pats my hand with a look that's too knowing.

"Go," she says.

"Go where?" I ask, already tense.

She smiles. "Go be young."

"I'm not—"

"Evie," she says, and it's the tone that has ended wars in this house.

I exhale through my nose. "Fine."

I leave the house with my hoodie up and my hands shoved in my pockets like I'm trying to disguise the fact that I don't know what to do with myself when I'm not responsible for someone else.

The festival hums louder now, closer to evening. The lantern frames overhead are ready. The scent of the ocean mixes with fried sugar and smoke and sweat. A radio somewhere plays the Harbor Lights jingle and my skin prickles again, that wrong familiarity skittering under my ribs.

Come back, come back—

People sing along without thinking.

I hate them for it.

I hate the song more.

At least after tonight the town will be safe again. No more demons.

I'm passing the games when someone catches my sleeve.

I whip around, ready to bite—

And it's *Kaia*.

Kaia herself, hood up, cap low, sunglasses on like she thinks she can cosplay as a normal person and fool the universe.

Security hovers a few steps back, pretending to be tourists. One guy is holding a corn dog with the rigid seriousness of a man who has been told *do not look like security*.

Kaia's fingers let go of my sleeve instantly.

Her voice is low. "Hi."

My heart slams so hard it feels like it rattles my ribs.

I force my face into something unimpressed. "Do you usually grab civilians in public now or am I just special?"

Kaia's mouth twitches. "Just you."

Those words should not make my stomach do *that*.

Behind her, the security guy with the corn dog shifts, eyes flicking around the crowd. People drift past us in a glittery blur, laughing, shouting, eating, living.

Kaia keeps her focus on me like the whole festival is background noise.

"I'm allowed a small break," she says, like she's reciting a permission slip. "'Controlled morale window.' Blaire's words. Not mine."

"Sounds... romantic," I say.

Kaia's eyes soften. "It's the best I can do."

My wrist warms faintly under the skin. Like it's annoyed I'm still near her.

I ignore it.

Kaia clears her throat. "Do you want to ride the Ferris wheel with me?"

I blink. "What? Really?"

She repeats it. "Yes, really, do you want to ride with me?"

I stare at her, trying to figure out if this is a joke or a trap or some elaborate PR thing that's going to end with my face on a fan account captioned *KAIA RHEE WITH MYSTERY GIRL??*

Kaia reads my expression and says quickly, "No cameras. Security can stand by the gate. Blaire bribed the operator to pause one cycle for... light testing."

"Light testing," I repeat.

Kaia nods, solemn. "Very serious."

A laugh almost escapes me. I clamp down on it like it's contraband. Kaia's gaze holds mine, steady, and her hand reaches out, fingers brushing mine.

"Evie... please?"

The word *please* does something unfair to me.

I cross my arms. "You're asking me on a Ferris wheel date during a demon festival."

Kaia's mouth twists. "When you say it like that, it sounds bad."

"It *is* bad," I say, but my voice is already softer and a smile tugs on my lips.

Kaia leans in a fraction, lowering her voice further. "I keep losing you in crowds."

My throat tightens.

Kaia keeps going, quiet and blunt. "And I don't want to."

I stare at her, angry at the ache rising in my chest.

Then, I glance at the Ferris wheel. It turns slowly, lights blinking, enclosed cars swinging gently in the wind. People inside laugh and press their faces to the glass.

A normal thing.

A small-town thing.

A thing Kaia and I used to do with cheap tickets and sweaty hands and stupid hopes.

My chest aches with something I don't want to name.

Then I sigh, like I'm giving in to gravity. "Fine."

Kaia's eyes flash bright. Relief. Hope. That stupid, dangerous warmth.

"Fine?" she repeats, like she needs to hear it again.

"Yes, fine..." I meet her gaze, cheeks warming. "I would like that."

We walk to the Ferris wheel with security trailing at a careful distance, forming an invisible bubble around us. People look, but not the way they'd look if they knew. Kaia keeps her head down. I keep my hands in my pockets.

At the gate, the operator lifts the little chain and waves us through like this is totally normal and not a logistical nightmare for a celebrity.

Kaia waits until I step into the enclosed car first, then follows me inside.

The door shuts with a clunk and the outside noise muffles instantly—festival chaos turned into distant, harmless sound. The car sways as it starts to rise.

Kaia sits beside me, not across. Close enough that our knees brush when the wheel jolts.

I stare out the window because looking at her feels like stepping into a fire.

Harbor's Edge spreads below us in lantern light and glitter. Booths like bright little islands. The main stage in the distance like a mouth waiting to sing.

Kaia's voice is quiet. "This looks like how it used to."

I swallow. "Except for the corporate branding everywhere."

Kaia huffs a small laugh. "Yeah."

The wheel lifts us higher. For a second, it really does feel like the old days—cheap tickets, sweaty hands, Kaia trying to look fearless and failing, me pretending I wasn't nervous about being that high up and lying badly.

I glance at her despite myself. Kaia's eyes are already on me.

"Stop doing that," I mutter.

"Doing what?"

"Looking at me like you're starving," I say, and immediately regret it because Kaia's breath catches.

She smiles, small and honest, then leans closer to me. "Maybe I am."

My pulse trips. Up close, she looks less like the posters. More like the girl who used to laugh too loud on this pier and shove her hands into my pockets because hers were cold.

We reach the top and the wheel pauses. The car rocks gently, suspended above the glowing festival. At the highest point, the festival spreads below us like a constellation. The ocean beyond is black and endless, reflecting faint lights like scattered stars.

Kaia inhales like she's about to say something important.

Instead she says, "Can I kiss you again?"

My heart punches my ribs.

I should say no.

I should say we can't keep doing this. That it's going to hurt. That tomorrow she'll be a poster again and I'll be a girl with a diner job and a wrist-binding and a grandmother who doesn't deserve demon fallout.

But we're in a glass box in the sky, and the world is far below, and my body is already halfway to yes.

So, I nod once, sharp.

Kaia's hand lifts—hesitates—and then she cups my jaw like I'm something fragile.

Her gaze drops to my mouth.

Mine drops to hers.

We hover there for a second, suspended, and it's ridiculous that we're both still scared of each other.

She leans in and kisses me.

It starts gentle, like she's testing whether I'll flinch.

I don't.

I grab the front of her hoodie and pull her closer, and Kaia makes a soft sound against my mouth that goes straight through to my stomach, then lower...

The kiss deepens. Hotter. Hungrier. Like all day's almost-glances finally got their teeth in.

Her thumb brushes my cheekbone like she's memorizing me.

My breath breaks.

"Kaia," I whisper against her mouth, half warning, half plea.

She answers by kissing me again, slower this time, like she's trying to make the moment last.

My hands slide up her shoulders. I feel the tension in her muscles, the way she's holding herself back. My heart pounds so loud it feels like it's shaking the glass.

I pull back just enough to say. "We're in a ferris wheel."

Kaia's eyes are bright, mouth swollen. "I know."

"This is insane."

"People kiss in ferris wheels all the time," she says.

"Well, this is my first time," I say.

"Mine too. But it makes sense…" And then she says, softly, like it's the most dangerous truth in the world, "Because it's you. It's always been you."

My throat tightens so hard it almost hurts.

I swallow. "Don't say things like that."

Kaia's gaze holds mine. "Why not?"

"Because—" I start, then stop. Because the answer is *because I'll believe you.*

Kaia leans in, forehead almost touching mine. "Evie, you're my home."

I laugh once, breathless and sharp. "That's—"

"I know," she cuts in, voice rough. "I know it sounds dramatic. I don't care. It's true." Her eyes meet mine. "Coming back here didn't feel like a homecoming until… you." She swallows. "Until I was sitting at your kitchen table eating pancakes. For the first time since I got back, the word *home* made sense again. *You've always been my home.*"

My chest aches so hard it feels like a bruise.

Kaia kisses me again, like she's trying to put the truth into my mouth so I can't spit it out.

I should stop.

I don't.

I kiss her back, harder, because if I start thinking I'll fall apart.

Kaia shifts closer until I'm pressed into the corner of the seat and she's between my legs, one hand braced on the seat beside my hip like she's holding herself back from doing anything that would scare me.

Her hair falls forward, hiding us from the window for a second like a curtain.

I hate how much it feels like last night all over again.

I hate how much I want it,

For a few minutes, the world is just this enclosed glass box and the taste of her and the hum of the Ferris wheel machinery and the way my heart is trying to break out of my body.

Then Kaia pulls back, breathing hard, and her expression shifts.

My stomach drops. "What?"

Kaia's hand stays on my cheek like she doesn't want to let go even while she says it. "You can't watch the show tonight."

I blink. "Excuse me?"

Kaia's eyes flick toward the stage in the distance, then back to me. "Promise me."

My pulse spikes, not in a good way. "Why?"

Kaia swallows. "Because I'm scared again."

That alone makes my throat tighten.

"Of what?" I demand.

Kaia exhales slowly. "A splinter breaking out again..."

My stomach drops. The diner. The TV glitch. The thing that came for my throat.

I stare at her. "You think it could happen at the festival?"

Kaia's jaw tightens. "I think it *might*. The wards are stronger, but... the Chorus adapts. It learns. And if a piece slips—" She stops, breath shaky. "If it slips into the crowd..."

She doesn't finish.

She doesn't have to.

My wrist warms faintly, like it agrees with her.

I swallow hard. "So you want me... where?"

"Not there," Kaia says, fierce and quiet. "Somewhere safe. Home. With your grandma. Anywhere else."

My throat tightens.

Part of me wants to argue because I hate being told what to do. I hate being managed. And I hate the idea of sitting out while she goes into danger.

But another part of me—smaller, softer, terrified—remembers being pinned under a table while sound tried to drown me... and how close I came to not breathing at all.

I look at her, really look. She's not asking because she wants control. She's asking because she's afraid she'll lose me.

I hate how that makes my heart ache.

I swallow. "And what, you're going to go sing out there like everything is fine?"

"I'm going to go do my job," she says, and there's steel under it now. "And then I'm going to text you the second I can."

My chest tightens. "Promise?"

Kaia nods quickly. "Yes. I swear."

I stare at her, anger and fear and longing all tangled together.

But I also... don't want to die tonight. I don't want Grandma alone. I don't want to be bait in a crowd.

So I swallow hard and say the words anyway...

"Okay," I whisper. "I won't watch. I'll go home."

Kaia's breath breaks.

She cups my face with both hands like she can't help it. "*Promise.*"

"I promise," I say, and it tastes like surrender.

Kaia kisses me hard—relief and fear and love all shoved into my mouth.

When she pulls back, her forehead rests against mine. "After," she whispers. "After... can we meet?"

My heart hurts because the question is *can we steal another piece of time?*

I nod anyway. "Yeah."

Kaia's smile flickers, bright and fragile. "Where?"

I swallow. "Text me. We'll figure it out."

Kaia laughs softly, then sobers. "I will."

The Ferris wheel lurches.

The operator unpauses the cycle. The car starts moving again, carrying us back down toward the noise.

Kaia squeezes my hand once, quick and private, like she's trying to anchor herself.

I squeeze back, even though my chest is already bracing for the moment she steps away and becomes the world's property again.

When the car reaches the platform, Kaia stands first, then turns and offers me her hand like she's a person and not a headline.

I take it.

Because I'm weak.

Because I'm human.

Because when she looks at me like *that*, I remember how it used to feel to be chosen.

Kaia leans in one last time, mouth close to my ear, voice barely there over the festival noise.

"Don't watch," she repeats. "Just... be safe."

My throat tightens. "Go do your job."

Kaia's eyes soften. Her hand squeezes mine, and I don't say anything else. If I open my mouth again, I might beg, and I refuse to beg. Kaia lets go and steps into the crowd, swallowed immediately by security and schedules and the pull of the stage.

I step out too, legs slightly shaky, lips bruised, heart pounding like I'm sixteen again and stupid.

Then I turn away from the lights, because I promised.

And because promises are the only thing holding me together.

I keep my promise.

I walk away from the Ferris wheel with my lips swollen, my heart in my throat, and my brain screaming that I'm an idiot for thinking any of this can exist outside a glass box in the sky.

I don't look back toward the stage. I don't follow the tide of bodies flowing toward the main grounds. I do the responsible thing and head home.

Like I'm not already breaking inside and filled with worry.

The closer I get to my street, the quieter everything becomes. Most of the festival noise fades into a distant roar. The lanterns on our porch sway gently in the wind like they're greeting me.

The front door is unlocked. That's the first wrong thing.

I never leave the door unlocked. Grandma doesn't either. Not since the storm two years ago knocked out the power, and a neighbor tried to check on her, and she chased them off with a broom.

"Gran?" I call, stepping inside.

The house is dim. Quiet. Too quiet. No TV murmuring. No kettle whistling. No shuffle of slippers.

My stomach drops.

"Grandma?" I say again, louder.

Nothing.

I move fast, checking rooms like I'm looking for a missing child. Living room. Kitchen. Bathroom.

Her chair is empty.

Her cardigan is gone.

Her *purse* is gone.

My heart slams so hard it makes my vision pulse.

"Shit," I whisper.

I whip back to the kitchen counter where her pill organizer sits. Today's compartment is empty. She took her meds, and then she left.

The floor tilts under me.

Even worse than her going on her own is that she doesn't know just how dangerous it is. She doesn't know about the demons. My wrist flares hot under my skin.

My hands shake as I grab my phone and call Grandma.

Straight to voicemail.

"Grandma," I say into it, voice already cracking. "Pick up. Please call me back."

I hang up and call again.

Voicemail.

I jam my feet back into shoes without tying them properly and bolt out the door. The porch lanterns rattle as I slam the screen behind me.

"Grandma!" I shout into the evening.

The street is alive with festival foot traffic. People walking in groups, laughing, carrying glow sticks and drinks and cotton candy.

No one looks like they belong in my panic.

"Grandma!" I yell again, louder, throat already raw.

A neighbor—Mrs. Delaney from two houses down—steps out onto her porch holding a red plastic cup.

She squints at me. "Evie?"

"Have you seen my grandma?" I blurt.

Mrs. Delaney's eyebrows shoot up. "Oh, honey, yeah. She just walked by. Fifteen minutes ago."

My stomach drops. "Where?"

Mrs. Delaney points down the street, casual as if she's talking about the mail. "Toward the festival. Said she wasn't missing the opening."

My blood turns to ice.

"No," I whisper.

Mrs. Delaney smiles like this is cute. "She was very determined."

I take off running before I can say anything else. My lungs burn, but that doesn't slow me down.

I cut through side streets, through little alleyways that smell like fish and salt, past people who glance at me like I'm weird and then go back to their funnel cakes.

I don't care.

All I can think is: *Kaia told me not to go. Kaia told me not to go and I promised and now my grandma is in the crowd and if something happens—*

The festival gates loom ahead like the mouth of something huge.

The noise hits me like a wave. Crowds. Shouting. Music. Lights. The air thick with sugar and sweat and anticipation. An emcee's voice blasts through the speakers, bright and booming.

"Harbor's Edge! Are you ready to light up the night?"

The crowd roars. The sound crawls under my skin.

I push into the mass of bodies, shoulder-checking my way through tourists and teens and vendors carrying trays.

"Excuse me—sorry—"

Someone bumps my elbow, and I nearly swing on them. My pulse is in my ears.

Then I feel it. A pressure at the base of my skull, like a thumb pressing into a bruise. Not pain. Not exactly. A sense of... *weight.*

Like the air is thickening.

My wrist warms again.

Hotter.

I shove forward faster, panic sharpening into anger.

"Grandma!" I shout.

No answer. Of course no answer. It's chaos. I scan faces like I'm searching for a specific star in a sky full of fireworks. Lanterns sway overhead. People hold glowing sticks. Booth lights flash. Screens flicker with sponsor logos.

Eon.

Eon.

Eon.

I hate the way the brand is everywhere.

The crowd hums under the noise, little bits of the Harbor Lights jingle slipping between conversations like it's stuck in everyone's teeth.

Come back, come back—

My skull pressure deepens.

I shove through a cluster of teenagers in matching Midnight Halo shirts and nearly trip over a stroller.

"Sorry," I gasp, not meaning it.

Then I see her. Grandma's gray hair. Her stupid lipstick. Her cardigan. She's standing near the center-left of the crowd, exactly where a short elderly woman should not be in a crush of bodies.

Relief hits so hard I almost sob. I sprint toward her.

"Grandma!"

She turns, startled, then delighted like this is the most normal thing in the world.

"Evie!" she calls over the noise. "There you are."

I grab her arm, shaking. "What the hell are you doing?!"

Grandma frowns at my language like she's about to scold me, then softens. "Oh, honey, don't look like that."

"I was *worried*," I snap, voice cracking. "I came home and you were gone and the door was unlocked and—"

Grandma pats my cheek with a hand that smells like hand lotion. "I left you a note."

"You did not," I hiss.

Grandma's eyes narrow. "I did."

I stare at her, furious and relieved, and realize there is absolutely a folded scrap of paper in her cardigan pocket that she is now pointedly not taking out.

I exhale hard through my nose. "Why did you come out here alone? You know better!"

Grandma lifts her chin like she's ten feet tall. "Because I wanted to see the Rhee girl sing."

My stomach drops. "*Grandma.*"

"Oh, don't you 'Grandma' me," she says, wagging a finger. "I watched her on TV for years. She's from here. She always looked like she had something sad behind her eyes. I want to see her in person."

My throat tightens, painfully.

I swallow. "It's crowded."

"So?" Grandma says, unimpressed. "I have elbows."

I look around wildly as if the crowd might suddenly become reasonable.

Then I spot the rest of my life scattered through the sea of people like landmines. Mr. Alvarez, near the front, holding a little lantern with both hands like it's a holy object. Gus, further back, arms crossed, pretending he's only here to supervise the food vendors, not because he cares. Tasha and three of her friends squeezed together in a cluster, all wearing merch and glitter and the kind of excitement that makes my chest hurt with dread. Tasha is literally bouncing, phone up, ready to record.

Faces I know.

People I can't lose.

The pressure at the base of my skull pulses again, deeper.

The emcee's voice booms.

"And now—our hometown hero. The voice of Harbor's Edge. The woman who took our little lights and made them shine across the world—"

The crowd screams. Grandma squeezes my hand. My wrist burns under the binding.

I shouldn't be here.

I promised.

But I'm here.

Because Grandma is here.

Because they're all here.

The lights onstage shift. The screens flare bright.

And then Midnight Halo steps into view.

They look unreal. Matching outfits that catch the lantern light like it's stitched into them. Four figures moving with the kind of practiced grace that reads like magic even before you know it is.

Jules, bright and kinetic even when she's standing still.

Remy, composed, gaze sharp like she's reading the air.

Mina, soft but steady, eyes scanning the crowd as if she's looking for something hidden.

And Kaia. Center. Perfect posture. Her face lit by stage glow, making her look like the posters and yet somehow more human because she's actually breathing.

My chest tightens so hard it hurts. All the noise fades into a dull roar.

Grandma whispers, "There she is," like she's talking about a miracle.

I can't look anywhere else.

Kaia lifts her gaze across the crowd, searching, like she's checking perimeter, like she's counting risks.

Our eyes meet. For one heartbeat, she goes completely still.

The world narrows to that line between us—stage to crowd, pop star to girl, past to present. Her expression flickers, alarm, longing, something almost like fear.

And I realize exactly why she made me promise. The pressure at the base of my skull deepens into something that feels like a hand closing.

Kaia's eyes hold mine.

And the lights flare brighter.

Kaia

The lanterns light like a thousand small hearts deciding to beat at once.

From the stage, Harbor's Edge looks unreal—glowing paper spheres bobbing above the crowd, warm gold drifting across faces, reflecting in phones held high. The ocean beyond the festival grounds is a dark ribbon, barely there, like the world ends at the edge of the light.

The emcee's voice booms again, syrup-smooth.

"Harbor's Edge! On the count of three, we light the sky—one, two—"

The crowd roars.

And on three, flame blossoms in lanterns further across the grounds.

A wave of heat rises. A rush of wanting, of wishing, of memory pressed into paper. My skin prickles under my stage makeup. The wards hum. This is what the Chorus likes. This is what it *feeds on*.

I force my smile wide enough to sell the moment to every camera in the world.

And then I see *her*.

Evie stands in the crowd, close enough that I can make out her face even through the lantern glow.

Her eyes are on me like a dare.

Her hand is on an older woman's arm: Grandma Calder. I see the familiar set of Evie's shoulders, protective and furious.

My stomach drops so hard it feels like it pulls my ribs with it. *No.*

I told her not to come. I made her promise.

She promised.

I can feel my expression flicker. I catch it and plaster the perfected smile back on like it's muscle memory.

Jules bumps my shoulder lightly in our opening formation, the gesture casual to the audience, a coded check-in to me.

"You okay?" her voice murmurs.

I keep my eyes forward. "She's here," I whisper back, barely moving my mouth.

Jules's gaze flicks once, fast and sharp, scanning the crowd like a hawk. Her smile never breaks.

"Oh," she breathes. "Oh no."

Mina's voice slips into my in-ear, soft but alert, on our private channel. "Evie?"

"Yes," I say, throat tight.

Remy's voice is a low blade. "That changes the risk profile."

"It shouldn't," I snap, too sharp.

Remy doesn't argue. She doesn't have to. We all know it does. The Chorus already tasted Evie once, and it will want more.

The emcee launches into a speech about hometown dreams and shining lights and how tonight is about coming back to what made you.

Every sentimental phrase is a match struck in a room full of gas.

My face stays calm. My body holds posture.

Inside, I'm already moving calculations around like knives.

Where is Blaire?

Blaire's voice should be in my ear right now, counting down, correcting my stance, telling me not to look at the crowd like I want to leap off the stage.

Instead, there's only faint static.

I press my thumb against the tiny in-ear button, the hidden comm switch. "Blaire?"

Nothing.

I try again, keeping my smile steady for the cameras. "Blaire, check in."

A soft hiss of interference answers. My stomach twists. Something is wrong.

The emcee lifts his arms dramatically. "And now—Harbor's Edge, give it up for your hometown hero and the world's brightest stars—*MIDNIGHT HALO!*"

The crowd detonates. Sound slams into the wards like a wave hitting a cliff. The barrier flares faintly, visible only to us, a shimmer threaded through the air.

My throat tightens as I step forward.

We take our positions. Stage lights snap on, bathing us in white-hot brightness. Cameras sweep across the crowd, across the lanterns, across the massive festival grounds that feel suddenly too open, too hungry.

I shift my in-ear from our private channel to the public one, the one that will project my voice across all of Harbor's Edge.

I smile.

And I start to sing.

The first song is bright. Up-tempo. The kind of thing that makes the crowd bounce and scream. The kind of thing that looks like celebration and feels like a lure.

Our choreo hits on muscle memory: sharp turns, synchronized steps, formations that look like art but are also geometry—ward shapes, binding patterns, sigils traced by our feet and the light rigs.

It's beautiful.

It's a trap.

Jules flashes me a grin, throwing her energy out like sparks, feeding the ward-lines with kinetic charge. Mina's movements are smaller but precise, her magic sliding under the choreography like a hidden blade. Remy sings her lines like scripture.

And I anchor it.

I amplify.

I hold the whole thing in my throat like a note I can't let crack.

The crowd screams the chorus back at us. And the air shivers. A wrong note slides under the music, thin at first, like feedback.

My skin prickles at the base of my skull. Remy's eyes snap toward the far right of the grounds, pupils narrowing.

The pressure shifts with the way the crowd's emotion is spiking too fast, too high, like something is pushing it.

The emcee's voice cuts in between songs, laughing too loud.

"That's right! Harbor's Edge, let's hear you! Louder! LOUDER!"

He shouldn't be on mic right now. He shouldn't be feeding the crowd like that. My gaze flicks to him. He stands at the side of the stage, face turned toward the audience, grin stretched too wide. And for half a heartbeat, his eyes go wrong. Not demon-glow wrong. *Hollow* wrong.

Like he's listening to something else.

Like there's a second voice inside him, shaping his mouth.

A chill slides down my spine.

As Mina and Remy harmonize, I drop back into our private comms.

"Mr. Bane?" I whisper into my in-ear.

Static. No answer. Blaire's channel is dead too.

The emcee laughs again, and the sound warps mid-chuckle into something that isn't human at all—an echo layered under his own voice.

The crowd doesn't notice. They cheer louder.

Because they think it's hype.

Because they think it's a show.

Because they don't know a predator just got handed a microphone.

The lanterns bob above their heads, glowing like bait. The air ripples. And then the Chorus arrives.

It spills across the festival sky like ink in water, a mass of faces and mouths and sound without bodies, old Harbor Lights jingles, forgotten love songs, lullabies, ad hooks, teenage recordings, a thousand half-remembered melodies stitched into one starving thing.

It stretches over the grounds, vast and hungry.

The crowd gasps—finally noticing something is happening—but they don't see the monster. They feel it though. And that's the thing about the Chorus... It feels like everything you miss.

Like the past reaching down to caress your cheek.

And people lean into it.

My stomach drops.

"No," I breathe.

The emcee's head jerks back like a puppet pulled by strings. His mouth opens, and when he speaks, it isn't his voice. It's a harmony of voices layered together, sweet and awful.

"Harbor's Edge," it croons. "*Come back~*"

My blood turns to ice.

The crowd laughs, thinking it's part of the act.

A woman near the front wipes her eyes like she's moved. A teenager starts singing along. And the Chorus *thrums,* pleased.

It drops down into the warding.

The pressure at the base of my skull spikes, like claws hooking into my thoughts.

I hear it in my ear, in my bones: *Come back, come back—*

Evie's face flashes in my mind without permission.

Evie at sixteen, laughing, hands sticky with lemonade, shouting my name across a rickety stage.

Evie on the pier, lantern in hand, eyes soft as she leans in.

Evie in the diner, throat pinned by invisible sound, eyes wide with terror.

Evie in a Ferris wheel, mouth warm against mine, promising she wouldn't watch—

But she's here.

She's here.

I force my voice steady into the mic, singing our next opening line like nothing has changed. The cameras catch my smile. The audience hears a pop anthem.

Only the girls hear the panic in the sub-channel, the magic beneath the music tightening like a noose.

"Time to transform," Remy says under her breath, barely moving her mouth.

The Chorus's mass stretches farther, a curtain of faces drifting toward the crowd edges.

It's trying to bleed into them. It's trying to get inside mouths, inside memories, inside throats. It wants to devour everyone here.

I feel Aurora pulse inside me, begging to be brought into the fight.

I keep singing, because if we break the performance, the crowd panics, and panic is an open door.

"Do it on the beat," I command in comms for the girls.

Jules grins wider, eyes bright with adrenaline. "Finally. The fun part."

Mina's breath trembles. "Kaia—Blaire isn't answering."

"I know," I say, throat tight.

The Chorus speaks again through the emcee, voice a velvet knife. "*Sing for me~*"

The crowd screams. The wards flare brighter, struggling. My vision flickers at the edges.

Aurora *demands* to be drawn.

I step into the next choreo formation, arms sweeping up in a move that looks like a dramatic dance break. And I reach into the air as if I'm grabbing light itself. Aurora flashes into existence in my hand, blade blazing, radiant and unreal. It looks like stage tech to the crowd, a prop catching the light, part of the show.

But I feel its weight. Its heat. Its link to my throat.

Jules spins beside me, her movement sharp and fast, twin short swords sparking into being out of nothing, Voltstep charged and ready.

Remy's blade appears with a flick of her wrist, Inkthorn black and rune-etched, trailing glowing script in the air.

Mina draws Heartglass like she's pulling a shard of moonlight from her own chest—translucent, shimmering, reflection bending around it.

To the crowd, it's choreography.

To the cameras, it's stunning.

To us, it's war.

The Chorus leans down, mouths opening wider, harmonies slipping into our ears like hooks.

I feel it tug at my thoughts.

Come back.

Remember.

Stay.

Evie.

Evie.

Evie.

I grit my teeth and raise Aurora, singing one clean note that rides under the pop track like a hidden blade. The note becomes a shockwave. A pressure barrier blooms outward, invisible to the crowd but very real to the thing above us.

The Chorus recoils, then laughs, a sound that ripples across the sky.

It likes resistance.

It likes a fight.

It likes that we're feeding it more sound.

"Kaia," Mina whispers, voice tight with fear. "It's in our heads."

"I know," I breathe. "Focus."

Jules darts forward in a series of spins that look like a dance solo, Voltstep crackling as she slashes through the air, cutting at the edges of the Chorus's mass where it's trying to drip into the crowd, trying to find the seams in the warding.

Remy sings her line, and the syllables become glowing runes that hang in the air like a net, tightening.

Mina's blade flashes as she angles it toward the crowd, the reflection in Heartglass flares, revealing the Chorus's tendrils as black threads trying to slip into open mouths.

And that's the problem.

Those threads shouldn't be able to get that far.

The wards are flaring—bright, hot, working—but the Chorus is still *finding purchase*, sliding through tiny gaps like smoke through cracked glass. It's not rushing the net. It's *cheating* it. Fragmenting, thinning, threading itself between the lines like it somehow knows where the lattice is weakest.

And if it can slip past the warding *here*, it can slip past it anywhere...

Evie.

My thoughts go to her so fast it feels like the demon yanked the string itself. And my gaze snags again on Evie. She's in the crowd, eyes wide, hand gripping her grandmother's arm. Her face is pale in the lantern light, and her eyes are locked on the sky full of mouths. Like she *sees* the Chorus now that she's marked.

"No," I whisper, voice breaking under the music.

The Chorus senses it—my spike of emotion, the tether between us. It turns its attention like a predator smelling blood. A cluster of faces in the mass swivels toward Evie's section of the crowd.

It leans.

Hungry.

And the emcee—possessed, smiling too wide—lifts his arm and points directly into the audience.

Right at her.

"*Bring her up here~*" the Chorus purrs through his mouth.

My blood turns to ice. The wards flare so bright I can see them even through stage lights. The crowd grabs at her, as if possessed as well.

Evie.

The only person in the crowd who looks awake enough to be terrified.

They tug at her. Not rough at first. Not violent in a way security would clock. Just... certain. Sleepwalker hands closing around her sleeves, her wrists, her elbows. The crowd shifts to make a path, like she's being offered.

My feet move before my brain finishes forming the thought. I step toward the edge of the stage. I'm still singing. My mouth is still on the lyric. My body is still on the mark. But my heart is ten feet ahead of me, already in the pit of the crowd, already reaching for her.

Evie's head jerks up. For a heartbeat our eyes catch through the distance.

I take another step. The wards react, pressure shifts under my boots like the stage is warning me. If I break formation, the lattice flexes. If I flex the lattice, the Chorus gets a seam. If it gets a seam, it bleeds further into the crowd.

Protect the town.

Protect *her*.

"Kaia—" Mina's voice catches in my in-ear, strained. "Stay—stay in the wards—We need you."

Remy's gaze flicks to me—quick, sharp, the way she looks when she can see the whole board and I'm about to flip it. She's in motion without looking like it. Inkthorn's runes hang in the air behind her like a half-written sentence, holding the demon's threads at bay. Her voice is steady in my ear.

"Don't," she says.

I take another step anyway.

Remy's hand closes around my arm. Her grip is cool through my sleeve, iron calm, the kind of touch that says: *If you move, everyone dies.*

I jerk my gaze to her.

"Evie," I breathe.

Remy doesn't even blink.

"I know." Her hand tightens once, just enough to hurt. "But if you leave the wards, it leaves everyone vulnerable."

My jaw clenches so hard my teeth ache.

Then something *snaps* in my ear. Static surges. An unfamiliar voice slides into the comms, low and wrong and amused, as if it's been listening the whole time.

"Hello, girls," it says.

My stomach drops.

Not Blaire. Not Council. Not even the Chorus.

Something else. Something watching. Something *hungry*.

My grip tightens on Aurora until my knuckles ache.

Jules' voice cuts tight into our private comms, panic disguised as sarcasm. "Uh... Tell me you're hearing that too."

"I'm hearing it," Remy says, voice like ice.

Mina's breath is a small, terrified sound. "What is that?"

I raise Aurora, voice leader calm, shaking only in the places no one can see.

"We have to kill it now," I say, and it's both an order and a prayer.

Because I don't know whose voice that is, but the show has become a battlefield.

And Evie is in the crowd, being pulled towards us.

And the Chorus has finally decided to stop playing.

For a second, my brain tries to pretend this is still a concert.

Lights. Music. The roar of a hometown crowd. Midnight Halo onstage like a myth someone invented to make this town feel important.

Then the emcee points straight at me.

Not vaguely. Not "front row shout-out." Not cute. His arm snaps up like a puppet string got yanked. And his mouth opens... and the voice that comes out isn't his.

"Bring her up here."

The words hit the crowd like a command coded into their bones. Around me, bodies shift. Not the normal "people pressing forward because the beat is about to drop" kind of shift. This is coordinated. Immediate. Wrong. Hands turn toward me like sunflowers snapping toward light. Someone grabs my elbow. Another hand closes around my wrist.

I jerk back, instinct screaming, and my own wrist—my *bound* wrist—erupts in heat like a brand. Pain spikes up my arm, hot and bright, and the thought arrives as clearly as a slap: The binding is the only reason I'm still me.

Everyone else is half-dreaming.

And I'm the only one awake enough to be terrified.

Because I can see it now.

Not a "bad feeling." Not static. Not the kind of wrongness you explain away later as panic.

I see the sky *moving*.

Above the lantern frames and the stage lights, something hangs over Harbor Lights like a second ceiling—thick as fog, restless as a storm. Faces form and un-form inside it: mouths open mid-song, eyes blank with devotion, expressions stitched together from old joy and old grief. It's not one creature. It's a crowd made into a monster. Songs leak from it.

The Chorus.

And it has tendrils.

Black threads snaking down through the air, slipping between bodies, brushing throats, and people *lean into them* as if they're being offered water. The air is full of them. They weave between the lanterns like spider silk and the lanterns sway in unison.

Someone yanks my arm harder.

"Let go," I snap.

The crowd chant starts again, and this time it isn't hype.

It's a machine.

"One more song. One more song. One more song."

Perfect timing. No lag. No variation. Hundreds of mouths forming the same syllables in unison like they share one throat.

My skull pressures at the base, like a hand is holding my head still. I twist, trying to find Grandma.

She's beside me—she *was* beside me—

My hand scrapes empty air.

"Grandma!" I shout.

I see her a few feet away, jostled sideways, shoulders bumped, her face tilted toward the stage with a too-bright smile. Her pupils are wide. Her mouth moves with the chant, slower, as if she's fighting through mud.

Someone shoves me forward again.

A woman's shoulder slams into mine.

A teenage girl grabs my sleeve and pulls.

"Bring her up here," the emcee repeats, smiling like he's announcing a prize winner.

My wrist burns hotter.

The binding keeps me safe from falling into the chant, but it doesn't let me speak freely either. Every time I try to yell something that sounds like "run" or "stop," the heat lashes my nerves like the magic is yanking my tongue back into my mouth.

It's a leash.

It's a muzzle.

And it is the only reason I'm not glass-eyed like everyone else.

"No!" I scream anyway, and pain knifes up my arm.

I snarl through it and swing my elbow backward. It connects with someone's ribs. They grunt and stumble—half-awake, half-not—and the crowd surges like it's annoyed I'm resisting.

Hands tug my hoodie.

Someone's nails rake my skin.

I shove with both palms like I'm trying to push back a wave.

"Grandma!" I scream again, voice cracking.

She turns her head, just a fraction, like she hears me through all the noise. For one heartbeat, her eyes clear.

"Evie?" she mouths.

Relief floods me so hard it's dizzying.

"I'm here!" I yell. "Look at me! Stay with me!"

But the chant rolls over us again, and her face slips like the wind blew out a candle. Her mouth starts moving in time with everyone else, and I'm tugged further away.

"One more—"

"No!" I shove forward, fighting the bodies between us. "Stop chanting. Stop. Please—"

My wrist flares hotter. The binding punishes the plea. The pressure at the base of my skull spikes too, like the Chorus doesn't like me refusing the script.

A voice tries to bloom in my head, sweet and familiar as warm syrup: *This is how it's always been. Lanterns. Music. Harbor Lights. Stay here.*

Images slam into me like waves.

The diner after hours—grease, laughter, fries.

Kaia leaning over the counter with a grin like she could swallow the sun.

The pier. Lantern light. Her mouth almost on mine.

The ache of being sixteen and thinking this town and this girl could be enough to live inside forever.

The nostalgia hits like a drug.

My knees go weak.

I understand, suddenly, with sick clarity: the Chorus doesn't just scare you.

It seduces you. It offers you a past where nothing hurts yet. It makes you want to be eaten.

My fingers loosen on the air. My mind blurs at the edges.

I inhale hard and dig my nails into my palm until pain sparks me awake.

"No," I whisper, fiercer. "No. Not like this."

It doesn't matter. Hands keep closing on me anyway—wrists, sleeves, elbows—gentle the way sleepwalkers are gentle when they're dragging you somewhere you don't want to go.

"Bring her up here," the emcee says again.

The chant swallows everything else.

"One more song. One more song."

My wrist *ignites* under the binding. Not a warning tingle—full, scorching heat, like the magic is trying to weld my bones into place while the crowd does the opposite.

I twist, trying to wrench free. I slam an elbow into someone's ribs. A shoulder. A hip. It's ugly and desperate and it barely slows the tide.

"Grandma!" I scream over my shoulder.

I see her only in flashes between bodies and lantern light—her small frame jostled; her face tilted toward the stage, that too-wide, half-beat-late smile. Then I lose her in the crowd. Something in my chest tears.

"No—Move—" I try to shout, but the binding flares so hot it steals my breath. Pain lances up my arm like a hand clamped on my throat.

I choke on my screams. The crowd hauls me forward anyway. I fight, clawing at sleeves, shoving faces, swinging on shoulders, but they don't react like people. They react like one organism adjusting around a rock in its path.

And I'm the rock.

I get yanked closer to the stage. The lights swallow the fog. The bass becomes pressure in my teeth. The closer I get, the worse the air feels—thick, sticky, hungry. Like the space itself has turned into a mouth.

People start to *kneel*.

Not everyone at once. Not dramatically.

One drops like their strings got cut. Then another. Then a cluster.

Knees hit the ground. Hands go slack. Faces tilt up toward the stage, eyes glassy, mouths still moving with the chant like prayer.

It's feeding on them.

Not biting, not tearing, *drinking*. Siphoning the heat out of their bodies through sound and attention and nostalgia.

And I'm being offered like a fresh cup.

"Bring her up here," the emcee purrs.

I'm close enough now to see the stage clearly, and that's when my brain makes one last pathetic attempt to pretend.

Lights. Smoke. A show.

Then the truth hits. Midnight Halo is onstage, still moving in formation, but the choreography is wrong in the way a smile can be wrong. Jules is moving like she's fighting a current, her blade flashing too bright, too hot. Remy's runes hang in the air like torn sentences. Mina's stance is braced—shielding, anchoring—like she's trying to hold the stage together with her body.

And Kaia—

Kaia drops to her knees too.

Not a planned dramatic moment. Not a performance choice.

Her knees hit the stage like something inside her gave out. Her head lifts slowly, and her gaze... isn't there. Her eyes are that electric purple and this time it *sticks*, unsteady, too bright, like her magic is bleeding through faster than the glamour can seal it.

Her mouth opens, smile still on her face as she looks up at the Chorus.

My stomach turns to ice.

Because I have seen Kaia owned before.

By contracts.

By schedules.

By a company that turned her into a product and called it destiny.

And now the Chorus is trying to do the same thing, only it's not asking for a signature. It's *killing* her.

The crowd jerks me forward again, and I stumble. Someone's hand clamps around my upper arm hard enough to bruise.

I'm almost at the front barricade now. Almost close enough that the stage feels like a cliff over my head.

I can't get to Grandma.

I can't even see her anymore.

All I can see is Kaia's empty gaze and the mouths in the sky and people folding to their knees like the town is bowing to be eaten.

And something inside me goes terrifyingly calm.

If I stay and fight the crowd, the crowd wins.

If I scream, the binding burns me silent.

And if this loop continues, everyone kneeling becomes everyone *dead*.

The Chorus's weapon isn't claws.

It's the sound, the chanting, the speakers turning emotion into a pipeline.

So I need to break the loop.

I need to kill the sound. A final shove pitches me forward, and for one blessed second, the grip on my arm slips. Someone's hand loses purchase on my sleeve.

I twist hard, duck low, and slam my shoulder into the barricade gap where the staff move in and out.

I'm smaller than the bodies trying to drag me.

I use it.

I slide through the opening, panic threatening to drown me, skin scraping metal, lungs burning.

Someone reaches for me—fingertips snag my hoodie—but I rip free and stumble into the narrow space beside the stage where cables snake like veins.

I don't stop. I don't look back.

Instead, I look at the festival grounds the way I've always looked at them: as a map. Power junction near the sound tower. Generator trailer behind the souvenir tents. A service corridor between the kettle corn stand and the PTA booth that only locals know because we've been sneaking through it since we were kids.

My wrist is still on fire.

My skull still aches with the pressure of the Chorus trying to pull me into rhythm.

But I'm not chanting.

I'm not kneeling.

I'm *moving*.

I catch one last glimpse of Kaia onstage, her head tilted, purple flaring too long, Mina braced in front of her like a shield.

And I make the choice that feels like ripping my own heart in half.

Hold on, I think at my grandma, wherever she is in that sea of bodies.

Hold on.

Then I turn and run for the sound.

Not toward the stage—that's what the Chorus wants. That's where the mouths are. That's where Kaia is trapped in lights and sound and a crowd begging to be eaten.

I run sideways, cutting along the edges of the festival where the booths are dense and the tents make narrow corridors only locals know.

Because this is my town.

Because Harbor Lights is a maze I grew up inside.

Because if the demon is using sound, then I'm going to take away its teeth.

I duck behind the kettle corn tent as a surge of bodies pushes forward toward the stage. Someone bumps my shoulder and snarls without looking at me. I shove back and keep moving. Past the ring toss booth. Past the overpriced lantern table. Past the "Hometown Heroes" photo wall that makes me want to vomit.

A staff gate sits behind the food trucks—cheap chain, padlock, a bored volunteer who usually waves locals through if they look like they belong.

Tonight the volunteer's eyes are glassy. His mouth is moving with the chant.

I don't slow down. I grab the gate and yank. It rattles.

Locked.

"Of course," I hiss.

My wrist burns hot, warning me I'm doing something I'm not supposed to, like the binding thinks "don't draw attention" is more important than "don't let everyone die."

I slam my palm against the latch edge hard.

Once.

Twice.

The latch pops and the lock drops, clattering onto the ground.

The volunteer doesn't even blink. I squeeze through the gate and sprint down the narrow service corridor behind the tents. The noise changes back here, less crowd roar, more mechanical hum, more generators. The festival's guts.

I know exactly where I'm going.

Main power junction is near the sound towers, behind the sponsor banners, by the maintenance shed with the "AUTHORIZED PERSONNEL" sign that everyone ignores.

I used to sneak back here as a teenager to steal extra lanterns.

I can find it blind.

The pressure at the base of my skull pulses, stronger now that I'm away from the crowd. The Chorus doesn't like losing its audience. The chant follows me anyway, ghosting through speakers and bodies, crawling down the corridors.

"One more song."

I shove past a stack of coiled cables.

A tech stumbles into view ahead of me, holding a flashlight like it's a weapon. He's wearing a headset. His eyes are too wide, too unfocused. He's chanting too, quietly, like he's trying to harmonize with something he can't see.

"One more—"

"Move," I snap.

He doesn't. He turns toward me with a smile that isn't his own. His mouth opens and a wrong harmony slips out... soft, sweet, layered.

"Come back," it whispers.

My skin crawls. For half a second, I see Kaia in my mind again—her mouth on mine in the Ferris wheel, her voice in my ear.

Don't watch.

Be safe.

My throat tightens.

"I'm not in the mood," I tell the tech, and slam my shoulder into him.

He stumbles sideways, hitting a crate. His flashlight clatters. I sprint past him. The maintenance shed is right there, half-hidden behind an Eon banner. I yank the door open. Inside is the power board—rows of labeled switches, breakers, and one big lever marked MAIN AUDIO FEED in thick sharpie.

Because Harbor Lights runs on prayers and duct tape.

My hands shake. The crowd noise booms through the walls like a heartbeat. Onstage, the Chorus is still feeding. The loop is still tight.

If I flip the wrong switch, I might plunge the whole festival into darkness and panic, and panic is also food.

But if I don't try, the Chorus eats everyone.

I stare at the lever.

My wrist burns hotter, like the binding is screaming now.

I grit my teeth so hard it hurts.

"Sorry," I mutter.

Then I grab the lever with both hands and yank it down.

The effect is immediate. The music drops mid-beat. The speakers go silent, not a gentle fade. A brutal stop, like a throat cut wide open.

For half a second, there's a vacuum. The crowd's chant stutters.

"One more—" a hundred voices start, then falter as the sound disappears.

The stage lights flicker. The big LED screens glitch. In the sudden silence, I hear something else, an ugly, furious sound overhead, like a thousand mouths inhaling at once and finding no song to ride.

The Chorus screams. It isn't audible like a normal scream. It's pressure in my head and vibration in my bones.

I stumble, hand gripping the shed doorframe as the soundless shock hits me.

Then the crowd reacts. People start to shout, confused, angry, afraid.

"What happened?"

"Is it a power outage?"

"Where's my mom?"

Someone laughs nervously. Someone screams. The spell breaks in pieces, unevenly. Some people blink like they're waking up. Others keep chanting without sound, mouths moving like fish.

I don't wait. I bolt out of the shed and sprint toward the sound tower itself, because cutting the feed might not be enough if the Chorus is already inside the rigs.

The back corridor is chaos now—techs stumbling, security yelling into radios, a generator whining like it's overworked.

I reach the base of the nearest sound tower and start climbing the metal stairs two at a time. A tech stands halfway up, hands on the console, eyes glassy. He's humming the Harbor Lights jingle under his breath like a prayer.

"Hey," I snap, grabbing his shoulder.

He turns his head slowly, too slow. His mouth opens. And that layered voice tries to slide out again, sweet as rot.

"Stay—"

I shove him. Hard. He stumbles back, catching himself on the railing with a startled, human sound.

His eyes blink, focus snapping in for half a second.

"What—"

"Go," I bark. "Get down. Now."

He looks like he wants to argue. Then the air ripples above us, and his face drains of color. He bolts down the stairs.

Good.

I slam my hands onto the console. It's a mess of sliders and buttons and glowing indicators. I don't know sound boards. I know coffee machines and cash drawers.

But I know one thing: If the demon is riding the speakers, I take away the speakers.

My gaze locks on the emergency shutoff switch—a red, plastic-covered button labeled SYSTEM KILL.

Of course it has one.

Because even Harbor Lights knows something could go wrong.

My wrist burns like fire.

I flip the plastic cover up. Then I slam my palm down on the button.

The tower goes dark. The stage lights flicker again. The big screens glitch harder.

A wave of murmurs rises from the crowd like a tide changing direction. And overhead, the Chorus's mass convulses, faces stretching, mouths opening wide with no sound to carry them.

For the first time all night, it looks *hurt*.

For the first time, it looks like it can't just feed and smile and pretend to be a pleasant memory.

My chest heaves.

I grip the railing, breathing hard.

Below, the crowd is starting to move—panic, confusion, people looking around like they just realized they've been chanting.

But the Chorus isn't gone. It's still there. Still hungry. And now it's *angry*.

I look toward the stage, toward the lights, toward the center where Kaia is. She's looking around, confused. Mina helps her up.

Thank god.

Now, she has to do her job. And I realize with a cold drop in my stomach: I just pulled the plug on the demon's control loop.

Now they have to kill it before it finds a new way to sing.

THE MUSIC DIES MID-BEAT. Not a planned cut. Not a dramatic pause. A brutal, throat-slit silence that rips the world open.

And me—

I realize I'm on my knees.

Not kneeling for the crowd. Not performing. Collapsed.

My hands are braced on the stage like I'm trying to keep myself from tipping forward into the dark. My heart is sprinting. My throat feels scraped raw from singing against a force that wasn't letting go.

For a beat, I can't remember how I got here.

The fog in my head thins in shreds. I taste blood like I bit my tongue somewhere in the struggle.

"Kaia." Mina's voice is right beside me, close enough to cut through the static still ringing in my skull.

Her fingers hook under my arm and tug—urgent, firm, pulling me out of the undertow.

"Kaia, look at me," she says.

I blink.

My vision stutters like a glitching screen, stage lights too bright, wards flaring too hard, the crowd a sea of faces suddenly wrong in a different way.

Mina's eyes are blazing magenta—too bright, too steady. Heartglass is still summoned in her grip, its reflection catching the broken sky like a shard.

I inhale, ragged.

The purple in my own eyes flares, then finally snaps back, like the glamour can breathe again now that the sound is gone.

"Mina," I rasp.

"Yeah," she says, relief and fear tangled. "Yeah. You're back."

Back.

The word lands like a punch because I don't know where I went.

I let her haul me up, my knees shaking as I get my feet under me.

And the Chorus—

The Chorus *shrieks* in the sky, its harmony collapsing into static. It's not sound you hear. It's pressure. It's the air suddenly wrong, like the temperature drops and your teeth ache.

The chant in the crowd stutters.

"One more—" voices start, then falter, confused by the absence of reinforcement. People blink. Heads shake. Hands lower. Some scream, suddenly awake and realizing they've been chanting like sleepwalkers.

The wards flare bright, then steady.

Jules's voice snaps in my ear, adrenaline edged with awe. "Okay. Whoever just killed the sound system is my new religion."

Mina's breath is shaky. "It's weakening."

Remy's voice is pure focus, clipped like she's cutting thread. "Harmony destabilized. Pattern is unraveling."

I know exactly who did it.

My chest tightens so hard it hurts.

Evie.

Of course Evie would rather rip the whole festival's power grid out of the ground than watch me get swallowed.

She should have *ran*, but of course she would risk her life to keep other people alive.

I should be furious.

I'm... something else entirely.

"Hold formation," I command, voice steady even as my pulse slams. "We strike now. While it's stuttering."

Aurora blazes in my hand, blade catching the flickering stage lights and throwing them back like dawn on broken glass. The Chorus convulses overhead, its faces rippling through old jingles and half-remembered melodies, trying to find a new hook, trying to latch onto the panic now rising in the crowd.

Panic is a banquet too.

"No," I snarl under my breath.

Jules launches forward, Voltstep crackling, twin short swords slashing through the air in a spinning sequence that looks like a dance solo to anyone watching, but every cut she makes is a severing of a thread.

She grins, wild. "Hey, no audio, no problem!"

"Jules," Mina warns, but her voice has steel now.

Heartglass catches the lantern light, reflecting the crowd in a prismatic shimmer, and in that reflection I see the Chorus's tendrils clearly, black threads trying to crawl into the crowd once more.

Mina angles her blade and slices.

The threads snap.

People gasp like they've been freed from underwater.

Remy sings a low, controlled line, no mic, no amplification, just raw spellwork encoded into melody. Inkthorn leaves glowing runes in the air, letters that hang and tighten like chains.

The Chorus thrashes against them, furious.

It tries to pour itself downward.

Toward the emcee.

Toward the crowd.

Toward—

My gaze catches movement at ground level near the edge of the stage. Someone small, angry, pushing through security chaos.

Evie.

My breath catches.

Evie shoves past a stumbling stagehand and storms straight toward the emcee, who is standing near the stage stairs with his arms lifted like a conductor again.

His mouth is still moving, still shaping wrong harmonies even in silence, trying to pull the crowd back into sync.

The Chorus has him like a puppet.

Evie doesn't hesitate. She pulls something from her hoodie pocket like she's been carrying it her whole life.

Pepper spray?

She plants her feet and raises it like it's a holy weapon.

"Back the hell up," she shouts.

The emcee's head jerks toward her. His eyes are black in a way that makes my stomach lurch. His mouth opens, and the layered voice slips out, thin now, broken by static, but still sweet as rot.

"Come back," it whispers.

Evie's face goes pale for half a second, then her jaw hardens.

"No," she spits, and sprays. "Go to hell."

A bright, furious stream of chemical fire hits the emcee directly in the face. He shrieks—human shriek, finally—and staggers back, hands clawing at his eyes.

The Chorus recoils too, like it can feel pain through him. The mass overhead jerks violently, harmony breaking further.

And something inside me *snaps*.

The last sticky tendril of the Chorus's hold on my thoughts tears loose, and suddenly I'm fully in my body again.

Fully myself.

Fully *angry*.

"Evie!" I shout, and it's not into a mic, it's not performance, it's raw.

Her head whips toward the stage.

Our eyes lock. For a heartbeat she looks like she's going to yell at me for being shocked she did something reckless. Then the emcee lunges.

Not fully himself. Not fully the Chorus. Both.

His hand shoots out toward Evie's throat like the diner all over again, like the demon wants to punish her.

My blood turns to fire. I move before I think. Aurora flares in my grip as I leap down the stage stairs, boots hitting the steps in a controlled drop that is absolutely not in the choreo.

"Kaia!" Jules snaps in my ear. "Formation!"

"Cover," I bite back. "Now."

Jules swears, but she's already moving, Voltstep flashing as she slices a crescent of kinetic energy across the front of the stage, creating a barrier between the crowd and the lower steps. Mina follows, Heartglass reflecting the Chorus's tendrils and cutting them as they try to dip.

Remy's invisible runes tighten, holding the mass overhead in place like a net.

They're doing their job, so I can do mine.

I hit the ground in front of Evie like a shield, body-checking the emcee. His hand releases her throat as he stumbled back. Aurora sings in my grip as I swing—one clean, brutal arc. Not to kill the man. To cut the binding. My blade doesn't slice flesh. It slices the tendril of the Chorus wrapped around him.

The air *cracks*.

The emcee drops like his strings have been cut, collapsing to his knees, gasping and coughing like he's just been pulled out of deep water.

The Chorus shrieks overhead, furious, starving, unraveling.

Evie stares at me, chest heaving, pepper spray still clutched in her hand like she's ready to fight God.

Her eyes are bright with terror and rage.

"What are you doing?" she yells.

"I'm saving you," I snap back, voice raw.

Evie's lips part.

For a heartbeat she looks sixteen again, shocked by how fierce I can be for her.

Then she glances past me, toward the crowd.

"I need to find my grandma," Evie says.

Evie starts forward. I catch her wrist.

"Evie," I breathe. "Wait."

She jerks back, eyes wild. "Let go."

"Wait," I say again, voice rough. "It's not over."

Evie's laugh comes out sharp and wet. "Of course it's not over. It's never over."

Above us, the Chorus thrashes, its harmony shattered into static, but its tendrils are still out, thin threads of sound and memory reaching for any mouth that'll take them. The wards are barely holding, but holding doesn't mean safe. Not yet. Not when the demon is wounded and furious and desperate.

"You run into that crowd right now," I say, "and it will use you. It will use her. It will use both of you."

Evie's eyes blaze. "But my grandma—"

"I know," I choke out. "*I know.*"

She yanks again, and this time I feel how hard she's shaking. The kind of shaking that comes when you're trying to hold your whole world in your hands and it keeps slipping.

"I don't take orders from you," she spits.

"I'm not ordering—" I start, then stop, because that's a lie. My whole life is orders. Even my care comes out like command.

Evie's chin lifts, daring. "Then let go."

I swallow. The words I want to say are too big and too late: *I'm sorry. I'm here. I won't leave.*

What comes out is smaller, meaner, because fear makes me sharp.

"Just listen to me for once!" I snap.

The second it leaves my mouth, regret punches me in the ribs. Evie's eyes go flat. Deadly. Familiar. Like we're sixteen again and I just stepped on the same landmine.

"Oh," she says softly, and it's worse than yelling. "There she is."

I flinch.

The battle is still happening around us, but Evie and I are locked on each other like this is the only fight.

I force my voice down. I force my hand to loosen just a fraction, not releasing her, not yet, but giving her room to breathe.

"Evie," I say, quieter. "I'm sorry. I didn't mean—"

"Yeah," she whispers. "You did."

Her gaze flicks past me toward the crowd. She tries to step forward again. I move with her, staying between her and the crowd without blocking her completely, protective.

"One minute," I plead. "One. Give me one minute to clear the tendrils and then I will help you find her."

Evie's breath shudders.

She looks at my hand on her wrist like it's a chain. Then she looks at the sky, at the Chorus twitching and spitting static, still reaching.

It's wounded, which makes it mean.

The mass convulses and the air fills with broken sound—feedback without speakers, memory without mercy. Tendrils lash toward the crowd in thin, desperate threads, searching for something that will stitch the loop back together.

And then it does the cruelest possible thing.

A melody slips into the static.

Not a jingle. Not a chant.

A soft, familiar sequence of notes—one I've never sung on stage, never handed to the world, never let Eon polish into a product.

Because it was never for them.

It was for *her*.

Evie goes rigid.

Her eyes widen, horrified in a way that has nothing to do with monsters.

The Chorus sings it wrong, half a beat off, the harmony warped, the vowels pulled too long like a mouth that doesn't know how to hold tenderness. But the words are the same. The phrasing is the same.

Breathe with me, breathe with me—

Evie makes a sound—small and broken—and slaps her hands over her ears like she can keep it out. Like she can stop memory from crawling into her skull.

"No," she gasps, voice cracking. "No, no—That's *mine*."

The word hits like a blade.

Not *ours*. Not *the town's*. Not something you can chant in a crowd and pretend it belongs to everyone.

Mine.

My throat tightens. "Evie—"

"You wrote that," she spits, almost furious through the terror. "After the storm—after the pier got flooded and we were soaked and you were shaking—"

I flinch, because the memory is too sharp: saltwater in our hair, lantern frames rattling, Evie giving me her hoodie because I wouldn't stop shivering, my hands numb around a cheap pen as I scribbled lyrics on a napkin like if I didn't get them out I'd drown.

"It was for me," Evie says, voice breaking on the last word. "You said it was—you said you weren't going to play it for any-one. You said it was just... for me. So how can it *know* it?"

"It tastes us," I say. "It tastes what we're thinking. What we're carrying. It's not singing your song because it found a record-ing." My jaw locks. "It's singing it because it felt it in me, because it felt *you* in me."

The Chorus drags the line out again, mangling it into some-thing sweet and rotten, like it's tasting her grief and my fear and deciding it likes the flavor. The demon isn't just trying to eat her. It's trying to wrap her in the softest thing I ever made and turn it into a leash.

I lift Aurora slightly. The blade hums, eager.

"I wrote that for you," I whisper, fierce and certain. "It doesn't get to use it against us."

Evie swallows, eyes shining.

I hold her gaze. "One minute. Cover your ears. Don't listen to it. Look at me."

Her hands tremble, but she nods once.

I feel my eyes flare purple—hot, violent, steadying—because rage is clean and easy compared to panic.

Aurora hums in my grip, hungry for an ending.

The thought in my head turns razor-sharp. *The thing that keeps trying to hurt Evie dies here.*

Not "save the town." Not "protect Eon's image." Not "contain the incident."

This is personal now.

The Chorus convulses overhead, trying to find another hook—panic, grief, nostalgia. It dips toward the paramedics like it can smell Evie's fear. Like it knows exactly where to bite next.

I step in front of her again, blade raised.

Her shoulders shake. She swallows hard. And she steps behind me.

The gesture is small, but it feels like trust.

"Girls," I say into the comm, voice steady. "We end it."

Jules' laugh is bright and vicious. "Finally."

Remy's voice is calm as a blade. "Pattern is exposed."

Mina's breath steadies. "Tell us where."

I lift Aurora, feeling it link to my throat like a second spine.

The Chorus's faces ripple overhead, mouths opening in silent hunger.

I taste the edge of its song in the air—old jingles, old love, old regret.

It reaches for Evie again like a reflex. Like it thinks her heart is a lever it can pull.

I bare my teeth.

"No," I whisper. "Not her."

Then I sing.

Not into a mic.

Not for a crowd.

For war.

One note—pure, amplified through Aurora—slams upward into the sky like a spear of light.

The wards flare in response, catching the note and turning it into a containment dome, tightening around the Chorus's mass.

It shrieks, trapped.

Jules darts in with Voltstep, blades charging with every step, carving through the demon's edges. Remy's runes snap into a circle, glowing script sealing gaps, forcing the Chorus's fragments back toward center. Mina raises Heartglass, reflection flaring, and in it, the Chorus's true shape shows: a knot of longing and hunger wrapped around the festival's jingle like a noose.

Mina's voice is soft and deadly. "There."

I see it: the core, the hook it keeps returning to.

I draw a breath so deep it hurts, and I think of Evie.

Evie's mouth on mine in the Ferris wheel.

Evie breaking the power to save strangers.

Evie always choosing other people over safety.

Evie, fierce and furious and alive.

The Chorus tries to whisper at me.

Come back. Stay. Never move on.

I lift Aurora. My voice drops into a note so low it vibrates the stage. Then I swing.

Aurora's arc is bright and final, cutting through the demon's core with a soundless shock that makes the air explode.

The Chorus shatters. Faces splinter into static. Mouths collapse into nothing. Old jingles fragment into harmless noise that scatters like ash.

The pressure in my skull releases all at once.

The crowd screams—human screams now, real, panicked, alive.

The sky clears. Lanterns bob, suddenly just lanterns again. I stand there breathing hard, blade humming in my hand, sweat cold under my makeup.

For a heartbeat, the world is quiet.

Then Evie's voice cuts through it, raw and shaking. *"Grandma."*

Evie

Hospitals always smell like someone tried to bleach fear out of the air and failed.

It's antiseptic and plastic and old coffee, layered over something human you can't scrub away. The fluorescent lights are too bright. The hallway floors shine like they're proud of themselves.

I hate it here.

I hate that I'm here because my grandma wanted to see 'the Rhee girl sing.'

I hate that I didn't drag her out sooner.

I hate that my promise didn't matter in the end.

Because when it was all over, I found her. Grandma hadn't just fallen. She was *hurt*. The kind of hurt that makes your brain go blank because it can't hold it.

In the ER, a doctor with tired eyes told me what happens when a crowd tramples an elderly body. Crush injuries. Broken ribs. A bruised lung. Internal bleeding they couldn't fully stop. Her blood pressure dropping every time they tried to stabilize it. Her heart working far too hard.

He said they could keep trying to force her body to stay, but it would be violence dressed up as help.

He said, very gently, like he was offering me a gift I didn't want, "We're going to keep her comfortable."

Comfortable is a word people use when they've run out of options.

A nurse finally opens the curtain and glances at me with that careful look people get when they've already decided what kind of grief you're allowed to have.

"You can go in," she says softly.

My legs feel like they belong to someone else. I nod once, because if I try to speak I'll make a sound that will embarrass me.

I push through the curtain.

The room is small, dimmer than the hall. A monitor beeps in a steady, indifferent rhythm. There's a thin blanket over her body, tucked too neatly.

Grandma looks even smaller in a hospital bed.

That isn't fair. She always took up space. She could fill a room with one raised eyebrow and a single sharp inhale. Now she's pale, hair brushed back, lips still faintly tinted like someone respected her stubborn vanity.

Her chest rises. Barely.

I step closer until I'm at her bedside, and my hands hover, unsure where I'm allowed to touch.

Then I take her hand. Her skin is cool. Not cold yet.

"Hey," I whisper. My voice comes out scratchy. "You scared me."

Her eyelids flutter, slow like she's fighting through water.

"Evie," she breathes my name, barely there.

"I'm here," I say quickly. "I'm right here."

Her fingers squeeze mine weakly. It breaks something in my chest. I lean in closer, pressing my forehead against the edge of the mattress as if I'm trying to anchor myself to her.

"You're not allowed to—" My voice cracks. I swallow hard. "You're not allowed to leave me."

Grandma's mouth twitches like she's trying to smile.

"You're... always... bossy," she whispers.

A laugh and a sob collide in my throat. I make a noise that is not dignified.

"Don't," I whisper, because the urge to beg is a tidal wave. "Don't do that. Don't make jokes right now."

Her eyes open a little more, unfocused but searching until they find my face. The clarity in her gaze flickers—there, then gone, then there again.

"You look," she murmurs, voice thin, "just like yourself... when you're fighting for something."

Tears blur my vision. I blink hard, but it doesn't help.

"I'm not *fighting*," I choke out. "I'm—I'm *scared*."

"That's... fighting," she whispers, like she's correcting my math.

Her hand trembles in mine. I squeeze back, too tight.

"I'm sorry," I say fast. "I'm sorry I wasn't there. I'm sorry I—"

Grandma's brows knit faintly, like she's trying to scold me through the fog.

"Stop," she rasps.

I freeze. Grandma's eyes hold mine for one lucid heartbeat.

"Don't let this place," she says, voice trembling, "hold you back."

My breath catches.

"Go," she whispers. "Go where... your heart is."

My stomach drops like the floor just fell away.

"Gran—" My voice breaks completely. "My heart is—my heart is with *you*."

Her gaze softens, and for a second she looks like herself again, fierce and tender and absolutely unmovable. She hasn't looked more like herself in years.

"No," she whispers. "Your heart is… bigger."

Her fingers squeeze mine once more. I press her knuckles to my mouth, choking back the sound I want to make.

"I love you," I whisper, desperate. "I love you. I love you. Please—"

Grandma's eyes flutter. Her hand loosens.

The monitor's beeping changes—not dramatic, not cinematic, just… different. Slower. Then it pauses too long between beats.

A nurse steps in quietly, but I don't look. I can't look. I feel it, the moment her hand goes slack in mine, the exact second the warmth leaves her grip.

I sit there holding her hand like if I hold on hard enough, I can keep her.

But the world doesn't care how hard you hold on.

A soft voice says my name from somewhere behind me. The nurse, maybe. Or a doctor.

I don't answer.

I just bow my head over Grandma's hand and shake.

I don't cry pretty.

I cry like something is being torn out of my ribs.

The next day, I'm sitting outside my house on the porch.

The night air is cold, damp, salt-heavy. I sit on the wooden steps with my arms wrapped around myself, staring at nothing.

I don't know how long I've been there.

Long enough that my eyes feel raw.

Long enough that my phone battery is almost dead from texts I didn't answer and notifications I didn't read.

Long enough that the adrenaline wears off, leaving only the hollow.

Footsteps approach. I don't look up. I already know who it is by the way my chest reacts, an old reflex, sharp as a wound.

Kaia sits beside me without asking. She doesn't touch me. She doesn't say "I'm sorry for your loss" like a greeting card. She just sits. Her hoodie is pulled up. No makeup now. No stage lights. No perfect posture. Just Kaia, breathing beside me like she's afraid if she stops, she'll break too.

For a long time we sit in silence. The quiet between us isn't awkward, but it is heavy.

I finally rasp, "Aren't you supposed to be somewhere... getting debriefed?"

Kaia's voice is low. "I left."

I snort weakly. "That tracks."

Kaia's breath hitches, like she almost laughs, but it dies before it becomes one.

The hospital yesterday was a blur. I didn't sleep much last night. And all day I've been ignoring Kaia and Gus's texts like silence could keep me from drowning.

Kaia shifts beside me, not closer, not farther. Just... there. Like she's trying to be a presence without demanding anything from it.

"I'm sorry," she says quietly.

Kaia doesn't rush to fill the space. She just watches my face like she's listening to everything I'm not saying. Then she adds, softer, more specific...

"I'm sorry I didn't see sooner how dangerous it was," she murmurs. "How... hungry. I helped bring this world into your world..."

My throat tightens. My jaw locks. Because if I speak, it'll come out wrong. It'll come out as blame. Or grief. Or both. And I don't know which one will kill me faster.

Kaia keeps going anyway, carefully, like she's walking on glass. "If I'd known—if I'd seen what the Chorus was doing sooner, if I hadn't—" She swallows hard. "If I hadn't been so good at doing what I'm told... maybe—"

"Stop," I rasp, and it comes out raw. "You can't 'maybe' her back."

Kaia goes silent immediately.

Good.

I hate that it's good.

I press the heels of my hands into my eyes like I can shove the tears back inside where they belong.

When I speak again, my voice is hollow. "She wanted pancakes," I say, and it sounds stupid and enormous at the same time. "She was... happy yesterday morning. She called you the singing girl like she was—like she was ten years younger..."

Kaia's breath shakes. I don't look at her. I can't. If I see her face right now, I'll either yell at her or cling to her, and I don't trust myself to choose the right one.

"She didn't even know," I whisper. "Half the time she didn't know *where* she was or *who* she was. But she knew she wanted you to eat."

Kaia's voice breaks, barely audible. "I did."

I nod once, staring at the asphalt like it might answer me. "Yeah. You did."

Another stretch of silence. It's the kind that usually would've made me snap. The kind I'd fill with sarcasm just to prove I'm still in control. But control feels stupid right now.

Finally Kaia says, quieter, "I kept texting because I didn't know what else to do."

I swallow. "I saw."

"You didn't answer."

"I couldn't," I say, honest and ugly.

Kaia inhales like she's trying not to make a sound.

I wipe at my cheek with the sleeve of my hoodie, furious that my face is still doing this.

I glance at her finally, one quick look, like checking a wound. Her eyes are red-rimmed. She's not crying the way I am. She looks like she already cried and then packed it away because that's what she's trained to do.

And something in me softens in the worst possible way.

"Why are you here?" I whisper, the question hitting harder now that I've let it exist.

Kaia's gaze holds mine. "Because you shouldn't have to sit out here alone."

I laugh once, weak and sharp. "That's not your job."

Kaia's voice drops. "It is if I want it to be."

I look away again because I can't hold her gaze and my grief at the same time.

My hands curl into fists in my lap.

I don't know what I'm supposed to do now. I don't know who I am without the routine of meds and schedules and pretending everything is fine.

All I know is Kaia is sitting beside me, and the quiet between us is heavy, and for the first time in a long time, she isn't asking me to make it lighter.

"I stayed," I say, voice flat. "I stayed here for her. Because someone had to. Because if I left, who was going to—"

My throat tightens. I force the words out anyway.

"Now she's gone," I whisper.

Kaia's hands flex on her knees like she wants to reach for me and is afraid.

"I'm sorry," she says again, but not like a platitude. Like she's bleeding the words out.

I laugh once, ugly. "You already said that."

"I mean it," Kaia whispers.

I stare at the parking lot. My wrist aches under the binding like it's reminding me that even in grief, I'm owned by rules.

Kaia's voice is careful. "You don't have to stay."

That gets my attention. I look at her, eyes narrowed, because there's a trap in that sentence. Kaia meets my gaze steadily.

"I'm not saying... abandon everything," she says, choosing each word like it matters. "I'm saying... you don't have to rot here out of obligation."

My throat tightens.

Kaia swallows. "You can come with me."

The words land like a punch. I stare at her like she's insane.

"Kaia," I whisper. "You live in hotels and schedules and—and there's demons."

Kaia nods. "Yes. But it's not just hotels." She swallows. "We have a home base."

I go still.

Kaia keeps her voice low, practical, like she's offering something real, not a fantasy. "It's a warded building Eon owns. Private. Security in the lobby, Council access, medical on-site, comms that don't leak." Her jaw tightens. "Rules."

"Rules," I repeat, tasting it.

"Privacy constraints," she adds, honest. "No random visi-tors. No telling people where you live. You'd have your own key card, your own space—" She pauses. "And if you come with me, you should know now: you're not walking into normal. You wouldn't be trapped, but there would be restric-tions." Her voice drops. "You can leave anytime. I won't ever take your choices from you."

I'm quiet for a moment too long.

"I can't bring her back," Kaia adds, voice cracking. "I can't— I *would*—" She swallows hard. "But I can—" Her voice drops. "I can stop running from you."

My chest aches so hard I think I might be sick. I press my palms into my eyes again, unable to think. When I lower them, Kaia is still looking at me like she's willing to sit here all night if that's what it takes.

My voice comes out small and broken. "If I go with you..."

Kaia leans in slightly, hope flickering.

I continue, harsh, because softness will kill me. "I'm not going to be your secret."

Kaia's eyes widen. "You won't be."

"I'm not going to be something you tuck away when it gets complicated," I say, voice trembling with rage and grief. "I'm not going to be the girl you leave behind again."

Kaia's face crumples, pain sharp. "I won't," she says imme-diately. "I won't leave you behind ever again, Evie. I swear."

I swallow, throat burning.

"If the thing that did this is tied to your world," I whisper, "then I'm not letting you fight it without me."

Kaia goes still.

I laugh once, wet. "I couldn't save her," I say, and it hurts so much my whole body shakes. "But I can make sure it doesn't get you too..."

Kaia's eyes shine.

She whispers my name like it's a prayer. "Evie."

I stare at her, grief ripping me open wide enough that I can't keep lying anymore.

"I loved you when we were teens," I say, voice raw. "And I love you now. I'm done pretending I don't."

Kaia's breath breaks. She looks like she's been punched and kissed at the same time.

"I never stopped," she whispers. "I just—I buried it under work. Under survival. Under being told it was dangerous."

My chest tightens.

"Everything with you is dangerous," I whisper.

Kaia's smile is shaky, devastated. "I know."

I look at her and the grief doesn't go away. It just makes room.

Room for rage.

Room for love.

Room for the fact that I am still here, still breathing.

I reach for her before I can second-guess myself, grabbing the front of her hoodie like I did in the Ferris wheel.

Kaia's hands come up to my face, gentle like she's afraid I'll break.

"Can I..." she begins..

I nod.

Kaia kisses me with the utmost gentleness. I cling to her, anchoring myself to something real. Kaia holds me like she's finally allowed to.

When we break for air, my forehead rests against hers and my cheeks are wet with tears.

My voice is small. "I'm so tired."

Kaia's eyes close briefly, pain and love written all over her face. "I know."

She presses a kiss to my temple.

"I've got you," she whispers.

And for the first time since the noise started, I believe her, just enough to keep breathing.

Kaia keeps her voice low, hand rubbing over my arm. "Do you want to go inside? It's cold out here."

I swallow hard. "Sure."

We stand.

My legs feel like they belong to a different timeline, one where I'm not walking away from my grandmother's death and toward my ex-best friend like the world hasn't completely lost its mind.

Kaia stands one step behind me, close enough that I can feel her warmth, far enough that it still feels like my choice.

The door opens. The house smells like lavender and old wood and the faint ghost of Grandma's tea.

It hits me like a shove.

My breath catches. I step inside and the silence is... physical. It presses against my ears.

I flick on the entry light. The living room is exactly as we left it yesterday. Grandma's chair. Her throw blanket folded neatly over the arm. A book open on the side table like she's just in the bathroom and will be back any second.

My throat tightens until it hurts. I take my shoes off because muscle memory is cruel.

Kaia follows, quiet. She pauses by the doorway like she's waiting for permission to exist in my space.

I hate that my first instinct is to snap at her.

But more than that, I hate that my second instinct is to pull her closer, so the house doesn't swallow me whole.

"Come in," I mutter.

Kaia steps in carefully. "Okay."

She closes the door behind us. The click sounds too loud. I stand there staring at Grandma's chair, and something in me caves.

"I can't—" I whisper, then stop, because what even is the sentence. I can't *what*? I can't do this? I can't be here? I can't be the only heartbeat in this house?

Kaia moves closer.

"Evie," she says softly.

I shake my head once, fast, refusing the tears.

Kaia doesn't touch me yet. She just stands in front of me, close enough that her presence blocks the chair from my line of sight.

"I can—" she starts, then stops, recalibrating like she's fighting the instinct to go into leader-voice. "I can make the energy quieter," she says instead. "Just... for a minute. So you can breathe."

I swallow. "Do whatever."

Kaia nods once.

She doesn't summon Aurora. She doesn't flare purple. She doesn't turn into anything mythic.

She just reaches into the pocket of her hoodie and pulls out a small, flat charm that looks like a cheap acrylic keychain. Eon's logo is on one side.

It looks stupidly normal in her fingers.

"They hand these out to staff," she murmurs. "Council slips sigils into the design. It's... not a full ward. Just an energetic hush."

"Of course they do," I rasp.

Kaia turns it over once, thumb tracing the edge like she's remembering instructions. Then she lifts it toward the nearest window and presses it to the glass.

No big flash. No dramatic glow. Just a faint shimmer that ripples outward—like heat off pavement—followed by a soft, low vibration I feel more than hear, settling into the bones of the house.

The air changes. Not sealed. Not *safe*. Just... calmer, as if someone finally closed a window that's been rattling in the wind.

Kaia drops her hand. The charm stays on the window.

"Okay," she says quietly. "It won't stop anything big. But it'll make the... edges less sharp."

I manage a rough, sarcastic exhale. "Great. My house is officially a magical bubble. Grandma would've loved that."

Kaia's mouth twitches, grief flickering behind her eyes. "She would've made you label it."

"For ghost," I mutter automatically, and the words punch me in the ribs because that's our old joke and I didn't mean to say it.

Kaia freezes for half a second, expression softening in a way that makes me want to bite her and kiss her in the same breath.

"I—" I start, then stop, because my throat is closing again.

Kaia steps closer. "You don't have to hold it in."

"I do," I snap, then my voice cracks and betrays me. "If I let it out, I don't know if I'll stop."

Kaia's gaze holds mine. "Then don't stop."

That's the thing. That's what she's always been good at, making me feel like it's safe to be a mess.

I hate it.

I *need* it.

My shoulders shake once, and then I'm crying in a way that's ugly and real, my hand flying to my mouth like I can physically shove the sound back in.

Kaia catches my wrists gently and lowers them.

"Hey," she whispers. "Let it happen."

I shake my head, tears falling anyway. "I'm so mad."

"I know."

"I'm so—" I swallow, choking. "I'm so *empty.*"

Kaia's eyes shine. "I know."

I grip her hoodie like I'm anchoring myself to cloth instead of air. "I don't know who I am if I'm not taking care of her."

Kaia's voice is rough now. "You're still you."

I laugh through tears, bitter. "Who the hell is that?"

Kaia touches my cheek, thumb gentle. "The girl who runs toward the sound tower when everyone else is chanting."

I flinch. "Don't make me a hero."

Kaia shakes her head. "I'm not. I'm just... seeing you."

My throat tightens again. I wipe my face with the back of my hand, furious at myself for crying like this in front of her.

Kaia doesn't look away. Doesn't make it weird. Doesn't try to fix it. She just stays.

After a minute, my breathing steadies into something survivable. I step back, still holding onto her hoodie like an idiot.

"Come upstairs," I mutter, because I can't stand the living room. I can't stand the chair. I can't stand the space where my grandma should be.

Kaia nods. "Okay."

We move through the house quietly. The stairs creak the same way they always have. My bedroom door sticks a little; I shoulder it open.

The room is dim. Ordinary. Mine.

I flick on the bedside lamp.

Kaia follows me. I turn to face her and realize my hands are still shaking, even now, even after the battle, even after the hospital, even after all of the crying.

Kaia notices.

She reaches out slowly, palm up. "Can I?"

I swallow. Nod once.

Kaia takes my hands in hers and brings them to her mouth, kissing my knuckles like it's a promise.

My chest aches.

"You don't have to be anything for me," she whispers.

I scoff weakly. "I'm being a disaster."

Kaia's mouth twitches. "Good. Be a disaster. I can handle it."

I stare at her. "Since when are you good at handling anything?"

Kaia exhales a small laugh, then sobers. "Since I stopped trying to do it alone."

The words land quietly, heavy with everything she's finally learning. My throat tightens. I step closer, and this time it's me who kisses her—slow, deliberate, not hungry-first. My hands slide up to her shoulders, grounding myself in the reality of her body here, warm and breathing.

Kaia kisses me back with the same care, like she's not trying to take anything from me. Just offer.

We separate on a shaky breath.

I whisper, "We're still here."

Kaia's eyes glisten. "Yeah."

"After everything," I say, voice breaking again. "We're still here."

Kaia nods, and her voice is rough. "Still here."

I tug at the edge of her hoodie. "Take it off?"

Kaia pauses, just a beat, checking my face. "Okay."

She helps me out of my hoodie first, slow. Like she's unwrapping something precious instead of just taking off fabric. Her fingers brush my skin and I shiver—not from desire, not exactly. From being touched gently after yesterday's violence and loss.

I swallow hard. "You're being... weirdly careful."

Kaia's mouth curves faintly. "You deserve careful."

The words make my eyes burn again.

I pull her hoodie up and over her head. Her hair falls free, dark and slightly messy, nothing like the stage.

She looks like *Kaia* again. Not the poster.

I brush my thumb under her eye. "You look tired."

Kaia leans into the touch. "I am."

"Good," I mutter. "Be tired with me."

Kaia's breath shudders like she's trying not to cry. "Okay."

We move together without rushing. Shoes kicked off. Layers folded or dropped without ceremony. Skin meeting skin in small, grounding touches, foreheads pressed together, hands on shoulders, a kiss to my temple that feels like an apology without words.

There's a moment where I hesitate, grief flashing up like a sudden wave.

Kaia notices instantly. She stills.

"We can stop," she whispers.

I shake my head. "No. I just... I don't want to feel alone in my own body tonight."

Kaia's eyes soften with something fierce. "You won't."

I let out a shaky breath. "Promise?"

Kaia kisses my forehead. "I'm not going anywhere."

The words move through me slowly, like warmth returning to a limb that's been numb too long. I hadn't realized how tightly I'd been holding myself together until that moment—how cold the house felt, how hollow everything inside me had been.

Without really thinking, I tug her toward the bed. We sink down onto the mattress together, not in a rush—just easing into it, like we're both remembering how to be close without fear. Kaia's arm slides around my waist immediately, pulling me in until my face ends up tucked against the curve of her shoulder.

Her skin is warm. Familiar. I breathe her in like I've been holding my breath for days.

The tightness in my chest doesn't vanish, but it loosens a little with every slow inhale.

The house is still empty. Too empty. But it doesn't feel like it's swallowing me anymore.

I press my mouth against the warm skin of her shoulder, letting the simple contact anchor me to the moment.

"Stay the night?" I whisper.

Kaia's hand tightens gently at the small of my back.

"Yeah," she murmurs against my hair. "I'm staying."

Something inside me settles when she says it. The promise sinks deep, past all the noise in my head, into the place that's been aching all day.

For a long while we just lie there holding each other. Her thumb moves slowly up and down my spine, tracing small circles over my skin through my shirt, patient and steady like she's coaxing the tension out of me one breath at a time.

Eventually she shifts, fingers lifting my chin so I'm looking at her. The way she kisses me now is different. Slower. Softer. Careful in a way that makes my throat tighten.

Her lips move over mine with quiet patience, letting the kiss deepen only when I lean into it. When I sigh against her mouth, she whispers the words again.

"I'm not going anywhere."

Her hand cups the side of my face, thumb brushing gently along my cheekbone before her lips drift to my temple. She presses a kiss there, then another, murmuring softly against my skin.

"You're okay," she says. "I've got you."

The reassurance slips into all the places that have been aching.

Kaia moves slowly as she helps me out of my clothes, fingers brushing my shoulders, my arms, the curve of my waist. She never rushes. Every time she pauses, her eyes flick up to mine like she's checking—making sure I'm still with her.

I am.

Every piece of clothing she removes is followed by another kiss. My temple. The corner of my mouth. The hollow beneath my ear.

"Still okay?" she asks quietly.

I nod, my hands sliding over her back as she leans over me.

Her mouth drifts lower, leaving warm, lingering kisses along my collarbone. The attention makes my breathing hitch, a quiet sound escaping me before I can stop it.

Kaia smiles softly against my skin.

"There you are," she murmurs, her voice low and coaxing, like she's drawing me back into my own body.

Her hands wander slowly over me—up my waist, over my ribs, cupping the weight of my breasts with a lingering, knowing touch. Her thumbs graze over my nipples, just enough pressure to make my breath hitch, before she drags her palms down again. Each pass of her hands loosens something tight inside my chest, melting me open under her.

By the time she settles between my legs, my body feels loose and warm and alive in a way it hasn't all day.

One of her hands slides up and threads through mine, fingers lacing tight, grounding me. Her grip is firm, almost possessive. Her other hand drags up my thigh, spreading me wider for her as she settles between my legs. Her eyes meet mine, a silent question, and I nod.

I feel her breath first—warm, teasing—right over my pussy, and it makes my hips twitch before she even touches me.

Then her mouth is on me.

A slow, deliberate lick through my folds that makes my whole body jolt. She groans softly against me, the sound vibrating straight through my clit, and I gasp, my free hand twisting into the sheets. Her tongue moves again, firmer, dragging up, circling, pressing exactly where I need it.

"Fuck—*Kaia*—"

My voice breaks as she keeps going, her mouth hot and wet between my thighs. She doesn't rush it. She drags it out, licking me slowly, then harder, then easing back just enough to make me chase it before giving it to me again. Every pass of her tongue makes my hips lift, grinding helplessly against her face.

Her fingers tighten around my hand when I start to shake.

Her other hand digs into my thigh, keeping me spread open while her tongue flicks over my clit, faster now, more insistent. The wet sound of it, the heat of her mouth—it's too much, not enough, and everything at once. My thighs try to close around her, but she holds me there, keeps me exactly where she wants me.

The pressure builds fast—tight, sharp, coiling low in my stomach until I can't breathe past it.

"I'm—Kaia, I'm gonna—"

She doesn't stop. If anything, she presses in harder, sucking, licking, driving me right to the edge with a relentless, hungry rhythm.

And then I snap.

The orgasm hits like a shock through my entire body, ripping a cry from my throat as my back arches off the bed. My hips jerk against her mouth, grinding hard as wave after wave crashes through me. I clutch her hand, nails digging in, my whole body trembling as the pleasure pulses, dragging on, pulling another broken sound from me.

She keeps going through it.

Slower now, but still there—still licking, still teasing my over-sensitive clit until I'm gasping, twitching, trying to pull away even as I can't stop chasing the feeling.

"Kaia—too much—"

Only then does she ease off, pressing one last soft, lingering kiss against my soaked skin before lifting her head.

I collapse back into the pillows, chest heaving, my body loose and wrecked, thighs still trembling around her. Everything feels too sensitive, too alive, like I've been stripped raw from the inside out.

Kaia presses one last soft kiss against my hip before climbing back up beside me.

"You didn't—" I start, still catching my breath.

She shakes her head, brushing my hair away from my face.

"I just wanted to make you feel good," she says quietly.

Something in my chest aches at the tenderness in her voice.

She pulls the blanket over us, then settles against me again, her arm sliding around my waist the way it was before. When I curl into her shoulder this time, sleep creeps in almost immediately.

Her lips press into my hair.

"I'm here," she murmurs again.

And for the first time since everything fell apart, I fall asleep without the fear of waking up alone.

$$Kaia$$

The house looks like a mouth that forgot how to speak.

Even from the sidewalk, I can feel it: quiet pressed into the walls, air too still, curtains open like someone tried to make it cheerful and failed. Harbor's Edge is bright outside, like it doesn't know what it cost to get here.

A few days have passed since the hospital. Since the festival. Since the world got loud and then went quiet in the worst way.

In those few days, the Council was busy with cleanup. Council teams moved through Harbor's Edge with Handlers in plain clothes standing in doorways with that dead-eyed calm, asking people to "repeat after me" until their fear became forgettable.

Eon's cleanup was different, but just as busy. Phones got flagged. Live streams vanished. Fan-cam accounts got hit with takedowns so fast it made the rest of the internet look polite. Press got fed a clean narrative: power surge, pyrotechnic malfunction, crowd panic, heroic security response. It's the kind of story that fits in a headline and leaves out the part where a demon tried to eat a town.

Even Blaire made calls. Not the PR kind. The real kind... Eon's "logistics" team showed up at Evie's house with boxes, tape, and a woman who kept saying "I'm so sorry" like it was a checklist item. Mr. Bane did a final sweep of the house and left another little hush charm on the window.

And Blaire—Blaire roped Gus into being in charge of the practical stuff with the same sharp efficiency she uses on tour schedules.

The plan is ugly, but it's a plan.

Gus will keep an eye on the house, collect the mail, and make sure nothing gets broken into while the paperwork moves. He'll also be the one meeting with the realtor on Evie's behalf. Blaire had the solicitor's number on speed dial before Evie even stopped shaking. She handled the "how do you sell a house when you feel like you're dying" part so Evie didn't have to.

All because I said, once, finally out loud and completely non-negotiable: *She's coming with us.*

Because I'm done pretending distance keeps anyone safe.

I let myself in with the spare key Evie pressed into my hand the other day.

The hush inside is immediate. Not magical. Not the hush charm. Something older than that. The silence left when a person who belonged in a place is suddenly nowhere in it.

There are boxes stacked along the wall of the entryway, each one labeled in Evie's blunt handwriting. KITCHEN. BOOKS. DONATE. TRASH. A roll of tape sits abandoned on the little side table by the door beside a glass bowl full of loose change and two hair ties.

I close the door quietly behind me and follow the sound of cardboard shifting.

Evie is in the kitchen. She's standing at the table in a washed-out shirt and old jeans, hair pulled back badly like she did it without looking in a mirror. The kitchen around her is half-packed and half-still-lived-in. Cabinets hanging open. A box on one chair. Another on the floor by her feet. The table is covered in small sorted piles that look impossibly intimate: recipe cards, takeout menus, a chipped mug, rubber-banded pens, batteries, a little ceramic lighthouse salt shaker, prescription bottles, a pair of reading glasses folded on top of a dish towel.

The room smells faintly like cardboard and stale coffee.

Evie has one hand braced on the table and the other wrapped around a mug like she forgot to drink from it.

She looks up when she hears me.

"You're early," she says.

Her voice is flat with exhaustion, but there's still enough edge in it to feel like her. Relief hits me so hard it almost makes me dizzy.

"I know."

Her gaze drops to the reusable grocery bag in my hand. "What's that?"

"Just groceries."

She nods and looks back down at the table instead. At the little piles of a life being divided into keep, donate, throw away. My chest tightens.

I have fought monsters in front of screaming crowds. I have bled under spotlights. I have stood in arenas and pretended not to be afraid.

This feels harder.

"I brought food," I say, because apparently when I'm terrified my solution is always to state the obvious like it's tactical.

Evie lets out a breath through her nose. "Kaia."

"I know."

"No, I mean—" She rubs at the space between her brows with two fingers. "You didn't have to."

"I know that too."

She finally looks at me properly.

The bruised exhaustion in her face is worse in daylight. The last few days have sanded her down to something sharper and quieter. But she's still here. Still standing. Still giving me that look like I'm one stupid sentence away from being told to get out of her kitchen forever.

Somehow that steadies me.

I step farther into the room and set the grocery bag on the counter. "Have you eaten?"

Evie glances at the mug in her hand like she's surprised to find it there. "Coffee."

"That's not food."

"It's bean soup."

I huff out a laugh before I can stop myself. Her mouth twitches.

The kitchen falls quiet again.

On the table, next to the reading glasses, there's a stack of recipe cards tied together with faded blue ribbon. The top card is written in slanted handwriting I don't recognize, ingredients ineligible, like whoever wrote them assumed they'd always remember the rest.

Evie follows my gaze.

"She wrote everything down," she says, and her voice changes on the sentence. Not much. Just enough to make something in me go very still. "Not because she needed to. Just because she liked pretending she was more organized than she actually was."

I step closer to the table carefully. "Sounds familiar."

That gets me a real look this time. Tired. Suspicious. A little helpless around the edges.

"I *am* organized. My gran, on the other hand," she says, with the ghost of a laugh, "was chaos in orthopedic shoes."

I smile before I can help it. Then I see the mug in her hand.

White ceramic. Blue stripe. The handle repaired once with glue so old it's gone yellow at the seam.

I remember that mug.

Grandma Calder used it the morning I ate pancakes with them. The memory arrives so sharp it hurts.

Evie must see something change in my face, because she looks down at the mug like it offended her.

"She used this one every morning," she says. "Even when I bought her nicer ones. Said this one was her favorite."

My throat tightens.

Evie sets the mug down too carefully. It makes almost no sound against the wood.

"I keep thinking," she says, still looking at it, "that if I pack the wrong thing first, the rest of the house will get mad at me."

The sentence is so raw and strange and honest that it cleaves straight through me.

I don't say I'm sorry. Everyone keeps saying that to her, and I'm starting to think the phrase has been worn smooth from overuse.

Instead I look at the open cabinets, the bare patch of wall where something used to hang, the boxes waiting with their little blank mouths open.

"Can I make you breakfast?" I ask suddenly.

She glances at me like I've suggested summoning a dragon into the kitchen. "You can cook?"

I narrow my eyes. "Rude."

"You're a celebrity."

"I'm half-Korean."

That startles a sound out of her—small, sharp, almost a laugh—and for one reckless second I love myself for being the one to cause it.

Then her eyes go glossy with exhaustion again, and the feeling in my chest changes shape.

"My mom used to make kimchi jeon when the house felt wrong," I say, pulling out the ingredients out of the bag one by one because it's easier to focus on my hands than on the look on her face. "After bad nights. After nightmares. If I came home hoarse from training or crying or being sixteen about something."

Evie leans one hip against the table, watching me.

I keep my eyes on the counter. On the bowl I've found. On the knife in my hand.

"She'd open all the windows and fry pancakes and tell me hot food chased bad spirits out faster."

Something in the room shifts. Not magically. Not like a ward catching or a sigil flaring. Just grief making space for one strange little story.

Evie's mouth softens.

"She actually said that?"

I nod. "Very seriously."

A beat.

Then, quietly, Evie adds, "Pancakes that fight ghosts."

The memory hits both of us at once. Gran at this table, delighted, declaring it like it was entirely sensible. I see it happen in Evie's face when she goes still. For one second I think I've done something cruel by bringing it back.

Then Evie swallows and says, "Okay."

Just that.

Okay.

I release a breath I didn't know I was holding.

"Okay?"

"Okay," she repeats, rougher now. "Make your ghost-repelling pancakes."

I move before I can overthink it. The cabinet doors are half-open but I still don't know this kitchen by instinct, and that hurts in ways I do not have time to name.

"Where's the flour?"

"Left of the stove," Evie says automatically. "Behind the tea."

I find it exactly where she said.

"Mixing bowl?"

"Under the counter by the sink."

Every answer comes fast. Easy. Worn into her by years of reaching without looking. Each one lands like a tiny proof of all the life that happened here while I was gone.

I whisk batter in a bowl older than I am. Chop kimchi on the cutting board by the window. Slice scallions too thin because my hands are steadier with swords than knives and always have been.

Behind me, cardboard whispers.

I glance over my shoulder.

Evie is sorting again, slower now. She picks up one of the recipe cards, reads half a line, and presses her lips together. Sets it gently in the keep pile. The reading glasses go next. Then the lighthouse shaker, after a moment of hesitation that says everything.

I turn back to the stove because watching her grieve feels too intimate, like seeing bare skin.

Oil goes into the pan. The first hiss when the batter hits it fills the kitchen. Warm, immediate, alive. The smell follows a second later, savory, sharp, familiar enough to make my chest ache.

For a few minutes, the room becomes something simpler.

Evie sorting at the table. Me turning pancakes at the stove and praying I don't mess them up. Boxes stacked like patient witnesses. Sunlight inching across the floorboards.

I plate the first two pancakes and set them down between us with chopsticks and soy dipping sauce I found after opening the wrong cabinet twice.

Evie looks at the plate like she doesn't trust it.

I drag out the chair opposite her and sit. "Go on, try it."

She picks up a piece with the chopsticks awkwardly, like it's been a while. Blows on it once. Takes a bite.

Her eyes close. It's such a small reaction it almost destroys me.

"Good?" I ask, trying for light.

She opens her eyes and looks at me over the edge of her grief, over the half-packed table, over everything broken and unfinished between us.

"Annoyingly," she says.

I grin despite myself.

She takes another bite, slower this time.

"She always overfed people when she was scared," she says. "Like if everyone ate enough, nothing bad could get through the door."

My chest pulls tight. "My mom was like that too."

A silence settles. Not empty. Just full.

Then she laughs under her breath, broken around the edges. "God. She would've loved you doing this."

I don't know what to do with that. I look down at my plate because it suddenly feels impossible to meet her eyes.

"I don't know how to help with this kind of thing," I admit. "The normal kind. I know how to fight. I know how to fix a formation when it breaks. I know how to make a crowd look where I want. I don't..." I swallow. "I don't know what to do with *this*, but I want to. If there's anything I can do, Evie..."

Evie goes quiet. When I finally look up, she's watching me with an expression so open it scares me a little.

"You're doing okay," she says.

The words hit somewhere unguarded. I nod once because anything else would come out wrong.

We eat in silence for a while longer, and when we're done, Evie unties the ribbon around the recipe cards and flips through them. She stops at one in the middle. Her thumb traces the handwriting.

I stand without thinking about it and move around the table. I don't touch her right away. I just stand beside her shoulder, close enough that she can choose.

After a second, she leans the tiniest amount into my side. It's barely anything, but it feels like being handed something breakable.

I exhale slowly, then slide my arms around her from behind. My chin settles on her shoulder. Evie goes still for a heartbeat. I press a kiss to her cheek—soft, almost reverent—and feel her swallow. Her fingers tighten on the recipe card.

"Okay?" I murmur, so quiet it barely counts as a word.

Evie's answer is a tiny nod, her body leaning back into mine.

We stay like that for a minute in the half-packed kitchen while the house breathes around us. Then Evie straightens first, wiping quickly under one eye like she's mad at it.

She snorts and nudges the recipe cards toward me. "Can you find a smaller box for these? Not with the books. I don't want them bent."

"Yeah." I pick up the stack carefully. "Of course."

The ribbon is soft with age against my fingers.

A few minutes later, the kitchen starts moving again.

Not healed. Not lighter, exactly.

Just moving.

The next day, Evie stands in the doorway with a cardboard box hugged to her chest.

It's not a big box. It's the kind of box you carry when you're trying to pretend you aren't leaving a whole life behind.

Her hair is pulled back. No makeup. A soft open sweater over a tank top.

She looks hollowed out and stubborn at the same time.

She sees me and makes a face like she's allergic to tenderness.

"You're early again," she says.

"I didn't want to miss it," I admit.

Evie snorts softly. "It's a key handoff. Very glamorous."

"I meant…" I stop, because if I say *I didn't want you to do this alone,* she'll either cry or snap at me. Possibly both.

Evie reads it anyway. Her mouth tightens. Then, very quietly, she says, "Thanks."

She steps onto the porch and looks back into the house one last time.

I don't rush her.

I don't tell her it'll be okay.

I just stand close enough that if she leans, I'm there.

Evie's fingers flex around the box edges, knuckles whitening.

Then she locks the front door. The click sounds final. Gus is waiting at the bottom of the steps with his hands in his pockets, looking like someone who got dragged into feelings against his will.

He's wearing his diner apron even though he's not working. Like armor. Like if he takes it off, the world will realize he's human.

Evie walks down the steps and stops in front of him.

For a second, neither of them speaks.

Then Gus clears his throat, gruff. "You sure about this?"

Evie's jaw lifts. "No."

Gus squints. "That's not—"

"I'm sure enough," Evie corrects, voice steady even as her eyes shine. "And I'm not staying out of fear."

Gus huffs like he wants to argue, but his gaze softens in a way he probably hates.

He holds out his hand. Evie slides the keys into his palm.

"House'll be fine," he says. "Blaire already set me up with a damn binder." His mouth twists like the word *binder* offends him. "And a realtor number. And instructions. Like I'm a child."

I bite the inside of my cheek to keep from smiling.

Evie's voice catches. "Thank you."

Gus grunts. "And diner will be fine too," he adds. "I've got it."

Evie swallows. "You better."

Gus's mouth twitches. "Yeah.."

Evie's eyes flicker—pain, gratitude, something like love she'd never say out loud.

Then Gus does the most shocking thing I have ever seen him do. He pulls her into a hug. It's awkward at first—Gus doesn't look like he's ever hugged anyone on purpose—but Evie clings for a second like she's trying to imprint the shape of home before it vanishes.

My throat tightens.

I look away, giving them privacy, hands shoved into my pockets so I don't reach for something I don't have the right to take.

When they separate, Gus clears his throat hard, like he's trying to shake emotion loose.

He nods at me without looking directly at my face. "You look after her."

My stomach twists.

"I will," I say. The promise tastes like steel.

Evie rolls her eyes, wiping at her face like it's just dust. "I'll look after myself, thanks."

Gus snorts. "That's what I'm afraid of."

Evie huffs a laugh, small, tired.

Then she shifts the box in her arms and steps back toward me. Up close, I can see the exhaustion in the lines around her eyes. The way she's holding herself together with sheer will.

My chest aches.

I lift my hand—hesitate—then settle it lightly against her back, not pulling, not guiding, just... there.

Evie freezes for a half-second. Then she doesn't pull away. It's a small thing. It feels like a miracle.

"Okay," she says, like she's speaking to herself. "Next stop: sentimental goodbye tour."

The Lighthouse Diner is bright when we walk in, sunlight slicing across the booths.

It smells like coffee and french fries and the exact kind of comfort that makes my chest tighten.

The diner is technically closed for another 'private event,' with the exception of the few invitees. Tasha is at the counter with her apron and a Midnight Halo t-shirt underneath. When she sees us, she squeals. Actually squeals.

"Oh my god," she says, hands pressed to her cheeks. "You're here. You're *all* here."

Jules saunters in behind us. Remy and Mina follow. Blaire comes in after them, scanning the diner automatically, earpiece in, posture annoyed by default.

Evie drops her box gently behind the counter and looks around. Mr. Alvarez is in his usual seat, wearing a clean button-up like he's attending church. When he sees Evie, he stands up slowly, face soft.

"Evie," he says.

Evie's voice goes rough. "Hey, Mr. Alvarez."

He opens his arms and Evie walks into the hug without hesitation, burying her face against his shoulder for a second longer than she probably meant to.

Mr. Alvarez pats her back gently. "Your grandma was a fierce woman."

Evie swallows hard. "Yeah."

"She'd be proud of you," he murmurs.

Evie huffs a laugh that almost turns into a sob. She pulls back and wipes her eyes with her sleeve like she's furious at her own face.

Gus grunts from behind the counter. "Sit down, all of you. Before the whole place turns into a group therapy circle."

Jules grins. "Too late."

Evie raises a brow at her. "Don't start."

Jules puts a hand to her chest, scandalized. "I would never."

Remy says, deadpan, "She will."

Mina nods solemnly. "She definitely will."

Jules gasps. "Betrayal."

Evie's mouth twitches despite herself.

It's the smallest crack of light, and I catch it like oxygen. Gus gestures at a booth, the big one by the window. "That one. It's yours."

Evie hesitates, then she slides into the booth first. I immediately slide in next to her.

On the wall near the register—already framed and leveled, as if it's been there forever—is the photo. The one Blaire took.

Me and Evie and Gus under the *LIGHTHOUSE DINER* sign inside, all of us pretending we're normal people, all of us failing in different ways.

Before I can mention it, Tasha bounces over with a notepad, vibrating with excitement. "Okay. Hi. Welcome. Can I start you with drinks?"

Evie lifts an eyebrow. "Are you... waitressing me."

Tasha's grin turns wild. "Yes."

Evie's eyes narrow. "Be normal."

Tasha nods rapidly. "Absolutely." Then she immediately fails. "Would you like our new signature latte, the *Midnight Halo Mocha,* served with—"

Evie cuts her off. "Coffee. Black. Just... coffee."

Tasha scribbles dramatically. "One black coffee."

We all order, and then Evie catches Mina staring at her.

Evie's shoulders tighten. "Why are you looking at me like that?"

Mina flushes. "Because you... uh... you saved everyone."

Evie scoffs. "I yanked a lever."

Remy's gaze is steady. "You broke the loop."

Jules points a finger-gun at Evie. "You absolutely did the hero thing."

Evie's mouth tightens like she hates praise. I reach under the table and take Evie's hand. Her fingers squeeze mine once, hard.

Not romantic.

Anchoring.

The food comes out in waves.

Blaire eats like she's offended by calories, whereas Jules eats like she's on a mission to clear the kitchen out.

At some point, Tasha reappears with a camera.

"I need a picture," she announces.

Evie's eyes go flat. "No."

Tasha ignores her. "Yes."

Jules cheers. "Yes! Picture! Picture!"

Tasha points the camera at us. Evie's jaw tightens, but she doesn't move away when I slide closer to her in the booth.

I tuck my arm around her shoulders, careful. Evie leans into me.

Tasha grins like she's about to explode. "Okay. Smile. On three. Three!" Tasha says.

The flash pops.

The moment freezes.

Evie and me, pressed together in the booth that used to be our whole world.

Jules throws peace signs. Mina looks like she's witnessing a sacred event. Remy barely tilts her head, but her eyes are soft. Blaire looks like she's being held hostage.

It's absurd.

It's *perfect*.

When Tasha shows the photo to Evie, Evie stares at it for a long second, then simply requests, "Send it to me?"

Evening comes like a slow exhale.

And then it's time.

We stand outside the tour bus on the edge of town where the road begins, the engine idling low like a heartbeat. The bus looks enormous in the dim light, sleek and black and completely out of place against Harbor's Edge's sleepy streets.

I'm standing beside the steps, palms damp, posture too controlled. Jules leans against the bus like she's posing for a photoshoot. Remy stands with her arms crossed, quiet and watchful. Mina glances down the street every few seconds.

Blaire is pacing with her phone at her ear, muttering about schedules and insurance.

I'm not listening. I'm staring down the street.

Waiting.

My stomach twists so hard it feels like it's tying itself into knots.

This is ridiculous.

I've done stadium debuts and award shows and live interviews with thousands of cameras.

But this—

This feels like the scariest entrance of my life. Because I want Evie to choose *this*. To choose me. And I'm terrified she'll change her mind at the last second and I'll have no right to ask her not to.

Then she appears.

Evie walks toward us with a duffel bag slung over her shoulder and a small box in her arms. Her face looks... blank. Not emotionless. Just... braced. Like she's walking into bad weather. She stops at the foot of the bus steps. Her gaze flicks over the girls, over Blaire, over the bus itself. Then to me.

"You ready?" I ask softly.

Evie huffs. "No."

I nod. "Okay."

Evie's mouth twitches. "But I'm doing it anyway."

Something in my chest loosens, sharp and sweet.

Blaire finally looks up from her phone and sighs like the universe is personally inconveniencing her.

"Evie," she says, brisk. "Ground rules."

Evie lifts an eyebrow.

Blaire ignores the tone. "You're not a staff member. You're not a civilian guest. You're... a security liability."

Evie's eyes narrow.

Blaire continues anyway. "So. You'll be registered as a private consultant under Eon oversight. It's temporary. You'll be briefed. You'll sign the addendum."

Evie stares. "I already have a magical NDA tattooed into my wrist."

"It's not a tattoo," Blaire says automatically, then sighs. "The point is: you'll be in the safe zones during shows. You'll follow instructions during incidents. You do *not* go rogue."

Blaire looks at both of us when she says that last part.

I step closer, voice quiet. "Evie. We'll keep you safe. But... you need to let us."

Evie's gaze holds mine for a long moment.

Then she nods once. "Okay."

Blaire exhales like she's survived a war. "Great. Everyone on the bus."

Evie hesitates at the steps.

I hold out my hand, because I want her to know she's not doing this alone. She doesn't even hesitate to take it. Her grip is firm. Determined. And we climb onto the bus together.

Inside, it smells like leather and coffee and travel. The other girls immediately scatter: Jules flopping onto a seat, Mina hovering near Evie like a shy cat, Remy slipping toward the back with her notebook already out like she's logging everything. Blaire disappears into the front lounge muttering about paperwork.

Evie stands in the aisle for a second, duffel still on her shoulder, box clutched tight. Her eyes dart like she's looking for exits.

I touch her elbow lightly. "Come here."

Evie follows me toward the small bedroom space near the back. It has our bunks, in case we need to sleep on the road. I close the door behind us, giving us a pocket of quiet.

Evie exhales shakily. "This is... insane."

I nod. "Yeah."

Evie's gaze sweeps the small space.

Then she looks at me. "Are you sure about this?"

The question hits me hard.

Not *are you sure I can handle this?*

Are you sure you want *me* in your life like this?

I step closer. "Yes."

Evie swallows. "Kaia—"

I cut her off gently. "I mean it. I'm sure."

Evie's eyes glisten but she blinks it away fast. I reach under my bunk and pull out a small box, worn edges, hidden like contraband.

Evie's brow furrows. "What's that?"

I sit on the edge of the bunk and pat the space beside me. Evie hesitates, then sits too. I open the box.

Inside are scraps of a life I pretended I didn't carry. A folded diner receipt, creased soft. I hand it to her first. She unfolds it carefully. The old teenage handwriting, hers, scribbled at an angle. My 'don't panic' list. Evie stares at it.

Her breath catches. "You still have this?"

I nod once, throat tight. "I kept it in my wallet for years. Then I started hiding it in places I thought no one would find."

She snorts, then reads out loud, voice dry. "'Drink water. Not energy drinks. *Water.*'"

"I told you that you've always been bossy," I say with a smile.

Evie's voice goes rough. "You're... unbelievable."

"I know," I whisper.

Quietly, without warning, she reads the last bit under her breath.

"'Your voice is my favorite sound.'"

The words hit the air between us and just hang there.

Evie's gaze meets mine. Her eyes are deep brown, the kind that always looked like they were holding a whole storm behind them even when she was pretending to be fine. There's no bite in her expression right now. No armor. Just something soft and exposed that makes my throat tighten.

She swallows, like the admission costs her.

"It's true," she says. "It is."

My chest aches so hard it feels like a bruise.

I don't know what to do with the fact that she just gave me something tender without making me wrestle for it.

Evie sets the receipt down, then she looks at me. For a second it feels like she's looking past the posters and the stage lights and the years. Straight at the girl she knew. Straight at the girl I still am when no one's watching.

"I love you," she says.

Two seconds. No qualifiers. No armor.

My breath catches.

Evie's voice stays quiet, but it hits like a vow.

"I loved you when we were teenagers and anything felt possible," she says. "I loved you when I hated you for leaving. I loved you in every stupid little silence where I told myself I was over it."

Her eyes shine, furious at the vulnerability of it, like she wants to bite the feeling until it behaves.

"And I'm done pretending that loving you makes me weak," she whispers. "It just makes me honest."

My throat pinches. My heart feels too big for my ribs. I reach for her hand—slow, asking without words. Evie lets me take it. Her fingers squeeze once, sure and steady.

"Your voice *is* my favorite sound," she says again, like she's choosing the words on purpose this time. "But you—Kaia, you are my favorite place to come back to. You're my home too."

I lean forward and press my forehead to hers.

"I love you too, Evie," I whisper, and it's small, and it's everything.

Evie exhales, shaky. Her fingers curl around mine tighter, like she's anchoring us both. Then she pulls back first and wipes at the corner of one eye like she's annoyed it dared to shine.

"Now" she says, brisk again, like she's saving herself. "Show me the rest."

I swallow, throat thick, and reach into the box. I pull out some old photos next. Most of them are us—blurry pier shots, the diner booth, the boardwalk at dusk.

One of them is my mom, in our old kitchen, arms crossed, hair tied up, glaring at the person taking the picture like she's judging their life choices. Evie's expression softens despite herself. "That's your mom."

I nod. "Yeah."

The very next photo is a younger me, maybe ten, sitting on the breakwater with a paper bag in my lap. My dad beside me, wind whipping his blond hair, both of us squinting into the sun. In the bag: foil-wrapped kimbap. We're mid-bite, cheeks full, laughing at something outside the frame.

Evie's breath catches again, softer this time. "Your dad."

I nod once.

My voice comes out low. "He used to bring kimbap and swore it tasted better 'because of the ocean.'"

Evie's eyes stay on the photo. "Did it?"

I exhale. "Yeah," I admit. "It did."

Then Evie finds more of us.

"You kept all of these too," she whispers.

"Yes," I say simply. "I kept... everything I wasn't supposed to."

For a second, she looks like she might break. Instead, she sets my keepsakes back gently and reaches for the small box she's been holding since Harbor's Edge.

She opens it. Inside is a small framed photo of her and her grandmother—Grandma Calder mid-laugh, Evie leaning in close, eyes soft.

Evie's fingers brush the frame like it's a wound.

She places it inside my box instead.

Our box?

My chest tightens.

Evie leans in. This kiss is quieter than the others. No frantic edge. No desperation. Just... intention. Like we're signing something with our mouths that the world can't invalidate.

When we pull back, Evie rests her forehead against mine.

"Okay," she whispers. "We're really doing this."

I close my eyes briefly. "Yeah."

Evie exhales shakily. "Don't make me regret it."

I smile, small and fierce. "I won't."

I kiss her again, then I whisper against her lips, "Welcome to the road."

Evie's eyes close for a second. Then she opens them, determination settling over grief like armor.

"Let's go," she says.

The bus engine deepens.

We pull away from Harbor's Edge like the town is exhaling us.

I sit with Evie in the back lounge now, her duffel tucked under her feet, her fingers laced with mine like she's still checking that I'm real. Outside the window, the last lanterns blur into distance.

And then—because Jules can't let anything be sacred for more than thirty seconds—she flops onto the couch beside Craig the skeleton and pats his ribcage. "Okay, Craig. We're leaving the haunted coastal town. How do you feel about that?"

Remy doesn't look up. "Don't talk to him."

Jules gasps. "He's family."

The plastic skeleton is strapped into the chair by the mini fridge, buckled in tight like he's a valued member of the team. He's wearing his Midnight Halo lanyard and his rhinestone sunglasses that are perched crooked on his skull.

Someone has also put a neck pillow around him.

Evie stares at the skeleton for a long beat, then looks at me with an expression that is half disbelief, half accusation.

"You didn't tell me you have an emotional support skeleton," she accuses playfully.

I squeeze her hand once. "Well, now you know."

Jules points at me like she's proud. "See? She gets it. Craig *is* an emotional support skeleton."

Evie's mouth twitches despite her best efforts. "You named him *Craig*?"

"Hey, don't make fun of his name," Jules says, offended on Craig's behalf. "He's very sensitive. Besides, I didn't name him. Mina did. Right, Mina?"

Mina sits across from us, knees tucked up, staring out the back window instead of forward. She's been doing it since we turned onto the highway.

Remy shifts beside her. "Mina?" she murmurs.

Mina doesn't answer. Her gaze stays fixed on the shrinking town lights.

"Do you See something?" Remy asks quietly.

Mina's throat bobs. She blinks fast. Then she shakes her head once, too quick.

"...No..." she says.

But her voice is wrong. Too thin. Too careful.

Jules's grin fades a notch. Even Craig, strapped in his chair, looks like he's listening.

Evie's grip tightens on my hand, sensing the shift even if she doesn't know why. I feel it in her fingers—instinct, alarm, the way she's learned to read danger without being taught the language for it.

I watch Mina a moment longer. Her shoulders are tense. Her eyes are wide. Like she's watching something follow us down the road that no one else can see.

"Hey," I say gently. "Mina. You okay?"

Mina flinches, then forces herself to smile, small, shaky.

"I'm fine," she says, too fast.

Jules tries to drag the mood back by sheer force and a wink. "Mina's always fine. Mina is literally made of *fine*."

Mina's smile wobbles. Remy's gaze stays sharp. Craig tips forward slightly as the bus hits a bump, his skull nodding in agreement.

I let it go.

For now.

Because Evie is beside me, and Harbor's Edge is behind us.

But in the dark beyond the bus windows, something feels like it's following us.

One Month Later

The first thing I learn about "home base" is that it's quiet in a way the world isn't.

Not small-town quiet. Not hospital quiet.

A curated, expensive quiet—thick carpet swallowing footsteps, soundproofing in the walls, security glass that doesn't reflect well. The whole building feels like it was designed to keep secrets from leaking through vents.

Eon owns it. Of course they do.

The lobby is all marble and soft lighting and a receptionist who could probably kill someone with a stapler. There's security at every choke point, men and women in plain clothes with earpieces and eyes that flick over you like you're a package being tracked. Nobody here is "a fan." Nobody here is "a civilian."

Everyone is... inside. The elevator opens onto our floor with a soft chime.

Kaia's door is three doors down from mine—except it isn't *mine.*

Not really.

My name is on the paperwork. I have a key card. I have access like I belong here.

But the place I actually sleep—the place my toothbrush lives, my hoodie hangs, my grief is allowed to exist without being watched—is Kaia's apartment.

Ours.

That fact still hits me sometimes, out of nowhere, and I feel like I'm waiting for someone to yank it away and tell me I didn't earn it.

Kaia's door clicks open before I can knock. She's barefoot and dressed in cotton shorts and a matching shirt. Hair damp at the roots, not styled, just *hers.* No glitter, no lights, no mask. She looks like a person who might steal your fries, not a person with billboards.

"Hey," she says.

"Hey," I answer, like this is normal.

It still isn't.

Behind her, the apartment is warm and lived-in in a way the rest of the building isn't. My shoes are by the entry bench where I keep leaving them. My jacket is on the hook because I never remember to put it away. There are throw blankets on the couch, a bowl of clementines on the counter, and a stack of lyric note-books near the coffee table like the words just... happen here.

And then there's my stuff threaded through it in small, stub-born evidence: a mug I stole from the common suite, a framed photo of Grandma on the shelf, my hair tie on the end table because I keep taking it out and forgetting where I put it.

Kaia steps aside to let me in. I toe my shoes off out of habit—like I've been doing it here forever.

She watches me with that look—the one that makes me want to throw something at her and kiss her in the same breath.

"What?" I demand, already defensive.

Kaia's mouth twitches. "You're settling in."

I scoff. "I live here."

Kaia's smile softens. "Yeah," she says quietly. "You do."

My cheeks warm. I turn away, shrugging my jacket off. "Where are the others?"

"Common suite," Kaia says. "Blaire's doing schedules. Mina's making tea like we're in a Victorian novel. Remy's listening to music, and Jules is—" She pauses. "Jules is trying to smuggle takeout in."

"That tracks," I mutter.

Kaia's eyes flick toward the hallway leading deeper into her apartment, like she's debating something. Then she exhales.

"I have... something for you," she says.

My chest tightens automatically. "If you say 'surprise' I'm leaving."

Kaia snorts. "It's not a surprise. Well, not... like that." She hesitates, then adds, smaller, "It's something I wrote for you."

I cross my arms to hide my hands. "Oh. Okay."

Kaia leads me down the hall into a small room that isn't quite a studio and isn't quite a spare bedroom. A keyboard tucked against one wall. A mic stand, plain and unshowy.

There's a couch against the back wall, plush and wide.

She gestures at it. "Sit?"

I sit, back to the cushions. Exit in sight even in a luxury tower.

Kaia stands by the keyboard for a second, not touching it yet.

I blink. "Are you... *nervous*?"

Her jaw tenses—yes, she's nervous, and she hates that I noticed. "Shush."

I almost smile. "No way."

Kaia exhales and finally reaches for the keyboard, fingers hovering as if she's afraid it'll bite.

"This is—" she starts, then stops. Her throat works. "You know the storm song? The one I wrote when we were teens?"

My pulse trips.

I keep my voice flat because that's safer. "Yeah."

Kaia nods once, eyes on the keys, not on me. "I rewrote it."

I stare at her hands. "Why?"

Her voice is quiet. "Because the old one was... me trying to love you without choosing you. Trying to make it safe... And then the Chorus stole it from us."

My throat tightens.

Kaia looks up at me then. No stage polish. No bright smile. Just Kaia.

"And I don't want to sing the old lie anymore," she says.

For a second, I can't breathe.

I force my voice to work. "Okay."

Kaia nods, taking that as permission. Then she plays. Soft chords. Familiar melody. It lands in my chest like a hand finding an old bruise.

Kaia sings, quiet as a confession. Not a performance. Not projecting. Just letting the sound exist in the room with us.

"Breathe with me—just breathe with me, if your chest gets tight, count one, two, three..."

Her voice is steady. Warm. The sound that used to make me feel like the world could be bigger than this town.

Then the revision comes.

The part that wasn't there when we were sixteen.

"I said I didn't have a choice, that's what fear sounds like when it dresses up as fate. But I did. I did. I chose the world because I was scared to choose you."

My eyes sting so fast it makes me angry. Kaia's gaze stays on me as she keeps singing, holding eye contact like she's done hiding.

"So breathe with me, breathe with me, if your chest gets tight, just count to three. If you wanna run, I'll run with you, but if you want the truth, I'm telling you: I'm here on purpose. I'm not letting go. I'm not a storm that leaves you broken."

My throat aches.

The building's quiet presses in around the notes, catching them, keeping them safe. No cheering. No cameras. No crowd noise. No demon hunger.

Just her voice.

Just me, sitting on a couch in a building I never imagined I'd step inside, letting a girl I love ruin me with truth.

Kaia's final chorus softens, almost a whisper.

"No promises like chains. No 'prove it.' No rules. Just me—still here—when the sky breaks loose."

The last chord fades.

Silence settles.

Kaia doesn't move. She doesn't fill it with a joke. She just stands there, hands still on the keys, watching me like she's waiting for the verdict.

My voice comes out rough. "You're showing off."

Kaia's mouth twitches, relief flickering. "Maybe."

I blink hard, furious at my own face. "That's... unfair."

I breathe once, twice, like the song told me to. Then I look up at her. She's still. Open. Real. And something in my chest unclenches just enough to speak.

"You know what's stupid?" I say.

Kaia's brows knit. "What?"

"I've seen you sing in arenas. I've seen you on screens." My voice wobbles. I hate it. "And this—this is the thing that makes me want to cry."

Kaia's throat works. Her eyes shine.

"Your voice," I add, quieter. "Is still my favorite sound."

Kaia goes still like I punched her and kissed her at the same time.

"Yeah?" she whispers.

I roll my eyes because if I don't, I'll fall apart. "Yeah."

Kaia crosses the room in two steps, drops to her knees in front of the couch like she's done being careful, and presses her forehead to mine.

Her hands cup my face, warm and steady.

"I'm here," she whispers. "I'm not leaving."

My chest aches. I manage, "You're literally leaving next week."

Kaia huffs a breathy laugh. "Okay. I'm not leaving *you*."

I swallow hard. "Better."

Kaia smiles—real, whole-face smile—and kisses me. Slow. Intentional. Like we have time. When she pulls back, she stays close, breathing the same air.

Outside, somewhere down the hall, I hear muffled yelling—Jules' voice, probably arguing with security about noodles. Life continuing. Ridiculous and ordinary and yet also not very ordinary at all.

Kaia brushes her thumb over my cheekbone. "Want to go to the common suite?" she asks, soft. "They're going to start a fight without us."

I snort. "Let them."

Kaia's smile turns wicked. "Or we could spend the rest of the day in here. In bed."

Kaia kisses me again, quick and bright, then stands and offers me her hand.

I take it.

And as she pulls me up off the couch, the building's quiet wraps around us like a shield, Eon's velvet cage, sure, but inside it, for once, there's something that belongs to us.

Not a montage.

Not a PR storyline.

Just a girl who rewrote her own song, and meant it.

A Note from Moira Darling

THANK YOU SO MUCH for reading! It genuinely means the world to me.

If you enjoyed Kaia and Evie's story, please consider leaving a review on Amazon. Reviews mean a lot to self-published authors! It will help others find the book too.

Free Bonus Content:

To read Chapter 6 (the diner rescue scene) from Kaia's POV, scan here:

Continue the Story With Pact (Halo Hearts Book 2)

Check out Jules's book, Pact:

One Last Thing...

If you would like to support me + get some cool bonus content and sneak peeks of upcoming projects, please consider joining my Patreon at: www.patreon.com/moiradarling

Thanks again for reading. I'm honored to have shared this piece of my heart with you!

With love,

Moira Darling

Also by Moira Darling

Her Fangs in My Heart series

A sapphic vampire romantasy series of interconnected stand-alones...

A Hunger Soft and Wild

A dangerous mercenary. A runaway vampire. A hunger neither can resist.

A Curse Bright and Breathing

A holy sacrifice. A faithless mercenary. A fate born of blood and moonlight.

A Heart Fierce and Blooming

A sunshiny vampire baroness. A grumpy lady knight. And six reasons to fight for something softer.

A Vow Cold and Kindled

A vampire knight. A fated princess. Twelve Nights of Yule to fall in love.

Halo Hearts series

A sapphic pop star paranormal romance series...

Halo

She broke my heart. Now she's famous and sworn to keep me safe... even if I hate her.

Pact